PRAISE FOR *LITTLE*

the inhumanity of barbaric sexual and physical trauma by those responsible for protection and unconditional love. It simultaneously horrifies and inspires and is a testament for anyone who survived through childhood, has trusted and been betrayed, loved and lost.

"*Little Girl Leaving* highlights Selma Fraiberg's concept of the *Magic Years*. She describes the awesome omnipotence of children, that they see themselves raising the sun in the morning and the moon at night by their own actions. Deidi's story highlights the universal need for attachment, love, security, and approval. Her story also reveals the protective mechanism of dissociation and how, in Deidi, it was essential for her survival.

"This story invites the reader to expand these dynamics to children growing up in war zones, suffering abuse through elders they are taught to trust, and for women and men everywhere who have not revisited their childhood trauma memories for fear they are being disloyal to those they love, not fully understanding that they are not responsible for their abuse.

"I applaud the author for her courage in telling this unvarnished and universal truth that is frequently kept secret or disbelieved. As a family therapist and family life educator, I believe that everyone living with or around children should read this book."

—Judith Landau, MD, former president, International Family Therapy Association; senior Fulbright scholar; consultant to the United Nations and World Health Organization

"*Little Girl Leaving*, Lisa Blume's debut novel, is sadly tragic, but deeply moving and evocative."

—Gabrielle Glaser, *New York Times* bestselling author, *Her Best-Kept Secret*; winner of the Award for Excellence in Journalism, American Psychoanalytic Association

"Frosted Flakes, Tang, crayons, Jiffy Pop, visits to Grandma and Grandpa, newborn kittens: the stuff of normal childhood flowing almost naturally—almost, there is the terror—into scenes of rape and physical and emotional abuse.

"In *Little Girl Leaving*, Deidi—awake and alive to the unending beauty of the world juxtaposed with its secret horrors—offers her colorful, confused, and conflicted memories from ages three to seven in short, snapshot chapters that deliver an extraordinarily powerful punch to the heart and the gut of the reader.

"This book is difficult to read, and yet Deidi's resilience can be felt on every page. Her deeply felt, expressively written story will help others find their voices and realize, perhaps for the first time, that they are not to blame. Nor are they alone."

—Katherine Ketcham, author, *The Only Life I Could Save: A Memoir* and *Broken: My Story of Addiction and Redemption*, with William Cope Moyers

"I was totally transfixed from the beginning of *Little Girl Leaving*. The book, with the beautiful and terrible side by side, is authentically written from the child, Deidi's, point of view. Many of her observations of the world around her made me laugh out loud. Then *Little Girl Leaving* would make me pound my fist and make me cry. I could not put this book down."

—Joyce Sundin, certified intervention professional; board member and former ethics chair, Network of Independent Interventionists

"*Little Girl Leaving* is a mesmerizing story—a page-turner, told by a beautiful child, little Deidi. You will love her voice. You will laugh, you will cry with her. Deidi will get inside of you and won't let you go, even after the last page is turned. That is the power in this story. *Little Girl Leaving* will move you, if you let it, to open your eyes to the child within you, your own children and family, to other children and families, so you will notice pain and fear in a child's eyes—and when they are saying, help, save me, do something.

"Deidi's gentleness, resilience, and thankful heart drew me to her. For Deidi, every day is a new day of wonder and excitement mixed with terror, confusion, and unknowing. The day and night before fly away like birds and disappear by the howl of a magnificent coyote, and the magic of Deidi's imagination makes each day a new possibility. *Little Girl Leaving* is an enthralling read, a brilliant read, a happy, sad read. I believe this story of Deidi and her family will be revered as a great classic; it will not disappoint. *Little Girl Leaving* delivers a fascinating story, excellent writing, and a charming and brave little girl you will never forget."

—Mary Dispenza, educator, activist, and national distinguished
principal; author, *Split: A Child, a Priest, and the Catholic Church*

"In her groundbreaking work, first-time author Lisa Blume nails it. *Little Girl Leaving* is a stunningly poignant first-person account. In this novel, told in the voice of a child, the reader hears, sees, and feels what it is like for a young child to live with, try to make sense of, and navigate within the secrets of a multigenerational abusive family system. As a former chaplain for police and sheriff's departments, I've seen the devastating impact of childhood sexual abuse, including in ministering to the families of adult victims who committed suicide.

"Through this important work, Deidi takes the reader by the heart and shows them the reality of her world in its pain and its beauty. Deidi's confusion, heartbreak, and indomitable spirit shine through."

—Kristi Schiroo, chaplain, Ridgeview Medical Systems, Minnesota; former
chaplain, McLeod County Sheriff's Department; founding member,
Crow River Critical Incident Stress Management Team

"Written in the diction and syntax of a very young girl in an abuse-ridden family, *Little Girl Leaving* is a sensory barrage. At first the reader might wonder how so many different family members could enact so many different forms of abuse. On the other hand, the vivid images and the distinctness of the different abusers' personalities form the braid of a convincing and disturbing narrative. The physical beauty of the child's world and Deidi's love for her erratically tender and remorseful parents is mixed with the terrible physical and psychological pain she endures at their hands from ages three to seven.

"Most wonderful is how variously the child's goodness of spirit tries to maintain itself. Through this saga of growing horror winds the clear thread of the narrator's growing comprehension of her situation, along with her compassion and her creative gifts. This is a page-turner, a book that will teach members of luckier families how abuse perpetuates from generation to generation, as victims and perpetrators and enablers conspire to hide the family evil."

—Sharon Solwitz, creative writing professor at Purdue University; author, *Once, in Lourdes*; *Bloody Mary*; and *Blood and Milk*; winner of the Carl Sandburg Prize and the Doheny Award of the Center for Fiction, finalist for the National Jewish Book Award

"In the voice of Deidi, a trusting child whose literal and emotional vocabulary evolves over the course of four formative years, Blume leads us in baby steps down a darkening corridor that ultimately opens to an excruciating paradox: the mysterious and wonder-filled, still-new world as explored by a happy, curious toddler and the harsh intrusion of family violence and sexual abuse. As the child's comprehension develops, we travel with her faster and faster into the darkness, nearly racing back toward half-light by book's end.

"How does one turn the unfathomable into the believable without lecturing, without seeding hatred, without sounding vengeful or outrageous—in a voice, even, of great tenderness? In *Little Girl Leaving*, first-time novelist Lisa Blume has done just that."

—Sally Anderson, editor-in-chief, Strategic News Service, FiReBooks, and FiReFilms; co-editor, *Poets Against the War*

"*Little Girl Leaving* left me literally speechless. The experience of getting to know the child, Deidi, made me have to think about so much that is good in the world. She is a righteous child. Her voice took me back to my childhood and memories about the importance of favorite toys such as Play-Doh. Overall, Deidi exemplifies a type of radical acceptance without ever receiving this particular form of therapy. Her increasing dissociation throughout multiple forms of abuse manifests her remarkable resilience. In the end, *Little Girl Leaving* offers a critical opportunity for understanding this virtual childhood epidemic that is colorblind, immune to socioeconomic status, and screaming for our attention."

—Ann Delgado, therapist, Community Psychiatric Clinic; former sex offender treatment specialist

"*Little Girl Leaving* is a read I will never forget. Gut-wrenching, heartbreaking, warm, humorous, and a book that will make your blood boil. Deidi, the little girl who tells her story of abuse and triumph, will make her way into your heart. Lisa Blume brilliantly positions her as the main character, trying to make sense of her abusers and those who enable them.

"I have figure skated at an elite level, and during my younger years I often competed against Tonya Harding. The Academy Award–winning movie, *I, Tonya*, showed her being abused from a young age. I saw it with my own eyes at the skating rink. It was painful and confusing for me, and I'm sure other kids skating with us, to see adults not do anything. We have such a long way to go—to act when abuse is obvious, and to recognize it when it's not.

"*Little Girl Leaving* shows us how the worst abuse is unseen, and how children usually endure it alone. It shows us that it often starts with the youngest children, which seems unthinkable. But *Little Girl Leaving* makes you do more than think about it. This riveting story of a wonderful little girl will inspire you to do whatever you can to stop it. I recently had the opportunity, with my husband and children, of being with Pope Francis at the unveiling of my husband's painting of the Pope greeting the refugees at Lesbos. As I think about this now, it reminds me of what *Little Girl Leaving* has left in my heart. Whether as nations, institutions, or families, we need to protect the children."

—Bente Stangeland Mullally, double gold medalist,
US Figure Skating Association

"Lisa Blume's book, *Little Girl Leaving*, is remarkable and profoundly moving. She is able to tell the story of horrible and inhumane abuse through the eyes of a child from the age of three to seven years old. What is truly extraordinary is that, to the very end of the book, the main character, Deidi, is present in a state that I call *Holy Innocence*. She speaks from her heart honestly and authentically, yet she does not blame or attack the people who are cruel and abusive to her or her brother or the animals in her life. Innocence is a gift of childhood, and there are special people who can maintain innocence on a spiritual plane that allows them to experience the cruelty of others without letting it touch their own soul. This quality is a gift that allows Deidi to survive and continue loving, to keep her heart open, and to maintain connection with the people by whom she needs to be loved.

"I highly recommend this book to all health and mental health practitioners, teachers, and parents. It is a call to action for all societies and cultures to wake up and take collective social action to stop the abuse of children."

—Laurie Moore, MD, American Board of Neurology and Psychiatry
Lifetime Certificate holder; fellow of the Royal Australian and
New Zealand College of Psychiatrists with special interest in
survivors of adversity and multicultural populations

"Ms. Blume has captured the experience of this child and her family and the abuse that occurred in a relatable way. Intergenerational abuse, domestic violence, lack of resources, secrecy, and lies are all portrayed. As an African American child who grew up in Eastern Washington in the '60s and '70s, the small-town, rural experience rang true for me. Feeling different and having no one to talk to about it rang true for me. It is not an easy read, but a sober reminder about what is happening in many families behind closed doors.

"Whether you're a professional, an adult, or a victim, this book will grab you and take you into a world that you may know nothing about, and inspire those who need it to get help."

—Johnna Lehr, psychotherapist, MSW, LICSW; former Child Protective
Services investigator, abuse and neglect; Division of Licensing Resources
investigator, abuse and neglect in Washington State licensed facilities

"A book may entertain you, but a good book informs and stays with you long after closing the cover. Lisa Blume's debut novel has done the latter.

"*Little Girl Leaving* is an important story that needs to be told. It is an inspiring story based on a young girl struggling to come to terms with and overcome her traumatic life. Written from a very young child's perspective, it captures the breadth of both childhood and the adversity associated with sexual, physical, and psychological child abuse and neglect. It also highlights how abuse is perpetuated throughout a family. However, most importantly, this story will touch the hearts and minds of all those who have been in a similar situation. It will hopefully give them the ability to find support and recognize they are not alone."

—Glenice J. Whitting, PhD; author of *Something Missing* and
Pickle to Pie, shortlist, Victorian Premiers Literary Awards and
winner, Ilura Press International Fiction Quest; creative writing
teacher, Godfrey Street Community House, Australia

"*Little Girl Leaving* is as innovative as it is disturbing. The narrative captures elements of child abuse which, all too often, are lost or not understood by justice systems. The author has succeeded in conveying the insidious malevolence and criminality of the adult perpetrators. Likewise, there is a skillful portrayal of how their acts are absorbed into and affect daily lives and routines. The long, slow erosion of innocence is particularly tragic. It is a harrowing account but one which all professionals working in this field should read."

—Raymond McMenamin, solicitor advocate; Shrieval Convener of the
Mental Health Tribunal for Scotland; appointed part-time judicial office
holder; former spokesperson for the Law Society of Scotland's vulnerable
witness legislation; former president of the part-time Sheriffs' Association

"*Little Girl Leaving* is a must-read book for clinicians, therapists, teachers, welfare workers, social workers, and any adult who works with children. *Little Girl Leaving* is a compelling story of a wise girl who describes early traumatic experiences of incest and sexual, physical, and emotional abuse in her own voice and under her own terms of endearment. In addition, she very genuinely reveals increasing dissociative episodes. Her story unfolds via vivid descriptions of interpersonal and intergenerational trauma and her desperate attempts to rescue herself, her brother, and her parents. Deidi is an amazing girl who knows right from wrong and has great insight beyond her years. Through her books, coloring, playing, animals, and being connected with nature as well as people, she overcomes the unimaginable. Her resilience is captured throughout the book as she tries to do good, no matter how painful and frightening life becomes, with the beauty of her essence always somehow enduring.

—Rocío Chang-Angulo, PsyD, co-director, Center for Trauma Recovery and Juvenile Justice, University of Connecticut; steering committee member, National Child Traumatic Stress Network; clinical advisor for the Jordan Porcow Foundation and Connecticut Public Broadcasting

LITTLE GIRL
LEAVING

LITTLE GIRL LEAVING

A NOVEL BASED ON A TRUE STORY

LISA BLUME

Published by Illumine LLC, Seattle
www.littlegirlleaving.com

Edited and Designed by Girl Friday Productions
www.girlfridayproductions.com

Editorial: Emilie Sandoz-Voyer, Ingrid Emerick,
Laura Whittemore, and Nick Allison
Interior and Cover Design: Rachel Marek
Image Credits: cover © By John D Sirlin/Shutterstock; © izzzy71/Shutterstock;
© My Generations Art/Shutterstock; © Yuriy Mazur/Shutterstock; © Chaykovsky
Igor/Shutterstock; © PopTika/Shutterstock; © SJ Travel Photo and Video

ISBN (Paperback): 978-0-692-10406-4
e-ISBN: 978-0-692-10407-1

First Edition

Printed in the United States of America

To my husband, Keith,
my love in this life and forever after, whose love, integrity, and courage have
brought more happiness to me than I ever thought possible.

To all in need of healing from their childhood.

To the nurturing of the next generation of children and all who follow.

CONTENTS

LEAVING ONE

A puff of dust follows the tumbleweed rolling in the pasture by our house. When we leave I'm not going to miss the wind that kicks up that dust. Mommy's calling my name, "Deidi, Deidi," and I know it's almost time.

Almost time to leave our house in Moses Lake to move far away. I feel like the astronauts going to the moon. I wonder if they ever lick their finger, stick it in the floating Tang jar, and suck off the orange powder when they're in space? I'm excited, scared, and sad. I don't know how these feelings go together.

My toes sink into the green island around our house, the smell of cut grass still in the air. It's peaceful here. Then I look at the dry pasture next door. It's like reading my *Busy, Busy World* book. The bunnies are driving too fast in their little red cars. The foxes direct traffic and blow their whistles. Bus horns keep beep, beep, beeping. Even the zigzags of tiny mice hats seem extra rushed. Does everything feel the change that's coming?

Birdsong pulls me back to my spot in the grass. The meadowlark's right next to me. I close my eyes when he stops. He sings again and stops. I turn toward the voice. He's perched on the yard light that stands at attention near the shed. I watch his bright-yellow chest lift a black V necklace, and the song starts over. His white tail feathers tell me he's leaving. "Goodbye, sweet meadowlark," I say out loud. "I'll miss your Charlie Brown shirt and Fruit Stripe coat." I stare into the blue sky until he's gone.

A voice behind me says, "Fruit Stripe isn't brown, Deidi."

I try to say, "Choooocolate Fruit Stripe, Matty," as if my brother's dumb. I'm seven and he's eight. My birthday's one week before his, so for one week we're the same age.

Matty says, "That's not a gum."

I say it should be and he says, "Yeah, it's called Bubble Fudge and doesn't have stripes."

He squats next to me.

"It's almost time to leave."

Matty slowly nods as he pulls up some grass. He sticks it between his teeth and walks back in the house.

We're moving to Bellevue, by Seattle. We've gone on trips there before. I remember how green everything was. There're a lot of huge trees. You can't see very far because of the hills, 'cause it's not flat like here. Mommy said they don't have a Tastee-Freez in Bellevue. I'll miss their cheeseburgers. She said people are smarter in Seattle because it's a big city, but Daddy said that's stupid. I hope they won't keep fighting about Nixon. Mommy hates that he wants to be our president again, but Daddy wants him to stay in the White House.

The grass is starting to make my bottom wet. I whisper, "Goodbye, Moses Lake, please take care of Hansel, because he can't come with us." I'm sad we're leaving our dog. This morning Mommy said we'll visit Hansel all the time, but I don't believe her. She said there isn't enough room for him where we're going. He's a German shepherd and runs in the pastures and farmland that go on forever like the ocean all around us. I remember when Hansel was in the newspaper because he saved a piglet that tried to cross the street by our house. Hansel saved my life too, but that wasn't in the paper. When they burned the rubble field in front of our house, I wanted to get closer to the fire, but Hansel bit my shirt and pulled me back.

Mommy said we have to drive across the mountains to get to our new house in Bellevue. I wonder if we'll see any snow at Sno-qual-mie, the name she said for the top of the mountains. I like to say the name over and over to myself because it makes my face and tongue feel funny. I wonder if "qual" is like "quail" that Daddy shoots with his guns.

I look around at the fruit trees, the pasture, the fields, and the house that I've seen every day. I wish I could come back whenever I want. I wish I could go anywhere, anytime. Not that long ago, I thought that maybe I could. Maybe I could twinkle my nose just like Samantha on *Bewitched*.

We haven't always lived here, though. Mommy and Daddy said we lived in Harrington after I was born in Spokane in 1965. Harrington is between Spokane and Moses Lake and has farms all around it. Daddy was mostly a wheat farmer since I can remember. I was still a baby when we moved closer to Moses Lake to a farm in Ruff. I had my first, second, and third birthdays in Ruff. I still have my Raggedy Ann doll from my first Christmas there. Mostly, I remember Ruff starting when I was almost three.

My heart hurts to see the name of that town in my head. It looks the same as a happy dog bark like Hansel's, but it sounds like the "roof" that covers our house.

Mommy and Daddy said they got Hansel on their honeymoon in the South where Mommy's favorite movie was. It's called *Gone with the Wind*. They knew each other in high school. Then they got married when Daddy came back from Vietnam. We got another German shepherd in Ruff that Mommy wanted to name Gretel, but Matty and I called her Snoopy instead. Hansel and Snoopy had puppies even though Daddy kicked Snoopy in the tummy when she growled at strangers. Our family were the only people she liked, and I don't know what happened to her or the puppies when we moved to Moses

3

Lake. That's where I started school and Mommy was a teacher, but not my teacher.

I was still three when we moved to Moses Lake. That was a million years ago. Okay, I guess only four years ago. I'm seven now. But it feels like a million.

When we moved to Moses Lake, Mommy told me it's named after Chief Moses. He was chief of the Indians who used to live here. I read at the library they had a war with the army a long time ago. Then they had to go somewhere else. Chief Moses said there were too many white men. Like too many grains of sand to count, he said. He was right. It's almost all white people in Moses Lake. In my classes at school there was only one Indian girl and one Japanese boy. There was one black girl my age in a different class. There were a few Mexican kids. But mostly, there were lots of white kids.

I've seen a place close to Moses Lake on the news. It's called Hanford. That's where mushroom-cloud bombs are made. Mommy says some doctors think people get sick from Hanford. She says not to worry. But maybe it's good we're moving.

The back door to the house opens and Mommy says, "Deidi, it's time to come in and finish packing."

I wave and say, "Okay, I'm coming," as she turns back inside. I weave through the boxes in the kitchen and living room to get to my bedroom. The hallway's empty, but my room looks like a tornado hit, as Daddy would say.

The cardboard box by my closet is taller than me and has a silver bar inside. Mommy said to hang my nice clothes on the bar. I pretend to work at Sears and press my dresses, slacks, and tops together on the rack. I push my stuffed animals into the bottom of the box like Mommy said. It isn't easy. I see Blankie at the back of my closet, grab her, and push her into the box. She looks like a ball of pink cotton candy. I think about all the places we've gone together. I want Blankie back. I almost disappear inside the box when I pull her out. Sitting

4

on my thick blue carpet and leaning against my bed, I spread Blankie over my lap. I wonder what color carpet I'll have in Bellevue. I squish my face into Blankie. She smells a little like baby powder and cigarette smoke. I used to wrap her around me in the car.

I think about how Daddy holds a cigarette in his left hand by the car window, cupping it like a letter C when he sucks the end, ashes flying outside with a flick of his thumb. He's a cool smoker, but she's not. Mommy keeps the cigarette in her right hand, even when she drives, and uses her pink polished pointer finger to tap, tap, tap the brown end into the ashes in the tray under the radio.

I hear Mommy turn the stereo on in the living room as I pull Blankie off my lap. The song plays. I know it. The lady's voice is pretty. *She's leaving on a jet plane . . . and she smiles for me.* It feels sad and happy at the same time.

I quietly sing along. I fold Blankie and put her back in the box. "Bye-bye. See you at the new house."

I take my white weave purse off the dresser, snap it open, and grab a pack of cigarettes. I flip the top just like Mommy and pull back the paper. I choose a perfect white stick and put it in my mouth. I light the cigarette and take in a big breath to hold as I put it between my peace fingers. I stare out my window like I'm thinking something important. I blow air into the chalky filter as a puff of white comes out the other end. I see Matty out of the corner of my eye. I hear the crackling wrapper on his rope of Bub's Daddy gum as he leans against my doorway.

He grins with a nod toward the red pack still in my hand. I nod and lift my eyebrows with a look at his grape gum. He nods, and I give my box a little shake like Daddy does when he shares. All the sticks pop up, so I hold up one finger. Matty gives me a thumbs-up, pulls one cigarette out, and hands me a twist of purple.

He turns to leave, and I see the Evel Knievel sticker on his shirt. I think about how much he wants to race motorcycles. Daddy said that

Evel Knievel used to live in Moses Lake. I ask Matty's back, "Are you scared?"

He shakes his head and doesn't turn around when he says, "No, but I don't want to go."

I see my dolls inside another brown box. Cinderella's sitting in her green rag dress on Dancerina's hot-pink tutu, and Velvet's long blond hair is tangled around Barbie. Baby's wearing the PJs I dressed her in a few days ago. She's on top of my Barbie case of clothes and shoes. I tell everyone to be nice and I'll see them at the new house. Everyone nods. We wave and blow kisses.

My books are stacked on top of my dresser. I know every story by heart. I pull out *The Adventures of the Three Colors*. This is one of my favorite books. It makes me a little sad because it's about Herbie and his dog, Angelo. I don't have a dog anymore because he belongs to the neighbors now. Herbie and Angelo see a big beautiful rainbow outside. The rainbow lasts forever, because it's "really a circle, you know." I didn't know. Herbie's an artist like me. I have my own easel and paints, but they're in a box now.

Herbie goes home to paint all the colors of the rainbow. But he only has blue, pink, and yellow paints. This is a problem. I like that he stops to think about what to do and Angelo pretends to help Herbie, but he's really napping. Hansel used to turn his big head to one side and stare at me when I painted, like he was helping too. Angelo keeps sleeping, just like Hansel did. Herbie starts painting. He paints a yellow dog, then a blue elephant, and by accident makes a green fish. Now Herbie has four colors, like magic. When he paints a yellow butterfly, then a pink pig, he makes an orange snail by accident. Herbie's so excited he splashes paint on Angelo's nose. That wakes the little dog up. I count six colors that Herbie has now.

He paints more and more animals. This creates more and more new colors, and more paint splashes on his clothes and Angelo's black nose. There's a brown alligator and a purple alligator between the yellow hippo and the blue kangaroo.

Herbie paints a super big flower at the end. He uses two shades of each of the first three colors he started with. It's like a kaleidoscope of rainbows and flowers all mixed together.

Memories of the past four years start floating through my head as I watch the flower's light blue, soft pink, emerald green, and lavender melt together like the colors I swirl with my paintbrush.

PART I: AGE THREE

CHAPTER 1

The Magic Face

I remember something from when I was a baby.

I can see her through the thin wooden bars that keep me safely inside. I want to touch her, but this hand of mine keeps moving the wrong way. I put some of it in my mouth. I see her again. She sees me, all of me, and I'm everything to her. I hear me laughing because I'm happy. I like the sound of laughing. She's different from all the other faces I see. There's nothing in between us.

She says the small sheet tucked into the crib beneath me is soft like her wings. *Can I touch you?* Her breeze brushes my cheek when she says, "This is me." A silky wing tickles my fingertip when she says, "This is goodness."

CHAPTER 2

Third Birthday Party

I count one, two, three candles. One candle looks like a blue bear with a hat. One's yellow. One's a brown pony. Maybe it's a giraffe, I'm not sure. This is a really big birthday cake. It smells like sugar. Mommy says sugar doesn't smell. Great-Grandma made my cake from scratch. Mommy said it means not from a box. She said Great-Grandma spent time with the cake. I wonder if the candles came from scratch. There're pink flowers and little leaves on the sides and top of my cake. I like the pink tulips outside. It's spring.

Maybe pink frosting tastes like strawberries.

Great-Grandma brought a cake for Matty too. Mommy said we're sharing our party. She said he was born close to me. I count Matty's candles. He has four. One's pink. He has more candles than me. But my birthday's first. Mommy said Matty's the oldest. It makes me mad. I'm first and oldest. His cake has white frosting too. I hear bubble noise on the purple counter. The coffee's ready for big people. It smells good. I watch Mommy get nice cups out of the wood door. I get in trouble if I touch those. She asks who wants cream and sugar. I put a sugar square in my mouth when she's not looking.

I like the curtains in the kitchen. They're like the chairs. My legs stick on the chairs if it's hot or I spill Kool-Aid. Mommy's sister has curtains like ours. I think she's beautiful. She has blue eyes. Her yellow hair's like mine. She has a pretty face. She doesn't play with me. Mommy's brown hair is like Daddy's and Matty's. I like to watch her spray and spray and brush and brush. She has a sticky bottle and comb. Mommy says I'm not like her, Daddy, or Matty. She says she picked me up at the store like a free puppy. This makes my chest hurt.

Matty's eyes are blue. Like his best shooter when we play marbles. I like his freckles. Mommy says I have freckles too. I don't have as many. Matty put the blue-green crayon by my nose. He said, "That's your eyes, Deidi."

My family's singing "Happy Birthday" to us. I don't hear "Deidi." I kind of hear "Matty." I don't hear "Deidi." Mommy looks at me. I blow on the animal candles. I'm happy for the claps. I'm the birthday girl. Matty's the birthday boy. We get first pieces of cake.

My grandma's my favorite. She's Mommy's mom. She says the cake's fluffy. I think, *My new birthday dress's sleeves are fluffy.*

I took my new dress out of the box this morning. I liked the sound of the paper. I put the dress Mommy gave me on my bed. It has a pink ribbon on a white bib. But not a baby bib. There are big flowers on it. Mommy said they're pastel. I pulled my tights on all by myself this morning. Mommy buttoned my dress and I buckled my best red shoes. Mommy sprayed water on my hair. She brushed it. She said it was good I took a bath last night.

My piece of cake's gone now, and I drink the rest of my cold milk. I wipe my face with a birthday napkin. I open the compact Mommy gave me. I put ChapStick on each side of my top lip. I make one stripe on my bottom lip. I press my lips like Mommy, and Grandma says I'm ready for a picture.

She rubs my hand with her thumb. She's taking me to the living room. The flowers she works on make her hands hard. She says mine are soft. The room smells like lemons. I see my favorite trees in the big windows. I tell Grandma one time I found a robin's nest. It was under the trees; it had three blue eggs.

Grandma lifts me up and puts me on Great-Grandma's lap. She has pretty lips like Grandma and Mommy. She kind of spits when she talks. Great-Grandma's wearing a purple dress. I want to touch the curls around her face. Grandma has brown hair like Mommy's. She's wearing a pretty dress with pink and purple on it. She lets me draw the colors on her sleeve with my finger. She tells me we have three mommies and their three daughters in the picture. She tells me a word for this, but I don't know it.

Mommy says people think Great-Grandma looks like the queen. And she even came here from England. Her family took a ship here. Their house burned down. Great-Grandma's mommy and daddy worked in the real queen's greenhouse. Her mommy died when she was born. Mommy's big sister said Great-Grandma should live in a palace. She said a prince did something in the greenhouse. That's why Great-Grandma's house burned down. I don't know what this means. Great-Grandpa was a farmer like his mommy and daddy. He said they came here on a ship from Germany.

Daddy says Davenport's close to Ruff. Great-Grandma started Davenport Flower Shop, and she had three greenhouses. That's all gone. Grandma has Davenport Flowers now. It's at her house. Grandpa works on farmer things. I love to play in their garden. Some flowers are bigger than me. Every color's in the yard. The fountain has frogs. The chimes play if wind blows. Their house's my favorite. Grandma gives Matty and me a little bag of marshmallows and candies when we leave.

Grandma wears glasses. She's pretty like Mommy. Great-Grandma wears glasses too. She's pretty, but she has a hair on a bump on her chin. Grandma says we must be clean, dress nice, and have combed hair. I'm glad that's how I am today.

One time, Grandma got mad at Daddy's mommy. She's my grandma too. Matty and I were dirty from her farm. Daddy's dad is my grandpa too. He grows wheat at the farm. Daddy helps him if they're not mad. Daddy said Grandpa's nephew fell in wheat when he was twelve. He drowned.

Daddy said Grandpa had polio. He said it means his legs hurt. Now Grandpa wears special boots. He stomps when he walks. Grandpa said he lost tops of three fingers. A bad machine cut them off. His fingers work, but the nails are gone. Grandma and Grandpa live by the house and barn my great-grandpa built on the farm. He moved here in a covered wagon. His grandma was Welsh like grape juice. His grandpa was from Germany. Grandma said her mommy and daddy are from Russia.

There's a covered wagon on a book about Laura and the little house. Somebody read it to me.

Daddy has one sister, no brothers. I have three aunts. Daddy and his sister are like Matty and me. He's the oldest. I don't see why Matty's oldest. My birthday's first. Daddy's sister has brown hair and blue eyes. She's shorter than Daddy. They grew up in the farmhouse Grandpa and Grandma made.

I see the windmill before I see the houses when we drive to their farm. It's not very far. It's by Harrington, where I was a baby. There's a big tree in the yard that looks like an elephant's leg. Mommy said it's a crying something. It looks like the tree in my *Miss Suzy* book. She lived there before red squirrels stole her house. Good soldiers took it back for her. Miss Suzy left the fancy dollhouse she found and went home.

Grandma's hands smell like the pink lotion in the bathroom at her farm. I like to push the top with one hand and a pink string comes out in my other hand. It smells good. Grandma says it's Rose Milk.

Mommy takes my hand. I tell her I think Rose is a pretty name. She says, "That's nice." It's time to take a picture of me, Mommy, Grandma, and Great-Grandma. *Flash!* Red dots in my eyes. I can't see.

Mommy tells her mom to stop fussing. Grandma's combing my hair again. She says I want to be pretty for more pictures. Grandma says we need a picture with her daddy. Grandma puts me on Great-Grandpa's lap. He's an old man. His mouth doesn't close. I wish I could push his chin up. I'd get in trouble, though. Matty stands next to Great-Grandpa. He points his cap gun at the camera. It looks like a real gun. Mommy says don't point it at her. *Flash!*

Grandma lifts me off Great-Grandpa's lap. I blink a lot. Great-Grandpa used to ride a horse to school.

Great-Grandma lets me sneak frosting on my finger before she covers what is left of my birthday cake. She whispers, "Don't tell anybody." She gives me a wet kiss and they say bye-bye. I like being happy.

CHAPTER 3

Go for a Drive

I dump my puzzle on the kitchen table. I got it for my birthday. I'm turning pieces to the picture side when Daddy says, "Let's go for a ride." I cross fingers on both hands. I hope we go to town. Matty and I race each other to Daddy's car. He wins. We sit between Mommy and Daddy on the front seat. Mommy doesn't like that there is no back seat, but I do. I don't like Mommy's car. I sit inside a box she buckles on me. My head and feet poke out. Mommy gets mad if I cry. Matty got in trouble when I screamed one time. Mommy thought he did a bad thing to me. He didn't, but I didn't have air.

Cars make the best sound on gravel. We drive by the fields of green baby wheat all around our house. When it gets hot, those fields will be gold. Little birds fly out of the tall cheatgrass by the road. Farmers hate cheatgrass. I hate the tiny needles that stick in my socks and scratch me. Daddy's driving to the store in Ruff. I see dust chasing us in his mirror. I watch Mommy put her pink lipstick on with one hand. She turns the knob on the radio and sings along, *Jesus loves you, wo, wo, wo.*

When Daddy parks in front of the store, I'm out first, but Matty beats me to the door. Mommy says slow down, just as the bells ring on the store door. They're like the bells behind Grandma's front door on the farm.

Daddy's work boots are loud on the wood floor. He says, "Pick out some candy, you two." I love chewy sticks of purple. I like to fold the wrapper. I suck the taffy to make it last. Daddy digs in his back pocket. He pays at the tall counter. He keeps money in his old brown wallet. It goes in the pocket he sits on. I get in trouble if I say "butt." He puts a paper bag in the back. I make my stick last all the way home.

I hear Hansel and Snoopy barking before I see them. They're wagging their tails when Daddy parks. He says, "C'mon, kids, let's wash this car!" Matty and I cheer. Mommy goes inside.

Daddy squeezes soap into two buckets. He fills both with water. And then he runs inside for clean sponges. I get to paint headlights with soapy bubbles. Matty paints doors. Then Daddy says, "Stand back," and he sprays the car with water.

Daddy's real tall. He has long arms. Mommy says he's handsome if she's happy. Daddy played college basketball. But his knee broke so he couldn't play anymore. He says there's steel in it now. He was in Seattle then. Daddy says it's bigger than Ruff. Daddy's a lot bigger than Mommy. My head touches his knee. Her head touches where his heart is.

CHAPTER 4

Brer Rabbit

Mommy's going to read a story to Matty and me! I love the book *Brer Rabbit and the Tar Baby*. We sit on each side of her on the green couch. Mommy calls it a sofa. She puts her feet up. I help her open the big book with one hand. Matty tells Mommy to talk southern. Mommy says, "It's called a 'southern drawl' and that's how people talk in the South where your great-grandpa came from."

Mommy tells us about Uncle Remus. She says he read to Miss Sally's son, like Mommy's reading to us. "Here come Brer Rabbit pacin' down de road—lippity-clippity, clippity-lippity—des fez sassy ez a jay-bird."

We get to my favorite part. Brer Rabbit tells Brer Fox, don't throw me in that briar patch. He says it after Brer Fox tricks him. He's stuck to the black tar-baby girl Brer Fox made.

Brer Rabbit thought tar-baby girl was deaf. Mommy said it means you can't hear. He thought tar-baby girl was stuck up. Mommy said it means she thought she was better than him. This makes Brer Rabbit very mad. He beats up tar-baby girl.

Brer Rabbit swings his paws at tar-baby girl. His paws get stuck. He's like Mommy and Daddy swinging their fists at each other. Daddy and Mommy swing fists at Matty too, and then he swings fists at me. Sometimes I swing back.

Brer Rabbit gets mad that tar-baby girl won't let go. "En den he butted, en his head got stuck." Brer Rabbit hits tar-baby girl with his head and then he gets stuck. I saw Daddy hit his head on Mommy one time. She fell down. Daddy shook her. She woke up and Daddy hugged her. He cried. Mommy hits Daddy's head too.

I know Brer Rabbit is scared. Mommy says you can tell because his eyes get big. Brer Fox laughs at Brer Rabbit. He says Brer Rabbit "sassed me for the very last time." Mommy says it's because Brer Rabbit talked back to Brer Fox. Brer Fox wants to roast, hang, or drown Brer Rabbit now. He says, please do all those things, but don't throw him in that briar patch.

Brer Rabbit knows Brer Fox is mean. He knows he'd do the meanest thing. Mommy says Brer Rabbit made Brer Fox think getting thrown in the briar patch was the meanest. That's why Brer Fox did it. Mommy says some people are mean like that.

Brer Rabbit sits on his log after Brer Fox throws him in the briar patch. Brer Fox tries to hear Brer Rabbit dying. Mommy says that a death rattle is a noise people make when they die. Brer Rabbit combs his hair. He calls Brer Fox. Brer Rabbit says he was born and bred in the briar patch. Mommy says that means Brer Rabbit grew up there. He knows all about it. It can't hurt him. I like that. I want to hug Brer Rabbit.

CHAPTER 5

MLK and the Kitten

I'm at the kitchen table with Daddy. Mommy's making soup for lunch. Daddy tells Mommy he can't believe they shot the king. Mommy stops stirring the soup. She looks up and says it makes her sick. Daddy says he didn't like the king. Mommy has a mad face all of a sudden, and then she calls Daddy a bad name. They're talking louder and louder. I slide off the kitchen chair and tiptoe out of the room. I wish I had pink ballerina slippers on so I could be more quiet, but I have boots on. I close the screen door behind me. I want to run back and stop the fight. I hear Matty say, "C'mere, Deidi. See what I found."

I run over the grass to Matty. He's sitting cross-legged by a big tree. There's a tiny kitten in his hand. The kitty's crying. Matty says it's hungry. He says he's getting milk for it. He puts the kitty in my hand and runs fast to the back door. The bad sounds get louder when he goes in. Now I just hear kitty cries. Her black fur's soft. I pet her and she purrs.

I jump when Matty yells. I put the kitty down and run to the screen door. It's closed. I see Matty pushing Daddy and yelling,

"No!" Mommy and Daddy's arms are flying. I see Matty fall. Daddy's kicking him.

Matty's running to the door, but Daddy beats him to it. Matty pushes the screen door open, and Daddy's big hand shoves his head out the door. Matty trips and falls. Daddy slams the screen door. He's yelling and fighting with Mommy. They're yelling bad words. It sounds like glass breaking. I start to go to the door, but Matty pulls my shirt.

I follow him, running back to the kitten. He scoops her up out of the grass and turns around. He bends back with the kitten over his head and throws her hard on the side of the house. He just stands there and then runs away. I walk over to where the kitten is. She's not crying anymore. My tummy hurts.

I find Mommy in the living room. I don't know where Daddy is. Her elbow is on the table and her hand is over her eyes.

"Mommy," I say quietly.

She just looks at me. She's been crying. I sit down and ask what happened. Mommy says, "A good man died." She says he got shot by a gun. Mommy says he helped people. I think about the guns my daddy, my grandpas, and my uncles shoot. Daddy says guns are for hunting, but Matty shoots my boots. I get pellets in my skin if he misses. It hurts when Mommy digs them out.

I tell Mommy, "I've been shot and I'm not dead."

Mommy says this was a different kind of gun.

Mommy shows me a picture of the good man. She says he was black. She says I haven't met black people. I ask Mommy if he's the same as the man hanging on the wall. Mommy says no, but that's a black man too. Mommy and Daddy got the black man's picture on their honeymoon. Both men look sad.

CHAPTER 6

Day and Night

Mommy says to go play; she's got things to do. The sun comes in through the living-room window. It makes me warm. I pull my See 'n Say from under the couch. I climb up on top to make myself comfy like Mommy. I move the arrow to the cat and pull the string. *Meow!* I turn the arrow to the cow. I pull the string. *Moo!* It's windy outside. I hear a little whistle by the front door. I turn the arrow to the dog. I pull the string. *Ruff, ruff!* I feel so sleepy.

The vacuum cleaner wakes me up. Mommy must be cleaning downstairs. Where's my vacuum cleaner? I find it in the closet. I push the vacuum happy face. The balls *pop, pop* inside. Mommy's coming up the stairs. I tell her I vacuumed the living room. She says, "That's a big help, thanks." I say I've got to run. I say my phone's ringing. She says bye-bye.

I pick up the red handle on my phone. I push the pulley string under the wheels. A lady's calling me. I say yes a lot. When I hang up, Mommy comes in. I tell her I'm busy. I say I'm sorry, I can't talk. She says okay. Matty's yelling at me. He wants me to come outside. I run to the back door. His hands are muddy. He says to follow him.

I hear field sprinklers go *click, stop, click*. Matty shows me where he's making pies. I see his blue bucket and shovel.

"Hold on," I shout, and I run to get my red bucket by the hose. Matty digs some mud for me and puts it in my bucket. I say my store will be down the street. Matty tells me to bake pies before I open. I say okay.

Mommy comes out with a red-and-white tablecloth. She says we need to wash up for lunch. Matty turns on the hose. He holds it for me to rub my hands under. I hold it for him. We both climb on the bench. Mommy puts purple Kool-Aid in my pink cup. I eat my tuna sandwich fast. I want to play more.

Matty goes inside after lunch, so I bake chocolate pies all day by myself. Daddy drives up in the truck. His door squeaks open and I run over with Hansel and Snoopy barking behind me. Daddy's boot steps on a cigarette. He smiles and swings me up in his arms. He says, "Looks like we both got a little dirty today!" I say I've been working all day and I'm bushed. Daddy says, "I'm bushed too!" We wash our hands under the cold hose. Daddy carries me inside. He tickles my bottom and I laugh. I hear chicken frying in the kitchen. Daddy says it smells good. He says let's see what Mommy's up to. I watch Daddy hug her. She bends a little and smiles.

After dinner, Mommy says it's bath time. I hear water running in the tub. I toss dirty clothes in the hamper. I get my PJs out like Mommy told me to and run to the bathroom. She's pouring pink powder from a pink box into the water.

"Yeah! We have Mr. Bubble!" I clap and Mommy smiles and puts a bath cap on my head. She lifts me into the tub with Matty. We play fishes. Mommy says our fingers are raisins. The towel smells like flowers when she dries me off. I'm sleepy. Mommy pulls PJs over my head.

Mommy says it's time for bed. Matty and I race to jump on our beds so monsters can't grab our ankles. I'm glad we share a room.

I might be scared by myself. Mommy turns on the night-light. It's supposed to keep monsters away. She tucks me in bed. She smells like Mr. Bubble and hair spray.

I think how good it feels to be in my warm bed after my bath. I fall asleep as fast as my eyes close.

Daddy wakes me up. The night-light's off. I can't see. I ask him to turn it on. He must've forgotten the monsters.

"Shhh," he says.

Daddy smells bad. He smells like the sour milk Mommy put on my Lucky Charms once. My favorite's the pink hearts. I save them to eat last with yellow moons, orange stars, and green things. I think it's the stuff Daddy puts in his lip. He spits a lot with that stuff. It's stinky. Why's Daddy pushing my covers off? He pulls my undies down. What's that sound? I hear his belt buckle. I make little fists. I'm going to get spanked with the belt. Why am I getting spanked? I try to think what I've done. He's not saying.

He turns me over. My tears get the sheet wet. He makes sounds like Hansel when he digs. There's no spanking. Daddy pushes his big knees on my bed. I hear Matty move a little. He's in his bed next to me. When's the spank coming? I hear sounds like a dog growling. My bed sinks. Something hard is on my bottom. I hear more dog growls. Daddy puts something sticky on my bottom. My bed goes back up when he gets off. He leaves. Is he coming back to spank me? I'm kind of cold.

CHAPTER 7

Daddy's Girls

Daddy put me in front of the TV after dinner. It has wood on the sides. He says it's "the best." He comes back into the living room with a brown bottle. "What's on the boob tube, princess?"

I smile. He's happy. I say, "Don't know."

Daddy lifts me up to his lap. We sit on the couch. I make an icky face. The bottle's stinky. He says it's his favorite beer. Daddy says it's alcohol and not for kids. He pets my head like a kitty. I curl up on his lap.

I say, "Meow," like my See 'n Say.

He laughs. I like it when Daddy laughs and when he rubs circles on my back.

Daddy puts me back on the carpet. I lie on my tummy. I like watching TV with my chin in my hands. Daddy lights a cigarette. He lies down next to me and pushes the green pillow under his head.

"C'mere," he says.

I scoot over. I smell soap and cigarettes. He squeezes my bottom. He pulls me close to him. I ask if I can play with his hair. His cigarette goes in the corner of his mouth. I hear a hiss like a mad cat. It burns red. He squeezes one eye closed and nods. Smoke rolls out of his mouth. I get up and skip to my room. I find clips and ribbon. I skip back to the living room. Daddy's back is on the couch. He takes a big drink from the brown bottle and tells me to wait a minute, that he'll be right back.

I hear Daddy's loud pee in the bathroom. He flushes and I know he's going to the kitchen from the floor sounds. Daddy's back with another bottle. It has water drops on the sides. He drinks it fast. He makes a loud burp and we both laugh. It smells like his drink.

"Okay, princess," he says. "Give Daddy a new do." I hop up on the couch and cross my legs behind his head. I forgot to get a comb, so I run to the bathroom. I'm running back and bump into Daddy's legs. He's leaving the kitchen with a new bottle. He laughs and says, "Slow down, speedster."

I brush his short hair. I wish his hair was longer. I'd make pig-tails with ribbons, but I use my clips. When Daddy goes in the kitchen again, I can't help giggling. His hair sticks up with my red clip. He gets more bottles. They're all empty when I hear the dogs barking. Mommy and Matty are home.

I open the door. Mommy's carrying Matty. He's asleep in her arms and she says it's late. She says, "Deidi should be in bed." Daddy says we're having too much fun. He lights a cigarette. I fix his hair. Mommy comes back in her bathrobe. She says it's time for bed. Daddy's voice is slow, and he hiccups. Daddy says let me finish his hair. He waves his hand. It flops on the carpet. Mommy tells him to put me to bed. She says good night, but she doesn't kiss me. My chest hurts.

I wake up on the couch. Mommy's lifting me up. The screen door slams. I hear Daddy's car turn on. She puts me in bed and kisses me good night.

I wake up and Matty's already out of bed. I run to the living room and plop down next to him on the floor. It's time for

Saturday-morning cartoons. He's smiling at the TV and bouncing his bottom on his feet. He doesn't look at me. Mommy says Matty gets glued to the TV. Mommy walks into the living room. She tells us to turn off the TV and get in the car. She has a mad voice. Matty's face is sad. We run outside in our PJs without any shoes on. Mommy has red eyes. Daddy's car's gone. Mommy gets in her car. We're not in boxes with buckles. She starts driving. She doesn't talk for a long time. We see Daddy driving to us. I wish we were watching cartoons.

I see a lady sitting by Daddy. He pushes her head down. Mommy yells she saw her. She's calling Daddy bad names. He slows down. Mommy goes faster. We're close to Daddy. She grabs her purse and gets lipstick. Mommy's lips are pink, but she colored outside the lines a little. She turns the car over the yellow road paint. Our car's in front of Daddy's now and he can't go around.

Mommy stops the car, jumps out, and slams the door. She runs to Daddy's car. She opens his door. A lady with long brown hair pops up. We hear more yelling. Mommy pulls Daddy's sunglasses off. She starts hitting him. She's trying to hit the lady too. I think Mommy's pulling her hair. Daddy's trying to stop her. He pushes Mommy away. She throws his sunglasses on the road. Mommy yells and stomps the sunglasses to pieces. My hands are shaking. They hold each other. Mommy runs back. She gets in our car. She's crying. She drives the car in dirt by the road. I can't see Daddy in the dust behind us.

Mommy doesn't talk all the way home. She tells us to get dressed and go outside and play. My tummy makes loud sounds. We didn't eat breakfast. Matty and I don't ask about lunch.

Daddy's back. We had dinner without him. My tummy's still unhappy. Daddy's in his chair and Mommy's in her chair. They aren't talking. Matty and I are watching TV. Mommy says it's time for bed. Matty's in bed before me. He's fast and I'm sleepy.

I open my eyes and it's not dark anymore. Mommy and Daddy are still asleep when Matty and I get up. Mommy comes in the living room. Her hair looks funny. She tells us to get our cereal. She says they were up late and need to sleep more. Matty makes me laugh when he says, "I'm cuckoo for Cocoa Puffs."

I play with my toys until Mommy and Daddy finally get up. I hear him go outside, and I see Mommy in the kitchen. I ask if I can have a piece of the candy Grandma gave me. Mommy says no. She gives a piece to Matty. Mommy says it's because the queen bee doesn't get everything she wants.

"Does that make you feel bad?" she asks.

My head goes up and down. I think she'll be nice, but Mommy says I need to feel bad. My chest starts to hurt. She says I'm not the only one who needs treats. Other people need things too, not just me. Mommy says just because Daddy treats me special doesn't mean I'm the only one. Mommy asks if I can remember that. My head goes up and down again.

CHAPTER 8

Uncle Drew

Today we're going to Grandma and Grandpa's house in Davenport. We drive by so many wheat fields. I wave out the window when we pass Harrington. My other Grandma and Grandpa might be in town getting their mail. I'm happy to see some cows and tell Mommy to look. She shushes me and points to the radio. We drive up a big hill and I see Davenport. It's bigger than Ruff or Harrington. I wish I could count all the green trees. I think the houses look happy here. There's lots of grass and flowers. White bedsheets wave like flags from clotheslines. I like that Grandma and Grandpa live on the top of a hill.

Mommy says first we're going to see Great-Grandma. She lives down the street. Mommy likes to go for drives. But I don't think it's fun to drive. My tummy feels sick from the car ride. When we finally get there and get out of the car, Mommy tells me be nice to Uncle Drew. He's Great-Grandpa's brother. She says people like Brer Fox are mean to him. Mommy says Uncle Drew can't help that he has a hole in his lip. He talks funny. There are stairs going down to Great-Grandma's basement. Uncle Drew lives down there.

Great-Grandma has poodles. She says they're toy poodles. The black poodle's name's Toy Yung Sunshine. Great-Grandma's poodles wear bows by their ears. The bows match the red paint on their nails. I wonder who paints doggy nails? I hear the poodles barking in the house. Great-Grandma's saying, "Stop it, stop, be quiet!" She opens the squeaky screen door, and I hear her TV too. It's loud. Great-Grandma's hearing isn't good. She kisses my cheek and says she's happy we came to visit.

Great-Grandma has a big picture in her living room. It's a forest with a mommy deer and Bambi. I like to touch the deer because Great-Grandma pasted them on her picture. She says it needed a little more life. Great-Grandma gives me two cookies from her big green cookie jar. It looks like an apple. She runs water into a green glass. It matches her cupboards, and the green squares in her carpet. I say, "Great-Grandma, how's your champagne today?" She says, "Very well, Deidi. Thank you for asking." Great-Grandma calls water her champagne. She told me champagne's really alcohol. She says she's never taken a sip of alcohol.

Great-Grandma has a gold couch in her living room. She calls it her davenport. I say, "But, that's where you live, Davenport." Great-Grandma says, "Yes, it is, Deidi." Mommy says it's a word for sofa.

Great-Grandma takes me in the pink bedroom. It's for "company." She shows me the new quilt she's making. I think it looks like all her quilts. I love that she makes them. Great-Grandma and Great-Grandpa have twin beds in their blue bedroom.

We walk back to the living room, and I see Uncle Drew sitting in the big gold chair. Mommy tells me to say hello and get in his lap. He pulls me by my arm. His hand's under my dress. He pinches my pee-pee. I say, "Ow!" I'm crying. Uncle Drew pulls me more. He says, "Don you like Unc Dew? Don be afay cause Unc Dew loffs you." Mommy gets up from the couch. She's walking to me. Great-Grandma's picking up the poodles. They're barking again.

Mommy picks me up. She takes me to the bathroom. She asks if Uncle Drew put his hand where I pee. I nod. Mommy pushes me down. She pulls my undies to my knees. She's mad at me. Mommy pokes my pee-pee. She says, "Did he do this?" It hurts, but I just nod. My chest hurts more. I know I'm bad. But I don't know how. Mommy says I better be nice to Uncle Drew. She says Great-Grandma won't let me be at her house. And I won't get to go to Grandma's. I want to go there so much. I wish I was there now.

Mommy and I walk back into the living room. Uncle Drew pulls me on his lap. He pinches me again. I'm not crying, though. Mommy's laughing and picks me up from him. She holds me on her hip and looks at her watch. I hear the bell ringing outside. This tells the town when it's lunchtime and if there's a fire. Mommy says we're meeting Grandma downtown in ten minutes. We say bye-bye.

I see Grandma outside the restaurant and run to her. She lifts me up for a big hug. She's wearing a short-sleeve top with red and yellow flowers all over it. Her stretchy pants are red. Her earrings are yellow. She wears happy clothes. Grandma calls me her favorite girl. She's the nicest to me of anyone. I sit next to her in the red booth and eat a grilled cheese sandwich for lunch.

Grandma and Mommy talk in big people voices. I pretend not to hear. Grandma says it's sad and now he's gone too. I scoot closer and she pulls napkins out of a red box. Mommy says a lot of people around here hated him. Grandma nods and spells, "A-S-S-E-S." Mommy wipes under her eye.

"Are you crying, Mommy?"

"No, but I'm sad. A really good man was shot and died." She's digging in her brown purse. Grandma hands her a pink Kleenex and she blows her nose. There's lots of snots by the sound of it.

"Was he black like the other good man?"

Mommy shakes her head. "No, he was white. But he tried to help people like the black man."

Grandma says he would've been a better president than his brother.

Mommy's voice gets a little loud when she says, "And now they're both dead."

"Who, Mommy?"

She says the good man's brother was the president. Mommy says that's who tells all the big people what to do. She says he was shot and died right before Matty was born.

"Was he good too?"

Grandma nods. Mommy sort of whispers, "Yes."

"Who shot the good men?"

Grandma squeezes my hand and says, "Bad men."

"Why?"

Grandma turns my chin to look at her. She says, "Because, Deidi, some people don't like good." She taps my nose and says, "It's nothing for you to worry about." Grandma hugs me and orders a milkshake. I like the lady with the pad of paper. She stuck a blue pen behind her ear when she brought our lunch over. Mommy lifts her white cup to the lady for more coffee.

Mommy says this restaurant used to be called the Mitten when she was young. I'm drinking a yummy chocolate milkshake. It has whipped cream and one cherry. Mommy looks at my drink and says they still use the same glasses.

CHAPTER 9

Band-Aids

Grandma in Davenport gave me paper dolls. I'm cutting a pretty girl out on the lines. I cut out a hat, a dress, and boots for her. I've laid them on the carpet. I like the quiet living room. I hear *clickety, clickety.* I'm thinking, *That's okay. He's far away.* But the *clickety, clickety*'s getting closer and closer. Matty shoots into the living room on his Batmobile. I yell, "Stop!" and dive on my cutouts. He yells, "Screeeech!" and stops in time.

Matty starts talking fast. He says he needs help. He says he's chasing bad guys. I say hold on and pick up my paper dolls.

"You're Robin," he shouts, and we race to catch bad guys. It takes a long time. Matty shoots one with his pop gun. He says that bad guy's dead.

I say, "Phew, good job!"

Matty says tie up the next bad guy with my jump rope. This is a big job. Matty says he'll be back. It takes me a long time. Matty drives up and says we got all the bad guys. We're done playing, so I grab my new coloring book off the table. I'm coloring Minnie Mouse's dress in the living room. Matty walks in and grabs my crayon.

"Give me back my crayon, Matty!"

Mommy's with Daddy in the kitchen. She says, "Be nice, Matty."

He breaks my crayon. I don't tell. I keep coloring. He'll be meaner if I tell. Matty crawls in front of me.

He whispers, "Your coloring's ugly, nah, nah, nah, nah, nah, nah."

"No, it's not. Liar, liar pants on fire." He's making me mad. I keep coloring. Matty stands up and steps on my coloring book. He turns his foot back and forth. Minnie Mouse rips. I get up, but he pushes me down. I'm mad, I don't like him. I get up and he sticks out his tongue. I kick his leg. He grabs mine and we fall over. I pinch his arm.

He says, "Ow!" and punches my arm.

It hurts and I'm crying.

Mommy says, "You two better not be fighting again."

Matty's biting my head! It hurts so much I yell, "Mommy, Daddy!" I push my fists in Matty's tummy. He makes a funny sound like *oof.*

Mommy walks into the living room. She yells, "Stop it!" and tells Daddy to get in here. My head's bleeding and my eyes are blurry.

Daddy grabs Matty's arm. His feet go off the floor. Daddy takes him out of the living room. Mommy gets the first-aid box. It has stuff to fix owies. She cleans my face and says she's mad at me. She says don't say a word. She keeps pulling my hair back. It hurts, she's too rough.

"I told you to stop fighting with him, didn't I?"

I nod.

She says if I fight again, I'm in big trouble. She says, "Are you listening to me, Deidi?"

I nod. I'm listening more to Daddy and Matty. I hope Daddy doesn't do bad things to Matty.

I jump when Matty screams, "Ow!" He's crying real loud. Daddy's yelling at him. He's says, "Now you know what it feels like!"

Mommy tells me to sit still. She takes paper off a Band-Aid and sticks it on my head just above my eye.

Daddy and Matty come back into the living room. Matty's holding his arm. Daddy says Matty better stop biting now. Matty's bleeding too. Mommy gets a big Band-Aid out of the box and puts it on his arm.

Daddy gives Matty a little shove. "What do you say?"

Matty says, "Sorry, Deidi." I see a red dot on his Band-Aid. It's getting bigger and bigger.

One time Matty bit Hansel. He got fur in his mouth. It stuck to his tongue. Mommy said Matty was lucky Hansel didn't bite back. She says most dogs would. Mommy says she wishes Hansel bit Matty. She says it'd teach him a lesson. She says maybe he's learned his lesson now. Daddy says he better have. Matty's not mad at me. He says Daddy bit him real hard.

CHAPTER 10

Wheat

Matty and I run outside. He breaks the top off a wheat thing. He rolls it in his hands. He shows me the wheat berries.

"Here, try it, Deidi." He gives me a top to roll in my hands. The wheat berries tumble out in my hand too.

The wheat's the same color as the sun. Matty says, "Shhh," and we're both quiet.

There's no sound.

He points to the big wheat field. Wind pushes parts of the field to one side. More wind pushes the other side. Matty whispers, "They're dancing."

This is fun. I love summer. But it's too hot.

We go back inside. We ask Mommy to read *Frederick* to us. It's about a field mouse and his family. They work hard to get wheat in their house. They need it for when it snows. They stay in the cozy house a long time. I say I've seen Frederick and his family outside. They're fast.

Matty says those are different mice.

I say, "No, it's Frederick and his family."

Mommy says, "Shhh," and keeps reading.

Frederick doesn't get in trouble when he sits and his family works. He doesn't get in trouble when he stares at the meadow. His family asks what he's doing, and he says he's working. He's making up poems and stories. One time his family asks if he was sleeping, but he doesn't get in trouble. They don't hit him or call him names.

After it's been cold out for a long time, Frederick shows his work to his family. He tells them about the sunbeam, the colors, and lots of other stories. He did so much work! The family's so happy. I love Frederick's family. I love Frederick. He hears the wind. He likes the big trees just like me.

Matty points to the wheat in the book. He says, "That's what they pumped out my tummy, Deidi."

I say, "Yuck."

He tells me they gave him big shots, or he would've died. Mommy says a shot is medicine. Mommy and Daddy say he ate bad wheat. I don't want Frederick's family to eat bad wheat and die.

Matty says he's sad Daddy didn't see him in the hospital. Mommy says they fix sick people there. It was far away. I think that was mean of Daddy. Matty got toys from people at the hospital.

Mommy says Matty and I need a bath. We're dirty from playing outside.

Matty's pushing me in the bathtub. He's being mean. He pushes his leg on my leg. He wants all the room. I push him back. He pushes harder. He says his floaty boat's doing big work. I tell him to stop it. He says stop it. I say stooooop it! I see Mommy putting makeup on in the mirror. She says use the washcloth and soap to make sure we're clean.

Where's the soap? I look for white soap in the bubbles. I like the white soap, it floats. Matty's not pushing now. I roll on my tummy in front of him. Matty rubs my back. I ask Mommy to paint pictures on my back. She says not tonight. It's time to get out. I like to guess what Mommy paints on my back with soap. Last time she painted a cat, but I guessed a horse. Mommy painted the flowers on the wall in the living room. She says they're sunflowers.

Matty stops rubbing my back. He pushes something in my bottom.

"What's that?" I say. It kind of hurts where I poop.

Matty just laughs, so I laugh too.

Mommy says, "Okay you two funny fishes. Time for bed."

CHAPTER 11

Princess

I'm in my bedroom, playing Candyland with my pretend funny friends when I hear Mommy's mad voice. I think, *Mommy's being mean to Daddy.* I don't know why. I trip down the hall to the living room.

Mommy yells, "Deidi, don't rub your eyes when you're walking!"

I see Daddy's shoulders shake. He starts crying. I go to hug him, but Mommy grabs my arm. Her pointy nails hurt.

"Ow!"

Why's she so mean? Daddy just sits there. Mommy takes me to my room. She yells I'm his little princess. She yells that doesn't mean I get what I want. Mommy pulls my pants and my undies to my feet. She sits on my bed and puts me across her legs.

Mommy's hitting my bottom hard. It hurts and I'm crying. I start to get up. She pushes me down. She yells this is all Daddy's fault.

I say, "Mommy stop!" She's scaring me. She's hitting me and yelling bad names. She stands up and I fall on the floor. It hurts and

Mommy yells for Daddy to do a bad word and "daughter." I see her hands shaking.

I'm bad, but why am I bad? Mommy says stop crying in her scary voice. She tells me to sit on my bed. To never do it again. I promise I won't. I don't know what I promise. Daddy leaves and doesn't say bye-bye.

I'm in my room a long time. I go back to Candyland and my funny friends. Mommy comes in and says Matty and I get TV dinners. She smiles at me. I want to cry.

After dinner, she lets me put dirty dishes in the washer. Matty and I watch TV, and then Mommy tucks us in bed.

Mommy's yelling wakes me up. I hear *crash* and *boom*. Holding Raggedy Ann, I tiptoe into the living room. Daddy's back. He's on the couch. Mommy's standing in front of him. Her arms are over her head. She looks wet. She sees me and points her finger at me. She says why don't you go do a bad word to the princess?

Daddy turns and looks at me. He is so sad. His eyes are sinking in his face. He's turning red. He grabs Mommy. I jump. Daddy throws her down. He sits on her like Matty when he's mad at me. Daddy's holding Mommy's neck. She's making funny sounds. Her hands grab his hands. I put Raggedy Ann's face in front of mine.

Daddy's yelling bad words. He's yelling shut up. He yells at me to go back to bed. I'm so scared. I go back to my bed. I fall asleep to Mommy and Daddy yelling.

CHAPTER 12

Harvest

It's too hot to play in the yard today. I got sunburned one time. It hurt. Mommy had to put stuff on me. She said I was a brave girl.

It's the end of summer. Mommy says men are coming to help with harvest. I saw the combine Daddy drives. It's a big tractor with things that cut wheat. He climbs way up to a chair at the top. His combine's red. And it's real loud.

I saw Daddy put wheat in a big truck. There's a man who drives the truck. Daddy says the truck goes to a place and dumps the wheat. Trains take it to boats, and boats take it to all over the world.

Mommy says the wheat gets squished up and then they can bake cinnamon rolls with it. I love Grandma's cinnamon rolls. I wonder if she bakes them with Daddy's wheat. Mommy's baking food for harvest. It smells good all day. I play in the kitchen in case she needs my help. She says I'm a good helper.

I'm looking at the black-and-white paper on the table. I think, *I need my egg.* I tell Mommy I'll be back. I know my egg's in my room. Here it is. I run back to the kitchen. I open the black-and-white paper. The kitchen table's brown. Mommy says this is a newspaper.

It has stories and pictures. I find a nice picture of a bunny. I take the top off my egg. I see Silly Putty inside. Mommy says the putty's beige. I like how the word sounds. I say it over and over. I press the putty on the paper. Mommy says stop saying beige. I pull the putty off. The bunny on the paper is on my putty. I stretch the putty with my fingers and the bunny looks like a giraffe. It makes me laugh.

Mommy asks me to get the napkins out. I'm happy I know where they are. She looks out the window and says she's happy it's cooling off. Mommy says it looks like the men are done working.

I hear Daddy and the other men coming home for supper. I see them in the window. I tell Mommy that they look like dust monsters. She smiles. I open the back door. It tastes like dirt outside and the big trees look sad. But the pretty sunset is making me happy. The blue sky's starting to turn pink. I can feel a little breeze.

We have a big swimming pool by the house. It's blue and tall, and there are big stairs to climb to reach the water. Mommy says I can't swim.

She carries tubs of soap and water to the table outside. I watch the men wash. Their arms are brown up to their short sleeves. I see white skin when they scrub and their sleeves go up their arms. I take the tubs inside when they're done to help Mommy. Matty likes to arm-wrestle with the men. They let him win.

I watch the men drink brown bottles with Mommy and Daddy. They squish cigarettes in the gravel. It looks like popcorn. The bottles are noisy when they throw them at the garbage can. Sometimes Daddy's arms go up. They say good shot. I say, "Yeah! Daddy!" He pats my head. We sit at the two wood tables outside for supper. I like it when we eat outside.

Mommy puts us to bed when it's all the way dark outside. She smells like the brown bottles and cigarettes. I hear Daddy laughing outside. That makes Mommy laugh when she kisses me. She's funny. I hear, "Go get 'um!" Hansel and Snoopy start barking. I hear Mommy laughing. I fall asleep happy.

Daddy wakes me up. I'm so sleepy. He says he has a friend. Who? They stink. I don't like this. My pee-pee hurts. I'm crying. I feel bad.

Daddy says, "Shhh. Don't get us in trouble with Mommy, princess."

He's nice and I like that.

They laugh. Daddy turns me over. He pokes my bottom. He's sticky. I hear Matty say, "Ow!" and "Daddy!" The friend says, "Shhh!"

Daddy says his friend's playing. I hear dog sounds like with Daddy before. Matty's bed makes squeaking sounds. They whisper bye-bye. They're laughing. I hear the screen door close. I'm dirty. I can't find my undies.

Daddy comes back. He says not to tell Mommy about his friend. He says she'll get real mad at us. I promise Daddy not to tell. He says I'll get a treat tomorrow. I fall asleep and wonder what it'll be.

CHAPTER 13

Move to Moses Lake

We had our last harvest in Ruff. We don't live there now. Mommy and Daddy say we have a new leaf in Moses Lake. I like our new blue house. Mommy says, "It's gray, Deidi."

I say, "It's blue, Mommy."

She says, "What?"

I say, "Nothing."

I see a big white tower. I hear tick-tock turning sounds. We're driving down our gravel road. It's squished between wheat fields. Daddy says the big tower has water inside. It comes out of our faucets.

Here's our big front yard. There's a wheat field between the yard and the park across the street. That's where the water tower lives. There's a school and church too. We have neighbors on both sides. But the wheat fields are so big, we can't walk to visit.

I love the trees in our yard. Daddy says some have plums. Plums are purple. Great-Grandma has Burpee's purple potatoes in her vegetable garden. I say "Burpee's purple potatoes" over and over. I don't let sound come out. Mommy and Daddy will tell me to stop. Daddy says there's a potato plant in Moses Lake. It stinks when we drive by. I think it should be the Burpee's purple poopy potatoes plant.

I walk by four white posts to the front door. They hold up the roof from the garage door to the front door. You don't need an umbrella here when it rains. Mommy says there're secret stairs inside the garage. "Can we see them?" I ask. "No" Mommy says. I ask if they're in-vis-ble. She says, "No, you have to pull them out of the ceiling." Matty says he'll find them. Daddy says, "Sorry Tiger, the attic is for big people only." Matty wiggles and says attics have icky spiders.

I count windows by the front door. Two are in the kitchen. One's in the bathroom across the hall from my room. It has a green bathtub and green toilet paper. One window is in the blue bathroom with the shower and the blue toilet paper. Matty's room's next door. There's a closet in the hall between my room and Mommy and Daddy's room. Their room is across the hall from the blue bathroom. Mommy said the house is shaped like the letter L.

There're two big windows and one small one in the living room. We have wood bookshelves around the fireplace. The brick fireplace's in the kitchen and living room. It's white in the living room. In the kitchen it's like the oldest piggy's brick house in the book. The wolf can't blow the brick house down. He tries to trick the oldest piggy. But piggy's smart. When the wolf comes down the chimney, he falls in hot water. Piggy boils and eats him for dinner. I've eaten a boiled egg. I liked it. I've eaten deer. I didn't like it. Daddy shot the deer. Mommy says they don't shoot Bambis. Matty says he'd shoot Bambi. I say that's mean. Mommy says no one will shoot Bambi. Daddy shot a buck and took the antlers off. He says that's the word for horn things on the head. Daddy and Grandpa shoot geese from Canada in a place on the farm. I don't know what Canada is, but I know they have ginger ale. Mommy gives me Canada's ginger ale if I'm sick. I don't like it. I like orange pop.

My new bedroom has a big window. I have two white closets for toys and clothes. My carpet's blue. Matty's carpet's green. He has a desk in his room. He has two windows. I have my own door.

Mommy and Daddy say they have a lot of work to do. Mommy says the big boxes in the rooms are made of cardboard. I like how they smell. We have a basement. It's dark, but you can see people's feet outside in the little windows. Mommy washes clothes down there.

There's white wood on the walls in the living room. Mommy says it's called paneling. She says the sofa and chairs work in there. I don't know what they do. She put the tall light with stripes on the covers by Daddy's chair. My favorite orange light's next to her green chair. It has a little chain I pull to turn it on. I can see the light bulb inside the orange bubble. I think there's a light like this in *The Jetsons* cartoon. My favorite chair has flowers on it. People put drinks and ashtrays on top of the long stereo table. The top opens, and records go in to play music. Mommy says it's a coffee table, I don't know why.

We have a pasture. Daddy said we'll have a horse! I saw a parade with horses. A pretty girl rode a horse. She had a sparkly cowboy hat, top, and pants. She had red boots like mine. I ride my play pony. I hold on with one hand. I wave to the crowd with my other hand. The end of my pony makes a tapping sound on the floor. In the parade, horses pooped on the street and didn't get in trouble. There were clowns with ruffles on their necks to scoop the poop up.

Mommy's going to teach school in Moses Lake. Matty and I get to go to school someday. I don't know what Daddy does in Moses Lake. I think he's a farmer. This house isn't a farm like Ruff, though. It has wheat fields all around, but they're somebody else's. I don't know who.

Mommy says we'll go to the library. We'll bring books and records home. When we're done, they'll go back to the library.

Mommy says there's a good Mexican place to eat in Moses Lake. She says they eat beans and rice. I like it when Mommy makes beans and hammocks. Mommy says it's beans and ham hocks. She says you lie down on a hammock. It's tied between two trees. She said you eat ham hocks. Matty says they're piggy legs. I don't want to eat a piggy's legs.

I'm sitting on the flower chair, and sun's in the living-room window. I pat a round pillow where the sun's coming in. The dust specks float and twinkle. The house's quiet and outside's quiet. Maybe I hear the Whos on the dust speck. Maybe it's the dust speck Horton hears in the book Mommy reads. I watch the specks of dust float like tiny clouds.

I hear Daddy and Mommy come in the front door. Daddy says he needs a new mower for all the nice new grass. Mommy says, no you don't. She says he needs to talk to the kids about the electric fence. I ask Daddy what "lectric" is. Mommy says, "E-lectric." It's the same thing in light bulbs but in the fence. The fence will hurt. I don't know why a fence hurts. Daddy says to stay away from the electric fence. It will hurt a lot if we touch it. I hope it doesn't hurt Hansel.

I'm happy at our new house. I'm happy Mommy and Daddy say this is a new leaf. They say that means good things.

CHAPTER 14

Drawing Pictures

Daddy's gone when I wake up and eat Frosted Flakes in the kitchen. After breakfast, Mommy gives me crayons, paper, glue, and scissors. She says to make a pretty picture. She'll put it on the fridge. I pick out paper. I cut and glue colors. I pick out crayon colors. I draw dots on the papers.

I hop off my chair to show Mommy. She says she loves it. She tapes it to the fridge. I dance in a circle. She says it's art. Mommy says, let's clean up. She gives me a red-and-white box. We put my glue, crayons, scissors, and pencils in it. I love my box. Mommy says I can draw on it. She tells Matty this is my box. He gets his own box. It's brown and he's happy too.

Mommy says we're going to play in the basement today. I say, "No. It's icky down there." She says, "It won't be if you follow me." Mommy grabs dish towels. She takes a brown paper bag off the desk. We go down the big steps.

We walk past the washer and dryer and past the big room to the scary room. Matty and I stop at the doorway. We can't see Mommy until we hear *ch-chick*. The room lights up. A string of little silver beads swings by Mommy's head. Matty points up and says, "Those used to be trees." I look up and see big pieces of wood. Some wires are poking out.

Mommy says he's right and "Now they're holding up the kitchen floor."

"Why doesn't this room have a top on it?" I ask.

She laughs and says because it's a storage room. Mommy's happy when she turns the paper bag upside down. Paint pots and pencils *tappity-tap* on the floor. My heart does a happy jump. These are pretty colors. Mommy says, "This room is made of cement, like the back patio. We can draw and paint here, but never on the back patio. Okay?" Matty and I nod.

Mommy takes lids off the pots for Matty and me. She picks up a pencil and says she's drawing a clown and balloons.

I dip my pointer in a pot. The paint's soft and cold. It smells good. I look at my red finger. I wish I could lick it, but I know paint tastes bad. I'm making the hard wall red. I want the red here and here. I stand back.

"Look, Mommy, all my marks made one red balloon!"

She says I've done a good job.

I put two fingers in the red pot. I make small balloons around my big balloon. The big one has friends. It won't be lonely. The sky's full of red balloons.

"There's plenty of paint for more pictures," Mommy says.

Matty says he painted a green balloon. I walk behind him. It looks like a big green pancake with a furry hat. The pancake's bigger than his head.

Matty says my red balloons need blue balloons too. I say okay, and we share the blue pot. I'm painting little blue balloons. Matty says his balloons are secret bullets. They're shooting my red balloons out of the sky.

"Stop shooting my balloons!" I'm going to cry if he doesn't stop. Mommy tells Matty, "Scoot over and paint something new."

Matty scoots and sits on his feet. My blue balloons are all done. Matty looks at Mommy. "I think I drew the 'bominable snowman." He looks back at the wall. Mommy looks and says, "I think you're right, Matty." I squish between them. I say, "It's the bom-ball snow-man." We all laugh. Matty says, "It should ride a horse."

And I watch him paint a blue horse.

"It looks like a snowman's riding a cat," Matty says, and that makes me laugh too. He looks at me and says, "It's not funny, Deidi," as he paints a stripe under the horse. "That's our pasture."

"Can I paint us in the pasture too?" I ask.

"Sure, but don't mess it up."

I tell Matty he can't look until I'm done. I paint him in front of the horse. I paint me behind him. We're both blue. I tell Matty he can look. He doesn't say anything at first. Then he points at the wall and says, "Is that me, Deidi?"

I nod.

"No. That's not me, that's a penguin."

I'm trying not to laugh.

He points at me on the wall. "What's sticking out of your head?"

I can't stop my laugh.

"Why are you floating? Why am I a penguin?" Now Mommy's laughing too. "Deidi, why'd you paint me a penguin?" he asks.

"It's not a penguin!"

We put the pencils and paints back in the bag, and Mommy says, "Job well done."

We go back up the stairs, and I hear Matty say, "It's a good pen-guin. Are there penguins in Moses Lake?"

Mommy says, "No, Matty. There're no penguins in Moses Lake."

He says, "Uh-huh, there's one."

CHAPTER 15

Snow

I'm happy it's snowing, and I'm happy because it's almost Christmas. I tell Daddy it's a good thing our new house has a chimney for Santa. Daddy says that Santa's not coming. He's too busy with his reindeer and all.

"What?"

Daddy smiles. He tickles my bottom and says, "Gotcha! Just kidding. Santa's bringing all kinds a stuff this year!"

Mommy's putting mittens, caps, coats, and boots on Matty and me. Daddy winks and asks if she'll dress him to go outside too.

My nose feels the cold as soon as we step outside. I hear Hansel barking. He's racing around the side of the house. Daddy says, watch out, here he comes! Hansel doesn't really run in snow. Matty says it's more like he hops. Hansel goes to Mommy, jumps up, and puts his paws on her shoulders to lick her face. His tail keeps wagging after she tells him to stop and to get down. Hansel looks at me. Before I can run, he's got me in the snow licking my face. His breath smells like dog food and fish. Matty's yelling, "C'mere, boy, over here." Hansel hops away.

We build a big snowman. Mommy says it's lopsided. I like that word. She helps me say it. Daddy says stop saying lopsided. I put the carrot in the middle of the snowman's head. Mommy says the snowman can breathe now. Matty and Daddy are making snowballs.

Mommy says, "C'mon, Deidi, I think the warm house is where we girls want to be."

I put my mitten in her glove and we go inside. She helps me take my coat off. Mommy grabs me with both arms and gives me a big hug. She squeezes me and says, "I love you so much, Deidi."

I say, "I love you so much too, Mommy." This feels the best!

Mommy's helping me into dry pants when Matty comes in crying. His hat's half off. He says Daddy threw a hard ball and it hit him in the head. His face is red. Matty says his ear's making noise. Mommy says be a big boy and it will go away.

Daddy comes in. He says, "Hey, Tiger, let's go back outside, that was getting fun!"

Matty shakes his head. He says, "No, I don't want to."

Daddy tickles Matty's head. He says, "Okay, baby boy, we stay in da house where it warm wi' mama."

Mommy tells Matty to help Daddy make a fire while she makes dinner. I ask if I can help her. She says to clear off the table. I like clearing off the table.

Matty helps Daddy build a fire. It makes me feel warm when we're eating dinner. The wood snaps and pops. I help Mommy clean the dishes after dinner. She says I was a big help. I go into the living room and Daddy is on the floor in front of the TV changing channels. Matty's in the middle of the room going around and around in a circle. He keeps saying Rudolph's on tonight, Rudolph's on tonight. Mommy walks in, looks at Matty, and asks Daddy, "What's he doing?" Matty says, "Rudolph's on tonight, hip, hip, hooray!" He's doing a wobbly dance now. He says, "Dizzy," and falls. Mommy says, "Let's get some Jiffy Pop and Tang for the special event!"

CHAPTER 16

Christmas 1968

It's the night before Christmas and I'm sitting at the kitchen table drawing Rudolph for Matty. I'm listening to the best voice sing *Si-lent night, Ho-ly night, all is calm, all is bright . . . Sleep in heavenly peace. Sleep in heavenly peace.* Mommy has the stereo on in the living room. She has the sound nice and loud.

I see Mommy's back as she's making a salad. She has a pretty dress on. She's wearing my favorite shiny shoes. She says they're "flats." Her hair's all poufy around her head. The ends are curled. I wish my hair was beautiful like Mommy's. My hair's short. Mommy says the hairs above my eyes are bangs. They stick up in the morning. Matty says I look like a Martian. I tell him I've seen *My Favorite Martian*, and I don't look like a Martian. He says, okay, well you look funny. I say he looks like Fred Munster. We laugh because that's stupid. Matty says he's going to his room to play with Legos.

I hear Daddy come in the front door. He says, "Hello, Bing!" He says that's the singer on the record.

"My name's not Bing!" I say.

He bends over and runs to me saying, "I'm gonna getcha, you little Bing girl." I run into the living room. Daddy catches me and swings me up to his face. He kisses my cheek and asks, "How ya doing, pretty one?"

I say, "Okay." I tell him about drawing Rudolph and getting ready for Santa.

Daddy says, "No, no, no. Santa only comes for good little girls. He's only coming for Mommy this year. Mommy says you haven't been good!"

This makes me sad, and I look down at my tummy.

Daddy says, "Now there's a sad face. I'm joking, princess. Santa can't wait to visit you!" He puts me down, and I run in circles like Matty when he's happy. Daddy says, "Be careful." I fall over. The room's spinning.

Daddy goes back in the kitchen. I follow him. I walk slow. I'm still dizzy. He gives Mommy a hug and says, "Don't you look pretty."

"Thank you, but you need a shower," she says.

Daddy says he'll be lickety-split but needs a little something first. I sit on my knees at the table as he opens the door to the fridge. I see his bottom and legs sticking out of the door. He's in there for a long time. I hear glass clanking and stuff moving.

Daddy stands up with his hand on the fridge door. He asks Mommy, "Hey, where're all my Buds?"

Mommy says she was too busy to pick any up today. She says, "You'd have a lot if you didn't drink so many last night." She says something about drinks where they're going.

Daddy's quiet. Now he says in a mean voice, "You know, I don't ask for much." He says words I don't know about school, clothes, and hair. "You do all these things that cost money. But you can't keep a few Buds in the fridge for me?" Daddy's voice is getting loud. He's swinging the fridge door. He says, "You don't even cook anymore. All we eat are damn TV dinners." He points at me. Daddy says in a quieter voice I still hear, "You don't even keep her clean. She's dirty all the damn time. She smells when I pick her up."

What? Do I smell?

Daddy bends back into the fridge. Mommy turns from the counter with a big bowl. *Crack!* She hits the side of Daddy's head, and he falls on the floor. She drops down next to him saying, "Oh, honey, are you okay? Oh my God, are you okay?" I run to Daddy.

He puts his hand to his head. He says, "Wow, you got me good!"

Daddy's okay.

I'm in bed now. I'm thinking about the presents under the tree. I'm trying to remember which ones mine are. I'm sleepy, but Daddy's in my room taking my covers off. His hands are cold. He pulls my undies down. He pushes me on my tummy, and I make a little sound. He says, "Shhh, princess. Daddy's here, everything's okay." He's making noises, but no words. I think the wolf sounded like him when he huffed and he puffed to blow down the piggy houses. He pushes his pee-pee in my bottom.

I'm thinking about our Santa mugs. I never see the mugs except Christmastime. Before, when I was a baby, I couldn't use a mug. Babies use bottles. Mommy's going to make hot chocolate. She'll put it in my Santa face mug. I'll put four marshmallows in the hot chocolate. Maybe she'll let me have five. Marshmallows are yummy. I wonder if they melt. I can't wait to have hot chocolate. Tomorrow I'll play a big person drinking coffee.

Daddy gets off my bed. His mouth is by my ear. He says, "Remember this is our special secret."

Is he talking about playing a big person drinking coffee? I fall asleep.

The light coming in my window from outside is extra bright when I wake up. I like it extra bright. My bottom hurts really, really bad. I don't know why. The big owies are making my eyes wet.

Maybe I can have Santa face hot chocolate and that will make the owies better.

CHAPTER 17

Christmas Morning

I've been waiting for Christmas for so long. It's here! All I see out my window is snow. I think it's pretty and hope we can play in it today. Grandma and Grandpa from Davenport are coming to visit.

Grandma gives us cookies and candies every Christmas. Matty says, "It's a sugar mountain." Mommy says her mommy works hard before Christmas. She makes all the treats from scratch. Each caramel is wrapped in paper called wax. Each chocolate has a curly thingy on top of the brown square. They're my favorites. Oh, but I can't forget the divinity. It's pink or white, and some have the tiniest pieces of nuts and some don't. I like no nut. I bite off a bit. It melts in my mouth. My favorite cookies are Grandma's sugar cookies. They have pink frosting every year. I also love the swirly round cookies she makes because they taste like cinnamon rolls.

Matty and I found Christmas presents from Mommy and Daddy hidden in the hall closet. We unwrapped little corners to see what was inside. I couldn't tell what they were. I was too scared to pull back any more wrapping. Mommy said she thought a mouse got into the presents when she put them under the tree. Matty and I had to cover our mouths to keep from laughing.

Mommy runs into my room and says, "Merry Christmas, Deidi." She has my hairbrush, a bottle, and a clip in her hand. "Sit still for a sec so I can fix your hair." She brushes and sprays and puts a pretty red flower clip on the side of my head. She snaps the clip closed and says, "There we are. Let's go see what Santa brought!"

Wrapping paper is all over the living room from last night.

Matty wants to put my new Barbie from Santa on his new red tractor, but I say no. My Barbie's beautiful. I can't wait to play with her. Matty's playing with his Hot Wheels now. He's happy saying, "Zoom, zoom," on the track. I wonder if Barbie can use my play makeup? The doorbell rings and Grandma and Grandpa are here. Mommy wishes her mommy and daddy a Merry Christmas and so does Daddy. He lifts packages from Grandpa's hands. They shake off the snow and Mommy asks, "Who wants coffee?"

Daddy says, "Don't mind Matty, he's pretty crazy right now." Matty's running in circles again in the living room.

"Isn't that what it's all about?" Grandma says. "Enjoy it because they grow up so fast!"

Daddy smiles and nods.

"You two need to get on Grandpa's lap for a picture," Mommy says, so I climb on one side and Matty climbs on the other. I hold Barbie tight so I don't drop her. Grandpa wears glasses that look funny when I see through them from the side. *Flash!*

I open my new makeup case. I put my finger on the color for eyes. I smudge like Mommy under my eyebrows. I think, *This will make them look better.*

My Grandma makes the prettiest presents in the whole world! She wraps them with special paper and pretty bows. I save her bows for when my hair grows long. Mommy said I could let it grow.

I'm happy Santa didn't forget Matty and me. I hope we left cookies for Santa and carrots for the reindeer.

LEAVING TWO

Somebody should let Hansel inside. He's barking a lot. My eyes open wide. Is that Hansel barking? I think I just heard him, what's happening? Why do I feel wet?

My right hand is stuck to the plastic page of colors on Herbie's super flower. I'm sweating. I slowly peel the page of blue petals off my hand and tell *The Adventures of the Three Colors*, "Please don't rip."

I'm seven years old. I'm seven years old. I'm leaving the places I've lived since I was a baby. I'm breathing so hard.

I talk silently to me. I'm okay. I'm still in my bedroom and I'm by myself.

I put my book in the moving box headed to Bellevue. I brought this book home after we visited there. I remember going to a department store downtown in Seattle and finding it on a table of books for sale. Afterward, I drank a milkshake at the Paul Bunyan Room. He cut down a lot of trees with his blue ox friend. Their picture is on the menu. It would be fun to go back when we move. The big store is called Frederick & Nelson. They have a lot of green carpets and sparkly lights hanging from high ceilings.

I guess I'm not really like an astronaut going to the moon. I've been to the moon. I feel like an astronaut moving to the moon.

I can't believe I'm thinking about so many things. Maybe I was dreaming too. I wish I'd heard Hansel barking.

I say it out loud, "Hansel's gone," and curl up on my side with my knees to my chin.

I roll onto my back and twirl a strand of blond hair around my pinkie finger. I couldn't do this when I was three. I count from three to seven. This hair's four years older. I wonder how it grew out of my head? I pull myself up to the top of my blue dresser and watch the busy world outside my big window for a minute. I'm surprised to see a yellow-headed blackbird holding a skinny tree limb. I've only seen them swaying on pussy willows by the lake. They make a strange sound, like a little piece of steel scraping on the sidewalk. Wind moves the pretty bird in a circle and off he flies. It feels like goodbye.

I bet the sparrows working in the grass stole my hair this year. I remember the nest I found on Grandma and Grandpa's farm. It looked like a cup of leaves and grass sewn together. Grandma said the birds weave hair with leaves and grass to keep their babies warm. I brushed my hair in our backyard just for them. Sparrows sing a lot in the morning and around dinnertime. It's so beautiful. Not like the shiny black-eyed bird I catch staring at me. He can't sing. The blue jay dips into the grass and pops up dangling a juicy pink worm. His bright-blue feather wings spread and lift like an elevator to the top of the plum tree.

I think I have that same color blue in a ribbon. I pull the knob on my top drawer and feel the loose bows inside. I lift a soft pile of pink satin, red fuzzy braid, and yellow ribbons as high as I can. I watch the colors float to their new home in a moving box. I've saved more ribbons than I've worn. I pinch a blue-jay-blue ribbon from the next pile and let the other blues, greens, and purples fall into Mr. Box. When I'm older I'll wear all my ribbons and bows because I won't need Mommy's help to do my hair anymore. Mr. Box eats my last ribbon. It's a creamy white color that looks like the warm eggs I've helped collect from different chicken coops.

The mama chickens didn't seem to mind when I took their eggs, but I always felt bad. I saw those eggs cracked over a skillet that sizzled the clear sides white. We hatched eggs that looked the same under a heat lamp at school. The shells cracked and tiny chicks pecked their way out. Their eyes were closed, but they knew what to do somehow.

I don't mind eating scrambled eggs because I know they're not baby chickens. I know hens need a rooster for that. My grandma from the farm told me so, and she showed me the big rooster she drew with special crayons. I think they're made out of fireplace ashes. Her rooster's beautiful. I told Grandma to put it on the wall, and she said, "Maybe, someday." I think I saw tears, but she turned away. I don't think other people like the things she makes. That makes me sad for her. My other grandma has two roosters in her kitchen. One is a clock on the wall, and the other stands on top of the fridge. Grandma says it's breakable. Both my grandmas say roosters are good luck.

I got mad after I ate veal one time and found out it was a baby cow. Why do we eat these animals? Why do we eat cows? Mommy said cows can't think like us, but I saw cows let out of the barn after a storm. They didn't go out like they're dumb. They knew the storm was over and jumped around in the grass. If cows are dumb, like she says, why don't they eat my hand when I feed them grass through the wire fence? Their thick, pink tongues tickle my fingers. If all the animals we eat are dumb and we're smart, how do they all know what to do without going to school? How do those birds know to leave Moses Lake before it's too cold outside? How do they find the warm place so far away?

Mommy said cows are grown for us to buy at the store and eat. I watched a kid at school hold up a big white-and-red ribbon for show-and-tell. He looked at his feet and said he won the ribbon at the fair for best cow. When another kid asked if he was sad, he got mad and said a company bought his cow to kill it for money.

I found three baby birds in our backyard after I heard loud chirping in the big green tree that doesn't have any leaves. I climbed up a few branches and saw three babies inside a hole. They were squeaking and tweeting with their heads straight up and mouths wide open. I didn't touch them in case it would make their smell bad for the mama bird. I climbed back down and waited until a woodpecker flew in the hole. When the babies were quiet, I fell asleep under the tree.

Mommy and Daddy and my grandmas and grandpas and all the big people say animals eat animals. They say that's nature and we're part of nature too. I guess so. I've seen hawks snatch mice out of the pasture, and I watched a coyote carrying a dead jackrabbit across a field. On TV, I've seen big cats attacking some kind of deer and eating them. I wish animals didn't need to kill each other to eat. I wish we didn't need to kill animals to eat. But I like hamburgers.

Big people say hunting is for food. Why? There's food at the grocery store. I asked this when I was little. Mommy and Daddy said it's what big people do. They said I'll understand when I'm older. I'm older and I don't understand.

I look out the side of my window. I can see part of my big tree from here. I must've run to it a hundred times. I hid under her branches sometimes when I was scared. My feet start moving because I need to say goodbye. I'm running through the house to the back door, across the cement and grass to the tallest tree, when I hit the brakes. A butterfly's landing on her. Its wings of black, white, and orange barely move. I get closer to see the tiniest arms busy around the face flinging specks of pollen onto pine needles. We're both still for a while. And then, goodbye.

I scoot my sad heart under my tree's branches and lie back on a bed of brown needles. It's summertime now and she smells different when it's warm, not like her Christmas smell. I love that smell too, it's just different now.

I close my eyes and the memories begin again.

PART II: AGE FOUR

CHAPTER 18

Spring Litter and Gus Gus

I'm happy it hasn't snowed for a long time. I'm four now. It's my first spring in Moses Lake. The fruit trees at our house have flowers on them. I don't have to wear mittens and boots when I go outside.

Mommy's throwing brown bottles in the trash. Daddy drinks lots of them. I tell Mommy that something smells sweet outside and she says, "It's spring." It smells better than all those brown bottles.

"Spring smells sweet, spring swells meet," and my tongue gets twisted.

Mommy laughs and says, "Yes, Deidi, it does. It smells better than winter. I like spring better than winter. You're smelling the flowers on the fruit trees when you go outside, because the blossoms smell sweet."

"Deidi, Deidi, c'mere!" Matty calls.

Mommy smiles and says, "You better go see what he's up to."

I find Matty in the garage bent over an old box in the corner. It's kind of dark in here. I can't tell what the sounds I'm hearing are, so I walk closer to take a peek over his shoulder. Inside the big old box is a whole litter of little kitties.

"Look, Deidi, look at what I found."

The kittens are the smallest I've ever seen. I sit down next to the box and look at their furry faces. When they cry, their tiny mouths show the smallest pink tongues and littlest, pointiest white teeth. Most of them are crying.

"Where's the mama?" I ask Matty.

He says, "Dunno."

"Are they hungry?" I ask.

He says, "Probably, don't care."

Why doesn't he care? I wonder.

Matty picks up two kittens and walks three steps to a wood wall in the garage. He stands in front of the wall and tells me to get a kitty and follow him. I pick up a little black-and-white kitty with funny-looking fur on its face. She's got big yellow eyes. I walk next to Matty by the garage wall. He says he's made up a fun game.

"Here're the rules," he explains. "You have to hold the kitty, toss it on the wall, and try to catch it when it bounces off. You have to keep tossing a kitty on the wall until it drops on the ground. Whoever throws and catches the kitty the longest wins the game!"

I don't think I like this game, but Matty likes it and that makes me want to play too. He says, "Let's see who can get the most tosses. Ready? One, two, three, go!" Matty tosses the first kitty and catches it after I hear it make a sound against the wood. I toss my kitty, but it doesn't touch the wall. It kind of floats in the air, twists to land, but drops to the floor. It hits the cement with a *pfff*. My kitty's lying on the floor looking at me with an open mouth, but no sound comes out. I see Matty's other kitty sliding down the wood wall to the floor. It's not moving. I remember when Mommy and Daddy were fighting and Matty threw the kitty. It stopped crying and it didn't move.

I turn around and yell, "Nooo!" I hate my brother.

I run to the door as fast as I can. I'm thinking, *Open the door, open the door, get outside and run, run to Mommy, fast, run fast. Look at the ground, don't trip, look up, don't hit a tree. Run.* There's Mommy. I see her in the kitchen window. I fly through the door to her. "He's, he's, trying to kill kitties!"

Mommy looks at me and says, "What did you say?"

I can't breathe. "Mommy, Matty's in the garage and he made me take a kitten. No, I took a kitten, he had kitties, so I took a kitty." I'm bending over, hands on my knees.

Mommy says, "What? Slow down. We don't have kittens. Breathe, I can't understand you."

I can't breathe. I say, "He said to play, to play the game, the wall, like a ball, throwing baby kitty balls."

Mommy says, "Baby kitty balls? What're you talking about?"

I say, "He wanted me to play the game, he played first. You need to stop him! He's going to kill kitties." I point my finger and say, "Garage!"

Mommy's running out the door with Hansel close behind and she's yelling, "Matty! Get out here right now!"

I can see Mommy pulling Matty out of the garage by his arm. Here they come. I'm scared Matty's going to be mad at me for telling. They're in the kitchen. Matty's face is red.

"I didn't do anything! I didn't do anything!" he's yelling.

Mommy says, "I know what you were doing with the kittens. You could've killed one!" Mommy's yelling that Matty can't go around killing animals.

Matty yells as Mommy takes his shoes off. "You're stupid. Stupid, Mommy."

He's in trouble now.

"Daddy kills aminals! Grandpas kill aminals! My uncles kill aminals! You eat killed aminals!"

Mommy just stands there looking at Matty. I'm thinking, *They do what he said, and we do those things.*

Mommy says in her nice voice, "Okay, Matty, just hold on for a second." He's crying as she pulls his coat off. Mommy sits Matty next to me on another chair at the kitchen table. She says, "Okay, you two, let's talk about this. Matty's right that we kill some animals to cook and eat them. There are other animals, like Hansel, that are pets. They are not for eating." Mommy explains that cats, dogs, and horses are pets that we don't eat. She says cows, deer, and chickens are the kind we eat. She says we can't kill animals. Mommy makes Matty promise he won't kill animals.

"I promise," Matty says, "but what if a bear comes to eat Deidi, and I have my BB gun?" Mommy says that's a good question. She says a BB gun won't stop a bear. And we don't have bears in Moses Lake. Mommy says if we had bears, grown-ups would make sure kids don't get eaten.

"What about spiders, snakes, daddy longlegs, or potato bugs?" I ask. "What about the bunnies and birdies that Matty shoots in the yard with his BB gun? Can we kill those?" Mommy says we can't kill those either. She says Matty can't shoot any animals. We can't touch animals that aren't pets. Mommy says to get a grown-up if something scares us. She says that's the rule. If we don't follow rules, we'll get in super big trouble for a long time.

Matty says he sees ghosts that scare him. But they're too fast and grown-ups are too slow.

Mommy says, "There's no such thing as ghosts."

Matty says, "Yes, yes there is. Grandma has a ghost in her basement by the fruit room, not the flowers."

"There's no ghost in Grandma's basement."

"Yes, there is. I saw the scary red face with big teeth!" Matty opens his mouth and pulls his lips to show his teeth. He squishes his face up and holds his hands by his head like claws. He says, "Grrr!"

Mommy shakes her head, and says again, there are no ghosts.

I remember when I had to get a jar of peaches for Grandma in the basement. I saw Uncle Drew fixing his belt buckle. His face was scary. Matty was crying behind him, coming out of the bedroom. Uncle Drew went into the bathroom and closed the door. Sometimes he comes to Grandma and Grandpa's house. Grandma doesn't like him. She gets a mean look on her face when she sees him. I think she lets him come to her house because he's her daddy's brother.

I ran to Matty and said, "Are you okay?" Matty shook his head and pretend-kicked the bathroom door.

Then he said, "Let's go."

I held his hand up the stairs. His nose started bleeding in the kitchen.

I think there are ghosts. I think sometimes bad ghosts are around people that hurt you. There are good ghosts, like my book about Gus the friendly ghost. He saves his mouse friend's life. Good ghosts can help people. I wish I had an army of Gus ghosts. If I had my very own ghost, I would name him Gus Gus, like Cinderella's mouse. She named her mouse Octavius, but his mice friends called him Gus Gus. They say the same word twice a lot. I'm not sure why.

Great-Grandma says that Gus is short for Augustus. She says Gus is a baby name from England. Great-Grandma says we have a big family in heaven I have never met. And there's lots of Augustuses and Guses up there. I asked if we have an Octavius. She said, "No. He's from a different country."

CHAPTER 19

Fairy Bubbles

I'm wearing my pink shorts outside today. It's getting warmer. "Ow!" My bottom hurts! I don't want to play tug-of-war with Hansel anymore. He let go of the rope and I fell hard on the cement. I lift one side of my bottom and push my hand down my shorts and undies. I can feel big bumps on my bottom from last night. I bet they're still red.

I remember how Matty and I got in trouble. Mommy and Daddy started fighting in the living room when we were watching TV. Daddy knocked over his brown bottles and grabbed Mommy's arms. He pushed her on the green chair. Mommy scratched his face and put her knee where he pees. She jumped up and grabbed the poker thing from the fireplace. When she jabbed his tummy, he pulled the poker from Mommy and threw her down. He stood up and took a burning cigarette from the ashtray. He tried to put it on Mommy's cheek. Matty ran into Daddy's legs. He pulled Matty to the floor by his shirt. Daddy rolled on top of Matty with the cigarette in his hand. He screamed the cigarette was going on Matty's arm. Mommy didn't move. I ran at Daddy and hit his hand with my shoulder as hard as I could. The cigarette went flying. Daddy shoved me and started to choke Matty. He kept calling him a sissy. He said little girls protect sissies.

Matty stopped trying to take Daddy's hands off his neck. His lips were turning blue. I screamed, "Mommy, make him stop!" Daddy let go and sat on Matty for a second. Then he stood up and told Matty and me to get our butts in the kitchen. Matty was coughing as he ran behind me around the corner.

Matty and I stood next to each other in the kitchen. Daddy yelled at us to take our pants and undies off. He told us to bend over all the way and grab our ankles. My legs were shaking. Daddy's belt was off. He hit our bottoms a lot. He called us little shits when he whipped us. Matty told me that means "poop." I wished I was poop so I wouldn't feel it.

This morning Matty told me not to help him again. He said it makes everything worse.

My pee place still hurts when I go potty. The belt hit there too. My hand's making the owies on my bottom feel better. I pull my hand out of my shorts when I see Daddy walk around the corner. He's holding a rag and pipe in his hands. "Whatcha doing, princess?" I tell him I fell when Hansel let go of the rope. Daddy says, "Hansel, that wasn't nice to do to Deidi." Hansel's ears stick up, and he turns his big head to one side. "See, Deidi. Hansel agrees that wasn't nice. I'd say he's sorry."

"Okay," I say.

The pipe clanks when Daddy sticks it in the dirt by the cement. He puts the rag in his back pocket and says, "C'mon, Deidi, let's go inside."

I take his hand and follow him up the step to the back door. In the kitchen, Daddy says we need to clean up. "How 'bout a shower, princess?" I don't want a shower with Daddy, but I have to.

He takes me to the blue bathroom I don't use. It has a shower, but no tub. He takes my clothes off and turns the water on. Daddy throws his work clothes on the floor. I know Mommy won't like that. I lift the lid and put them in the hamper. He smiles and says thanks. He works on getting the water just right. He has hair on his legs and I touch it. He laughs and says it tickles. Daddy says this'll be fun. He's always happy before a shower with me. I get happy too.

We're in the shower and Daddy rubs soap everywhere. He starts to clean my bottom and I say, "Ow, that hurts, Daddy!" He says he'll be more careful. I watch the drain suck up the last suds. I wonder where they go. I know it's time to practice. Daddy always says remember it's like a hot dog. He holds his pee-pee up. Daddy says taste it. I lick a little. I always say it doesn't taste like a hot dog. He always says put more in my mouth like a bite of a hot dog. Like I'm hungry and he always says don't bite, don't bite. That'll hurt Daddy. I think about going to the store. Daddy will take me there when we're done for a surprise. Last time I got a short Barbie dress with flowers all over. It ties at the neck and has big sleeves. There's pink, yellow, orange, and a little green on the dress. A matching scarf ties around Barbie's head. I'm thinking about the new Barbie clothes I might get. My throat hurts when I throw up in the shower. Daddy says it's okay. He always says to remember I'll get used to it.

I get a star for having a good practice with Daddy. But he doesn't really give me a star. He pours baby shampoo in his hand, I love the smell. He washes my hair. This is my favorite part. He says, "Here come the fairy bubbles, Deidi!" There're bubbles everywhere. Daddy says, they're special fairy bubbles just for me. He always says, "The fairy bubbles don't come out for anyone else but you. There ya go, pretty one."

Daddy says to put my feet on his blue towel. He pats my sore bottom when he's drying me off. Daddy always says to promise I'll never, ever tell Mommy about our showers. He always says it's a special secret for Daddy and me. I promise I'll never, ever tell. I remind him I'm four, so I'm a big girl.

"Daddy, 'member when I was three and kind of a baby?"

He nods.

"'Member when I said I'd tell Matty the shower secret?"

He laughs and says he remembers.

I say, "You said, no, no, no, you can't never, ever say that to anyone 'cause my fairies go bye-bye from the bubbles."

Daddy hugs me and says that's true. He asks, "And do you want to lose the fairy bubbles?"

I shake my head and say, "Never, ever."

CHAPTER 20

More Drawings

After breakfast, the house is quiet. I remember I haven't snooped in the kitchen desk for a long time. I'm pulling out each big drawer, hoping I find a stick of gum. There are lots of papers and gold bullets. Maybe I'll make a house out of paper clips. I stand three bullets in a row. They'd make a good fence around a house. Wait a minute, here's a nice red marker. It looks new. Here's a new blue marker. I love new markers. I don't know why. I'm thinking of things to draw, but I can't find any paper without stuff on it already.

I hop off the chair and walk to the hallway. There might be some paper in the living room. I look at the big white wall. I sit cross-legged in front of it. I use the red marker to draw a round shoe like Mommy's clown in the basement. I use the blue marker to draw stripes for his pants. I'm doing a good job. Matty's door opens down the hall and he skips over to me. He's standing in front of my drawing with his mouth open.

"Oh, oh, Deidi, you're going to be in sooooo much trouble!"

My tummy flip-flops. "Why?"

"We're not s'pposed to draw on walls, that's bad!"

"Are you going to tell?" I ask, and he shakes his head no. His eyes get big when Mommy walks into the living room. I grab both markers. Mommy turns and sees us in the hallway. She says, oh my God, oh my God. I try to say I did it, but I'm not loud enough.

Matty says, "Sorry, Mommy, we thought you'd like it."

She asks if he did this. The markers are in my hands. Matty nods, but I shake my head because he didn't. I'm too scared to talk. Mommy says, Deidi's saying she didn't do it. I shake my head again, she's wrong. She yells, look at what's in my hands.

Mommy's staring at the wall a long time. She steps back and looks at us. Mommy says Matty didn't do this. She says Matty can help her clean it because he lied.

"Young lady, you're in much more trouble," she says and tells Matty to wait while she takes me downstairs. I feel sick when I hear "downstairs."

I can't move. Matty gives me a push and nods his head like it'll be okay. Mommy goes fast down the big stairs to the basement. She pushes me into the cement room. She says to sit here and think about telling lies until she comes back. I jump when the door slams. I hear her stomp up the stairs.

It's cold in here. I'm scared there are monsters behind me, or ghosts, like in Grandma's basement. I see a scrap of green chalk in the corner. I crawl over to sit on the floor next to it. I draw a small green flower in the grass on the wall. I hear the dryer turning clothes by the door. I hear feet walking back and forth above me. Mommy and Matty are laughing. I'm sad. I'm drawing more flowers when the door bangs the wall. I jump up and turn around. Mommy yells she knew I'd be doing something I'm not supposed to do. Mommy says I need to stay down here longer. She yanks me up by my arm to my tippy-toes. I drop the green chalk on the floor. She pulls me under the light bulb. She says I need to sit down and not move from this spot. I need to think about the bad things I've done.

She says to look at how dirty I am. She's told me over and over to never draw anywhere. Mommy slams the door and I hear her stomp up the stairs. Why didn't I hear her come down the stairs?

I touch my bottom and it's wet. I peed my pants a little when she scared me. I wipe my hand on the cement and scoot my bottom a little to wipe off. I am dirty. I feel a big hurt in my heart. I have an owie from my head to my tummy. It feels like *boom, boom* inside. I'm stupid to forget Mommy said never to draw anywhere. I'm bad and I'm dirty. I say it over and over in my head. The hurt makes my eyes get tears. My lower lip's sticking on my teeth.

I sit here a long time. I see the pictures Matty, Mommy, and me made on the wall when we first moved here. I follow the lines with my eyes. Then I close my eyes and draw the lines in my head. I do this over and over. It makes me feel better. I can't feel my legs under my bottom. I pinch my tummy to stay awake.

I jump when I hear *stomp, stomp, stomp* down the big stairs. I wait for Mommy to open the door. She's there, but I can't see her face. She walks over to me. Now I see her, she looks scarier than before. I pretend I stuffed cotton clouds in my ears. I see her mad and yelling, but I don't hear her. I wonder what it's like outside on the grass right now? I see me drawing flowers on white paper in the sunshine. The yelling stops after a long time.

I'm in my room now and I can't go out. I lie down on the carpet and close my eyes. I'm hungry, but I don't care. I wish I had a blue fairy like Pinocchio.

CHAPTER 21

Eyes

I'm in the hospital in Wenatchee. The room is cold. It's getting hot outside, so this feels good. Mommy said it only took an hour to get here, but it felt like all day. The nurse tells me to put on a gown. I don't think that's a gown. I saw Miss America's gown. Her hair is the same color as mine. She wore a blue dress that touched the floor. She wore white gloves on her elbows. She had a crown on her head. The thing I'm in is not a gown.

Dr. Pare's here. I remember when he put drops in my eyes. Everything was blurry. He said my right eye isn't as strong as my left eye. I'm not sure which is which. He said I need an "operation" to fix this. I don't know what that is. I'm staying overnight at the hospital. I hope I get toys like Matty did when they pumped out his tummy. I get a shot to sleep while they fix my eye. Dr. Pare said I need to wear glasses. I want glasses like Grandma's. They're "cat eyes," she told me. I like looking at them on her when she's working with the flowers in her shop.

I heard Mommy say to Daddy that his sister was right about Deidi's eyes. Mommy and Daddy said she saw my eyes cross in a picture.

The thing in my head that talks to me is my brain. That's what Dr. Pare says. I like him. He wears a bow on his neck. Daddy says it's called a bow tie. Dr. Pare says my brain talks to my eyes, and my eyes talk to my brain. I don't hear them talking. One of my eyes doesn't talk with my brain so good. Dr. Pare is going to help my eye and my brain talk better.

Mommy says Dr. Pare went to school with her older sister, and she says he's the best doctor.

I'm on my tummy counting tiny ducks on a sheet. There's five ducks. I don't like what I smell. Someone's rubbing cold on my bottom. A voice says, "Just a li-tt-le poke." *Ow!* They poked my bottom. I'm sleeeeepy.

I wake up. What are these white bars around me? Am I in a crib? I'm not a baby! Something's on my eye. It won't open. I feel it with my hand. It feels like a big Band-Aid. It's good I have two eyes. Dr. Pare says I did great. I don't know what I did. He says that's a patch on my eye. I have to wear it. Matty will call me a pirate. *Peter Pan* has pirates. I'm sleepy now. Night-night.

I open my good eye. I'm seeing lots of colors running around. I know Mommy and Daddy are with me. I can hear them. Daddy says, "We have a surprise for you, Deidi." I blink my good eye and feel something on my hand. Now I see a pretty box. It's a doll! She's beautiful.

Mommy says, "It's Cinderella, and she looks just like you, Deidi." She has on a green dress and orange apron. She has an orange scarf on her yellow hair. She looks just like Cinderella in my View-Master. I tell Mommy and Daddy, "Thank you, I love her." I'm so tired. Night-night.

Where am I now? I feel cozy. I open my good eye a tiny bit. I see my white bedspread with blue roses. This makes me happy.

I know Daddy's here. I can smell him. His knees are pushing my bed down. Something's warm on my legs. I'm not cold. I'm falling asleep until Daddy flips me on my back. I'm like a pancake. What if I'm a pancake and not a little girl? Someone puts butter on me and maple syrup. It goes around and around in a smaller circle. I'm hearing Daddy's dog sound. He's shaking my bed. Up we go as he's getting off the bed. My face has warm icky wet on it. It smells like pickles and bread. My eye in the patch is going *boom* and hurts. Daddy's wiping my face and my patch with his T-shirt. I say, "Owie, Daddy, that hurts." It makes me start crying. I say, "I want Mommy."

Daddy says, "Shhh, princess, Daddy's taking care of you. You made Daddy so happy! You like that, right?"

I nod and fall back asleep.

CHAPTER 22

Barbie's Dresses

Barbie doesn't have any clothes on. Her skin's pinker than mine. Where's the silver dress? I'm good at seeing through one eye now. I look through the case I keep especially for all of Barbie's clothes and shoes. I like playing by myself in my room. I pick up a long green-and-white dress with a big ruffle. I don't think it's very pretty, but Mommy said it's special because it's handmade. I asked her if the silver dress was handmade. She said a machine made that one.

Here it is! I pull the stretchy silver over Barbie's head. She says, "My favorite dress." I put silver boots on her feet. They go up to her knees. I look at my knees and bend my leg. Barbie's legs bend, but she doesn't have any knees.

Barbie's done, so I take my doll off my dresser. Her name's Baby. I need to change her wet diaper. I go into my closet and take out a box of baby clothes. Some were my baby clothes. I was so small then. I'm a big girl now. I take off Baby's wet diaper. She doesn't have any clothes on. Will I have a baby when I'm big like Mommy? I've seen real babies and they cry a lot.

Matty took Baby one time and made me cry. He took off her clothes and pulled her legs off. Daddy fixed her. I say no now if Matty asks to play with Baby. He hurts Baby just like he hurts kittens and me. I dropped his Matchbox car on the cement and chipped it. He pulled my arm back and said, "I'm breaking it." Daddy came out and stopped him. He got in trouble.

Matty hurts Baby and kitties. They can't hurt him. Matty says it's fun to hurt kitties. Daddy hurts Mommy, Matty, and me. Mommy hurts Matty, Daddy, and me. I wonder if my grandpas and grandmas hurt Daddy or Mommy when they were little? I wonder if my grandpas and grandmas hurt each other? Pictures come in my head. Go away, pictures. Go away!

I love Baby. I feel hurt in my tummy when I think of baby me. Daddy says he dropped me on my head. Mommy laughs when he says this. Mommy says she almost died after I was born. The doctor was drunk and her bottom was bleeding. But she got all better and came home. Mommy said "drunk" means he had too much alcohol.

I'm careful with Baby. I won't ever hurt her, or kitties, or real babies.

I love animals. Daddy says animals love me. He calls me Elly May because of *The Beverly Hillbillies* on TV. All the animals in their big house love Elly May. We have the same hair.

I can feel animals when I see them. Lots of animals have owies, like me. The hunters hurt Bambi when they killed his mommy. His daddy was Prince of the Forest and helped him. I would've helped Bambi; I wouldn't shoot him or his family. Daddy shoots Bambi families with both my grandpas and my uncles. Matty will go hunting for Bambi families when he's older. I hate hunting. Bambi's daddy had antlers. My daddy has antlers from a Bambi daddy he shot hanging on a wall.

I told Daddy I want to hunt with him, but I don't really. He likes it when I say things like that. He's nice to me. It makes him happy.

I don't want to hunt, but I will hunt if Daddy really wants me to. Matty says girls don't hunt. I say that's stupid.

Mommy doesn't like hunting. She says it's for boys. But she says girls can go if they really want to. Matty says, no they can't. Why does Mommy say it's for boys, but girls can go? Why isn't it for girls the same? Why do boys or girls want to kill animals? My head's fuzzy. I don't ask. I don't want Mommy or Matty to be mad.

Baby is all done, so I pick up the *Sneetches* book on my dresser. Some Sneetches have tummy stars and some don't. The stars are green. The star-tummy Sneetches put their noses in the air. They don't let the other Sneetches eat hot dogs with them or play with them. Mommy says they're stuck up. Just like when Brer Rabbit thought tar-baby girl was better than him.

Then the Fix-It-Up Chappie comes and changes everything. He has machines that put on stars and take off stars. At the end, the Sneetches are all mixed up. They're happy to say the stars don't matter starting that day. One Sneetch isn't better than the other Sneetch.

The Sneetches book is fun to listen to even when the Sneetches are being mean. The words sound good together. Mommy says Dr. Seuss "rhymes." I love the rhymes, and I love that all the Sneetches love each other at the end.

The book made Barbie sleepy. I put a hankie over her so she doesn't get cold. This one is pink with purple flowers on the corners. The hankie kind of smells like old perfume. It's sweet. Maybe Barbie needs two hankies tonight. Here's a white one with pink ribbons on one corner. It doesn't have any smell.

My grandmas gave me hankies they em-broi-dered. That's a big word. My grandmas say it's putting thread with colors in cloth to make pictures. I've seen both my grandmas put a needle with thread in and out and in and out of a wood circle. That's how they sew my hankies. Hankies make the best Barbie blankets. I think *hankie blankie* and laugh. I look over the top of my bed to see Blankie. I love my Blankie.

I think about machines like Chappie's. I think about the sewing machines my grandmas push fabric into. I think about special and not special. My hankies are special because my grandmas made them. My silver dress is special because it's for my Barbie. Chappie just wanted money from his machines. He didn't care that the Sneetches got mixed up in a bad way at first. Then the Sneetches liked that they got mixed up and were the same. They didn't need Chappie's machines. I guess his machines were special in a way.

Outside my window I can see the wind moving the leaves on the trees. I like that. I wish I could float on the wind to a soft nest at the top of a tree.

I pull the silver dress off Barbie and lay it on the carpet next to the green-and-white dress. It's shorter and shinier. If Barbie wore the silver dress, kids would like her. If she wore the green-and-white dress, they'd make fun of her.

I don't like that. I wish everyone was just nice.

CHAPTER 23

Another Operation

Mommy says Dr. Pare needs to do another operation. I say, "I just had one!" Mommy says, "It's been months, Deidi." I say, "Dr. Pare's mean." She says, "He's not mean, he's helping you, Deidi." She can't hear me think in my head, *He's mean.* Daddy says, "Dr. Pare's making sure you don't go blind like Helen Keller." I ask him, "Who's Helen?" He says she's a girl who couldn't see or hear. I want to know why, but I don't ask.

I'm at the hospital again. I'm in the waiting room. I guess that's the name because I'm waiting to see the nurse. I look at my *Highlights* picture book. There's a cat, a bat, and a hat. The hat looks better when I make it red.

Cold air's blowing on me. I don't want a shot. Shots scare me because they hurt. I don't want an operation. My eyes itch. I don't want a patch again. I won't be able to rub my eyes like now. I was happy to stop wearing a patch before. Patches smell funny, like Cream of Wheat and glue. I think I'm sleeping here again too.

The nurse takes me to the smaller room for the operation. She's wearing white shoes with white laces. The radio is noisy and beeping. I ask who's talking on the radio. She says it's an "intercom." I see red lipstick on her teeth. The paper on this bed's noisy too. I'm smelling the bad smell. She's rubbing the bad smell on my bottom. I hear paper tearing and cupboards closing. I'm lying here for a long, long time. Needle poke! I'm so sleepy.

I'm trying to open my eyes. One's stuck. I see blurry. I feel like I'm floating, but not fun floating. Like too much floating. It looks like the nurse is bending over me. She has red hair. It's stacked on her head like *I Dream of Jeannie*, but red. Her hair's pretty. It's shiny like Breck girls in Mommy's picture books. I think I said she's pretty and shiny out loud. She's smiling. Is that a hat way up on her hair? The nurse with red hair says, "Sleep" and something, but I'm bye-bye.

I'm awake, but my good eye's asleep or stuck. Both eyes itch. Someone's holding my hands. I can't itch, but it's okay. I fall back to sleep.

I wake up feeling sick in my tummy. I'm in the car lying down. I'm too hot. My skin's sticking to the seat. I'm not crying, but there's water on my eye. Is the car stopped? My pee place feels warm. I see Daddy touching me there out of my good eye. He says, "You keep sleeping, princess." He turns me over and my hair pulls off the sticky seat. The seat's bumpy under my cheek. It pushes on my patch, and my eye hurts. Daddy's pushing on my bottom back and forth and back and forth. I'm a big eraser. I throw up a little in my mouth. I swallow. My tongue tastes like dirt. My eye feels like it's burning. What if something bad happens to my eye? I feel mad. I feel so, so, so sleepy. Sleepy. Sleeping.

I see branches of trees moving in the dark outside my bedroom window. I stretch on my bed and roll on my side. I think I've been sleeping forever. I don't know what day it is. I softly touch the patch on my eye. My face feels asleep. I'm looking at the wall by the door. I see the picture. It's the only one in my room. I don't know why. It looks like dark colors smeared together. There's a little pink-and-purple part. It's like a tiny sun snuck into the big dark place. I wonder where that is. I like looking at the sun part. My eyes close.

Loud noises wake me up. Mommy and Daddy are yelling. I feel Blankie and my bedspread in my hand. I sit up and feel the rug on my toes. I don't want the mad voices to find me. I slide my drapes together and drag Blankie into the closet with me. The closet by the bedroom door's closed. I shut the other door, pulling on one of the rows of wood. No one can find us back here in the corner. I yank my favorite purply sweater off the hanger. I'm warm and Blankie is under my head. I hear a click and see blurry light stripes on my leg from the row of wood on the door. The other closet opens and closes. My stripes leave when Daddy's hand shoves Mommy's extra dresses she keeps in my closet. He smells like a big brown bottle. The light's too bright. His hand's grabbing my arm. He's got more sweater than me. He pulls so hard it rips apart. I'm on my knees. I'm flying over the floor and my bed. I land on my side by the wall. I'm glad I didn't drop Blankie.

Daddy's squishing me and making dog sounds. My eye owie rubs on my bedspread's blue roses. It hurts like fire on my eye. I go away to the time I got a tick in my back. Mommy said ticks live on deer. I wonder how many deer have ticks. I wonder if Bambi had ticks. A tick tried to live on me, but not for long. Someone lit a match, blew it out, and put it on my back. Ticks like that smell, the black bug came out. I come back to now. I jump when Daddy gets up. He kisses my head. He covers me with my blankets and says, "Love ya, Deidi."

CHAPTER 24

Preschool Daycare

Mommy takes Matty and me where kids stay when mommies and daddies work. I like it here. This is Beverly's house. She has white posts by her front door like mine at home. Her eyes close when she laughs. Her smile makes me feel warm, like the sun when my face is cold. She's always nice to me. Beverly's not mean if we break the rules. Her house has a lot of rooms and toys. All the kids go downstairs. We can see the lake through the big windows. Beverly keeps toys and crayons in tubs. Not like the tub for a bubble bath. These are tubs I carry by myself.

Lots of kids go to Beverly's. I like playing with Shirley and Holly. We're going to the same school next year. Shirley has brown hair. Her mouth stays open when she's not talking. She has big brown eyes. We're both bigger than Holly. She's small like a fairy. She has short hair and kinda looks like a boy. Two of the boys at Beverly's will go to our school next year too. They both have blond crew cuts. Matty's playing with a boy his age. His hair's longer like Matty's. Sometimes we climb the big tree in the front yard. Mostly we play in the backyard when it's nice outside. The girls go to their own place to play without the boys. Holly, Shirley, and I love coloring books. Beverly's downstairs has wood panels like mine at home. But her panels are brown. The downstairs is real big. It feels cozy when it's stormy outside.

The wind and rain make noise on Beverly's big windows today. Shirley and I are playing tic-tac-toe with purple crayons. I hear Beverly call me upstairs. Shirley says, "Bye, Deidi." I say, "Bye."

I run upstairs to do my special work with Beverly. She pats a chair for me at the big table. I climb up and she lays the newspaper out. Beverly gives me a red pencil. It has a sharp tip. Beverly asks me to please find the letter S. Matty runs in and says, "Pirate Girl!"

Two boys follow him saying, "Ahoy, matey!"

Beverly says, "Get downstairs, boys. Deidi, please find another S for me."

I draw a red circle around another S. "Found it."

Beverly says, "That was quick. Good. See if you can find a T." She says my eye's getting stronger. "I'll see you downstairs for lunch, Deidi."

Beverly makes the best baloney and Velveeta sandwiches for lunch. She puts mustard and mayo on Wonder Bread, just the way I like. She pours purple Kool-Aid in my green cup. I'm so happy at Beverly's house.

After lunch, the boys say, "Got any gold, Pirate Girl?" I tell them to go away. Some girls giggle. Are they laughing at me?

Holly says my pink patch makes it look like I have one eye, but just from far away. I say that's not so good, but she tells me that I'm still pretty. Holly's nice.

After we play, Beverly calls me upstairs again. She turns the newspaper over and says, "Tell me when you see a word you know." I look at the paper and see the word "can." I circle it with my red pencil and say it out loud. Beverly says I'm doing a good job. Newspapers make my fingers black. I can't touch my face. Beverly makes sure I always wash my hands when we're done.

Sometimes I can't see very good after my eye operation. But I can hear, smell, and taste things more. Dr. Pare says that's a surprise for kids that get to have operations like mine.

Beverly asks me about smells, tastes, and sounds after my operation. She says, "Tell me about summer." I love this game. I say summer smells like skunk sometimes and snapdragons in Grandma's garden. I tell her how I make finger puppets with the small flowers. I say summer tastes like the strawberries I pick. Summer sounds like wheat trucks and sprinklers. Sometimes, it sounds like the ice-cube tray when Mommy makes popsicles.

"Okay, time to wash your hands," Beverly says. We go to the kitchen sink.

The water's too cold! I turn the knob with the red dot to warm it up. Beverly helps me push my sleeves up. She's holding my arm. "Where did these bruises come from, Deidi?" I say I don't know. I don't remember what thing made them. Beverly looks at my other arm. "Deidi, did someone bite you?" Shoulders up and down again. I just want to wash my hands, but she wants to know about my scratches. I say I got scratched playing hide 'n' seek. Is Beverly mad at me? I push my glasses up and look at her face. She smiles. It's a sad smile, not a happy smile. Is she sad for me? The water's warm now. I see Beverly in the window over the sink. It's like a mirror, but it's not. She's shaking her head.

Mommy shakes her head too when I get in trouble. I remember when Matty was being mean to me. He snuck up and yelled, "Boo!" I jumped and dropped my juice. He knows I can't see people if they sneak up on my patch side. I called Matty a big booger and pushed him. I ran down the hall to the bathroom. He chased me. I couldn't close the door. Matty pushed me on the bathroom floor and ripped my patch off. I yelled, "Ow!" He grabbed the green soapy stuff and squirted it on my eyes.

"Mommmmmy!" I screamed.

Matty jumped off and ran out. I got up and washed the soap out. It hurt. I couldn't get my patch back on. It kept sliding.

I saw Mommy in the hallway with a clothes basket. She was shaking her head. "Were you two yelling?"

I shook my head and she put the basket down. She came in the bathroom and grabbed my arm. I fell off the stool and she yelled, "Why is your patch off?" She yelled that I want to be cross-eyed. She told me to go to my room. Her nails put scratches on my arms. I couldn't tell on Matty because he'd get beat up again. Daddy came home drunk the night before. Mommy got in a big fight with him, and I ran into Matty's room and hid in his bed. He said, "I'll protect you, Deidi." Daddy came in and grabbed my arm. My feet weren't touching the floor when he threw me in the hall. The rug burn hurt more than my arm. He slammed the door, and I heard Matty crying, "Daddy, stop," all the way from my room.

"Deidi, are you listening to me?" I hear Beverly say.

"Sorry, I didn't hear you," I say.

She says, "Never mind," and pats my head and shuts the water off.

I dry my hands and arms with the soft pink towel. I hear Mommy's voice. "Hello, hello." I run and hug her. Beverly walks in and tells me to clean up downstairs before I leave today. I walk loud down the steps. I sneak back up to listen. Am I in trouble? I'm scared.

Beverly tells Mommy she saw some marks on my arms. I hear Mommy laugh and say she's not surprised. She says how active I am. She says I'm always trying to keep up with my big brother. She says they all know how rambunctious Matty is. Mommy says something about me being clumsy because of my eyes.

I'm not clumsy. Puppies and kittens are clumsy. They fall over. I don't.

Beverly says something about her four kids. She says she knows about bumps and scrapes. Her telephone starts ringing. They walk away. I can't hear words. I go downstairs. There's nothing to put away; it's all clean. I look at the lake. I sort of like that Beverly asked about my owies. But they'd take Beverly from me if I told. Maybe it's better when nobody asks.

CHAPTER 25

Davenport Flowers

I love going to Grandma's in Davenport. That's the third hawk I've seen on this drive. It takes too long to go from Moses Lake to Davenport. Mommy's been smoking and singing the whole time. I've seen four big trucks and one had horses inside. There are more fields between Moses Lake and Davenport than Carter's has pills, like Grandma says. I don't know who Carter is, but they must have a lot of pills. Grandma says funny things like that.

Today Mommy drops me off there. I run from the car as soon as it stops, across the greenest grass I've ever seen. I see Grandma's car in the open garage. Grandma's home! But Grandpa's white work truck isn't in the driveway. He's probably helping farmers and will be home for lunch. I race up the side steps, grab the silver handle, and push the button to pop the screen door with the curly things in the middle. I turn the big glass knob and push the half window, half dark-wood door wide open. I don't even have to knock because Grandma says I'm family. I take one step up to the kitchen and smell Grandma's house, the best smell ever. She's cooking something sweet in the oven. The kitchen is clean and the sun's coming through the big windows.

"Grandma! Where are you?" I yell from the kitchen.

"I'm downstairs in the fruit room, Deidi. Be right there!" I can't wait and race down the carpeted stairs to find her. I turn and see her standing in the fruit room with her hands full. I run in and wrap my arms around her legs.

"Hi, Grandma!"

"Well, hello, Deidi! Are you ready to help me in the shop today?"

I say, "Yep! Can I carry stuff?"

She says, "Yes, you can carry the strawberry jam, how's that?"

"Good!"

Grandma hands me a glass jar with a gold top. I can see the strawberry seeds inside mixed up with the red jelly. I watch Grandma's short brown heels take each step, one at a time, from behind her. I like the swishy sound her dress makes.

I climb up on my favorite kitchen chair. I watch Grandma put things in her white cupboards with tiny round glass knobs. Her curtains match her dishes. Mommy says they are Spode dishes. I like the pictures of houses and trees on them. Grandma has yellow flowers on the kitchen table.

"These are pretty, Grandma," I say.

"Thank you, Deidi. I have a bushel of them in the fridge downstairs."

Grandma has big glass fridges in her store and extras downstairs. She says they keep her flowers fresh.

Grandma hands me two sugar cookies on a small plate, and I say, "Thank you." She pours a cup of milk and sets it on the table with a pink napkin.

My mouth is full, and she says, "I know, 'Thank you.'" She's funny.

Grandma's chairs are blue, green, and brown colors all mixed together. I tell Grandma about how Hansel got sprayed by a skunk. I stop talking for a second to count the buttons on the tall back of my chair. "One, two, three, four, five, six buttons."

Grandma says, "Good counting, Deidi. What else is new for you?"

I say that I learned a new song from my library record about a robin. "It's kind of sad, do you want to hear it?"

Grandma says, "Yes, I do."

I sing her the song. *She came to my window one morning in spring. A sweet little robin, she came there to sing. And the song that she sang was sweeter by far. Than ever was heard on a flute or guitar.*

I stop and say, "I have to hum this part, Grandma." She nods her head, and I hum and then sing again. *How happy, how happy the world seems to be! But just as she finished her beautiful song . . .*

I stop singing again. "I don't know some words, Grandma, but a man with a gun shot the robin." I sing, *She'll sing never more at the break of the day.*

Grandma looks at me with a sad face, and I nod as I keep singing. *Oh robin, oh robin, oh robin redbreast.*

Grandma claps and says that I sang beautifully. She says if anyone tries to shoot her robins, they'll be in big trouble!

I like that.

I finish my cookies and Grandma says, "Let's go to the shop."

People pay Grandma for flowers at her shop. Grandpa put a big sign on top of the garage. It says DAVENPORT FLOWERS and lights up when it's dark out. Grandma tells me she needs two spools of ribbon. She says, "One pink and one yellow." I say, "Okay, just a sec, Grandma," and run downstairs as she says, "Thank you, Deidi."

Grandma's shop stairs go to the basement just like her house stairs do. I see the wall of ribbons on big pegs. Grandpa made this just for ribbons. They look like big spools of thread from Grandma's sewing machine. I pick the prettiest pink and yellow spools and race back up to Grandma. She's at her big table with pink, yellow, and white carnations, white and pink roses, yellow mums, and tall yellow glads from the backyard. She has a stack of green fern leaves too. I point to each set of flowers and say their names, and Grandma says, "Very good memory, Deidi." I give her the ribbons and she says, "Thank you, these are perfect." Grandma says this is a good time to run my own shop while she finishes the birthday bouquet, which she says is a French word.

I get all my pretend flowers ready for a really big wedding. Everything must be just right. I run up and down the stairs a hundred times. The customer is fussy, but we work it out. Grandma says, "That's the best way." Next, I make two big round things to put on stands. I use white carnations and bows. I like how they smell. I ring up the customer. I say it's going to be a beautiful wedding, like Grandma does. I take care of my books and answer the phone, "Davenport Flowers."

Grandma's bells chime on her door, and a real customer walks in. She talks to Grandma and asks, "Who's your little helper today?"

Grandma tells her. And I say, "Nice to meet you." Just like Grandma taught me.

The lady says, "My goodness, what lovely manners you have, Deidi."

I say, "Thank you. I must return to my job."

She says she understands. The lady says she loves Grandma's bouquet, pays for it, and waves bye-bye.

I hear Grandpa's truck in the driveway. I run outside and see Grandpa hop out of the truck.

He says, "Hello, Deidi!"

I say, "Hi, Grandpa!"

He says, "No hugs, sweetheart, Grandpa's been crawling in the dirt and grease all morning working on the combines."

I say, "That's okay."

Grandma tells him to wash up and lunch will be ready in the kitchen. I hear Grandpa whistle all the way down the stairs to his bathroom. He has a shower, toilet, and sink downstairs. He says Grandma makes everything off-limits until he's cleaned up. Grandpa says he doesn't ever want to get in trouble with the boss, and I know that's Grandma.

We eat tuna sandwiches on Wonder Bread with potato salad. And the best dill pickles in the world that Grandma makes. We have orange drinks Grandma gets from a truck that sells food and drinks. Grandpa says he must get back to fixing a tractor on somebody's farm after lunch. He hopes he doesn't have to order any parts. I say I need to get back to work with Grandma, and he laughs and we say goodbye.

Grandma says, "Deidi, I need to go back in the shop for a minute. I'll be right back."

I run inside the house, skip to the guest room, and open the pretty wood door. The glass doorknob looks like a magic crystal ball.

There she is, flying on the wall. She's a little angel with wings on her face. She's been on the wall since I can remember. I pull my shoes off and climb on the guest bed to sit below her.

I tell her how much I think about the first time we met. I was in the baby crib in this room and she talked to me. I start crying. I remember how she needed me to know the one thing. I can't stop crying. The magic face said I'm good. But why is so much bad?

I don't know so many things, magic face. I curl up on the bed on my side. The door opens. The swoosh sound tells me it's Grandma, and I pretend to sleep. She turns the big light off and lays a quilt over me. She says, "Oh my goodness" in a whisper to herself, and I can smell her mint breath. She pats my head and leaves. I'm sort of sleepy, but I want to talk to the magic face more.

The face and wings are bright like a light turned on! Her face is sweeter than the best candy. One of her wings stretches to touch the top of my head. Her voice makes me warm like Blankie, but even better. "This is goodness."

CHAPTER 26

Grandma's Book

I'm helping my other grandma, my daddy's mommy, bake today. She says she won her kitchen from Betty Crocker. I don't know who Betty Crocker is, but I like Grandma's kitchen. I scoop flour out of a special drawer with my pink cup. I thought Grandpa made her kitchen. She says Betty Crocker did after Grandpa did. Grandma says she made her molasses crescent cookies and won a kitchen. She says Betty came to the farm from far away and gave her a new kitchen for her cookies. I tell her that I like to win things too.

The green carpet warms my toes in Grandma's living room. I climb on the flowered couch next to her, and it's quiet. Grandma's reading a big book to me. It doesn't have any pictures, and the pages make noise. Grandma says I need to know about a man who died for me. I say, "I don't know him," and she says, "That's why I'm reading the book." It's called Bible. Grandma says, "His name is Jesus, and he was a very good man."

Oh! I remember. I tell Grandma, "He was the black man. He got shot by a gun and died. I know a song about him." I sing and hum the parts I don't know, *Here's to you . . . hmm hmm hmmmm . . . Jesus loves me, I know, wo, wo, wo*, and put my leg in the air, and then my arm. My foot's taller than my hand.

Grandma's not talking, and her face looks funny. I can't see her lips.

Grandma starts talking and her lips come back. She tells me Jesus is not the black man who died. She says this man died because he loves me.

"What?" I say.

Grandma says, "That's how much God loves us. He let his son die for us."

That's kind of mean, Grandma, I think to myself.

Grandma reads a story about the man who was dirty and sick, and people were mean to him. They hit him and made him live in a rock. Her hands shake. Grandma says, "Jesus made him clean, and people were nice to him." Jesus told the clean man not to tell, but he did. Grandma says, "No, he didn't get spanked for telling."

Grandma says, "Christmas is the birthday of Jesus."

I think maybe Jesus is Santa, but I don't say it. I think Jesus has magic powers, like in *The Witch Next Door*. It has pictures and she has magic powers. She turns the ugly, mean people into pretty, nice prince and princess people. I like when the kids in *The Witch Next Door* get mad and don't get in trouble.

Grandma says Jesus helps people all the time and he's perfect. I say Mommy says no one's perfect, and Grandma says Mommy's wrong. She points her finger at me and says in a not-nice voice that one person's perfect. She says people like Mommy and Daddy are going to hell if they don't follow Jesus. I don't know how they find him. Her finger's close, not close, close. I'm giving Grandma cross-eyes when the finger comes close again, but she puts it on her book and taps it.

I say, "What's hell?"

Grandma says, "Remember when Matty burned his leg and he cried when I put butter on the burn?"

I say, "Yes, that scared me."

She says, "People burn like that all over in a dark place called hell. Forever." Grandma says people are in trouble for not doing things for God.

I say, "Wait, who's God?"

She shakes her head and says he made me and everything and everybody. She smiles and says he's everywhere. I say he must be re-ally big. She says he is and he knows everything. I think maybe that's not so good and squish my face a little. Grandma smiles and says not to worry; it's Mommy and Daddy who are in trouble, not me.

I say that scares me, and Grandma says, "It's scary." She says we need Mommy and Daddy to go to church and do good things so they don't have to go to hell. Grandma says, "Church is where Jesus is." She says bad people go to hell when they die. Grandma says children go to hell if their mommies and daddies don't take them to church. That made me scared, but she just said not to worry. My head hurts now.

She's making me feel grumpy and sleepy. Grandma tells me to take a nap on the sofa and gives me a soft gold pillow. I close my eyes and think maybe Hansel is God.

I wake up to Grandpa's black lab, Lucky, barking outside. I run to the window and see Mommy's car pull in the driveway. Grandma is cooking and it smells yummy.

We sit down at the big table in Grandma's kitchen for supper. I tell Mommy that Grandma says we're going to hell. We'll get bad burns like Matty's if we don't go to church. Mommy says, "Huh." She asks me to pass the carrots, and I see Grandma's cheeks are pink. I say Grandma's Jesus makes a dirty man clean. Mommy nods. I think about my other grandma, and she says I'm dirty when she takes me to her house from the farm. I say if I go to church I will get clean too, and that makes Grandma smile. Mommy says I'm not dirty and we don't need church. I can see her teeth.

I'm happy Mommy says I'm not dirty. She says I'm dirty and smelly a lot. Daddy does too.

Mommy calls Daddy's picture books from the store "dirty." She gets mad that he looks at those dirty books. Matty and I've seen them. They have pretty ladies in bikinis, but some don't have clothes. The ladies smile and have lipstick on. I like their bikinis. I wish I had a yellow bikini or a pink one. I have a blue-and-purple swimsuit, and it covers my tummy. I like it when Mommy puts my hair in pigtails. It's like the hair on the pretty ladies Daddy looks at.

CHAPTER 27

Irish Spring

There's the creaking sound in the hallway I've been waiting for. Matty's up. I climb out of bed, grab my slippers and my pink quilted bathrobe. I'm happy it's Saturday morning. It's time to watch cartoons with Matty.

I find him in the kitchen, and he gives me a big smile and asks what kind of cereal I want. I tell him I want Frosted Flakes. He always makes a little boom sound when he hops off the counter. My job is to put spoons by the bowls and Matty gets the milk. We always walk slow to the living room so we don't spill and get in trouble. Mommy and Daddy haven't made a peep, so we keep the sound low on the TV. If we're lucky, sometimes Mommy or Daddy makes pancakes on the weekend.

Matty says he forgot napkins, and I say I'll get them. I jump up and grab four napkins, just in case. When I come back into the living room, Matty looks at me and says, "You're the best sister in the world, Deidi." I like that and say that he's the best brother. A Play-Doh commercial is on. Yellow, green, red, white. Mommy said a commercial shows things to buy. Matty asks me if I ever wish Mommy and Daddy would help us in the morning.

I look at him and nod. I tell him, "But I'm still the luckiest sister because you're my big brother."

Matty gives me a hug and starts tickling my sides. I hate it when he tickles my sides, so I start squeezing his sides, and he kicks his cereal bowl over. I see a shadow move over the carpet. My neck's cold. It feels like needles are sticking in my skin.

"Matty!" Daddy yells, and I almost pee.

Matty looks at me and nods to the floor. We wipe up the little bit of milk that spilled on the carpet with our napkins. Before we can finish, Daddy's yanked Matty up by the back of his PJ shirt and made him cough.

Daddy puts Matty in his chair and starts taking his belt off. Matty's crying and Daddy yells, "You better knock it off and act like a man." Mommy's rubbing her eyes in the hallway and asks what's going on in a whisper.

I'm counting the hits on Matty's bare bottom with Daddy's belt. I'm at eight when I look back at Mommy with her arms folded.

She says, "Oh, stop it, that's enough."

Now I've counted eleven. Matty's stopped crying. Daddy's putting his belt back on and says maybe he'll act like a man now and not a baby. Matty lies on the carpet with his PJ bottoms and undies around his ankles. Daddy tells Mommy not to wait up for him tonight, and the front door slams behind him.

I remember the last time Daddy and Mommy made me and Matty pull our pants and undies down in the kitchen when we got in trouble. We forgot to put the milk back in the fridge. We both had to bend over and grab our ankles. I had red bumps on my bottom for two days. It hurt to pee. I remember when I got in trouble before that and didn't know why. Daddy was so mad. He yelled, "strip and grab your ankles." He said I wasn't bent over all the way.

I had to touch my head to my ankles. He hit me and hit me. I think about how Daddy does this to Matty and me a lot. I don't want to think about it anymore.

Mommy tells Matty and me to go get dressed. I whisper to him, "Race you back to cartoons?"

He nods and rubs his eyes.

I make sure he's back in the living room before I go back. He'd do the same for me. He says, "Beatcha, Deidi."

Matty lets me hold his hand when we watch our cartoons again.

I'm in my room when I hear Mommy tell Matty, "You need to put your Hot Wheels track away, Matty. We've got to get going and it's in the way."

Matty says he's watching something on TV when I walk into the living room.

Mommy says, "I don't care what you're doing. Get up and put those toys away. Now."

Matty gets up super slow and stretches and yawns. Mommy starts walking down the hall. Matty walks to his toys and says, "She's an asshole." Mommy stops and turns fast. She grabs Matty by both arms, lifts him into the air, and sets him on the green chair. Matty says, "Whoa! That was fun! Do it again!"

Mommy is really mad now and says, "What did you just call me?"

He says, "Asshole." She wants to know where he heard that word and Matty says, "Hundred times from you and Daddy." She's just staring at Matty, so he says, "'Cause you're both assholes. He says you're asshole, and you say he's asshole, so you're both asshole."

Mommy says, "Get up, you're coming with me." She takes him down the hall to the bathroom and tells him to climb up on the stool in front of the sink. I'm peeking around the door. Mommy opens a cupboard and takes out a box. She opens one end and slides a big bar of soap with green and white stripes onto her hand. She turns the faucet on and lets it run over the soap for a long time. Mommy tells Matty to open his mouth. She says, "Next time you want to call me a bad name like that, you better think about this soap in your mouth first, because it will happen again, only worse."

Mommy pushes the big bar of soap into Matty's mouth. He's yelling with no words, but she isn't taking it out. Her hand squeezes the back of his neck so he can't move. I see tears going down his cheeks.

I go back to the living room. I don't like looking at the cartoons now.

CHAPTER 28

Farm Visit

I'm in the car with Mommy, Daddy, and Matty going to Grandma and Grandpa's farm. It's windy. The car slows and turns onto the gravel road that goes to their house.

We drive up the big hill, I see the old windmill turning. Grandpa told me it doesn't work now, it spins. I don't know what "work" it did. Matty points to Daddy from the back seat. We know what he's going to say. I nod to Matty, and Daddy says, "This old homestead and barn was built by your great-granddaddy." We both giggle. Matty points again. Daddy says, "This newer house and barn was built by your Grandpa." I bend over and squeeze my mouth shut. Matty's covering his mouth. Matty says without sound the same words Daddy says. "And all this wheat land has been farmed by this family." Matty and I burst out laughing. Daddy's looking in the mirror at us, and Mommy turns around smiling. She says we're here. Lucky's barking by Matty's door.

Daddy says he and Mommy need to have adult talk with Grandma and Grandpa. Matty and I stay outside to play. We go to the little barn where they used to have chickens. There's a lot of wood and wire. I run over to the swing. Grandpa tied it to the big tree by the front door. The rope holds a wooden seat. I can go so high. I sing, *The morning I wake up . . . I put on my makeup I say a little la, la, la, la, la, la . . . how I love you.*

I'm thinking how much I love singing this song. Now I see Grandma in front of me. She's like *Bewitched*. She came out of nowhere. Her face looks scared. I drag the tops of my shoes on the grass to stop swinging. She says, "I didn't know what the noise was. I thought you were, uh, hurt or something."

I tell her I was singing, and she says, "Oh, well, back to it then." She turns sort of slow. She gives me a little wave bye-bye. I'm not going to sing so loud. I think something's wrong with Grandma sometimes. I don't know what.

I'm twisting back and forth on the swing and I remember when I asked Grandma about her toe. I was squatted on the kitchen floor and she was peeling potatoes in the sink. She has one toe that's the wrong size. It bends the wrong way. I touched her toe in her sandal, and she told me she's the "eleventh child." She said there were twelve kids in her family. Her big sisters and brothers liked to push her in the closet. She was a little girl like me. They shut the door on her foot a lot. Grandma said it scared her. I asked if it hurt, and she said it did. She said they broke the bone in her toe many times. I said that's a lot of breaks for a little bone. She looked sad and nodded. I told Grandma that I was sorry they were mean to her. She cried.

That's the only time I've seen her cry. I've seen tears in her eyes before, but she didn't cry.

I've never seen Grandpa cry. Daddy says he's never seen it. He must've cried when he was little and got polio. Mommy said Grandpa's lucky he can walk with boots and it didn't wreck his legs. People were mean because he was different. That makes me sad too.

I need to pee and run up the front stairs to the front door. The gold bells Grandma has ring when I walk in. I smell coffee. The bathroom's next to the kitchen. I pee, wash my hands, and steal pink lotion from Grandma. I open the door. I hear Mommy and Daddy, Grandma and Grandpa in the kitchen. They're mad. I don't want to listen now.

I run out the front door. I hear an engine. Matty's on the big green lawnmower. I jump on behind him. We ride around and around the yard, hit a big bump and both laugh. This is so much fun!

Mommy comes outside to tell us it's getting dark and it's time to go home. We say bye-bye and get in the car. As we back out of the driveway, I hear Mommy say to Daddy that Grandma was mean. I like Grandma, she doesn't get mad and she smells like baby powder. Matty says he's her favorite. I hear Mommy and Daddy say bad words and call Grandma names. They say Grandma said Mommy cooks bad. I don't like Grandma now because she made Mommy feel bad. I tell her that I don't like Grandma anymore, and Mommy says that makes her feel better because Grandma's not being nice. Matty's quiet and looks kind of sad. That makes me feel sad too.

Now they're calling Grandpa "greedy" and "asshole." Mommy says Grandpa does bad things. I don't know what bad things Grandpa does to get in trouble. I like Grandpa. He gives me lemon candy from a box in his pocket. Grandpa tells me I'm a pretty girl and I like that. He stomps when he walks because of his boots for the polio. I've seen the shiny bars over his boots. He told me they're "braces." He wears overalls with stripes. I have overalls too. Grandpa built their house on the farm, and my swing. Matty whispers that he likes Grandpa, and Mommy and Daddy are stupid, but I can't like Grandpa now because Mommy and Daddy say he does bad things.

I'm getting sleepy and my head falls to one side. I think about how Grandma one time let me call Grandpa with the old phone on the kitchen wall. She said the phone's an antique, and that means old. Grandpa was in the new barn with Matty. I held the black cup to my ear, and Grandma said turn the arm, it looks like a leg to me, around and around. Ring, turn, ring, turn, ring. Then I heard Grandpa say, "Hello," and I said into the little black horn, with my loud voice, "Hi, Grandpa, it's Deidi calling!"

He said, "Hello, Deidi!"

I said, "I'm calling to tell you that supper is almost ready."

He said, "Thank you very much, and we'll be right down."

I said, "You're welcome. Bye-bye."

He said, "Bye-bye."

Then I put the cup thing back on its hanger thing on the side of the phone. Grandma said I did a very good job. My cheeks get happy warm. The other kitchen phone is yellow. It has numbers and letters inside a plastic circle with holes for my fingers. Sometimes I hear the neighbor talking to people if I pick the phone up. Grandma tells me not to "eavesdrop."

I close my eyes and hear Mommy singing with the radio. She's singing, *Love child . . . never meant to be.*

CHAPTER 29

Big Girl on the Farm

Today's a special day for me. I'm back at the farm with Grandma and Grandpa, all by myself. I'm big like Matty now. I don't know how I got so lucky, like Grandpa's dog, Lucky. He's chasing me around the yard. When I stop running, Lucky stops. He barks to go again and stomps his front paws. I love running. Lucky's right behind me. Past the fruit trees, gooseberry bush, clothesline, and the barbecue Grandpa built. Gooseberries are sour.

I fall on the super green grass breathing fast. I'm trying to catch my breath. Lucky's catching his breath too. He lies down next to me with his head on my tummy. I see blue sky with white puffs and elephant-tree leaves. I like lying on the grass. I roll my head to one side. My ear squishes into the grass and it tickles. Grandma says Grandpa's finicky about his grass. I say "finicky, finicky, finicky" out loud. It goes from my lips, to my tongue, to the middle of my mouth, and out. I stare at the big elephant leg. Grandma told me the tree's real name again, but I forgot. The branches remind me of a giant's wig. Jack and the Beanstalk's giant could wear long, pretty, green hair on his head.

I feel my cheeks. One side's smooth. The other side's dented by Grandpa's grass. I wonder how much my head weighs. Maybe I could lay my head on a scale. I don't know how I'd see the number. My tummy's growling under Lucky's sleepy head. I'm hungry. I bet Grandma has lemon bars in the cupboard. Sorry, Lucky, I'm going to move you.

I run up the steps to the back door. I poke my head inside. Ooh, it's quiet. I think, *Don't slam the kitchen door*. I tiptoe through the kitchen. It smells like butter rolls. I hear the wall clock's tiny *tick, tick*. I turn toward the hallway and see Grandma's bedroom door cracked open. I see silver curls on her pillow. The blanket she made covers her shoulders. Daddy's mommy likes to take naps. I've never seen Mommy's mommy take a nap.

I tiptoe by the closet of coats, brooms, boots, and the vacuum. I know, I've looked. I sneak past sleeping Grandma and the basement door. I wonder if Grandpa's downstairs? He could be working on his electric train. I'll check later. I'm going to watch TV until Grandma's up.

I hear a little wind outside and walk into the living room. There's Grandpa reading the newspaper. He's sitting in his big chair. He says it's leather. That comes from a cow, but I don't know how. That's a rhyme. The foot thing is up. I see his brown boots that lace up from his toes all the way up his shins. I say hi in my quiet voice. He folds the newspaper and smiles at me.

"Hello, Deidi. Come over here and sit on Grandpa's lap."

I climb up on his blue-and-white-striped overalls. I just ran by some overalls hanging outside to dry. Grandma says, "They're on the line." She uses clothespins to keep them on the string. I can almost touch the string on my tippy-toes.

Grandpa says, "I wonder if there's anything in Grandpa's pocket that Deidi likes?"

I smile.

He says, "Better check for yourself."

There's nothing in his bib pocket. I check each front pocket. Nothing. I shake my head.

He says, "Make sure you put your hand aaaall the way in the pocket."

I lean toward him and push my hand into a front pocket again. This is a big pocket. I feel something. Not candy, and not in, but under the pocket. Grandpa says, "Yes. Grab that. Keep ahold of that. I'll give you special candy if you hold that like I say." Grandpa pushes my hand back and forth, back and forth. His face is red and his eyes close a little. He says, "Come closer." He puts the hand with all the fingers down the back of my pants.

I think, *It's good I have my flower stretchy pants on. The button on my jeans would hurt my tummy with his big hand there.* He puts his finger in my pee place. He moves it around and I say, "Ow."

Grandpa says, "Shhh. You're my special girl, Deidi." He makes a funny noise. He takes his hand out of my pants. Grandpa sits up more. He pulls a blue bandana out of his back pocket. He wipes his forehead and hand. He says, "Now let's go get some special candy. Just for my Deidi. Nobody else gets this. I'll keep it just for you."

I jump off Grandpa's lap and go to the bathroom. I close the door and wash my hands and face. My face isn't happy in the mirror. I want to go home. I open the yellow bathroom door. I don't hear or see anyone. I race through the kitchen to the back door. Good thing Grandma never put bells on this door. I'm almost outside. I push the squeaky screen door open and close the white door behind me. Lucky runs up, and we play until Grandma calls me in.

I walk up the stairs and say, "Yeah! Grandma's awake." She says she's glad too and points to a yellow kitchen chair. I sit next to a bowl of green corn. I know my job; Grandma already put the newspaper on the floor. I get to shuck the corn and throw the husks on the paper. Grandma says I'm chatty today. She says that means I talk a lot. I ask if that's a bad thing. She says, "I love when you're chatty." I ask Grandma if she gets lonely on the farm. She says that happens. But there's always work to do. I ask her if she likes the work to do. Grandma smiles and says, "Sure." She looks sad to me. I ask why what she likes is sad.

"It's not. Well, maybe it is. A little," she says. She stares out the window for a long time. She doesn't talk when I say her name. I pull her apron and she shakes her head a little. "Yes, Deidi, what is it?" I tell her it's nothing and we go back to work. I think Grandma wishes she wasn't here sometimes. Like me, I wish that too.

CHAPTER 30

Whistle

Matty says, "Make an O with your lips and pull your tongue back." He tells me to blow. No whistle. "Try again." He holds one ear and says he heard something. I think he's being nice.

We're sitting in the grass by our swing set in the backyard. We both see it at the same time. Matty puts one finger on his mouth. I nod. The bird's sitting on the fence post. Birds are too smart to touch the electric. I'm thinking that Charlie Brown has one shirt and this bird stole it. I want to tell Matty, but he gave me the "Shhh" sign.

The bird's head squishes down, comes back up, and sings. I've heard the song before. I didn't know it was from a Charlie Brown bird. It sings again and sounds like *chirp, chirp, chiiirrrpitty, chirp.* It's singing loud, and then it stops. Is it waiting for another birdie to sing back? I hope it isn't lonely.

Matty says, "I wish I knew what it said," as the bird flies.

I say, "Me too. That's a Charlie Brown bird."

Matty says, "No, it's a meadow something. Grandma told me it's her favorite."

I ask which Grandma, and he says Daddy's mommy. I tell him again, it's a Charlie Brown bird.

He says, "No, really, it's called meadow something. I can't remember."

I say, "Charlie Brown bird."

Matty says, "*Deeedeee*, Grandma says so, it's meadow something."

I say, "Charlie Brown bird times a hundred. Do you think he has a belly button?"

"Who?"

"Charlie Brown," I say, and his shoulders go up and down.

Matty says, "Make an O, but pull your top lip down a little more."

I hear a tiny whistle come out.

He says, "You did it, you did it!"

His whistle is good, mine's funny, but I'm whistling!

He says, "Just keep practicing."

We go inside and Matty tells Daddy, "I showed Deidi how to whistle, Daddy. Watch."

I whistle, and Daddy says, "No, that's wrong. That's not how you whistle." Daddy says Matty does it all wrong. He says to curl my tongue. I try it, but it doesn't work. Daddy says what Matty taught me was bad. Daddy is "undoing the mess." He sighs a lot.

Matty looks sad. He says, "Sorry, Deidi," and goes into the living room. I go to my room.

I'm in my room a long time. Mommy's at the beauty place. I'm mad that Mommy's always gone. She goes to school or teaches. She's gone a lot. I want to be gone a lot. I want to go to school. Matty goes to school. He's in kindergarten. I'll go next year. I want to go now.

Daddy opens my door, "Dinnertime, princess." He smiles at me and I'm happy now.

CHAPTER 31

Shopping

Moses Lake has lots of stores, and Daddy's taking us all shopping downtown. Mommy's sad today but she smiles when Daddy says he needs to get her something special. Matty and I are excited when Daddy says he needs to get us something special too.

I see so many stores as we drive. I like seeing the trees and grass by the lake. I like when the street lights change from green to yellow to red. Here's a place that sells cars. Mommy says, "Uh-oh," because Daddy loves cars. Matty says he's car crazy too, and Daddy says the boys need to stick together, and we laugh. Moses Lake is sooooo much bigger than Ruff was. I like all the people I can see when we drive by.

Daddy parks the car and holds open the big glass doors we walk through. I like the music playing inside. It smells like perfume and floor wax in here. Daddy tells us to follow him. Lots of clothes are hanging everywhere, and tall dolls with pretty dresses stand in the corners. Daddy pulls clothes off the racks with lots of colors for Mommy to try on. I start to follow her into the pretty dress room, but she says to stay with Daddy. He's picking out more things.

I look for Matty, but I can't find him. Then I hear, "Psst, over here."

I can't see him anywhere, so I whisper, "Where?"

"Straight ahead," he whispers.

I squeeze between the clothes racks, and there he is sitting cross-legged inside, all the clothes and colors in a circle around him. He tells me we have to whisper. He says maybe we should scare somebody, and his shoulders go up as he laughs without noise. I shake my head, no, we'll get in trouble. I hear Mommy saying, where's Deidi?

I run out to see her. She's putting on pretty clothes, and Daddy keeps giving her more. I get to sit on the soft cushiony thing by the mirrors and watch Mommy. She wants to know what I think. She says that's called my op-in-i-on. It sounds like an onion.

A nice lady in a blue dress and with red lips is helping Daddy find clothes for Mommy. She's wearing a square pin with letters on it, she smiles at Daddy a lot. I like the clicking sound her blue shoes make when she walks back and forth. I like the *k-sh* sound of hangers as she slides them on the silver bar. I watch her press the front of each piece with her hand.

The nice lady tells Daddy I'm a pretty girl, and he smiles at her.

She asks me what my name is, and I say, "Deidi," as I roll over on the cushiony thing.

Daddy tells me, "The nice lady can't understand you when you squish your face in the seat and talk."

I roll back over and say, "Deidi," to the ceiling.

Daddy and the lady are talking, but they sound like grown-ups in Charlie Brown, *wonk, wah, wa, wonk, wah.*

I keep staring at the ceiling without blinking. I need the practice. Matty says my eyes will turn into potato chips if I don't blink. I wonder if they will? I think it looks like someone poked holes in their ceiling, I wish I was tall enough to touch it. I ask Daddy if he can touch the ceiling as he walks by with red-lips lady, but he doesn't tell me.

Mommy says she's picked her special outfit. She's so beautiful. I can tell she put her lipstick on since the last outfit she tried. Daddy's happy and whispers to her. Mommy lifts her shoulder with a smile. Daddy gives her hair a pat and says he's going to corral Matty. Mommy tells me to wait. The nice lady tells me I'm lucky to have such a wonderful father. I don't say anything, but Mommy says from the dress room to say thank you, Deidi. I say, "Thank you, Deidi." The nice lady's eyebrow goes up on one side. I say, "Sorry, thank you," and try to raise one eyebrow without the other going up.

I tell Mommy I like the dress room, and she says it's a dressing room. I say, "Like salad dressing?" and she says no. Daddy runs up. He says he can't find Matty. I tell Daddy where we hid, and we look inside the rack of clothes. Matty isn't there. Mommy tells Daddy to get the manager. Pretty soon the pretty music's gone and a man's voice says Matty's name and he needs to go to the place he was with his mother and father. We keep looking through the big store. I jump when red-lips lady makes a loud noise and says, "Oh my gosh, you scared me, young man!" just as Matty comes out from between the skirts. We all laugh.

Now it's time to get special things for Matty and me. I love looking at the dolls and clothes. Matty loves looking at Legos and car toys. Matty hugs me with one arm, and we smile at each other.

CHAPTER 32

Secret Room

Matty and I are playing at Grandma's in Davenport. It's a lot colder than the last time I was here. Christmas is coming soon!

Grandma's helping a bride in the flower shop. She says the lady's getting married. Matty's playing with the big monkey. I don't like that toy. The head's too big. I'm putting away the tea set. I like playing upstairs in Mommy's old bedroom. It has two big beds and a vanity with a mirror. Mommy says that'll be mine someday. She says I'll keep makeup and girl things in the drawers.

Matty puts the monkey down and says, "Hey, let's go to the secret room, Deidi."

We run downstairs to the hallway. I close the bathroom door. Matty closes the door to Grandma and Grandpa's room. I close the door to the living room. Matty closes the door to the upstairs and then the guest room. I count five closed doors. They all have glass doorknobs. No one can see us inside the secret room.

"Are we spies, Matty?" I ask. He doesn't say anything. I can hardly see him. My eyes get used to the dark. "Hey, where're your pants, Matty?" He tells me to take off my pants.

"I don't want to. I want to play the spy game," I say.

But he says, "Take your pants off, Deidi. Now."

He doesn't sound nice. I want to say he's a meanie, but I'm afraid he'll punch me, so I take off my pants like he says. Matty puts his hand on my pee place. I think I hear something. Grandma opens the door to the living room. Everything lights up real bright.

"Stop that!" she says in a mad voice. "Put your clothes on right now. And come right out."

I'm sick to my tummy. I pull my undies and pants back on fast as I can.

Grandma's in the kitchen, and she tells us to set the table for dinner. She's being nice, but I feel icky. She's not saying anything. I feel like I've done something so bad. I think Matty does too, but I don't know for sure. He won't look at me.

We have pork chops, mashed potatoes, and carrots for dinner. The carrots and potatoes came from Grandma's vegetable garden. Dinner's yummy good. Grandma warms up her homemade apple pie after dinner. She asks who wants homemade vanilla ice cream with it. I raise my hand and say, "Me, please."

Grandma smiles at me. She squeezes my shoulder when I sit down. I'm getting ready to play my favorite game, Memory. She winks one eye and I know everything's okay. I still feel icky.

CHAPTER 33

Late Christmas Tree

It's almost Christmas and we still don't have a Christmas tree. Matty and I already watched *Rudolph the Red-Nosed Reindeer*, *A Charlie Brown Christmas*, and *How the Grinch Stole Christmas*. We always have a tree when we watch those shows. We've been asking Mommy over, over, over for a tree. I don't know where Daddy's been. Mommy says he's working someplace. I don't know where "someplace" is. She says, "Daddy was supposed to be home hours ago. We'll just have to get the tree ourselves." Matty and I don't care that she's mad. We jump around with happy hoorays.

Most of the trees are gone at the tree place. I feel sorry for the ones that are left. No one wanted them. Mommy says she found one. Her tree is not very nice. You can see right through it. It's not thick and green all over, like we always have.

Matty says, "No! That's not the tree we get!" He points to a small bushy tree that you can't see through and says, "That is."

I nod.

But Mommy says, "No. We're getting this tree. Now shut up and be quiet, both of you."

Matty's face gets red. I see tears in his eyes. I hold his hand, but he pulls it and says, "Stop it, Deidi." Matty kicks the bottom of another tree really hard.

Mommy yells, "Matty, get over here right now."

He walks over and she grabs his arm and pulls him with one hand while she hits his bottom with her other hand. Mommy's car keys are inside the fist she hit him with. Matty yells, "Ow!" and wiggles away from her. She tells him to wait by the car. I follow Matty. No one talks on the way home.

Mommy tells Matty to help her get the tree inside. The little sad tree is heavier than they thought. They drop the tree. They pick it up. They drop it. They pick it up. Tree pieces are all over the ground like a trail of bread crumbs from "Hansel and Gretel."

Mommy takes a long time to get the tree up in the living room. It keeps falling over and she keeps saying bad words. She's like the Grinch when he's mad at the Whos. He tried to steal Christmas. Doesn't Mommy remember you can't steal Christmas? Maybe her heart is too small too. But it can grow bigger like Grinch's heart! I'll ask Matty what he thinks.

The tree is crooked and I don't think it can be straight. But Mommy keeps turning the silver turns on the holder. She makes funny noises under the tree like *oof.* She's calling Daddy bad names, but he isn't home. If she wasn't a big person, this would be a tantrum, like she says about Matty and me. She'd be in trouble. Our Christmas tree reminds me of Linus's tree from Charlie Brown's Christmas show. That makes me feel better.

Matty's mouth opens with a loud yawn. I'm staring at the pretty stripes on the TV screen. I wonder what's on the other side of those colors. I want to go inside the TV. Matty's yawns make me yawn and stretch. In my book, *Eloise*, she yawns a lot, too. She lives in the Plaza in New York. It's a hotel. Mommy says stop yawning and help her get the ornaments on the tree. Matty says he wants to do tinsel.

It's not the best tree, but I kind of like it. I think it's sweet. Mommy says, "That's enough, time for bed." Matty and I don't even race to our rooms tonight, we're too tired. Mommy kisses me good night, and I thank her for getting the tree. I tell her she did a really good job putting it up without Daddy. She makes a sad smile, pats my head, and says, "Thanks, Deidi. Good night." I can smell the tree all the way from my room.

I wake up when I hear voices in the living room. I yell, "Daddy's home!" I hop out of bed and run to the living room. Daddy bends his long legs, stretches out his arms, and gives me a big hug.

"Hello, princess!"

I stand back and tell Daddy, "I really missed you."

He stands all the way up and turns his back, saying, "Me too."

Mommy tells Daddy to come with her into their room. Matty walks into the living room and turns on the TV. We hear them yelling, and Matty turns one of the big knobs on the front of the TV so it gets louder. I like that because I forget about the fight. I hear Mommy and Daddy's bedroom door open, and I lean over to see Daddy walk into the hallway. Mommy's still yelling in the bedroom. Daddy's head's down as he walks by and out the front door that slams behind him. Matty looks at me and squishes one side of his mouth and nose. I lift one shoulder to my ear. I like silent talking. I'm sad Daddy didn't say goodbye. I wonder when he will be back.

CHAPTER 34

Closet Mountain

I don't want to get up today. My room's a big fat mess. It needs to be cleaned. Mommy told me it's "priority," which means first thing. She wants clothes, toys, books, and dolls put where they belong. If I don't clean this morning, I'm in trouble. Daddy's still gone. I don't like it when I don't know where he is.

I stretch and listen for any bones to pop. I like that sound. Mommy says it's because I'm growing so much. I swap yellow shorts for my PJ bottoms and a blue T-shirt for my PJ top.

I pick up my Easy Curl kit. I put each green-and-pink roller in a holder. I wish I could set up a play hair store, but not today. I drop a can of red Play-Doh in a box with two more cans. Dried yellow Play-Doh is stuck to the rope-making thingamajig. Grandma told me they used Play-Doh to clean her wallpaper on the farm a long time ago. But then she said it was before they made Play-Doh. I don't know what she meant.

I push a stack of board games into my closet. Candyland's on top of the pile. That's my favorite game. Last time Matty and I played, he cheated. I remember when I said, "You cheated." He lied and said he didn't. We both knew he did, though. I was mad and said it again. The game went flying and Matty jumped on me. He pushed my neck to the floor and hit my head on the stereo. He punched my tummy, jumped up, and ran away. I lay on the floor crying. Mommy came into the living room and asked what happened. I told her what Matty did, and she asked how he cheated. I couldn't remember and didn't care. Mommy said that meant he didn't cheat. I had to tell Matty I was sorry and go to my room.

It feels like I've been working a long time. I'm wrapping my jump rope up when Mommy yells her ten-minute warning. What? I just got started! A lot of toys and clothes aren't put away yet. She knows I couldn't be done that fast. I look at my extra closet. I know I shouldn't, but there's no time. I open the white doors and see that there's nothing on the floor in here. I start pushing toys and clothes in the closet. I know I'm not supposed to. I know each thing goes one place. I tried, but it took too long. I better speed up before she walks in. My heart starts beating faster. I grab the last toys and clothes. Get the coloring books. She'll check under the bed. One more pile to push, close closets, make bed, sit.

Mommy opens the door as my bottom hits the bed. She walks in and looks around. My head's saying over and over, *Please don't look in the second closet.* Mommy's head checks under the bed. She says I've done a great job. She's happy with me. I'm happy, but I feel bad. I make a promise to myself to clean the second closet tomorrow. Mommy's giving me a frosted cookie for my good work. I feel bad about my mean thoughts about Mommy. She's smiling at me and petting my head.

I wake up the next morning and look at my closets, thinking, *I should put the stuff away.* But Matty's laughing in the living room, and it sounds like he's watching something funny on TV. I run down the hallway and sit next to him.

The commercials are on, so we race to get breakfast. We plop in front of the TV with our cereal bowls in our hands right when *Penelope Pitstop* starts. Mommy's yelling my name and saying to come right now. Matty looks at me and says she sounds mad.

I run down the hall and stop in my doorway. I see Mommy in my room with both closets open. She's standing between the closets with her hands on her hips. She looks at me and starts talking fast. Her arms fly with the words. Then she stops. She's not talking. She's shaking her head back and forth, looking at the closet. Mommy says she told me to clean up my room. She gave me a treat for my good work. She says she finds my clothes and toys not hung up, not put away, not where they belong, but in a huge mountain pile! Each word gets louder than the one before.

Mommy uses words I don't know after "You're the most . . ." I'm bad. Her hands squeeze her hips as she leans over the mountain in the closet. Mommy's talking, but I can't hear words. Her arm swings behind her as she throws things without looking. One hand grabs and one arm tosses.

The mountain I made flies all over my room. Things land on the floor, on my bed, on top of the dresser, on the knobs on my dresser. Some things hit the dresser and fall on the floor. Some hit the wall and fall on the floor. I think about how the clothes she throws are quiet, but my dolls make big thumping sounds. Toys like my play telephone make a lot of snapping, ringing, and cracking noises.

I wish I couldn't hear Mommy's mean words now. She hurts my insides. I'd plug my ears, but I know she hates that.

More clothes and toys fly by my head and I'm thinking, *Mommy's right! I am bad. I should've known better like she says. Fun days are for other kids, not me. Kids that are better. They're nicer, smarter, prettier, and stronger. Lots of big people love them. They make the big people happy. Not like me.*

The mountain's gone when Mommy stands back up. She says to follow her into the living room. She flips off the TV, and Matty says, "Hey!" Mommy says she's sorry, but this is my fault. She tells Matty the bad things I did. Mommy looks at me and asks where I got all the nice things I tried to destroy. I'm trying to think what "destroy" means. Does it mean "destroy" like Matty's Battleship game? I'm not sure. I lift my shoulders. She yells louder how she bought me those things. She did. She got the money and bought the things. Mommy keeps pointing at her head. She says something about how she tries hard and says words like "spoiled," "queen bee," and "Daddy's princess."

Mommy says this happens to things spoiled children don't take care of. She reaches over to the Christmas tree and grabs the middle with both hands. She makes an *uuuugh* sound and pulls the whole tree over. Branches and glass are breaking. Lights blink on the tree and go off. Mommy points at the tree on the floor and says to Matty that it is my fault. He looks at me, then Mommy, then the fallen tree, three fingers are hanging out of his mouth.

Mommy tells Matty to put his boots on and grab his coat. She says they're leaving. She unplugs the tree lights and says to me the tree better be up and the mess cleaned up before they're back. Mommy slams the front door when they leave.

I'm scared to be alone. I sit down cross-legged in the middle of the living room. I bend way over my legs until my head touches the carpet. I tuck my arms under my chest. I'm really scared to be alone. Hansel's locked in the garage. I think about what to do, and then I remember Cinderella. I run to my room and see her upside down by the dresser. She was alone, she had to clean, her family was mean to her, her mommy and daddy were gone, and she was scared.

I sit Cinderella on top of the stereo table, push her gold hair away from her face, and spread out her green rag dress. I'm glad my doll's like me. She's not Cinderella at the ball after her fairy godmother's magic. She's like me. I don't care about a pumpkin carriage with horses and the big party with a prince. I'd rather have the bluebirds and mice for my friends. I bet Frederick the field mouse wouldn't want to be turned into a horse. Cinderella's mice protected her from Lucifer, the mean cat.

I'm happy Cinderella's here to talk to. I start cleaning up and tell Cinderella her story. I say someday she'll wear a big, beautiful, blue-and-white ball gown that sparkles. I crawl around the tree. I say she'll have long gloves, like Miss America. There are a lot of broken ornaments. I say that her pretty blond hair will be fancy. I pick each broken piece out of the rug. I tell her about the glass slippers she'll wear and the pretty choker for her neck. Water from the pan got the rug and some presents wet. I tell Cinderella all about the party. I move the presents that are dry by Mommy's chair. I tell her about the prince. I'm careful when I take the wet presents out. I tell Cinderella about "midnight." I try to dry a wet present with my PJ top, but the paper kind of rubs off. I say that she lost one of her glass slippers when she ran away. I remember how I stand on the vent if I'm cold after a bath, so maybe that will dry the presents. I tell her about the prince looking for her. I tell Cinderella they live happily ever after because I need to get the mess cleaned up.

I take each wet box and put the wet side on top of each vent. Four vents have presents on top. Before I push the tree back up, I take off the unbroken ornaments. I get two towels from the linen closet and lay them on the wet carpet. The sideways pan's empty. It makes me wonder how a tree drinks water?

I try to pull the tree up from a branch that's not under it. The branch cracks and breaks in my hands. I stand and face the middle of the tree and grab it with both hands. I pull as hard as I can. The tree won't go up.

My heart goes *boom* when I hear car tires on gravel. Where can I hide? There's not enough time. The front doorknob clicks, and a burst of cold air makes me shiver. Daddy walks in the front door. His cheeks are real red and he looks happy to see me.

He takes off his coat and asks where Mommy is. I lift my shoulders and say, "Don't know."

He walks into the living room and says, "What the hell happened here?"

I start talking fast, like Mommy did. He sits on the foot thingy in front of me. I like his hands on my shoulders. I tell Daddy all the bad things I did with my closet mountain. I say how I'm in trouble. I say Mommy made a big mess in my room. She pulled the tree down. She took Matty and left. I've been so scared, but Cinderella's been helping. I've tried and tried to get the tree back up. I say I can't figure out how to do it, and Mommy will be mad if it's not cleaned up. And the presents got wet, not all, but some did, and I had to put them on vents or they rip if I try to wipe them off. Then Mommy would be even madder.

I feel the tears all over my face when Daddy stands and lifts me up to his waist. He says everything's going to be okay. Daddy carries me on his hip over to the tree. He lifts the tree with one hand and straightens it out. I say, "Daddy, you're strong." He kisses the side of my head. The tree looks even badder than before.

Daddy says, "Hold on, sweetheart," and puts me in Mommy's chair. He checks each light bulb on the tree. He says a couple are broken and he'll be right back.

I say, "Noooo!" and start to get up because I'm scared he'll drive away.

Daddy says, "No, no, I'm just going to the kitchen, hold on." He comes back in with one red and one green bulb. He twists them into the string and plugs the lights back in. They work!

Daddy helps me hang the ornaments and fix the tinsel. We stand back. He shakes his head a little and says we did a good job. One long branch sticks out of the bottom of the tree. Another long branch pokes out of the middle to the wall. It looks like a robot tree that broke and got put back together wrong. We sit down on his big chair.

Daddy lights a cigarette with one hand. He hugs my head to his chest. It goes up and down real fast.

Daddy says that Mommy shouldn't have pulled the tree down. He says she got too mad and did the wrong thing. Daddy says he's sorry Mommy did that to me. I start crying again. I keep crying while he pets my head and smokes. I almost can't stop crying and make funny noises when I try to catch my breath. Daddy keeps saying, "It's okay now." Daddy says Mommy's been having a hard time because he's had to work so much. He says that big people do stupid things sometimes. Daddy says that things have been hard. His mommy and daddy promised to help and broke their promise. I'm not sure what that means. I hear him talk about it. He sounds sad, but I don't know what he's saying. I'm getting sleepy now. I'm sure my eyes have fat sleepy fairies sitting on top of them. They won't let me open my eyes. I fall asleep on Daddy's lap.

CHAPTER 35

Christmas 1969

I've been waiting a long, long, very longest time. It's finally Christmas Eve and our tree has piles of presents. We get to open them all tonight!

I saw an Easy-Bake Oven in the Sears catalog. Mommy told me to mark something if I liked it. I drew a little X next to it. My fingers are crossed.

I just got the Easy-Bake from Mommy and Daddy for Christmas! They're setting up my very own oven in the kitchen. Daddy says we can bake a chocolate cake. Matty's hollering in the living room, "I don't wanna bake a cake!" Daddy's yelling back at him that it's Christmas. He tells Matty to get his fanny in the kitchen.

It looks like Daddy's putting a light bulb in the Easy-Bake. I think it helps cook the cake. I'm mixing water and brown powder in a silver pan. I have a little pink spoon. Matty's sitting on his knees at the table. He's trying to look like he doesn't care. I know he does. Mommy's taking lots of pictures of us. I tell Matty he can make the frosting if he wants. He says, "Sure, I can do that." Matty eats most of it before the cake's done. I don't mind. We go back to the living room after everyone has finished their chocolate cake.

We all go to bed, and I close my eyes and sing, "Here Comes Santa Claus" in my head.

It's Christmas morning. Santa gave me the most beautiful doll in the world! Mommy says her name's Dancerina. She's a real ballerina. She has a pink crown and blond hair like me. Daddy says, "She looks like you, Deidi."

Daddy's sitting on the floor next to me. He says, "Let me grab some batteries. Just a sec." I ask why he needs batteries. He tells me I'll see. Mommy says to check the kitchen drawer. We all know she means the junk drawer. It has paste, tape, scissors, paper scraps, coins, clips, bullets for Daddy's different guns, and my favorite gold-star stickers. Mommy puts stars on our artwork sometimes.

Daddy finds the batteries and sits back down next to me. He takes my doll and turns her over his lap. He pulls the long zipper on the back of her tutu dress. I can see her skin when Daddy clicks open a door above her bottom. I say she has little bottom cheeks like me. He says she sure does. I laugh and get on my knees. I hold his shoulder and lean over to see inside. It's an empty box with silver curly and pointy things. Daddy says, "This is where the batteries go."

He puts the batteries in the door. He clicks the cover closed and zips her dress up. He stands Dancerina on her toes. She's wearing light-pink ballet slippers over pink tights. They match her top and fluffy tutu dress. She has pretty flowers on part of her top and on her tutu. Daddy says to hold the middle of her crown with my hand.

Dancerina's as tall as my tummy when I stand next to her. I put my hand on the pink knob inside her crown. Daddy says, "Turn it." Dancerina starts moving. Her head turns. Now her body's turning. It goes head, body, head, body. She's dancing!

I give Daddy a big hug and say, "I love you. She's the best doll ever!" Daddy says he loves me too and he's happy I like her. I get up to give Mommy a hug, but she's helping Matty with his toys and shakes her head like she doesn't want me to hug her.

"Honey, I'm helping Matty right now," she says, putting one arm out. I bend a little and hug her with both arms.

I say, "I love you, Mommy."

She says, "I love you too, Deidi. Now let go of me." Mommy smiles and says, "Hey, Matty, here's the green Lego you're looking for."

I try to make my hair like Dancerina's. I'm standing on a stool in front of the bathroom mirror. I push my hair up with clips and bobby pins, but it keeps falling down. Mommy walks by the bathroom door and I say, "Mommy, could you please help me?"

She pokes her head in the door, "What, Deidi?"

"Could you please help me make my hair like Dancerina's? I've been trying. I can't do it."

Mommy walks into the bathroom, takes my pink brush, and starts brushing my hair, hard.

"Are you mad, Mommy?" She stops brushing and looks at me in the mirror. "No, Deidi, I'm not mad. I just hate how horrible your hair is."

She starts brushing again. I feel bad. She hurts my head when she starts brushing the hair back like a ponytail that's too tight. My eyes are getting wet. I tell them to stop, stop! I look in the mirror and my hair looks like Dancerina's. I forget the owies because it's so pretty. I can be like my doll and like a ballerina. I turn to see the side. Uh-oh, I look more like the Old Maid hair on my card game.

Mommy says, "What's wrong, Deidi? Now what?" I think she can see the wet under my eyes now.

I say, "I love it, thank you, Mommy." I wonder if that's a lie or not. I think it is. Mommy says something I can't hear, tosses my brush in the sink, and walks out.

I look down and see a piece of pink plastic in the sink. The brush's chipped on one corner. I cry a little and say, "That's stupid," to me in the mirror. My face says back that it's because Grandma gave me the brush with a comb. I say, "Stop being such a baby." I pull my hair down. Why'd I try to be like Dancerina anyway?

CHAPTER 36

Date Night

Mommy and Daddy are going out tonight. I'm watching Mommy put makeup on in front of her special mirror. I count one, two, three, four, five, six circle lights on each side. Daddy gave her the mirror. The lights change colors. Mommy says you match the light to the time of day you're getting ready for. She says there's a morning color, day color, or night color. I like watching her. "You're so pretty, Mommy." She says thank you, and her red lips smile. Mommy's "Avon lady" sells makeup. I love to look at the little book she gives Mommy. The lady gives me little white lipsticks. Some have red inside. Some have pink. I love my lipsticks. I keep them in my white weave purse. I only put them on dolls for the most special things. I draw on lips just like Mommy does.

Daddy has some new clothes on. He looks nice. I watch them put on coats and talk to the babysitter. They tell Matty and me to behave. We say bye-bye.

Matty and I get to watch *Love, American Style* because babysitter is on the phone. I like singing the song.

Matty tells me to stop singing and watch the fireworks. I sing it quietly, but he says, "Still hear you." I don't know what the show's about, but everybody's happy. They're pretty people. One lady looks like a Barbie doll.

I'm sleepy when the colors are on TV. The babysitter's laughing in the kitchen. I think she has a boyfriend. I brush my teeth and get in bed. I think about Mommy kissing me when they get home. I fall asleep fast.

Loud noises wake me up. Is Mommy crying? Why's Daddy yelling? I sit up in bed when I hear Mommy say, "No, no, please don't." She says, "Stop, please stop." Daddy's yelling bad words at her. Mommy's crying. He sounds real mad. I get out of bed. I watch my feet go to the floor. I think about how I love the ruffles on my PJ pants. The floor shakes with each boom and bang. I jump when Mommy yells, "Noooo!" I tiptoe to the hallway a little faster. I'm squeezing Blankie tight in my hands. The rug's a little scratchy on my bare toes. I look up and see Matty coming out of his room. He has his stuffed tiger from Daddy.

The light from Mommy and Daddy's bedroom makes a yellow door on the hall floor and wall. Matty and I look inside. Mommy's sitting on the carpet between the closet and the tall dresser. Why's she there? I see Daddy's bare bottom in front of us. His arms fly around as he yells.

Mommy sees us and Daddy turns around fast. I see his pee thingy. I jump back and push Blankie in my mouth. Matty says, "Ahhh." Daddy's mouth is shiny. One cheek is really red. His eyes are red and black. Mommy's face isn't sad or scared. It's nothing.

Mommy lifts one hand when Daddy's not looking. I see her pee place. Her hand makes a "shoo, shoo" at us. Where are Mommy's clothes? Daddy's getting closer to Matty and me. He's in front of us now and I can't see Mommy. My eyes water. Daddy yells so loud at Matty and me I can't hear what he says. I know it means "leave" by the way his arm is pointing. We walk backward into the hall and out of the yellow door. My body's shaking one way and my head's shaking another.

Matty grabs my hand. We're in the hall. Not moving. We're by the bedroom door.

Daddy turns and runs to Mommy. He squats his bottom on the carpet. I think, *He's going to take care of Mommy because Matty and I helped.*

I see Daddy grabbing Mommy's arms. He stands and lifts her into the air. He throws her on the bed. She looks like my Flatsy doll with her arms and legs sticking out. I see Daddy grabbing the pillow. I step toward the door but stop when Mommy's arms go up in front of her. He falls on top of her like a great big tree chopped down in the forest. Before the pillow hits her head, she says, "No, no, no." I hear louder Mommy sounds and no words.

Matty grabs my arm when I start to run in. "You can't go in there, Deidi. He'll kill you!"

"He's killing her," I whisper. Matty shakes his head. I try to pull away, and Matty yanks me back. The sound of loud dog growls stops me. Matty's face looks scared when I cover my ears and push my head into his chest. I can't move. I can't watch. I can't hear.

Matty's hug loosens. He tells me it's over. Mommy's quiet now. Is she dead? "Matty, is she dead?" He leans toward the door and shakes his head. Daddy says something about cleaning Mommy. His voice sounds bad. Matty pulls me to the door to his room. Daddy's dragging Mommy into the bathroom.

We hear yelling and booms, then splashes. I tiptoe behind Matty to the doorway. He peeks inside and pulls back fast. His back is on the wall. His eyes are real big. He's shaking his head at me, but I look anyway. Mommy's on her knees in front of the green toilet. I see her pretty hand on the toilet seat. I see Daddy's bottom when he bends over and pushes her head into the toilet. He lets her up.

Wet brown hair covers Mommy's face. She makes sounds. Daddy yells and pushes her head back in the toilet. Her knees are under the green bowl. Her hands look like they're clapping the seat. Daddy's saying bad words. Matty pulls the back of my PJ top. Daddy's hand moves and her head flies up. I turn my head to look at Matty. He's shaking his head at me.

Mommy moves the wet hair stuck to her face. Black makeup smears her cheeks. Daddy's standing behind her. His legs are spread like the Jolly Green Giant on a can of peas. Big tears pop out of me when I remember how happy Mommy was tonight. She said she took "extra time" to put her makeup on. Daddy pushes both hands into the back of Mommy's head. Water splashes out the side. She gets up on her knees and grabs his wrists. Her body's wagging back and forth like Hansel's tail. I watch her pink fingernails dig into the side of his arm. He lets go and jumps back. I see dots of red where her hand was. She pushes herself away from the toilet. He washes his arm in the sink. Mommy puts something on the floor next to her.

Peeking at her wet and black-smeared face I go backward in my head. I'm in her bedroom lying on the bed. Mommy's so pretty in the light of her new mirror. She asks me if Daddy will think she's pretty tonight. Daddy's screaming brings me back to now. I see Mommy putting her leg-shaving thing in front of his face. Mommy's voice is mad. Daddy walks backward. I feel warm tears rolling down my hands to Blankie.

Matty's trying to pull me away. We run to his room. I think I'm hearing birdies outside. I curl up behind him. He says, "Go to sleep, Deidi. I'll watch out for Mommy." I wake up in the same place in the morning.

LEAVING THREE

Something's tickling my cheek. I open my eyes to see dry pine needles falling from a green branch and remember I'm lying under my favorite tree. I brush her brown needles off my glasses and think about how I still hear morning birdsong.

I'm shaking a little. This happens sometimes when I think too much about too many hard things. I don't like this, but sometimes I can't help it. This time I can't help it more than ever. I tell myself that no matter what happens in Bellevue, there'll be birdies I can listen to.

I wish I could take a branch of my tree and plant it in Bellevue, but I'd never hurt her. I run my hands along the low branches and smell her. It's hard to say goodbye, but I better get back to packing before I get in trouble. I shake off the needles and put a scoop in my pocket. I kiss her goodbye and run to the back door. I'm walking as quietly as I can to my room.

The door closes behind me as everything starts spinning. A little barf taste is stinging the back of my throat. I'm squeezing my wet hands together.

I'm remembering something.

Why's Mommy yelling at Daddy in my room?

She's not. She's just super loud.

I put Blankie on my head and peek in the hallway. Everything's dark except a skinny line of light around Mommy and Daddy's door. Empty bottles of alcohol, big ones, are still on the floor. So is the pillow I put under Daddy's head when he was passed out in the hallway. Now he's gone.

Mommy's yelling, "Do it!"

Her laughing sounds mean. Their bed's knocking on the wall. I hate that sound. I barely hear Daddy saying, "Stop," between his sniffles.

Knock. Sniffle. "Stop." Knock. Sniffle. "Stop."

I hear Mommy's voice. "Poor little mama's boy."

The spinning stops.

My face hits the blue rug.

Blue, blue sky, think. Blue feathers, birdsong.

Blue roses on my bedspread. I'm okay.

Blue spot in my heart.

I roll my head from side to side. Sometimes it helps to empty bad memories out my ears.

I stop when I see a corner of white paper under my dresser. I stretch my arm and grab it. Inside the fold is a giant red-and-white candy cane. I remember this. I painted it on my easel when I was five. There's a black scribble where the candy cane curves, and I remember how Matty wrecked my drawing. I was trying to show it to Mommy at the kitchen table. Matty leaned over and said he wanted to see. He scribbled his black crayon on my drawing and sang, "Yum, yum, I ate your candy cane. I ate your candy cane." I pulled his hand off my candy cane with one hand and grabbed the crayon with the other, but it was too late. Mommy said, "Oh Matty, stop it." I looked at him with a sad face and he stopped smiling.

My head's floating back to Christmastime. It's like a movie. Mommy says Daddy's meeting us at the Elks Club. Matty has his long-sleeve gold shirt on. He's wearing his favorite brown-and-gold-striped pants. His hair's combed and he looks nice. I have my blue turtleneck on with my brown skirt and tights. My hair's clean and smells like baby shampoo. I pull the hall closet open and grab my mittens, shoes, coat, and we're out the door. It's cold outside!

We drive past dark stores with CLOSED signs on doors, and windows lit with blinking lights. Mommy says the road is icy. She drives so slow over the bridge above the black lake, I wonder if we'll ever see Santa. We turn into the big parking lot for the Elks Club. There's lots of cars here. People are walking fast to get inside and out of the cold. I wonder if I smell like cigarettes after Mommy smoked the whole way over in the car. I feel kind of sick. I'm glad for the fresh air when we get out. We walk past the front of the Elks' wall of big gray bricks. There aren't any windows in this wall. Mommy says hello to some people and pushes the glass doors open.

A man sits at an important-looking desk. I stare as he runs his hand through the dark hair covering his right eye. He looks like one of the Beatles. He smiles at Mommy and tells us where to find Santa. Matty and I follow her clicking heels down the hall of shiny floors and pictures. Everywhere I look, old men are shaking hands with other old men in big frames. All their faces look at the camera while they hold hands.

There's lots of flags in pictures and in stands around here. I hear "Jingle Bells" playing in the big room ahead of us. I see Daddy and run to him. He's talking with a blond lady in a red dress and too much perfume. He puts his brown drink with lots of ice cubes on a table and lifts me up for a hug.

I see myself in the big mirrors behind all the glasses, different-color bottles, and a real long counter. It has stools where people sit. I know those big bottles are alcohol, and this is a bar. I know kids aren't supposed to be in bars. I guess this is a special occasion, like Daddy said. He knows the man's name behind the bar and orders Shirley Temples for Matty and me and something "on the rocks" for Mommy.

The bar makes me think about the time Daddy didn't come home for a while. Matty said he was working at a bar called the Pantry.

142

Matty told me Mommy said he had to be the man of the house because Daddy was gone. How can Matty be the man of the house when he's a little boy? It made me feel icky inside, like when Mommy calls me queen bee or when she makes me stay home with Daddy while she takes Matty to the grocery store.

The perfume from the lady standing next to Daddy makes me breathe through my mouth. He tells me the lady's name. He says they've known each other a long time. I say I like her Santa pin, and Mommy gives me a mean look. Daddy hugs Matty, kisses Mommy's cheek, and says, "Speaking of Santa, let's grab those drinks and go find the old guy before he heads back to the North Pole."

Santa gives me a stocking with candies and toys inside. The stocking is made of red net with a tag stapled to the top. Matty got a harmonica, and I got a puzzle of a snowy forest.

This room's getting louder. A lot of people are laughing. Mommy and Daddy know a lot of people. Matty's pulling my hand to hide with him and some other kids. We run behind some big flags on stands and play spying games until Mommy says it's time to go. I ask Mommy why they call this the Elks Club, and she says something about brothers I don't understand. She says we need to go. She says Matty's riding with her and I need to go home with Daddy. I want to go home with Matty, but Mommy points and says in her mean voice, "Get in that car right now." There're cramps in my tummy. I don't want to go home.

Time for the movie to end.

I'm singing "Jingle Bells" and looking around my room.

I squish my candy-cane drawing into a ball and shoot over the moving boxes for my garbage can. "Two points!"

I think about the Indian girl in my class, Mary. None of the men in Mary's family can join the stupid Elks Club, even if the town we all live in is named after an Indian chief. Daddy said only white men can join.

Mommy likes going there. But she says everybody should be treated the same. She doesn't make sense.

I lie on my back and stare at the white ceiling. I wish I had skin like Mary's. It's the same color as those square caramel candies wrapped in clear plastic. I shut my eyes and all I see is black behind my eyelids, open and it's all white ceiling. Close, black, open, white, close. I can almost taste the melting caramel sugar in my mouth.

It's summer now. It was hot outside when I ran to my tree, but cool in the shade. It's about time for Grandma in Davenport to make her caramels for Christmas. She makes them way early. Big silver pots bubble on her stovetop when the white lilies and roses the size of my face bloom in her garden. I bet she still has daffodils and probably purple pansies from early spring. I repeat "probably purple pansies" out loud. This is my favorite time of year to play Thumbelina in her garden. She's a tiny fairy that lives in the flowers outside. But last time we had to wait forever for a pink-beard hummingbird to finish eating at the reddish-purple snapdragon cafe. I want to put Grandma's garden smell in a bottle for the Avon catalog. It would smell like roses, lilacs, and the flowers that smell lemony.

I see *Thumbelina* in with my books. She marries the prince at the end and is happy. Lots of stories end like this. But she was happy by herself too. I love that she saved the robin. Then the robin saved her.

My cousin Sophie gave me *Thumbelina* for my birthday. None of the pop-up pictures are torn in this book. I love Sophie and smile when I think that she lives in Bellevue. I've slept on the trundle bed in her room and listened to music on her record player when we visited Bellevue. She's one year older than me. Her mommy gives my mommy the clothes she grows out of. They always smell nice. Sophie and I have the same color hair. Her mommy is my mommy's older sister. She's a teacher, and her daddy grew up in the same town as my daddy. I wonder if my aunt and uncle hurt Sophie. She has a cat named Tigger and a dog named Chloe.

I remember when Sophie came to my fifth birthday party at Grandma and Grandpa's in Davenport. We were excited to eat the prettiest doll cake made by our great-grandma. The first piece was cut for me, and long strands of hair from the doll pulled between the cake and the piece on my plate. I made an *ugh* sound when I gagged. Great-Grandma thought I said something because her hearing's bad, and she kept saying "Eh?" Sophie covered her mouth. When we looked at each other we burst out laughing.

I heard Grandma tell Mommy that was the last time Great-Grandma was going to bake a birthday cake. Grandma doesn't like Great-Grandma. I think I sort of know why.

Grandma's the oldest of five. Mommy said she helped Great-Grandma raise her younger sister and three brothers. Grandma also helped Great-Grandpa with farming. Mommy said when it was time for Great-Grandpa to stop, he and Great-Grandma gave all the wheat land to the three boys. Nothing for Grandma or her sister. I heard Mommy say this hurt Grandma a lot.

I saw Grandma take care of everything for her mommy and daddy. She said no one else would do it. Just because Grandma's a girl, she can't have any land. I think that's the dumbest thing I've heard. I hate that it hurt Grandma so much.

My daddy's family has a lot of land, like Grandma's family. Daddy says that his mommy and daddy are giving him half their land and half to his sister. No stupid "boys only." Daddy says when he gets his land it will be Mommy's too. Mommy and Daddy say half their land goes to Matty and half to me.

But they say only if we keep our secrets.

Sophie and I were lucky to visit Great-Grandpa after my birthday party because he died before Halloween. That's the last time he gave us gumdrops. He gave these to us every time we saw him. Great-Grandma was sad. Mommy said Uncle Drew died almost the same day the year before Great-Grandpa died. I didn't care. Somebody said that Uncle Drew fell down the stairs going to his room in Great-Grandma's basement. Great-Grandma said, "There was blood everywhere." I wonder if someone pushed him.

When Sophie and I played at Grandma and Grandpa's house, we pretended Davenport Flowers was our business. We made flowers for weddings and funerals. We rode bikes in front of the house and made figure eights on the tennis courts behind the house. Whenever we got to a corner, we had to turn our signals on. They sounded like *tick-tock, tick-tock*.

I have four cousins, including Sophie. Daddy's sister has two kids, and they're younger than me. We don't see them much because they live in Seattle. Mommy's younger sister has a little boy and she's pregnant. I know that's the word for when mommies have babies and their tummies grow big. Mommy told me it takes nine months to grow a baby.

There are always lots of animal babies around the time of my birthday. I've seen cow babies walk on wobbly legs with hay stuck to their new noses. I've seen kittens, puppies, fawns, and colts. I've watched noisy baby birds hungry to be fed. But I've never seen a baby skunk, which I know are called kittens too. I wouldn't want a skunk kitten because when they spray, it's the worst smell ever. We were on a drive the last time I smelled a skunk. It was hot outside like today, so the car windows were up to keep out the dust. Daddy was smoking, Matty was chewing grape bubble gum, and Mommy's perfume was strong. The skunk smell hit the car from outside like a punch, and I barfed red tomato soup on the carpet. Daddy stopped, and when Mommy opened the door, dust blew in and turned the barf gray. Mommy got mad at me, but I said I couldn't stop the barf or wind. Daddy made me say sorry to Mommy for being a smart-ass, but I crossed my fingers when I said it.

I guess the Easter Bunny uses eggs because they're like new babies, but you can hide chocolates inside. I hope our move to

Bellevue is wrapped in a giant Easter egg, I hope it will be nice and sweet like Easter at my grandma's in Davenport.

I pull a pile of clean clothes under my head for a pillow. I wish I had a chocolate Easter Bunny right now. I'd bite its ears off.

I remember one time when Matty and I wanted to hunt Easter eggs.

I start a new movie in my head.

Matty and I are excited to go across the street for an Easter egg hunt. I know there's no such thing as the Easter Bunny. I know big people hide Easter eggs at the park and by the church. The eggs will have candy inside. Matty and I hunted for eggs in Grandma's yard in Davenport before. We got so much candy because we had our birthday party when I turned five, he turned six, and Easter was at the same time. Grandma put lace tablecloths and pink egg candles on the tables.

I pull my favorite light-blue dress off the hanger in my closet. I lay it at the end of my bed and smooth the wrinkles with both hands. I put clean white knee socks next to the dress.

Matty runs in my room and says we need to go outside. I follow him out the front door and halfway down our road. He stops and says we need to be ready. I ask him how, and he says pay attention. He's being serious, so I'm serious too. Matty points across the street and says the water tower's a good place to find eggs, we should start there. He says to check the big trees by the tower next. He's still pointing and talking, but I'm bored and wondering what kind of candy will be in the eggs.

We go back inside. I race into my dress and socks. I run into the bathroom and brush my teeth. I brush my hair into a ponytail. I look nice! Matty flies through the bathroom door and says, "We've gotta hurry, they're starting!" I turn off the water and follow him to the kitchen. Where's Mommy and Daddy? He shrugs and sits down to pull his shoes on. I say we better go check. Matty follows me back down the hall, and we hear the shouting behind Mommy and Daddy's closed door. Matty runs in place and shakes his hands. He says we're missing everything. Their voices are louder and something just hit the wall. I wave Matty away and we head out the front door.

There're a lot of people across the street. I hear laughter. I watch girls in white dresses race to show an egg to their mommy or daddy. Older kids are helping little kids fill their baskets. A teenage girl's wearing a long dress covered in yellow flowers. She has a circle of flowers and ribbons on her head. A little girl with a big bow on her tummy's holding her hand and trying to walk. I wish she was holding my hand too. I wish she was watching me squat by the big tree to pick up candy-filled eggs for my basket. Matty's head's lying on his arms.

Two words appear in my head: The End.

The clean clothes have slipped from under my head.

I'm lying flat on the floor as my head goes back in time.

PART III: AGE FIVE

CHAPTER 37

No More Tangles

Big girls brush their own hair. That's what Mommy said, and I'm five years old now. I'm a big girl and brush my own hair. My hair's long. I look everywhere to find my pink brush and my No More Tangles spray. Both are in the bathroom. I giggle to myself. Mommy would say, "Um, yes, because that's where they belong."

Johnson & Johnson makes my spray. Mommy says I look like the girl on the bottle. We have the same long blond hair. I take everything to my bedroom and climb on top of my bed. I take my compact out of my white weave purse and open it to see the mirror. I don't look like the bottle today. I look like Eloise. She has funny hair in her book. I want to stick a little pink bow right on top of my head like she does and leave the rest alone. Better not, I'll get in trouble.

I think about Mommy getting mad when my hair is tangled. She brushes hard and makes my head move. I look like puppets that sing baby songs on TV. She says, "Stop it, Deidi. Don't move," and then she pulls harder. I move again. She says, "We need to cut this rat's nest off." She always says that. My tummy ribbons tie knots that hurt.

When I'm with Mommy at the store or the Tastee-Freez, grown-ups say Mommy has adorable kids. I like that. They say, "Your daughter's hair is beautiful." Mommy always smiles and thanks them. Mommy says it makes her happy when people are nice like that.

If she cuts off my rat's nest, grown-ups will stop liking me. She will stop being happy at places we go. I'll be sad and ugly.

I say stop looking at the mirror and go to work. I spray a lot. No More Tangles smells good. Spray more. And some more. This squirter's more spit than spray. Now for the brush. I pull on my head a little. I get all the tangles out and look in my mirror. My hair looks real close to my head. Mommy will say it's flat. I don't care.

I'm running to tell Mommy to go to the store today. My spray is going bye-bye. I may not have enough tomorrow. Mommy's in the kitchen at the table smoking. She looks sad. I touch her back.

"Mommy, are you sad?"

She says, "I'm not sad, I'm happy."

I take my hand off. I tell her she looks sad.

She says, "No, I don't. Stop saying that, Deidi. I'm happy, so stop it. Stop it right now."

Mommy gets up and walks out of the kitchen. Her chair's still warm when I sit at the table.

I think in my head, *I'm five now. I'm not a dumbbell. I know the difference between happy face and sad face.* I always knew the difference. When Mommy or Daddy's face was happy, I was happy. When their face was sad, I was sad. Sometimes I think Mommy might be a dumbbell.

There's a mommy that's mean and a dumbbell at Beverly's. Her son plays with Matty sometimes. Matty says his friend says the mommy does things that aren't nice. The friend doesn't have a daddy because his mommy's drunk a lot. I heard Beverly talking on the phone one day about this mommy. She said this mommy picks the boy up from her on Tuesdays. Beverly said the mommy's an idiot. She told me it means the Tuesday mommy's dumb. Beverly said maybe she can't help it, maybe something's wrong. She says some people are born a dumbbell. Mommy could have a little dumbbell in her. Like I have a little Russian from Daddy's mommy.

Now that I'm five, I know things. I know about mommies and daddies. I know they're called "parents." I watch *The Brady Bunch* on TV. The mommy, Carol, and the daddy, Mike, are nice to Marcia, Jan, Cindy, Greg, Peter, and Bobby. They feed and take care of six kids. Carol and Mike don't hurt them. The brothers don't hurt the sisters. There's also Alice. I think she's a maid. She always wears a blue dress and white apron. I don't know anybody with a maid. Alice lives in the kitchen room and she helps everybody. The mommy and daddy help their kids when things go wrong. One time all the kids had measles. Mommy says I haven't had measles. The Brady kids had red dots on their faces and had to stay home from school.

Doctors go to people's houses where the Bradys live. The girls had a girl doctor. The boys had a boy doctor. I have an eye doctor. The girls don't want a boy doctor, and the boys don't want a girl doctor. My eye doctor's a boy. The boys said that girls aren't doctors, they're nurses. The girls said boys are nurses and girls are doctors. They fight, but they don't hit. The mommy and daddy run up and down their big stairs to take care of the kids. The Bradys have a nice, clean house. They keep both doctors. They say that's fair.

The Bradys have a big dog. His name's Tiger. One time he went away. They said Tiger's part of the family. Everyone tried to find him. Hansel's part of my family. But I don't know if Mommy and Daddy would help find Hansel if he went away, like the Bradys looked for Tiger. Their doggie came home after he'd been helping a mommy dog with puppies. He was the daddy doggie. The Brady family was happy. It made me wonder if Hansel's sad that Snoopy and their puppies went away. It makes me sad. Mommy and Daddy never told Matty or me until they were gone.

The Brady Bunch has a kind of hard thing happen each show. They don't pretend it didn't happen, like Mommy and Daddy do. If the Bradys hurt each other, they talk. Mike and Carol help the kids. They're all happy at the end. It's not pretend-happy. I go to bed sad or scared or mad a lot. I think the Brady kids go to bed happy a lot.

Our family has secrets. Maybe the Bradys do too. Maybe that's a part we don't see on TV because it's secret. I'm glad I'm five so I can know things. Maybe other families and kids are keeping secrets too. Maybe there's more than one mean mommy or daddy at Beverly's.

I wonder if Mike gives Marcia new Barbie clothes for not telling bad things. I'm happy when Daddy does that. I like it when Daddy's nice to me. Matty gets mad sometimes when Daddy's nice to me. I don't like that. Daddy's nicer to me. Mommy's nicer to Matty. I don't know why.

I wonder if Marcia, Jan, or Cindy use No More Tangles? I wonder if they ever have to strip and grab their ankles when they get spanked, like I do? It's probably secret and we can't see on TV, I bet.

CHAPTER 38

Hide 'n' Seek

We just ate beef stew for dinner. It was really good. I like it when Mommy and Daddy do the dishes together. She's at the sink with a green dish towel on one shoulder. Daddy shows Matty and me one finger on his lips. That means be quiet. We watch him sneak up behind Mommy and kiss her neck. Mommy does a little jump. She says that's sweet and touches his cheek. Matty and I think this is funny.

Now Daddy's sitting on the brick bench in front of the fireplace in the kitchen wiping his big gun with a cloth. Mommy is petting his head like I pet Hansel. Matty sees it and whispers Mommy thinks Daddy's a dog. We laugh, and Daddy says, "What are you two up to over there?" and we laugh even more. I like it when Mommy and Daddy are happy.

Daddy says, "Okay, you rascals, let's play hide 'n' seek." It's still light out, and there are pretty colors in the sky. The sparrows just finished their dinnertime song. I love the sounds of springtime. Daddy says to get our shoes on and he'll meet us outside. Matty and I pull our shoes on as fast as we can. This is fun.

We run out to the front yard, and Mommy says have fun. Daddy's in the yard holding his big gun. It's long and has shiny wood. I like the bullets that have green bottoms and gold tops.

Daddy tells us the rules: we can't go in the house, garage, or shed to hide, and we can't leave the yard. Daddy smiles and says he's it first.

He says, "I'll count to ten while you run and hide. Off you go, rascals!"

It's good that Daddy's counting slow. Matty and I run together around the side of the house by the fruit trees. We hide behind a bush. I hear Daddy say, "Ready or not, here I come!" Daddy sounds close when he says, "You two are really good hiders." I like that he says that.

I don't hear Daddy or Hansel for a long time.

I hear Matty ask, "Are you still there?"

And I whisper, "Yes."

I hear Hansel barking, and Daddy says to him, "Let's go find those two."

Daddy's voice sounds scary now. He sounds like the scary child-catcher from *Chitty Chitty Bang Bang*. He says, "I'm going to get you two. Where are you, little children?" I'm scared. I think about that scary movie . . . *BOOM!*

I jump and pee my pants a little. My ears are stuffy from the boom. It smells like fire and it's dusty. I see a big hole in the grass, and there is a little smoke coming out of it. The hole is close to me. Mommy's going to be mad I peed my clean pants a little. She says I make her wash clothes too much.

I don't hear any sound. Where's Daddy? Where's Mommy? Did they hear the big boom? Do they know there's a big hole in the yard? Where did Matty go?

I hear Daddy say, "I won't miss next time." He sounds mean. I'm so scared I can't move and my feet are stuck to the grass. I shake my head a little and say to myself that Daddy shot his gun. That big boom was Daddy shooting his big gun. That hole over there was from Daddy's big gun! Why did he shoot his gun in the grass when we were playing our game? Is the game over now? Daddy says that guns are for hunting. Why did he shoot his gun for hide 'n' seek?

Okay, I better run fast as I can! I need a new hiding spot. I run around the side of the house and squish behind a wood pile. I listen. Nothing. *BOOM!* Another gunshot.

Now it's quiet. I put my hand on my heart and I can feel it, like Thumper's paw in *Bambi*. I hear Matty crying, and Daddy yells, "Go inside." Oh no, Hansel is in front of my hiding spot. I whisper, "Shoo, Hansel, go away."

Hansel's ears go up and his big head turns. I know someone's coming. I sink down. I have dirt on my wet pants now.

There's Daddy. I pee a little again. He's in front of the wood and says he's done and to go inside. My right hand shakes. I crawl out from behind the woodpile. He's holding the big gun and says, "I have important things to do."

He leans down, face next to my face. He whispers, "Remember, never tell anybody about things that are our family business." He doesn't move. I pinch the sides of my legs to stop shaking. "Okay, Daddy," I say. He pats the top of my head, says "Good girl," and walks away.

Mommy's in the kitchen when I get inside. She tells me to go to my room. Matty's already in his. She doesn't get mad about my pants, and I'm glad.

CHAPTER 39

Grab the Electric

Where's my jump rope? I thought I put it back in my closet, but I can't find it anywhere. I hear Mommy and Matty yelling. He was supposed to clean his room and didn't. It's a smelly mess. I'm glad my room's clean. I open my other closet. I see my red-and-white rope hanging and grab it. I run through the living room to the front door. Mommy tells me to slow down. I slow to a walk until I am down the front steps and out in the yard. Hansel chases me around the side of the house.

I slow down to look at the hole Daddy shot in the yard. I think it was from the last hide 'n' seek. I don't know. It's happened a lot. My head starts to hurt. I run past the porch and the pasture and find a smooth patch of grass to jump rope on. Mommy and Daddy say family business is private. It means don't tell anybody anything. But what if Daddy shot Matty or me? My head's a sloppy joe. I jump faster and faster.

Mommy's yelling at me to come inside. I don't want to. She yells again and again. I growl to myself because now I've lost count of jumps. It's her fault I'm starting over. I toss my jump rope on the grass behind me to start again. Twirl, jump, twirl, back-door sound, stop. I turn to look and here she comes. Mommy's mean face's getting bigger. I drop the red wooden ends of my rope. I'm walking backward, but she's getting closer. I'm in trouble. Why'd I do this?

Mommy's grabbing my shoulders and turning me to the electric fence. She says bend and grab my ankles. She's pulling down my shorts and undies. Her hand hits my bottom and part of my pee place over and over. Mommy yells, "Grab the fence."

I let go of my ankles and my hands look little. I grab the lowest wire in between the X parts. I'm bending and something's coming up from my tummy. I don't barf, but all the stuff inside shoots up my bottom and down to my head. It's a balloon with too much air. I'm going to pop.

I feel Mommy pulling the back of my shirt. I stand, but my legs are sinking. I'm falling on my side in the grass. I hear Mommy's voice. I've got a bag of cotton in my ears. I don't know what she's saying. My mouth's full of pennies. Mommy's hands are pinching my armpits. We're moving until I feel a kitchen chair under my bottom.

Mommy's putting squishy cold on my face. I can't see. The cold's making me feel better. I think it's a wet rag on my face. I hear the phone ringing. Mommy's voice sounds nice, they're lucky. The phone's still ringing. She's not on the phone. She's talking nice to me! Mommy says I need to be a good girl. She says don't tell Daddy, and I nod.

Mommy's kissing the top of my head. The phone rings again and she answers. I wonder why it feels like I'm eating pennies when I grab the wires? Mommy says goodbye, and I hear the cupboard open and close. She says to open wide. I taste two little circles on my tongue. Mommy says, "Now chew." The baby aspirins taste good. How'd she know my head hurts? She's pulling me on her lap. I'm curling up and pushing hair off my face. My hair feels wet on top. I say, "Are you crying, Mommy?" She says just a little. I'm happy she's sad for me. I hope that's not bad.

CHAPTER 40

Pool

It's summer now. The sun gets to stay up late, and the moon gets to sleep in.

Matty and I are watching *Scooby Dooby Doo* when Mommy comes in and says we need fresh air. She turns the TV off and says to go outside and play. Matty and I hop up. He puts his shoes on faster than me and says he'll see me outside. He calls me "slowpoke." I watch Mommy follow Matty out the door. Where's she going? Mommy mostly never plays outside with us.

I like the words "saltwater sandal." I don't like that my strap is stuck. I'm pushing at the pokey silver thing when Matty yells at me. I can't hear what he's saying. I yell, "What?" back. He runs inside with a big smile on his face. He's wiping off his mouth like he does when he gets all excited. He keeps saying thanks to Mommy. My sandal's making me mad, and he's making me mad. What's he so happy about?

He says that he can't believe Mommy got us a pool. I drop the sandal strap. What? I'm thinking he better not be teasing.

Matty and I have been asking Mommy and Daddy for a swimming pool. Like they show on TV. A pool you can buy at the store and take home. You put the hose in it and fill it with water.

He says it again, "Mommy got us a pool."

"You better not be teasing," I say.

He says, "C'mon, hurry up."

The sandal buckle flaps up and down as I skip and hop outside behind him. Matty's not teasing. We have a swimming pool! It's big. Bigger than a baby pool. Like a real little-kid pool. It's blue inside. There's water in it. The top of all the water has magic sun sparkles. It's just like we wanted.

Mommy's standing by the back door. She has a big smile on her face. I run over to hug her. She lifts me up under my arms. I say thanks a bunch. She puts me down. I say she's the best Mommy in the whole world. She wants to know if we're just going to stand there or if we're going to put our bathing suits on and go swimming? Matty and I yell, "Swimming!" at the same time.

We both say, "Jinx, you owe me a Coke," and laugh.

Matty says, "Last one back's a rotten egg!"

Matty wins the race to the pool. Mommy puts two big towels on the grass, one for Matty and one for me. The sun's right over our heads when we put our toes in the water. It's cold! It feels nice because the sun's so hot. I have on my favorite light-blue-and-purple bathing suit. Mommy says my bathing suit is "seersucker." That word makes me laugh.

Matty and I make a deal. No splashing until we're both in. I'm slower than he is. Matty stands in the pool and his head's above water. I stand in the pool and the water covers my nose. It's fun to blow bubbles with my nose underwater.

Mommy tells Matty to keep an eye on me. She tells us not to drown. I think she's joking. She closes the door before we're done saying okay and no drowning.

Matty's pointing at the top of the water. I walk and pull the water with my arms and hands to get to him. I see a black bug swimming on top of the water. I say that bug's a good swimmer. Matty nods and disappears. Something tickles my tummy. I look underwater and see his hand. I take a big breath and go underwater. My arms stick out like a frog. We swim around and around. Matty's pointing at me. I think he just said I look like Kool-Aid with bubbles coming out of his mouth. He points his finger up. I know that means to meet him up top.

I'm up first, and then Matty's wet head pops up. We take big breaths of air. We're smiling. I ask Matty why he said I look like Kool-Aid. He shakes his head and laughs. He says no, he said "mermaid." He says he thinks I look like a mermaid. That makes me smile so big. I think about being a mermaid. They can swim all over the world. They do what they want and breathe under or above water. They're strong and beautiful.

We eat lunch on our towels. Mommy says we have to wait to go swimming. She says the food has to digest in our tummy. I go inside the house, get my spray for tangles and my brush. I feel like a big girl when I sit on my towel and spray my hair. Now I'm brushing all the tangles out. I'm like a teen girl at the beach on TV. I've seen them sit on big towels and brush their long hair. This is the most fun ever. Matty's scooping swimmer bugs off the top of the water. He holds them close to his face before he gives each a toss.

I lie on my back on my towel. The sun feels really good. I'm getting sleepy.

I remember when we went to the house of one of Mommy and Daddy's friends. They had a big pool in the ground. We played in it all day. Daddy tried to teach me how to dive. They have three kids, a boy and two girls. One girl is a teenager. She's never home.

Daddy likes their bar. Mommy said that's where alcohol drinks are. They have big mirrors around lots of alcohol bottles. When

Daddy stands there, grown-ups tell him what they want. He's like the waitress at Tastee-Freez when she takes our order. Daddy doesn't have to write it down on a pad. He's smart. Mommy says he mixes the best drinks. She gave me a sip of her drink once, and it made me gag. I said it tasted like gas. Matty said he likes gas. He loves going to the gas station. I hate the smell, but I love when we get free toys. I'm collecting Dolls of the World every time we get gas now.

I couldn't figure out how to dive in their swimming pool. Daddy said I belly-flopped. Mommy said I don't have any "depth-ception" because of my eyes.

Mommy and Daddy drank with their friends. The kids watched TV in the family room. I twisted back and forth in the chair that looked like someone cut an orange in half, took out the wedges, and puffed the peel with air. I thought about diving. I remember what I did next, but I don't remember why. I got on my knees, and then I stood all the way up. The chair was wobbly. I put my arms over my head with my hands together in a V like Daddy showed me. I pushed with my legs like he said, and I dove right into the orange carpet on the floor.

It made a big boom when I landed. Daddy lifted me up and took me to the living room. He told everyone I was okay. I heard Mommy say maybe my body was. She said a bad word and something about my head. The grown-ups laughed.

I hear a meadowlark and come back to now. I can't think about this anymore. I look at our new pool with the cold water. My face is burning, not from the sun. I want to jump in the water, but I can't move. Pictures are in my head about before we went in Mommy and Daddy's friend's pool. Pictures fly away! Fly away like the meadowlark.

I roll over on my tummy on the towel. I lay my head on my cheek. The towel's soft on my face. I feel the warm sun all over. I hear the meadowlark singing far away and fall asleep.

I wake up hearing *huh, huh, huh* behind me. I lift up my head and see Hansel lying in the shade. I put my chin on my hands. I watch Hansel's big pink tongue hanging out the side of his mouth. He watches me. Mommy says dogs pant to stay cool. Hansel has a lot of fur. He is shedding now, and Mommy doesn't like him coming in the house.

Mommy opens the back door and says we can go back in the pool. I'm so excited.

Matty and I pretend I'm a mermaid and he's a fisherman. He's trying to catch a fish. I keep saving the little fishes. The fisherman dives into the water to find fishes. He sees the mermaid.

Matty says the fisherman wants to catch her. He wants to hook her on his fishing pole. Then he will win a trophy. Mermaid swims too fast for him. He tries to catch her for a long time, but she's too fast. Mermaid swims away and is happy playing with all the little fishes.

CHAPTER 41

Moonshine

Matty and Mommy are walking, but I'm running into the best library in the world. I don't think I've been to another library, but I bet this is the best one. The white roof looks like a hat from *The Flying Nun* on TV. I like the big walls around the windows. Somebody had to stack a lot of rocks. It's like Bedrock, where the Flintstones live. There's a sign inside the first glass doors. It says the library was built in 1964. That's the year before I was born. I like the bench under the sign. It's a wood bench. You can see the floor through it.

I take a big breath when the second set of glass doors closes. It smells like books and window cleaner. I love the smell. Sun comes inside from the top windows of the nun hat. I trace the colors of the glass by the doors with my fingers. It reminds me of Grandma's bottles on the farm. Red, green, blue, yellow, and orange glass. My favorite is the big blue bottle in the middle. Grandma has round, tall, and square glass. Grandpa built a shelf on the window for her bottles. When the sun comes up in the morning, the glass colors go on the kitchen table.

The library floor is always shiny. There's wood on the walls like our living room. But this wood's brown and our wood's white. Mommy and Matty come inside and we go to the kid area. I sit in front of all these books. I bend my neck all the way back. I can see how far the books go up. The shelves are taller than me.

I like that it's quiet inside the library. No one ever scares me here. I think it's good how grown-ups work to keep the library clean. I never see smudges on the windows. I always put my garbage in the trash can. That's what you're supposed to do. Sometimes I borrow a pencil from the front desk because they let me.

There are so many books here. I choose three books to check out, like Mommy says. I get to take these home with me. I choose two records to take home. I watch Mommy write her name on the pink cards. We'll bring everything back when we're done.

As soon as we get home, Mommy starts reading *Sam, Bangs and Moonshine*. I think I like this book. When Mommy's done, I ask, "What's moonshine? Why did it almost kill Sam's friend?"

Mommy says, "Moonshine is another word for a lie in this story." She says Sam's daddy called her story about her mommy being a mermaid "moonshine," which means a lie. She says, "Sam was so sad that her mommy died, she made up the moonshine because it was easier for Sam to have her mommy be a mermaid than dead."

I say, "That's really sad."

I wonder about what Mommy read. Sam told the moonshine to her friend Thomas and said her mommy mermaid lived in a cove. Thomas went there and the tide came up and he almost died.

I ask Mommy if Sam wanted to hurt Thomas.

Mommy says, "No, she didn't want to hurt him. That's why she said she was sorry at the end." Mommy says that's why we can't lie. "Because people can get hurt."

I ask Mommy if she ever lies, and she says, "Only if telling the truth will hurt somebody's feelings." I say that Grandma from the farm told me that people go to the hell place if they lie. Mommy says, "Grandma doesn't know what she's talking about." I ask Mommy if I will get in trouble if I lie, and she says, "Yes, you will, Deidi. You and Matty have to learn that you always tell the truth."

Matty says, "But what if it will hurt feelings?"

Mommy says she needs to get lunch ready and, "That's for grown-ups to figure out, not for kids."

CHAPTER 42

Pasture Punishment

Matty and I are in the living room building Legos. This brown rug's scratching my ankles, so I move around a lot. The sun's moving around a lot too. Matty turns on the lamp. It has a tall white shade and a round table in the middle of the pole it stands on. Now I can see what I'm doing. I stretch across the Legos to grab the green piece I need. He reaches for a Lego piece by my foot. I know he's going to try to tickle me again.

I swat his hand.

"Hey, that hurt!"

I say that's what he gets for being sneaky. Matty grabs my arm and pinches it.

"Ow!" I holler and punch his arm just as Mommy walks in.

She sends me to my room and says I can't come out until she says. We're both in trouble, but he started it. Matty's a big meanie and I get in trouble. It's not fair. I hear Mommy in Matty's room. His door's open a little. Mommy's saying Matty's fighting other kids, me, and her. I walk slowly down the side of the hallway so I don't make any noise. I want to hear more, but Matty's door flies open. I freeze.

Before I can talk, Mommy whispers in her mean voice to get outside. She says not to leave the pasture. She says, "Do not come back in this house." She says she will get me when she's done. Why do I have to go to the pasture? Why can't I just be outside?

I stomp to the door a little, run down the steps, and head to the pasture. I look at my toes in my sandals. Daddy says there might be rattlesnakes in the pasture. I remember the first time I saw a rattlesnake at Grandma and Grandpa's farm. Grandma told me they're called rattlesnakes because they rattle before they bite. She said if they bite me, I'll die. She says run away if you see or hear one.

If a rattlesnake bites my toe and I die, Mommy will feel bad that she's mean. I don't want a snakebite. But I want her to feel bad. I whistle and call, "Hansel." I hear his panting before I see him. He's happy to see me. I rub his big head and he licks my hands. I love him so much. He's never mean to me. We squeeze through the gate to the pasture. I look for a good stick to toss for Hansel. Here's a good one. I give the stick my best throw. I'm walking when Hansel comes back wagging his tail and wiggling the rest of him. He drops the wet stick on my foot. I give it another throw. Hansel's back again and panting. I toss the stick, he runs back. I'm bored. This pile of wood looks like a good chair.

I sit down and watch Hansel's back sit on the dirt in front of me. I stare at the pasture and practice my whistle. Hansel's ears shoot up, and I hear the *ch, ch, ch* too. I've heard the sound before. It's a rattlesnake. Hansel lifts his back slowly and points his head to the sound. Hansel doesn't move when the sound stops. We hear the *ch, ch, ch* again, but it's farther away this time. Hansel sits back down, and his ears twitch front, side, front.

I'm thinking there're a lot of tumbleweeds back here. I was on the farm once with Grandma, and she told me a long time ago a bad weed grew all over. She said the weeds died and turned into big tumbleweeds. She said tons of weeds turned into tumbleweeds and blocked roads. I see a mountain of prickly tumbleweeds in my head. Grandma said the weed's gone now because planes spray stuff to kill them. We still have other weeds that turn into tumbleweeds.

I've heard grown-ups say plane spray makes people sick. Matty and I watch them from the fields. The spray got in my mouth one time and I gagged. It smells bad. I hear something moving in the weeds. Hansel stands up again. I'm pulling my feet under me on the wood pile. I think it's the snake, but there's no rattle. Hansel's growling in a quiet way he does sometimes. I see a little gray mouse face poke out of a bush. Something doesn't look right. I see his paws sticking out. The little mouse mouth opens, then it's gone. A bigger snake mouth just ate the mouse head! The snake head flops on the dirt. I see the shape of the mouse in the snake. Hansel's barking. He stops when the snake stops moving. It's pushing the mouse inside. I wonder if the mouse is alive in there. It'd be dark and scary. Poor mouse! No, it can't be alive. I'm stupid. I know snakes are pois-o-nous. Marlin Perkins said so on *Wild Kingdom*.

I hear Mommy calling. Hansel and I look at the house. Mommy's walking toward us and pulling Matty's arm. He's crying. Hansel's tail wags, but he's back to watching the snake. I tell Mommy to shush and point at the snake. She says, "Oh, shit," and grabs my arm too. She's pulling us toward the gate. She stops.

Mommy wants to know what I'm doing in the pasture. I say she told me to go here. She says she never said that. Mommy says she told me not to go in the pasture. She's asking why she'd tell me to go to the pasture. I say I don't know. Mommy says don't talk like that. Matty says he heard her tell me to go to the pasture. She says he's as bad as I am and yanks his arm. She gives us a shove and lets our arms go. I'm falling on the electric. My hands go out to grab the middle wire and stop my top half from following. *Owww!* My head's blowing up like a firecracker when Mommy pulls me off. She's yelling at us not to touch the electric. I barely hear her. I'm gagging from the pennies in my mouth.

We're in the kitchen. I don't remember walking here.

Matty's crying louder than me. Mommy's shouting at us. She says we both grabbed the electric. My insides are big rope knots.

I say softly, "Mommy, you made us grab the fence."

Mommy's pulling my arms to her. I know she's going to spank me. No! I don't want to be spanked. I don't deserve to be spanked. I pull back from her and she stops. Mommy says she'll just let Daddy do it.

I stop.

She tells me to sit on the brick bench and wait for him.

I say, "I'm really sorry, Mommy."

She says I'm too late.

I'm not crying. I'm too scared. I wish I could tell Daddy how Mommy told me to go to the pasture. How she lied and said she didn't say it. How she got mad when I said she did. How she pushed us and made us grab the electric fence!

She's a liar, she's a liar! She's Mommy moonshine.

I've been watching the front door forever. I hear Daddy's boots on the cement outside. He opens the front door, and Mommy runs to him before he takes off his coat. She's whispering in his ear. I hear hangers move in the hall closet. She walks back into the kitchen. She doesn't look at me. The closet doors bang together and Daddy walks in. He yanks me up by my arm. He drops me and says, "Strip and grab your ankles!"

I bend to pull my undies and pants down. I almost tip over when I grab my ankles. I hear Daddy's belt getting unbuckled. I see Mommy's feet and legs behind him. She tells Daddy something about how bad I need this.

"Go to your room," Mommy says when he's done.

I can't sit on my bottom; it hurts too much. I know it will take at least two days to go away. I remember from last time. I get on my tummy and slide my arms under my bed. I pull out the big sheet of paper I put there. I look at the picture I was drawing and coloring for Mommy's classroom. It's a picture of me. I wanted to be with her when she's teaching. I wanted her to not forget me. I tear it and tear it and tear it. I cry and yell in my head that I'm a stupid baby.

CHAPTER 43

Terry Tiger

Daddy says, "Arms up." He pulls the pink sweater over my head. I say this is my best pink. It's "more pink than pink."

He laughs and says, "That means it's ve-ry pink," tickling my tummy. Daddy grabs Matty's hand and says, "C'mon, Tiger, time to pile in the car."

I hear Mommy's hair spray spraying in the bathroom. Daddy says we'll see her outside. Mommy says she'll be right there. I skip to the car, and Daddy asks Matty, "How 'bout we go see my mom and dad?"

Matty says, "Yeah!"

Mommy's the last one in the car. She smells like the pretty bottle in her room. She puts her hand on Daddy's cheek and says, "No whiskers."

Matty says, "Hansel has whiskers."

Daddy says, "That's so he won't bump into things."

I think about the needles Hansel got from the porcupine. Matty says it out loud, and I squeeze his arm and say I was just thinking the same thing!

I know Grandpa has a train in the basement that whistles. Grandma has pickles down there. She says the pickles, beets, pears, and my favorite peaches are "canned" in big glass jars. I helped pick Grandma's peaches and pears from their trees in the backyard. I help Grandma when she tells me to go to the fruit room. We made strawberry jam one time with sugar and hot water.

Daddy has to stop the car because Matty's carsick. Mommy unbuckles him and climbs out with him. I can't see him, but I hear him throw up. They get back in the car, and Daddy tells Mommy to crack her window. Matty says he's okay and smiles after Daddy says we're almost there. I hold Matty's hand and he squeezes tight.

The golden wheat on the way to Grandma and Grandpa's house has all been cut. The combines have gone home to their barns.

Daddy's parking in front of the garage when Matty says, "Oh, wow!" He sees Grandpa sitting in a big car thing with no top. It's got lots of big wheels. We jump out of the car and race over to him. He tells us to jump in. Matty pushes me down and starts to climb in front with Grandpa. I get up off the grass and say, "No fair, meanie!" Mommy tells us to stop it. She makes Matty get in back because he pushed me. Matty says he's sorry, but I know he doesn't mean it. I get in the front. Grandpa says he calls this a "Terra Tiger," and he says it will go anywhere, even in water.

Grandpa turns the key to start the engine. We drive down the gravel road to the big barn, where I know owls live.

Grandpa speeds up when we get to the stubble field. We're going fast and it's bumpy. Dirt, dust, and wheat scraps fly out behind us. It's fun to drive in the dirt field. Grandpa's slowing down. He cuts the engine and tells us to be quiet. He points a good finger straight ahead.

Not far away is a big gray coyote standing on a rock. The coyote looks a lot like Hansel. It's looking right at us. Matty whispers, "Sure wish I had a gun right now." Grandpa laughs a little. I give Matty a bad look. Grandpa says to stay quiet. There's something moving behind the coyote's back legs.

Three, four, five coyote pups wobble under the big one. They're over half as tall as the big one's tummy. The puppy fur looks golden in the sun. The big coyote's head goes straight up and a long howl comes out. Five little heads copy the big one with little howls. Grandpa's turning back to the house. He says the coyote pups were born blind, but they start seeing after a couple weeks. That was a long time ago.

The bumps make my voice funny. I hear Matty holler, "I love Terry Tiger, Grandpa!" and I say, "I love Terry Tiger too," and we all laugh.

CHAPTER 44

Kindergarten

There are nineteen boys and only five girls, including me, in my kindergarten class. I don't know why there are so many boys, but I like the girls in my class. We say we need to stick together because there're too many boys. Five of the boys have crew cuts, but most of them have longer hair. Jose has shiny black hair; it's nice. He says he's Mexican. He's the smallest boy in the class, and he dresses the nicest. He's never mean to anyone. I like him and his hair.

Two of the boys are bullies. They're mean to the boy with the big face. He holds his fingers a lot. The girls tell on the bullies. Two girls in my class are taller than me. And I'm taller than the other two girls. The shortest girl's my friend Holly. The tallest girl, Shirley, is my friend too. Melissa's my friend and she has pretty hair, different from Jose's but pretty.

The name of my new school is Lake Hill. Mommy says Lake Hill is better than the school across the road from our house. I don't know why it's better, but she says so. My teacher's name is Mrs. Browne. She says she spells it with "an extra 'e' on the end." I like Mrs. Browne. She's the nicest teacher. I told her my mommy's a teacher. I told her Mommy's gone a lot because she teaches and goes to school. Mrs. Browne said that happens sometimes.

There's no upstairs or downstairs at my school. It's low and flat and there are big trees by the playground. I counted seven all in a row. I walk inside and outside to my classroom. The bricks on the walls are beige and brown. The sidewalk's covered so we don't get wet if it rains. There's a kitchen at my school and a gym with a panther on the wall. I see a lot of pictures of black panthers at school, like the kind in *The Jungle Book*.

Mrs. Browne has the alphabet on top of her chalkboard. Each letter is on a little light-green card. I stare at the letters all day. I draw them in my head over and over and over. I know most of them from the black-and-white paper at Beverly's. I have my own hook in the coat closet for my coat, and my own desk and chair too.

Dr. Pare said I needed new glasses for my eyes. Mommy says he picked out my frames. They're round circles and kind of a dark brownish color. I love my glasses. I can see a lot through them.

Mommy says I'm done with operations. She says my eyes should get better and better. Dr. Pare says my eye might wander when I'm real tired, and it won't be as strong as my other eye, but it shouldn't be too noticeable. Matty said he was glad to hear it because he didn't want a cross-eyed sister.

I like going to school. I go the same time every day. People are nice to me. I know that bad things with Mommy, Daddy, and Matty don't happen there. Mrs. Browne reads us stories, and we get to write the letters of the alphabet, and we get to draw and color things. Matty's in the first grade at the same school as me. We still get to go to Beverly's house after school, and some of my friends from kindergarten go there too.

My best friend in kindergarten is Melissa. She has the prettiest blond hair. It's almost white. We love each other. We're like sisters. She's real smart. We know lots of words. We read and play games. She wears jumpers to school with tights the same color. I told Mommy I want a jumper with the same tights.

Melissa says she'll play at my house and I'll play at her house. I said okay, except I don't have kids play at my house. Too many bad things can happen. The things would make them not like me. Maybe I can just go to her house instead. But what if her mommy and daddy know I'm icky? That would be bad because Melissa would find out, and we wouldn't be friends. I would be so sad if we weren't friends. Maybe it's better not to play at our houses at all.

But what if she wants a friend that'll play at houses? Then she won't want to be my friend because a better friend will make her more happy. This is making my head hurt. I thought friends help make each other happy. This isn't making me happy.

I'm happy to be with other kids at school. But I'm sad I don't really have friends. Mommy says, "You'll have lots of friends when you get older." I can't say things about me. I don't know what other kids will ask me. I wonder if other kids at school have secrets with their mommies and daddies? Melissa is real nice to me, and she doesn't ask about bad things, so maybe we can just be happy together.

CHAPTER 45

Suffocating

It's bedtime, but I'm not sleepy. I'm in my bed thinking about school. Melissa looked pretty at school today. She wore a red jumper with a white turtleneck, red tights, and white go-go boots. I've seen go-go dancers on TV in the same boots. Sometimes the dancers have Hula-Hoops like mine. I wonder what Melissa will wear to school tomorrow? I should wear my purple tights with my brown skirt. I'll ask Mommy if my turtleneck's clean when I wake up. I hope so, that'll look nice.

I hear somebody close the front door. It's probably Daddy. Mommy said he didn't eat dinner with us tonight because he's too busy.

I jump when the wall by my bed shakes. Daddy opens my door. "Hey, sweetheart, Daddy's home."

I sit up with Blankie and say, "Hi, Daddy, I missed you. Where've you been?"

He walks in and closes the door behind him. He's having a hard time taking his jacket off and says there's important work to do. I don't know what that means. Daddy leans over to kiss my head with both arms behind his back. He's wobbly and almost falls on me.

I say, "Daddy, are you okay?"

He says he hasn't felt good. He pulls me out of my covers and says he needs a hug. I don't want to be out of my covers. I hug him and try to sit back, but he's squeezing me. His shirt button's poking my cheek. I'm not listening to Daddy now. I have a little part of me listen to say okay and uh-huh so he won't get mad. The rest of me thinks about my cheek and what it would look like in a mirror. There would be a circle inside another circle with two dots inside.

Daddy almost tips over when he stands up. He's pulling off my nightie and my undies. My tummy's squeezing the macaroni Mommy made for dinner. I try to get back under my covers. Daddy's voice is saying, "Stop it, Deidi. I said turn over."

He sounds mean. I turn over and his big hand covers my face. I can't breathe! I twist, but he yanks my neck back. My mouth and nose and eyes feel like the roof fell on them. I'm falling into a dark hole in the floor. It's time to go.

Maybe I won't wear my purple tights tomorrow. I wonder if my blue sweater's in my closet. Mommy said I left it in her car. I might have to look for it in the morning. That's okay, I'll find it. I should wear long sleeves in case I have any bruises. Last time Daddy said sorry after being too rough, and I got my Liddle Kiddles doll. She's smaller than my hand and she has a tiny red dress. She has big red hair with a white flower in it. She lives in a bottle with a red cap and smells like perfume. Maybe I'll get a surprise tomorrow if I have owies after Daddy goes night-night. Time to go far away.

Fairies with sparkly dresses are carrying me. We're flying into the night sky where their sparkly dresses match the sparkly stars.

Mommy lets me wear a long-sleeve dress to school today. I ask her to put my hair in pigtails, but she didn't have time.

I'm in my class and everyone's standing up. The boy behind me keeps tapping me. I turn around and he's pointing at the back of my dress. He says, "There's something on your dress." I pull the back of my dress around as much as I can. Something feels wet on my hand. There's a little red spot in the middle of my dress. I say, "I must've sat in something." I look at the boy behind me, and he shrugs.

I think he's a nice boy. He doesn't talk a lot. Some boys in my class talk too much. I like his big brown eyes. They remind me of chocolate Tootsie Pops. When I suck on Tootsie Pops they make me feel sleepy. I don't know why. Chocolate and grape Tootsie Pops are my favorite. I save the wrappers that have a shooting star because I can get a free Tootsie Pop at the store. I squeeze the spot in my hand and run up to Mrs. Browne. She bends over me and touches my shoulder. She asks the lady helping her to watch the class. She opens a big drawer and takes out a small paper bag.

She puts her hand on my back and we walk out the door and into the hallway. The big classroom door closes. She kneels down in front of me, her nice dress on the floor. Mrs. Browne doesn't seem to mind. I like that. It makes me feel like I'm important. She says we're going to see the school nurse. I'm glad she tells me that I don't have to get a shot.

The nurse looks at my bottom. I say I have a hard time pooping sometimes. The nurse says that's all it is. My dress and bottom are cleaned up. The nurse gives me clean undies to wear. I'm supposed to give my dirty undies the nurse put in a paper bag to Mommy when I'm home.

Mommy isn't taking us to Beverly's today. Mommy's not talking to me. She takes us straight home and tells me to go in the bathroom. She's following me. She says to take my undies off and lie on the rug. I'm thinking, *I don't want owies on my pee place today.* I almost start crying. Mommy says she has to put medicine where I poop.

I ask if that's because of the blood and she nods as she opens the medicine box.

She takes out a spoon thingy and squeezes white stuff on it. Mommy bends down to look closer at my bottom. She pushes my legs apart. Mommy says to relax and this might be cold.

I pinch the soft part inside each arm on my chest. She pushes something in my bottom. It hurts, but my pinches hurt more. I'm happy about that. It feels like I'm pooping wet Play-Doh out of my bottom.

Mommy tells me to stay still for a few minutes. She says she'll be back. She doesn't close the door. I'm staying still like she said. Matty's voice says, "Are you okay, Deidi?" I tell him I'm okay. I tell him what happened at school. I say I'm lying here because Mommy had to put medicine in my bottom. Matty wants to see what it looks like and I say, "Yeah, I guess." I see his sneakers walk around me. He sits in front of my knees.

I tell him not to touch it. He pulls his hand back fast. I want to know what it looks like. Matty says it's all slimy and white. He says I smell a little weird. He stands back up and says that he'll beat up any kid that's mean to me. I say, "Thanks." He tells me to meet him in the backyard when I'm done.

Mommy comes back in and wipes my bottom with a cold washcloth. She tells me to get up. She says I might need to change my undies a few times from the medicine. She says if anybody asks me what happened at school tomorrow, I need to tell them I got an owie when I fell on my bottom. I don't remember when that happened.

CHAPTER 46

Smell

I like sitting at the desk in the kitchen. I'm playing office by myself. Mommy hollers from the living room, "Deidi, you got a card in the mail." I did?

I run into the living room and pick up the stack of mail. There's a nice white envelope with my name on it. I push my finger under the flap in back. I've seen Mommy and Daddy do this. Inside is a pretty blue card. It has a big yellow happy face and the word "Party!" on the front. "Mommy, please read this to me."

I can read some of the black letters. But some of them are in cursive. I'm not a good cursive reader. Mommy says, "You're invited to Shirley's house for her sixth birthday party." She's reading, but I don't hear. I get to go to Shirley's birthday party!

I'm hopping up and down. Mommy says, "Deidi, let's go shopping. You'll need a new dress for your first party." She says I can pick out a present for Shirley too.

We're driving downtown and Mommy says I need new dress shoes! This is the best day. Mommy's making me laugh. I tell her a knock-knock joke I heard. Now she's laughing too.

We're having fun! Mommy helps me pick out a light-blue dress. It has tiny white flowers all over. She's paying at the counter for white Mary Janes and socks. I picked out anklets with a pink flower on one side.

Now we're looking for the birthday present. I find a Barbie outfit Shirley will love. It has a long blue coat with a fuzzy neck. Mommy says it's a "maxicoat." There're tall blue boots and a striped minidress. We're leaving the store and Mommy says, "Let's swing by Arctic Circle, okay?" I say, "Yeah!" She buys a vanilla ice-cream cone for me and a Pepsi with extra ice for her. We talk about the party all the way home.

The toilet flushes and brings me back.

I see my white undies by my pillow. Daddy must've just left. I pull my undies back on under my covers. I better go to sleep now.

I hear Mommy saying, "Wake up, Deidi. Let's go." She says to hurry because it's late. I push my covers off. I can taste the bad smell. I think my throat has a cramp.

I got in trouble last night because I asked for a bath. Mommy and Daddy were fighting again. Matty said I stink. I need a bath. Kids will be mean to me.

"Mommy, please can I take a bath? I'll be fast, I promise."

She's stuffing peanut-butter sandwiches in paper bags. She says, "You have two minutes to get dressed."

I run in the bathroom, get a wet rag, and squeeze Phisoderm on top. I rub the rag between my legs. I put it in the hamper and pull my pink-and-brown pants on. Where's my pink sweater? Mommy's yelling that she's leaving. Here it is. I grab socks and run out.

CHAPTER 47

Grandpa and Hirsch

I love all the yellow, red, and orange leaves. They're starting to fall. I love jumping in piles of colors and making paintings with my feet. My nose is runny, and Mommy says I have a cold. Grandma's looking for a pack of Kleenex to give me. She says she doesn't like germs. Matty and I are staying at the farm with Grandma and Grandpa until Mommy and Daddy can pick us up. "Achoo!" Grandma says, "Gazoontight." She says that's German for "God bless you." People say that because our hearts stop when we sneeze, that's what Grandma says.

She hollers at me, "Don't slam the screen door," when I run outside to find Matty.

"Sorry, Grandma," I holler back over my shoulder as I jump down the steps. I'm thinking he might be at Hirsch's house. He's Grandpa's hired man, and they're cousins. He came here from Virginia and doesn't talk much. He spits a lot because he always has Beech-Nut in his lower lip. He calls it "snus." I saw Hirsch drive the combine one time, and he looked like he had a tennis ball in his lower lip.

I hear Matty yelling somewhere. It sounds like he's in Hirsch's trailer house. He lives in a long red-and-white house behind Grandma and Grandpa's. I start to run when I hear Matty yell again. I can't tell if he's mad or scared or playing. I run up the stairs to Hirsch's white door and knock. I don't hear anything, so I call Matty's name. Nothing.

I leave the porch and check both little barns, but no Matty. I'm turning to go back to the main house. Hirsch's door flies open. I walk back and nobody's there. I walk closer to his steps. I can see a case of big guns on the wall across from the door. Antlers are hanging above the guns. Matty says Hirsch has the biggest gun collection. I hear somebody moving around inside. I call Matty's name again.

Matty slides in front of the door like someone pushed him. His hair's all messed up and his cheeks are red. I ask what he's doing, and he plops down in the doorway holding his socks and tennis shoes. He pushes his pant legs up and pulls on white socks with two blue stripes on top. He says, "We're just playing a game. I won." He ties the strings on his tennis shoes. I ask where's Hirsch, and a deep voice answers real slow from inside, "Just sittin' here havin' a smoke, Deidi."

"Matty, why didn't you answer the door when I knocked?" He says because he was in a headlock and couldn't talk. I ask why Hirsch didn't answer, and he shrugs his shoulder.

I tell him that's weird. Matty sounds sad when he says, "It's not as weird as other stuff Hirsch does."

I say, "Like what?" He's walking fast past the fruit trees and I have to run a little to keep up.

Matty tells me he doesn't want to talk about it.

I say, "C'mon, just tell me."

Matty turns around and shoves me up against the side of the barn by my neck. He squeezes hard and says, "Don't ask me again!" He pushes his knee hard between my legs.

I push his shoulders and he lets go. I rub my snotty nose on my sleeve.

After supper, Grandpa tells Matty to follow him to the basement so they can work on the electric train.

I ask, "Can I help too?"

Grandpa says, "Nope, tonight's just us boys."

Matty says, "Maybe next time, Deidi." He looks sad.

Why isn't he happy to go downstairs? Maybe because he knows I wanted to go. Now I feel better after he was mean in the yard today.

Grandma asks me to help clean up, and I forget about the electric train.

Grandma and I take her sewing basket to the dining room. She shows me the towel she's embroidering. It's blue with a tiny frog at the bottom. She says she needs to add a lily pad under the frog and it will be done. I ask if she just heard a yell from downstairs. Grandma says she didn't. I get out of my chair and walk through the hall to the basement door. Grandma says I need to come back to the dining room. I say I'll be right there. I open the basement door. The stairs are dark until the light above my head shines down from the wide-open door.

Matty flies out of nowhere, grabs the stair rail, and jumps three steps at a time.

I hear Grandpa's boots on the hard floor in the basement. I see him through the railing when he stops. His overalls are down below his bottom. He's holding them with one hand. He's reaching over his shoulder with the other hand to grab the strap hanging in back.

I step away from the door and listen to his boots on the stairs. He doesn't close the door to the basement when he gets to the top. I'm hiding behind it.

I come out when Matty opens the bathroom door.

"Are you okay?"

No answer.

Matty says, "I get to drive the lawn mower."

"Really? In the dark?"

"Yep."

I watch him run through the kitchen and outside with Grandpa. I can barely see him driving up the main road as Grandma and I put her sewing kit away.

CHAPTER 48

Matty at Night

Mommy says, "Stop eating so fast or you'll choke."

I say, "Okay, Mommy," with my mouth full of tuna casserole.

She gives me a look and says, "One more of those and you won't be playing with any Legos for a long time."

I swallow and say I'm sorry. I want to get back to playing Legos with Matty. I'm thinking about putting more beds in my house.

Dinner's done and we're racing down the hall.

Matty's built his spaceship. He tells me to hurry up because he's bored. He says that a lot now. I know it means he can't think of what to do.

"Two more pieces and I'm done, Matty."

He's standing at his desk. I hear a *swoosh* sound.

"Matty, I smell a match." I hear *swoosh* again.

He says, "Yeah, I smell it too."

I see him throw something, and then I turn and see Mommy coming down the hall. She's in the doorway before I can say a word.

"What's going on in here?"

Matty jumps and turns around. He's got the matches behind his back.

"You're lighting matches again!" Mommy says in a mean voice.

Matty says, "No, I'm not."

She grabs his arm and pulls him out of the room. Matty drops the matches on the floor. I kick them under the bed. Mommy's yelling for Daddy. Matty's dragging behind her yelling. He keeps saying he didn't do anything. They turn into the kitchen.

I see Mommy shove Matty at Daddy. She's yelling about Matty lighting matches. She says something about burning the house down. Daddy's face is red when he crushes his cigarette in the tin ashtray. I jump when he slams the newspaper on the table. Daddy tells Matty to shut up. He starts to undo his belt. He yells at Matty to strip and grab his ankles. Daddy's belt's in his hand when he walks behind Matty's bare bottom. Matty's shaking a little. I plug my ears and close my eyes. If I push my ears in and out and in and out, I can't hear. I wait and open my eyes a little. Daddy's still whipping Matty's bottom with the belt. I squeeze my eyes shut.

I'm scared about Matty's lighting matches. He's been lighting fires outside at the farm too.

I look again and it's over. Daddy's shoving Matty back to his room. He tells Matty to stay there the rest of the night.

"Deidi, Deidi, wake up." Somebody's pushing me. I open my eyes and see airplanes and helicopters flying on two knees. It's Matty in his PJs sitting on my bed. His legs are under his bottom. "What?" I ask, rubbing my eyes soft. I can't see good right now.

Matty says he wanted to wake me up.

"Why?" I ask him.

He says he wants to see my pee place and touch it. He pulls my covers down. I want to go back to sleep. I think to myself, *He'll be mean if I don't pull my bottoms down.* He touches my pee place with his pointer finger. He says I should touch his pee-pee too. I say his pee-pee's icky. Matty's shoulders go up and down. He pushes my hand with one of his on his pee-pee. His other hand touches my pee place. He says, "I want to look in between this." He pulls my pee place with both hands and puts his head down real close to it. It kind of tickles. It feels like I have to pee, but I don't. He touches the more inside place.

The floor creaks in the hallway. I grab the covers and he pulls his pants up. Matty rolls into a ball on his side next to me. His breath smells like Red Hots. I know he hides candy in his room. I found jawbreakers under his bed one time. Jawbreakers change color when you suck them. Matty likes to crack them with his teeth, and Mommy gets sooooo mad.

We hear the toilet flush, water's on then off. More creaks, then quiet. We wait, just to be sure. Matty gets up slowly and gives me a little wave. He's off the bed and I can tell he's on tippy-toes because his arms stick out. He's walking slow. He looks like circus people. They wear tight clothes that sparkle. Way far up in the sky, they walk on strings. He looks back when he gets to my door. I wave and he nods. I'm happy I can't hear any sound when he goes to his room.

CHAPTER 49

Never Tell

The leaves are crunching under my shoes. It sounds like fresh apple bites or if I accidentally step on a stinkbug. The air feels cool on my face walking to Beverly's after school.

I'm in Beverly's family room drawing a leaf with a stem, five points, and lines in the middle when I hear Mommy's voice.

She's mad. I see her talking to Beverly. They're talking for a long time. Matty walks up to me. I ask what happened, he shakes his head. His face looks like he knows. I turn my head sideways and look at him. Matty says he did something dumb. I ask what. Nothing. I say he knows I'll find out. Matty says he beat up the boy with the weird hair. He says the boy called him bad names, like "stupid." Matty says he didn't want to hit him. He says he couldn't help it.

Matty says he won marbles fair and square. He says the boy's a bad loser. He kicked Matty's wiener. Daddy calls his pee thingy his wiener sometimes. Throw-up stuff comes up my throat. I point to Matty's zipper and say, "That's your wiener?" He says, "Yeah, Deidi. It's a wiener." He says that kick hurt so bad, he went crazy. He says he got the kid down and punched his face a lot. Matty says there was some blood. He heard Beverly say stop, stop. She said to get off him. He says Beverly's husband pulled him up. I ask if the boy died, and he says no, he doesn't think so.

Matty sits down and starts crying. He looks so sad. He wants to know why everybody but me is so mean. I shake my head. Matty says he wants to know why he has to be stupid. I squat down next to him and tell him it's that boy who's stupid, not Matty. I tell him that boy can't even play my Old Maid cards. Matty laughs. He wipes his face with the back of his hand. Snot stretches from his nose to his hand.

"Eeww!" I say as he tries to wipe it on me. I tell him I'm too fast. He falls over and reaches my pant leg. Yuck!

I start thinking how mad Matty gets. I never start fights with him. He just goes crazy sometimes. He's hurt kids at Beverly's before. I think of a lot of things he's done to kids, animals, and me. Mommy's been on the phone at home and I've heard her get mad at his teachers. I know he's had a lot of fights on the playground. Mommy always says it's not Matty's fault. She says there are mean kids at the school that start fights with him. I don't think she's right. I've seen Matty start fights. Boys' sisters I know tell me that Matty starts fights. One boy wanted to be Matty's friend, but he punched the boy in the face for no reason. Mommy said the boy was mean to Matty, but that's not true. I know he really liked Matty.

Matty fights Daddy to help Mommy and me. He fights Mommy to help Daddy and me. He's helped me when I've made a boo-boo. One time I squeezed Phisoderm lotion all over the toilet in our bathroom. I don't know why, I thought it needed to be painted white. Mommy was screaming at me when Matty came in the bathroom and said he did it. He said he squeezed the Phisoderm. She grabbed him so hard he had five purple bruises on his arm the next day.

I hear Matty saying, "Deidi, Deidi, take it." He's handing me a Kleenex for my pant leg. I say, "Thanks."

Mommy walks in and tells us to get our things. We get in the car without saying goodbye. I watch the house, and Beverly pulls the curtain back. She waves from her window. Matty and I wave back.

Mommy says she's taking us to her friend Sherry's house. Sherry has blond hair like mine, but it is more yellow and real poufy. Sherry smokes like Mommy does. They talk and talk and talk. Sherry wears a lot of rings. Her drinks have lots of ice cubes. They're noisy.

Sherry can drink with the same hand she holds her cigarette in. The lip marks on the ends of her cigarettes match the lip colors on her drink glasses. She must put a lot of lipstick on.

Daddy says he hates Sherry. He told Matty and me, never go to Sherry's house. I heard Mommy promise she'll never take us to Sherry's. Mommy was fighting with Daddy when he made her promise. I saw him sitting on top of her in the living room. He had the bottom of his arm squished into Mommy's neck. He kept saying bad words. He said, "Promise me, promise me." Mommy sounded like a frog and said she promised. When Daddy got off, she coughed. She breathed real loud. Her voice was gone, but it came back.

Daddy gave Matty a black eye before he hurt Mommy's voice. Matty had talked back to Mommy, so Daddy punched Matty's face. Mommy tried to help Matty, and Daddy jumped on her. Matty told day-care kids a bigger boy gave him the black eye just to be mean. Then he said he beat up the bigger mean boy by our house. That was a lie, but I didn't tell. They think he's cool now.

Beverly asked me about the black eye, and I shrugged my shoulders. She asked me again and I shrugged again. I know it's a secret. Those are secrets you never tell.

Mommy says baddest things will happen if I tell. Daddy says those are special just for us. Nobody else can know our business. He says families have special secrets. He says the best families stick together and never tell their secrets. He says bad things always get better when you never tell.

I think, *Daddy doesn't like Sherry because she's a women's libber.* The TV says they want jobs like men jobs. Mommy says women can only be nurses or teachers. I want to be a teacher. Or maybe an astronaut. Why can't I be an astronaut? I've seen women's libbers on TV and they burned bras in a burn barrel. I don't know why. Both my grandmas and grandpas have burn barrels. Mommy's mommy tells Grandpa when to burn the barrel. That's when it's full of trash. I like to watch the fire in the barrel. If you stand in a bad spot, the wind blows smoke and it's stinky.

I don't know why you would want to burn a bra. Mommy has pretty bras in her dresser. Her bras have stuff like Grandma's table-cloths. They smell like Mommy. I hold Mommy's bras up to me and look in the mirror. I look like I have boobies like Mommy. Matty told me that word.

Boys like boobies. I wish I had some. Mommy says I will some-day. I don't know when "someday" is. Daddy looks at lots of boobies in magazines. Mommy made Daddy take his booby magazines out of the living room after Matty kept looking at the naked ladies. She makes him keep them in their bedroom. But Daddy leaves them in the bathroom and the living room sometimes. I look at the pic-tures. I can read the *Little Annie Fanny* cartoons. She always loses her clothes. Men chase her. They're sort of like Daddy. I feel sorry for Annie Fanny.

The TV says women's libbers don't like Miss America. Mommy has a friend Daddy likes. She helps girls be in Miss America. She helped a girl in Moses Lake be Miss Washington. She was in the newspaper. She got a crown, a car, and a charm class. I asked Mommy why she got a candy class. I like Charms hard candies, but sometimes I choke on them. Mommy said it's not candy. She said it's to teach her manners. That's how to be nice, I think. She learns how to be charming, Mommy said. She told me that's how to be nice too, but different than manners. It's smiling and acting like you like people so they'll like you.

I don't care what Daddy thinks, I like Sherry. She gives us Oreo cookies and milk. She gives me coloring books and crayons. Matty gets to play with a box of Legos. I can sort of hear Mommy and Sherry talking in the other room, but just parts of what they are saying. Like when you turn the radio down. Mommy says, "He's out of control and mean, and he's going to kill someone." I'm not sure if Mommy's talking about Daddy or Matty. I twist the sides of my cookie and pull it apart.

Sherry says, "Leave." Mommy says she knows. They sound like they're mad. Then they don't. I'm scraping the white icing off my cookie. I hear Mommy crying. I go in the room to say I have to pee. I lie because I want to know if Mommy's okay.

They both look sad. Mommy tells me to go to the bathroom if I have to pee. But I don't move. I just look at her for a long time, until she says she's okay. She says it's a hard time and blows me a kiss. She hasn't done that for a long time. It makes me cry when I'm in the bathroom. I look in the mirror and my front teeth are black,

When I come out, Matty's waiting in the hallway. He says, "C'mon, Deidi" and pulls me into a bedroom. There're two beds in here. One against each wall. They have nice blue bedspreads folded over the pillows. There's a brown desk on one wall. Matty tells me to take off my shoes, and we each climb on a bed.

Matty starts jumping up and down and up and down. He tells me to jump on my bed too. I start going up and down like Matty. He's going high. I can see his bed moving against the wall. *Jump, thump, jump, thump.* I like the sound. My tummy feels funny when I'm in the air. It makes me laugh a lot.

"Stop it right now!" Mommy yells from the open door. Sherry's looking over her shoulder. Mommy wants to know what we're thinking. I don't think I should say what I'm thinking. She asks if we forgot we are at somebody else's house. No, I didn't forget. I don't think Matty forgot. We don't talk.

Matty sits across from me, and we're each on the edge of a bed. I think I'm sweating a little. Matty is, and his face is all shiny with red cheeks. I touch my cheek and it's a little wet.

Mommy says, "Deidi, I'm talking to you too. Look at me when I'm talking."

I turn my head to see her. But I want to look at my feet. I kick one foot forward and one foot backward, back and forth against the side of the bed and in the air. One foot goes higher each time. Mommy tells me to stop it.

I think, *Mommy's ugly when she's mad.* She reminds me of the green witch in *The Wizard of Oz.* I still have scary dreams about the bad witch. I love Glinda, she's the good witch. The bad witch likes being mean. The bad witch wants Dorothy's sparkly red shoes.

Mommy pulls Matty out of the room, points at me and says, "You stay put." When Mommy closes the door, I really want to start jumping on the bed again. But Mommy would get madder, so I take a nap instead.

Somebody's squeezing my shoulder and I wake up. Mommy says, "Deidi, time to go."

Mommy tells Matty and me we can't tell Daddy where we've been tonight. She says he'll get mad and they'll have a big fight if we tell. Mommy says to say we went to Tastee-Freez and the library. We both say okay, but my head's thumping like my feet jumping on the bed.

Mommy and Daddy say never tell about our secrets or bad things will happen to us. Daddy sometimes says never tell Mommy because she'll get mad. Mommy says never tell Daddy because he'll get mad. Never tell. Never tell. Never tell. I say it over and over to myself and think of the rhyme sound "ell" until I don't think about anything else.

Daddy's smoking at the kitchen table when we get home. Mommy sends us to our rooms. Daddy doesn't say anything to any of us. I close my bedroom door and wait a little. I think I hear Mommy and Daddy's voices in the other room. I open my door a tiny bit and stick my ear in the crack.

Mommy's telling Daddy about Matty's fight at Beverly's. She keeps saying how scared she is by what Matty's doing. I don't know why she keeps saying he's "violet." I love that color, and Matty's not that color! Mommy says if Matty keeps fighting, Beverly won't take him anymore. She says if she has to stay home with him we won't have any money. Daddy says that's not true. Mommy says they don't have Daddy's money. Mommy says that Daddy's mom and dad never keep their promises. He says he knows. She says we've been hurt by them, over and over. Mommy says no one else can "bail him" this time. She says the drunk friends at the Elks Club aren't helping. She says Daddy gets drunk too much. I know this means too much alcohol. I think about how much I've seen Daddy drink it from brown bottles and from bigger bottles poured in a glass. Daddy doesn't talk. Nobody's talking.

Daddy says he needs to have time with Matty. He says he'll take him hunting. Mommy says that's good. Daddy says if they shot a buck in Harrington, it would feed the family this winter. Mommy doesn't say anything.

I crawl away from my door when I hear Mommy and Daddy start walking down the hallway. I can tell by the floor noise they're going into Matty's room. They close his door. I try to listen but can't hear anything.

I stay in my room and wait to hear them leave his room. I wait a minute after they pass my door and then run to Matty's room.

I push his door open with my pointer finger. He's sitting on his bed flipping his Slinky in his hands. I sit next to him with my shoulders and palms up. Matty says he can't get the rocket he was going to build with Daddy because of the fights. He smiles and says the good thing is Daddy's taking him hunting. He says they're going to get a rifle from Grandpa so he can shoot deer when they hunt. Matty's happy. He says he can't wait to shoot a deer. I squish my nose up like something stinks. I hate it when he talks like that. He gives me a big smile and shrugs.

I skip down the hall to help Mommy get dinner ready. She's making lasagna and a salad. We all eat dinner together at the table in the kitchen. Everyone's happy tonight.

CHAPTER 50

Hallway Mommy

My head is on my pillow and I'm tucked under my blankets in bed.

I'm thinking about how Daddy comes and goes from home a lot. He talks on the phone and writes numbers on yellow paper. Sometimes he comes home dirty and says he was working on a combine all day. He's mostly mad at the people he works with. I don't know who they are. I don't know what he does. Most of the time he doesn't talk about it, and Mommy doesn't either. Whatever Daddy does, Mommy calls it "not enough." She goes to work every day that we go to school. She loves going to work and says it makes her happy. Daddy's work things make them both mad.

I'm falling asleep.

I wake up in my bed to hear Daddy whisper, "Shhh, princess, I just want to tell you how much I've been missing you. I'm sorry I've had to work so much." I tell him it's okay. His words seem like they're touching each other when he talks.

Daddy tells me to keep sleeping and he's going to scoot me over a little. He's being nice. My legs are hanging off the side of my bed. My bottom's cold until Daddy gets behind me. I squish Blankie under my head. I feel cozy. Daddy's rubbing his pee thingy in my bottom cheeks and pushes on me kind of hard. But he's nice to me. He's calling me sweetheart.

I go see the birds and kittens in my head, and we talk about happy things.

I'm back in my bedroom. How did I go away? How did I get back?

I hear the sound of the floor creaking in the hallway. Daddy's dog sounds are getting quieter. I lift my head and see Mommy's head in the dark by my door.

Daddy's done. I'm so sleepy. I can't keep my eyes open.

Mommy's waking me up. It's too early. I don't want to get up. It's not time to get up. It's still night. She pulls me out of bed and takes me in the bathroom. Mommy tells me to lie on the fuzzy bathroom rug. I don't want to, but her voice is mean. I lie down and cover my eyes. The light's too bright. She pulls off my PJ pants and undies. She says she needs to check me. She gets a bottle of something and some fluffy cotton balls from the cupboard. They're baby clouds. I remember the cold cotton balls on my bottom before the shots for my operations.

Mommy's twisting the top off a bottle. The smell makes me feel sick. It's the icky stuff the nurse rubbed on my bottom before shots poked me. I start to sit up. I need to get away from her. "Stop it, Deidi, what are you doing?" Mommy says.

"Are you giving me a shot?"

Mommy says no, she just needs to fix where I pee.

I ask if it's broken.

She says kind of and it's unhappy. She doesn't want to see me itching anymore. It embarrasses her when we're in public. She says if she doesn't fix it, I will start to stink. She says I don't want to stink, right?

I nod my head.

Mommy says to lie back down, and she tips the smelly bottle on the cotton ball.

I hate the smell.

Mommy says, "Open your legs, Deidi."

I open my legs and she starts to rub the cold, smelly stuff on my pee place. It starts burning.

"Owww! That hurts, Mommy!"

She says to stop squirming and it won't hurt.

I don't move. It still feels like my pee place is burning. I keep my eyes squeezed shut. She rubs more coldness on me. More burns hurt me. I hear the lid turn on the smelly stuff. The cupboard clicks closed. I smell the soap she washes her hands with. I peek, but she's not looking at me. Water sprinkles my bare skin when she tells me to pull my bottoms up. She wipes one side of her hands then the other on a green towel. I feel a soft *whoosh* on my cheek when she walks out.

I pull my bottoms up and stretch my body. I'm almost as tall as the fuzzy rug. My feet almost touch the cold floor under it. I cross my ankles and hold my pee place with both hands. The fuzzy rug's itching the back of my neck.

Tears I don't want roll into my hair. Another tear rolls right in my ear. Is Mommy coming back? She didn't say. She didn't tell me what to do next. She didn't say good night. I'm cold.

I get up and walk back to my bedroom, climb in bed, and pull the sheet and blanket tight next to my sides until the shivering stops.

CHAPTER 51

Christmas Eve 1970

I'm lying under the Christmas tree watching the blinking lights and singing along with records on the stereo. I love this song. *Fall on your knees, oh hear the angel voices . . .* I don't know some of the words. I love all Christmas songs. I can't think of any I don't love. I love the Christmas tree too. It makes the house smell good. Daddy says it's like bringing the forest inside. I scoop up a handful of tinsel that fell. I put it back on the tree carefully, like Mommy said.

Tinsel on the inside branches makes the tree sparkle more on the outside. We have a lot of orange balls and candy canes hanging on the tree this year. Matty's putting big piles of tinsel everywhere. I don't think he could have too much tinsel. He's stepping over me. I watch his hands picking up the tinsel I missed. His shoes stop next to me, and he throws a wad of silvery strings at the tree. I can see the pile from inside.

Matty's grabbing my ankles and saying, "Time to come out now." I laugh as he slides me out from under the tree. Matty says he'll help me put the packages back. I push a big box with purple-patterned paper and two bows on top to Matty. He says this is a big present and moves it against the wall. He says I need to give him smaller packages next. I slide a shiny green box with a gold bow and then a white, green, and red box with no bow. I slide three more packages back to Matty, and we're done.

Mommy and Daddy say it's time to go to bed. Matty says no way, and I say nope! Everybody laughs and we sit around the tree. Mommy told me that some families open their presents on Christmas morning. I'm glad we open all our presents on Christmas Eve so Santa can come in the morning. I think if he knows we won't have presents in the morning without him, he won't forget us. I think what that would be like and stare at the brick fireplace. I don't want to think about it.

I like the wood mantel on the fireplace. It's the same as the wood shelves next to it. Mommy has two people on the shelf. She said they're called Hummels. She said it means "figurines." One's a little boy for Matty, and one's a little girl for me. Mommy says a nun in Germany made them. They're like hard dolls. I can't touch them because they'd break.

I wonder if the nun looks like the nun on TV. Her big hat helps her fly. Sometimes men nuns visit her convent on TV. When I was little I didn't know they were priests. The priests always want to tell on the TV nuns. The priest men are bossy. I've heard old people say nuns and priests are Catholic. I was born in a Catholic hospital. The nuns were the bosses there. Mommy said they have statues of Mary, the mommy of Jesus, and not just at Christmastime in the manger.

My grandma in Davenport keeps a figurine of Jesus's mommy on a shelf. She wears a white dress and light-blue cape that almost touches the ground. I remember when I asked who she was, Grandma whispered, "Her name's Mary, and she's the mother of God."

I whispered back, "Why're you whispering?"

Grandma laughed and said she didn't know.

Grandma goes to the Lutheran church. I've been there with her, it was boring. She told me, "The Lutherans like Mary, but the Catholics love her."

Sometimes I stare at Mary. She doesn't look happy or sad. I don't know why, but I bet she's strong. I wish Mommy looked the way Mary does. I wish I had a light-blue cape and big Flying Nun hat. I wonder if Mary's a nun?

I like the Jesus in a manger we have in the living room at Christmastime.

Grandma sells mangers at Davenport Flowers. We have a little barn with baby Jesus on hay with cows and sheep. All the barns I've been in smell sort of bad. I bet Jesus's mommy and daddy were happy he got presents that smelled good from the three men following the star over his barn.

We wear nice clothes for Christmas. Mommy has a pretty red, purple, and more colors dress on. It has a lot of white dots on red. It has some string on the front. Her shoes are pink. Daddy has a beige shirt on. He says it's warm. It feels soft. He has light-blue slacks on. He's handsome, and Mommy's beautiful. I like Matty's bright-blue shirt. It has long sleeves and white buttons on the front. He's wearing his brown shoes and pants. Everybody always says Matty's the cutest kid. He couldn't care less, that's what Mommy says. I guess he's cute, sometimes. I'm wearing my blue sweater with the red-and-white pattern. I love this sweater. Mommy bought it from Sears. Daddy asks if anybody wants to open presents. We all say we do!

Daddy's in charge of passing presents out this year. He looks funny crawling around the floor on his long legs. Matty's opening a big box. He tears paper up like a wild man when it's his turn.

Wow! He got a race-car game. It has a big steering wheel on one end and a little red car that you drive down the road. I'm not sure how it works, but it looks like fun.

Daddy hands me a purple package with a gold bow on top. I peel the paper back where the tape is and try not to rip the wrapping. I pull the paper off, and the box tells me what's inside. I've wanted one of these for so long. It's a beautiful Small World doll from the Avon lady. She has yellow hair on a head that pops off, and there's perfume inside. Mommy shows me how to spray my wrists and behind my ears. She says I smell good. I give Mommy a hug and then Daddy. I say thank you and I love this so much.

Matty and Daddy go in the kitchen while Mommy and I stuff wrapping paper into the garbage can. We save some of the good bows in a brown bag. Matty and Daddy walk back with the tray of Grandma's Christmas treats. Mommy says her mommy has made them since she can remember. She says we can each have one.

"Matty's already had three chocolate-covered caramels," Daddy says.

Everybody, except Matty, laughs. I push the bump on the side of Matty's cheek, and he opens his mouth to show the caramel and chocolate stuck to his teeth.

Daddy hands me a flat box with shiny red ribbons on top. I pull the wrapping off, and inside is the prettiest red-and-white dress I've ever seen. I lift the top and it keeps going. It's a maxi dress! It's real long with puffy sleeves at the shoulders. The top part is mostly white with a red pattern, and the bottom part is mostly red with a white pattern. It has a blue belt at the waist. I'm so excited I pull my sweater off to my tank top and put the dress on over my head. It's too long, but Mommy says I'm growing so fast it will fit before I know it.

I love smelling the tree when I go to bed. And I can still hear Christmas music playing. Some Christmas songs make me feel sad. I don't know why. The song at the end of *How the Grinch Stole Christmas* always makes me sad.

I wonder what'd happen if the Grinch stole our Christmas? What if he took our presents, candies, records, tree, tinsel, lights, and candy canes? I think Mommy and Daddy would be mad if he stole our Christmas. I don't think they'd be happy like the Whos in Whoville. I don't think we'd sing any songs. The Grinch's heart wouldn't grow back. He wouldn't return our stuff, and he couldn't cut the roast.

The Grinch cut the roast beast because the Whos didn't punish him for stealing. Grandma on the farm said they forgave him. She says stealing's a sin. And sin means doing something bad. She says Jesus forgives our sins. I don't know how he does it. Sometimes Matty steals. It's good Jesus forgives him. I want to steal sometimes, but I'm too scared of getting caught.

If Jesus forgives Mommy and Daddy for their sins, I don't think that's fair. The Grinch took everything back to the Whos. He did it because his heart grew after he stole everything and heard the Whos singing instead of crying. He couldn't wait to give everything back. The Whos showed him Christmas doesn't come from a store. I think he loved the Whos and couldn't wait to show them his new heart. I'd forgive the Grinch too. If Mommy and Daddy's hearts grew and they flew down from a mountain with a sleigh full of things they'd stolen, I'd forgive them. Like Jesus forgives them.

Mommy and Daddy said Jesus was born to help people. They said he was a good man, but the churches messed everything up. I don't know what that means. I don't know if Jesus helps me and my family or not. I've asked him to help us. The manger has two angels on top of the barn. They're both naked. One has a little horn. The other angel has a ribbon. I pet her head sometimes. I like the warm feelings she gives me. She reminds me of something.

I sing "Happy Birthday" to baby Jesus and float to sleep thinking about the manger angels.

CHAPTER 52

Broken Living Room

I wish it was spring. Christmas is over and it's too cold out. I hear the furnace turn on, and I fall asleep.

My eyes open. I hear a big noise. There's no light in my window. It's night. I hear Mommy and Daddy fighting. I wish I could hide between my mattress and the other box thing. Then no one could find me. I rub my Blankie and hum a song I make up as I go. I fall back asleep.

When I wake up, the birds are singing. I think about the fight Mommy and Daddy had last night. I think about the little bird next to the fruit on the living-room shelf. I love this bird. I can almost hold it with both hands, but if I get caught, I'll be in trouble. I sneak touches because I like the feeling of the brown glass in my hands. I love the teeny-tiny beak on its round head. I think the birdie is looking for sunshine with its head up, and then in a minute it will peck the dirt for another worm. I see birds do this in the yard if I sit quiet as a mouse. The sides of the birdie are darker by the head and lighter by the tail.

I'm scared and can't get up. The house is quiet now. I think I heard Mommy break the birdie last night. I'm scared. I wonder if she broke it, and sad gets bigger than scared in me.

I say to myself, *Get up, stupid, and see if it's broken.* I tiptoe out to the hall and into the living room. The sun is starting to come through the big window, and I can see the mess Mommy and Daddy made. It makes me mad now, more than sad. I want to run into their bedroom and punch them in the head and call them stupid and mean! I whisper to whatever can hear me out there, "I hate them so much."

I see the birdie is still on the shelf. I want to cry now. Mommy's chair is on its side, the lamp is on the floor, records and squished papers are lying everywhere, here's Daddy's black sock. Why are Mommy's undies here? I feel dirty like icky, wet, covered in dust when I see her undies, and I don't know why.

Daddy's picture books with naked ladies are torn up on the couch and the floor. I see boobies in pieces and feel even dirtier. I want Samantha and Darrin from TV to be my mommy and daddy. I haven't seen their house look like this. I haven't heard them fight all night and beat each other up. Their house always looks nice like Grandma's house in Davenport and Grandma's house in Harrington. My aunts' houses don't look like this.

I walk over by Daddy's chair, and the black man's picture is on the floor with broken glass on the carpet. I walk backward away from the broken glass and slip on a record cover. My bottom hits the floor. It didn't even hurt, but I can't stop crying and my chest goes up and down real fast.

The tears stop after I close my eyes and start thinking about the time I sat on the carpet in this spot, when the living room was clean and nice, and the sun was shining. A big beam of sun made a straight line to the gold glass fruit on the shelf next to the fireplace. I could see the fruit balls glow like they had magic candles inside.

Each pretty ball was tied together by a wire that looks like leaves. It makes me feel better to think about it.

I stand up and start picking up all the records. I see big scratches on some. I know they won't sound right next time they're on the stereo. I put the picture books that aren't ripped back on the gold rack next to Daddy's chair. I carefully put all the torn pieces on the floor next to his chair in a little pile under the rack.

I pick up Mommy and Daddy's clothes and put them in a neat pile on the floor where the hall starts. Now I take each empty bottle, glass, and dirty ashtray to the kitchen one by one, just like Mommy always tells me. That's so I won't drop and break something. I pick up newspapers, why are parts of them wet? I squish empty cigarette packs in my hand. It makes me sad that my Hansel drawing for Daddy is crumpled here. I dump everything in the trash.

I get a rag from under the kitchen sink, hop on the cupboard ledge, and stretch to push the shiny faucet handle with the tip of my finger. I get the rag a tiny bit wet and go back to the living room. I wipe the stereo. There're a lot of ashes, wet spots, and rings of stickiness on top. It takes me a long time to get it all clean.

I put the pillows back on the couch and chairs. I pick the cigarette butts and bottle caps out of the carpet and throw them in the trash. I push the foot things back to the chairs and take the squished paper next to them to the kitchen desk. I smooth them with both hands and leave a pile on top of the desk. Under one of the foot things is Kleenex with bright red all over. Was someone bleeding? My tummy flips and flops, and I feel sick. I gag a little looking at the red part, and that stuff that stings my tongue comes up in my mouth. I pinch a white corner of the Kleenex with my fingers and carry it to the trash.

I go back to the broken glass. I'm careful as I crawl close to the picture of the sad black man. I stop and look at him. I don't think I've ever been this close to his face before. He's looking at me. I don't think he's had much to eat, and his suit is nice, but not shiny, new nice. His face is old, but I don't think he's old. I don't know why. He looks like a nice man, and I wish he was my daddy. I wish he would stand up and walk out of the paint and hug me. I wish he would make all the owies go bye-bye and make people here happy and not mad and sad and mean and bad.

Someone's walking in the hall. The toilet flushes and Mommy walks into the living room. Her hand is covering her mouth, and I'm scared. Am I in trouble? Should I have left the mess? Is she mad at me? She's standing there and I'm crawling away from the broken glass toward her. Mommy drops like a sack of potatoes to her knees with her hand still on her mouth, and I see tears. I scramble up to my feet and run to hug her. She wraps her arms around my waist and cries and cries, saying, "I'm so sorry. I'm so sorry."

I think I forgot a little how good it feels to be hugged by Mommy.

CHAPTER 53

Velvet and Telling Mommy

The furnace was quiet most of the day today inside. The birdsong is getting louder because it's a little warmer outside.

Mommy and Daddy gave me a doll that has hair like mine. Her name is Velvet. Her hair grows long out of the top of her head. I can make it short again by turning a knob on her back. It's long now, and I'm brushing it into a ponytail. I am careful so I don't hurt her head. I wish I had a purple ribbon to match her purple dress. Mommy told me her dress is "velvet."

I told Mommy, "No, that's her name, Velvet."

Mommy said her dress is made of velvet too. I'm thinking about that again. What a silly name. Maybe they should call the next doll Wool.

Velvet and I are sitting on my bed listening to *That Darn Cat!* I got the record from the library. Some of the songs on this record don't have words. I like the music so far, but the song that just started playing is kind of scaring me. There aren't any words. But the sounds are telling me a bad monster is coming to get me. I crawl to the corner of my bed and get under my quilt. Maybe it won't see me here. It's good my bed is in the corner of my room. No one can sneak up behind me. I didn't think monsters came out in daytime. I roll in a ball. I'm hoping the bad monster won't see me. Maybe I could scare it away. What can I do to scare it? The only thing I can think of is to jump out. Maybe I'll surprise it. The music's even scarier now.

Maybe I'll surprise and scare the monster so much it won't know I ran out. That could give me time to get away. Okay, I count to myself. One, two, three, jump! I race out from under the quilt, run over the top of my bed, turn, and pull my doorknob. I'm out the door. I say sorry to Velvet because I just whacked her head on my door. I'm running down the hallway to the living room. I see Mommy sitting on her green chair watching the TV. I fly onto her lap, and I don't care if she gets mad at me.

She wants to know what's wrong. It's her nice voice, I got lucky. I tell her all about the monster that came into my room with *That Darn Cat!* I say the monster got in my room when the scary song played. I start crying like a baby while I'm saying what happened. I don't care if I'm a baby, even a big baby. I feel like a baby because that song and its monster scared me. I'm crying because Mommy's being nice to me too.

Mommy's hugging me tight. It makes more big hurts inside push out, and I cry harder. She's making me feel owies that live down by my bottom. I can feel some moving up by my heart. Now they're in the back of my mouth. I wonder what they'll do next. Am I talking? I hear words coming out of me.

I'm letting each owie out of my mouth. All I can think is that I'm not supposed to. But it's too late, more bubble up from my bottom part to my heart part to my mouth and out. I can't stop now. It's coming out like barf does. Before one owie flies out my mouth, another one's bubbling up. I can't feel anything around me. I feel real tired inside me. I think the owies are slowing down. I feel mixed up. I feel big tears, my super-snotty nose, and the bubbles of owies pushing again.

I'm quiet now. Mommy is still hugging me, but not the same way she was. She's heard all the scary things that've hurt me. I told her about Daddy when he comes into my room. I told her he's been doing it for a long time. I told her Matty does it sometimes too. I said how I get in trouble if I don't do things. I don't like being in trouble. I wish they wouldn't do things. I say they hurt my pee place and bottom. I feel icky and yucky. I don't like it.

Mommy's not petting my head anymore. She's not squeezing me in a hug now. She says to get up and get off her lap. Is she mad? She stands up and holds my hand. I can't tell if she's mad or not. We walk down the hall to my room. The record's still playing. It's not a scary song now. Mommy turns the record player off. I don't see any monster. I ask Mommy to check the closets and under the bed. She says it's all clear. She sits on my bed and pats a spot next to her. I climb up to the spot she patted.

Mommy says she's madder at me than ever. Her voice is quiet and shakes a little, like it's cold and mean at the same time. She says it's bad to tell lies about people, especially lies that can really get people in trouble. She says if I told anyone the things I said in the living room, Matty would be taken away to a scary place. She says a lot of bad people would hurt him all the time. She says the same thing about Daddy. Mommy says they would take him away to such a bad place she can't tell me, it's so bad. She says it would give me nightmares like the child-catcher and the green witch did. Mommy says the monster that was here would be nice compared to the monsters Daddy and Matty would have.

Mommy asks if I want them to be taken away to live with monsters. I shake my head. She says she's still mad at me, but I'm a good girl and she loves me. Mommy says it's impossible Daddy and Matty would do what I said.

She asks if there was a monster in this room today. I think, *This is a trick.* I don't say anything. I need to give the right answer. I tell myself to think. I think how she said bigger monsters would get Daddy and Matty. Does that mean she knows the monster was real? But I think the answer is "not real." She's saying I need to answer. I need to guess, so I guess not real. I sort of shake my head. But I'm thinking how much time the monster had to go after I ran out. I can't say that. I don't want to make her madder.

Mommy says that's right.

That means I was right. But I'm thinking I was right to say a wrong thing. I don't know if a monster was there. I was afraid there was. So I ran just in case. Then I told Mommy all my owies. They're real. Maybe the monster is them.

Then Mommy says that if I keep saying bad things about Daddy and Matty, I might have to go someplace bad too.

I start crying again.

Mommy says that should scare me. She says it needs to remind me that I can never again say the things I said today. She asks if I understand, and I nod. Mommy says that's good. She makes me promise I will never tell these lies again. I promise. My head feels like she punched it.

Mommy tells me things are going to be better. "You'll see." She says she's sorry I've been scared by monsters and bad things.

This makes me feel better.

Mommy says she's here if I need her. I like that she says that. Mommy says I must always keep my promise to her. Not to tell anyone these things I said.

I nod.

Mommy asks me to help her make dinner. I'm happy to help her. She's being extra nice to me tonight. After dinner, we watch TV, and Mommy says it's bedtime. She's tucking me in. Blankie's not on my bed, and I ask Mommy if she can see her. She finds Blankie wrapped around Baby. I forgot I put her in Blankie for a nap.

Mommy says she's glad we talked. She says I'm not in trouble for saying the bad things. She says she loves me and we need to do some girl things together. Just the two of us. That makes me cry because I'm so happy. Mommy says to think about what I might like to do with her. I go to sleep thinking about the best, most fun things Mommy and I will do together.

I wake up and yawn and stretch. It's morning. I remember I need to tell Mommy what my ideas are for having fun together. Then I remember the things she said about the bad things. My tummy hurts.

I got in trouble for telling. I think about the times Mommy's been in the hallway. She knows. The monster's coming back. I'm under my covers. I twinkle my nose like Samantha, and I'm with Mommy shopping, laughing, and she's holding my hand. It's a sunny day.

My head's starting to hurt like it was punched again. I need to ask Mommy for chewable aspirin. Sometimes my headaches get so bad they make me throw up. I threw up last time I was on the farm with Mommy and Daddy and Grandma and Grandpa. I barfed right in the kitchen.

I'm running down the hallway to tell Mommy my ideas for fun girl time.

LEAVING FOUR

My eyes feel heavy. I'm a giant Flatsy doll lying in a blue rug field. Legs straight and arms by my sides. I lift myself up, fold my legs in front, and stare at my hands. Tears make it easy to slide my glasses off. I wish I'd kept Blankie out of that big box. Tears are in charge. Tears for Matty, for Mommy, for Daddy, and for me. A tiny drop for every memory I saw. If I could see me, I would watch teardrops roll to my cheek and down my chin or straight into the blue of my rug. Each tear knows where to go. That makes me cry harder and feel better all at once.

I push my glasses back on my wet nose.

I see the light-yellow side of *The Velveteen Rabbit* in my unpacked stack of books. I grab it and scoot back to a patch of sun on my floor and flip to the end.

And a tear, a real tear trickled down his shabby little velvet nose and fell to the ground.

The sun coming through my window's warming the book in my hands.

As I look through the pictures I'm remembering how Velveteen was a beautiful stuffed toy. He was loved by a real little boy. They went everywhere together. Once, the little boy left Velveteen in the forest by accident. He met real rabbits and wanted to play, but the real rabbits knew something was wrong. Velveteen looked like them but wasn't like them. They ran away to play without him. Sometimes kids at my school are like those real bunnies. I watch other kids and try hard to be like them. Sometimes I say I know things or do things that aren't real. I think kids like me if they think I'm better than me. I see kids stay friends a long time, but my friends leave to play with other kids, like the rabbits running from Velveteen.

Velveteen lived with toys and other stuffed animals. They became real if the little boy loved them more than just a toy to play with. Velveteen became a real rabbit because the boy loved him like that. Velveteen doesn't need to pretend to be real anymore.

I pretend a lot. So do Mommy and Daddy and Matty. Mommy and Daddy always say we have to look good when we go out. They never care when we're home. No one visits very much. Daddy says we have to have nice cars when we drive through town. Mommy gets upset if our clothes look worn-out and other people see us. We can't be dirty when we go out or we'll get in trouble. She always wants us to smile and be happy when we're all out together. Mommy talks a lot about what other people think. I don't know how she knows what other people think.

I roll on my tummy, squish my cheek in the blue carpet, and close *The Velveteen Rabbit*. I think about different rabbits. I'll miss the jack-rabbits when we move. I wonder if they have jackrabbits in Bellevue.

I love books. I can read a lot of words. I think of all the times I read and felt better. I think of all the times I looked at the row of colors on my dresser from all my books. I should put this stack of books in the box. Not yet.

I colored *Goldilocks and the Three Bears* when I was a baby. I must've thought my red crayon scribbles helped the pictures. Mommy said I didn't know any better. Matty drew purple storm circles on the same book and got in trouble. I guess he wasn't "didn't know any better" anymore.

I laugh to myself and flip the pages. The papa bear reminds me of Smokey the Bear. He's on TV all the time. He says, "Only you can prevent forest fires." I remember when Matty said Smokey should've talked to Daddy before he drove his car into a telephone pole down the street. It sent a spark through the wires into our basement and lit a box of lint on fire next to the dryer. Matty said Smokey should've told Daddy, "Only you can prevent house fires."

I remember Mommy shaking my shoulder and telling me to wake up. The electricity was out, and smoke was coming upstairs. We ran outside in our PJs. That's when we saw Daddy's car up the road with smoke coming out the front. It looked like a telephone pole was stuck in the hood. Hansel was trying to bark louder than the sirens on the main road. Mommy told us to sit in the grass by the trees and stay away from the house.

Mommy was calling Daddy a lot of bad names. He walked up the driveway like he was on a boat in big waves. Mommy grabbed him, and the wind blew her words at us. She said he could've killed us, but he should've killed himself.

Daddy pushed her away and wobbled to us. He sat between Matty and me with his long arms over our backs. He started to cry. "I'm so sorry, you guys! I love you two so much. You know I would never try to hurt you, right?"

Matty and I nodded. His breath smelled like poop.

I remember he said, "This's important. You two need to know about me. I wasn't treated right by your grandpa. Fact is, he was, uh . . ." He sat there for a long time.

I said, "Daddy?"

He shook his head. "Anyway, yeah, I need you to know. I was no older than you two when he'd kick the daylights out of me. Real bad."

Matty said that's bad, and Daddy nodded.

He took out his white handkerchief and blew his nose. I remember thinking it sounded like a bubbly trumpet.

"What about your sister?" I asked. "Did Grandpa hurt her too?"

Daddy nodded real slow.

"What did he do to her?" I asked.

"I don't know. Not gonna talk about it."

Then he said, "I went to Nam to get away from Dad and Mom. And Nam was bad."

Matty and I leaned in closer to see what Daddy was staring at. He didn't blink. Matty waved a hand in front of his face.

"Yeah, what? Okay, the war in Nam, it was ree-al bad. It just wasn't as bad as my dad, as they say."

I asked, "Who?" and he said, "Who what?"

I said, "Who says that?"

Daddy said, "Who says what?"

I said, "The 'not as bad' thing, who says?"

"I don't know." He squeezed us and said, "I need you two to grow up different. Not a drunk like your old man. I'm just sorry as hell for, uh . . ."

Matty asked, "Why did Grandpa beat you up?"

"I don't know. His dad was a mean son of a gun. His brothers kicked him around, oh, for being a cripple and all."

I asked, "Does Grandpa love you, Daddy?"

He shook his head. "Some people have bad in their heart, Deidi. You just got to know which ones."

I asked him how.

And he said, "How what?"

I said, "How do we know?"

He said, "Know what?"

I said, "Which have bad . . ."

But Daddy didn't let me finish and said, "Right, right, bad in the ticker. I don't know."

Matty and I said he was the best Daddy, and he cried. I remember when he leaned over and kissed my head. He whispered, "I'm sorry, princess." He cried so hard it sounded like he was choking. I remember the day after the fire I asked Daddy why he went to Nam to get away from Grandma too. He told me he never said that and I need to mind my own business.

When I stay overnight at Grandma and Grandpa's farm, they sleep on the main floor. The door to the upstairs is in the living room by the TV. The steps have a circus pattern with lots of dots of colors. Mommy said the floor is called "lin-o-leum." One side upstairs has lots of drawers where Grandma keeps sheets and blankets. The other side is a hallway to Daddy's old room. My aunt's old bedroom is at the top of the stairs, that's where I slept. There's a big square hole in the floor in front of it. It's a vent, and I can see the hallway downstairs. I can't sleep in when I'm upstairs because the smell of bacon comes up and makes my tummy growl. I like to listen to people talking in the kitchen.

There's a heavy curtain door to the bedroom. It's like a robot door, only it doesn't move itself. There's a cushy velvet chair in the corner and a big bed with a slippery bedspread in the middle. A big brown dresser with a mirror on top is on the other side of the window. There's a white doily on the dresser too. Grandma said she made it herself. The window looks over the front yard and garage, and all the way up the road past the old house and barn.

There's a little door in the wall by the big folding door. It has a white shelf inside. I always crawl in to push another door open to the hallway. Matty plays in there too. You can lock the big folding door to the room, but someone can still come in the little door. It doesn't lock. I wonder if Daddy spied on his sister when they lived here. I wonder why there's nothing from my aunt in her old room. I couldn't ask anyone. I always feel scared and icky in her old bedroom.

Mommy and Daddy always talk bad about Daddy's sister. I've asked what it was like when he grew up with her, but he won't say. He talks about playing basketball, driving cars, and his friends. He won't talk about growing up with his sister. I don't know why they don't like her so much.

Daddy's old bedroom is past a white crib with baby blankets. It has a weird door too, mostly glass so you can see inside. There's lots of things from Daddy's growing-up still in the room. His wooden toy box is by the door. Daddy said his desk's the same. He made the copper square on it with his initials when he was in high school. There's a wooden box with his marbles inside. Old pencils stick out of a brown cup. There's some kids' books and pieces of paper in the drawers.

Daddy said the cowboy picture on the wall was there when he was little. The name of his high school is on the wall above his dresser. Daddy said it's a pennant. The extra-long twin bed in the middle of the room is the same he had growing up. There are cowboys on the bedspread. Daddy said pretty much the whole room's the same. There's one window that looks over the top of the fruit trees in the backyard. Daddy said you can see their wheat fields going for miles and miles.

I feel sad when I go in Daddy's old bedroom. Sometimes I see him walking around these rooms when he was a boy. I get a scary feeling in his room too. Matty sleeps in Daddy's old room when we stay over. He said he likes it sometimes, but most of the time he doesn't.

I need to stretch my aching legs. Mommy says they hurt because I'm growing. Sometimes she rubs them for me before I go to sleep, but that's if Daddy's not home. I don't know why. I stretch out on my carpet between tall boxes and link my hands under the back of my head. I wonder how tall I'll be.

I'll probably be taller than Mommy when I grow up. I remember when she said she had big, red owies on her hands, arms, and legs growing up and would fake sick to stay home from school. Mommy said the owies itched all the time, and she was always embarrassed. Sometimes I hear her telling Daddy that she can't do anything right for her mommy or daddy. Mommy's daddy was the boss of something about schools in Davenport when Mommy was in school. She told Daddy that Grandpa always said he was ashamed of her. I heard

Mommy tell someone on the phone her parents hate Daddy and think she married a loser and a drunk.

I saw a picture from their wedding in a drawer in their bedroom. They look like the people on TV after their house was flooded. They look like it's after their biggest fight ever. Daddy's hand is on his forehead and Mommy's face is mad. She's staring at something. They got married at Grandma's church in Davenport. I know because I've been there. Grandma did the flowers for their wedding. Mommy doesn't look like the pretty brides I've seen in Grandma's pictures, in magazines, or on TV. Weddings are supposed to be happy. Mommy and Daddy look sad and mad.

I heard Mommy say on the phone her blond older sister was smarter and more popular than her in school. She said her blond younger sister was a pretty cheerleader everyone loved. Mommy said she was the plain, brown-haired middle girl who was always sick. I've seen pictures of Mommy in high school and she was beautiful. She was going to marry the undertaker's son in Davenport, but she said she went crazy instead. I know from Grandma that an undertaker buries dead people. She does flowers for funerals. I don't know what Mommy did, but she wasn't the "right girl" for the undertaker's son anymore.

I sit up and reach for the next book, *Poky Little Puppy*. The Poky Little Puppy wasn't a happy dog when he missed dessert. He had to go to bed hungry. I like the blanket he sleeps under. It has different-color squares all over it. My great-grandma made a quilt with different squares for me. I've gone to bed hungry before. My tummy hurt and made noise. I think Mommy and Daddy forgot to feed us before bedtime. They were fighting, so Matty and I didn't say we were hungry. I've told Mommy I'm hungry. When I was little, she was nice sometimes and got a snack for me. Mostly now I get my own snack. Sometimes she used to say uh-huh, but she didn't do anything. I don't like being hungry.

What if Daddy takes Mommy's food money? What happens if we don't have food? We don't have a farm or gardens like my grandmas and grandpas do. Our fruit trees aren't very big. I've never seen a family on TV not have food, so I don't know what people do. Daddy says Grandma and Grandpa on the farm don't like to share, so we wouldn't have any wheat. Not unless they died and Daddy got his part of the land.

Would kids at school share lunch with Matty and me?

Would God give my family food if we run out of money?

There's a girl on this book called *Are You There, God? It's Me, Margaret* who looks like me, but she's older. I can't read it yet. All I know is she needs something from God. Does she get help? If I knew God helped Margaret maybe I'd know how to get help too. I can't wait to read about Margaret.

I see my big red book, *The Story of Ferdinand.* Ferdinand doesn't want to play-fight with other bulls. He's happy under his tree smelling flowers. His mommy worries that he's lonely. I'm lonely when Mommy and Daddy fight and when they're mean to me or Matty. I'm lonely when they fight with my grandmas and grandpas, aunts and uncles. I hope they won't fight with Sophie's mommy and daddy in Bellevue.

Sometimes I wonder if Ferdinand got hurt when he was a little bull like I did. I wonder if he won't fight because of that. Sometimes when I get hurt, I want to be by myself.

I have books about animals, but I don't think I have any books about horses. We had a horse named Candy. Matty said she was his horse, but he was too small to do anything with Candy. She was white, and I thought she was a ghost horse because I didn't see her very much, even though she was in our pasture. Matty said Candy hated Daddy, except when he gave her beer. I've seen Daddy give Matty beer at lunchtime. Matty said he likes the way it makes him feel. He asks Daddy for beer if Mommy's gone.

When I used to feel lonely like Ferdinand, I would lie on the floor in the living room with Hansel. He always made me feel better. He put his head on his front paws and curled his tail around his bottom. I wish I could lie down with him now, but I can't. He's gone.

I lean against my dresser and pull my knees to my chin. I close my eyes and know he's watching, head resting on golden paws. He's the only one that likes it when I read out loud. I ask Hansel if he wants to see a picture and up goes his head. Sometimes he sits all the way up until I turn my book around. I show the picture page, he sniffs it and lies back down. We do the same things every time. I say "gobbledy-gook" for a word I don't know yet. His head turns to one side, and I hear him thinking, "That's not a real word, is it, Deidi?" I nod as if it's strange but true. I ask, "Should we read another book?" His answer is always the same. He scoots closer and pats my foot with his paw. I rub the spot behind his ear and pick the next book.

My eyes open to see Hansel's empty place on the rug. I pet the air and say, "Goodbye."

I see the shadows of leaves and sunlight through the window dancing on my rug. I wonder how many times I've seen this in all the years I've been here.

I start remembering again.

PART IV: AGE SIX

CHAPTER 54

Sixth Birthday Party

I didn't think today would ever get here. I've been waiting and wait-ing for a long, long time. I'm so happy my friends came all the way to my house for my sixth birthday party.

Holly, Shirley, Melissa, and Sissy are here. All the girls are dressed up in their nicest clothes, shoes, and hairdos. And I am too. I'm so happy Mommy gave me a pretty new dress for my party. She always gives me a new dress or outfit for my birthday. She says it's from Daddy too. My dress has a light-blue-and-white pattern all over it. The fabric is so soft. The long sleeves are poufy and have white lace at my wrists. There's a blue ribbon on the front of the dress. It's tied in a bow. I got my hair trimmed a little so my bangs don't cover my eyes. My hair's brushed and shiny. I'm wearing my fancy white Mary Janes. I think I look beautiful in the mirror.

Holly and Shirley are both wearing cute skirts, vests, and white blouses. Mommy gave me an outfit like that for my birthday last year. Holly's vest has different-color diamonds all over it. Shirley's vest has different-color stripes. They both look pretty. Shirley's mommy put her brown hair in a ponytail and tied a matching ribbon around it. She has bangs like me. Holly told me her haircut is called a "pixie cut." That means it's real short. She says her mommy likes a lady in the movies who has real short hair. Melissa's wearing a yellow plaid dress. She has a matching yellow bow on top of her head. She said her mommy curled her hair a little just for my party. Sissy looks beautiful today. Her mommy put her hair up in a fancy bun. Her light-blue dress with white lace on the neck, arms, and around the waist sort of matches my dress. She has white tights on with shiny black shoes. The shoes have little straps, but Sissy says they're not Mary Janes.

Mommy put all my presents in the living room. The pretty packages are on the floor in front of the brown couch and our TV. There are lots of presents. I sit on my knees by the TV. I can't help smiling at all the pretty boxes. I'm thinking about how everybody picked out each present just for me. I love every present and I haven't opened any yet! One present is wrapped in red-and-white-striped paper with red ribbons. I bet it's a book. Another present is wrapped in white paper with pink flowers. I have no idea what it is. Two presents have purple, pink, and yellow kitties on white paper. A funny-shaped present is wrapped in yellow paper with gold ribbon.

I want to wait a long time to open the presents because I'm so happy right now. All the presents have shiny ribbons tied or taped to the top. I feel like the luckiest girl!

Holly, Shirley, and Melissa are sitting on the carpet with me. Sissy's sitting on the couch. She says she needs to keep her dress clean or she'll be in trouble with her mommy. I tell Sissy that my mommy vacuumed the carpet not too long ago.

Someone hands me a present. It's wrapped in white paper with pink roses all over. There's a soft ribbon tied around the box and into a bow on top. I am excited to open it, but now I'm thinking about the carpet. Why does Shirley look worried? I think because she wants me to like her present. The goldish color of our brown carpet looks different in places. It's because of the stains. Holly says she likes the roses on the paper. The carpet stains are mostly from bad fights between Mommy and Daddy. I say I like the roses too. Shirley's almost sitting on a long piece of tape running down the carpet behind her and Holly. I pull one end of a pink ribbon that feels like satin. Another long piece of tape crosses the other on the floor behind my friends. The ribbon slides off.

Mommy and Daddy had to tape extra carpet to cover the worst stains and burns. Holly says the pink ribbon will be pretty in my hair. I think Mommy and Daddy's cigarettes burned the rug. I nod and lift one taped end of the paper without tearing it. I rub my hand on the carpet a little and look at my palm. It's dirty. I don't want to touch the white paper with my dirty hand now. I lift the other taped end with my clean hand. What if everybody's white tights and knee socks are dirty when they stand up again?

I look at Holly, she's staring at me. Shirley's face still looks worried. Melissa's on her knees facing away from me. She looks like she wants to go. I turn to look at Sissy on the couch. Her ankles and knees are tight together, and she's holding one hand on her lap with the other hand. She's looking down. Her face's like mine if I'm waiting for something bad to happen. I look back at the taped-and-stained carpet.

I feel my cheeks getting red. I see everything happening, my friends' unhappy faces, the stained and ripped rug, my dirty hand. A room that looks like the basement on the farm that nobody cares about being nice. I'm ashamed. I want to cry, but if I cry, my friends will know I know what's happening. Maybe if I pretend like all this doesn't bother me, then it won't bother them. I try to pretend, but I don't think it's working.

I want to say, "It hasn't always looked like this. It was nice and clean when we moved in." I want to say my mommy and daddy get in such bad fights they break things and ruin things like carpet. I want to say they hit each other with their fists and feet and knees and bowls and bottles over and over. I want to say they hit Matty and me, and Matty hurts me like the boys he beats up at school. I want to say Daddy's a drunk and burns us all with cigarettes. I want to tell them that Matty throws lit matches, and Daddy beats him up more. I want to tell them I've seen blood from each of us on the carpet after bad fights. I want to say I've tried to scrub the stains away with soap and water. I feel like I'm dirty. How can my house make me feel dirty? Why was everyone but me seeing this before?

I'm in bed tonight after today's party.

I still feel dirty. Maybe the best thing is for me to stop being friends with the girls who came here today. Then I won't have to hear the bad things they'll say about me and my house.

CHAPTER 55

Bicycles

When I was three, six sounded like being a grown-up. Now I think six is smarter than grown-ups. They know more things, but they act stupid a lot. Some do. Some don't. My hands and feet are stretching. I'm getting taller. My eyes see things from higher. I can see higher. I'm getting bigger.

Matty and I are riding our bikes across the main road today. Mommy says to be careful and look both ways.

Bicycles with banana seats are the best. My bike has a white seat and the prettiest pink and red roses all over. I have a tall wire that goes way up to the sky and has an orange flag at the top. That's so people can see me coming. I have shiny handlebars that get even shinier if I rub my T-shirt on them. That takes all my finger smudges off.

The sun is shining when we pull our bikes out of the garage. Matty gets on his bike, and I get on mine. I like to ride behind him. Pedaling down the gravel road, I sound just like a car sounds on gravel. I pretend I'm in one of those cars that doesn't have a top. I have big sunglasses on like the girl in *Love Story*. I have a scarf on my hair so it doesn't get messed up. I love feeling the wind on my face and seeing everything.

Matty and I stop at the main road at the end of the gravel road from our house. Highway 17. We can see it from our house. We can see across the street to the water tower, park, school, and the white pointy top of the church. Highway 17. When I was little, I didn't know its name. Now I think it's our own road. In the phone book, it just says "Highway 17" by Daddy's name.

Matty says, "Wait till I say we can go, okay?" I say, "Yep." Hansel sits down next to me. He's waiting for Matty too. "Okay," he says. "Let's go." We run our bikes across the road to the sidewalk. Hansel's pink tongue's hanging out the side of his mouth. Matty says, "Follow me, Deidi." I say okay.

We ride everywhere. There's lots to see on this side of the highway. We ride past the school we didn't go to, the water tower, and the big trees in the park. On this side of the highway, the houses are close together. They can walk out just a little on their front lawn and touch their neighbor. The houses we pass are painted yellow, green, white, or blue. All the yards have grass, flowers, and trees. I can smell roses and lilacs.

We ride by a lot of houses. I know we're almost at Frank's Market when I see the lake at the bottom of the hill. We pull up to the store. It's shaped like a big box. There's a square sign on top with Frank's name on it. Next to that is a funny thing that sticks up with two orange balls on it. Frank says it's like the Jetsons. He sells the best penny candy. I click my kickstand down, Matty opens the glass door. I hear the bells chime on the glass.

We say hello to Frank. He's always behind the counter. He says, "Hello, you two," with a happy voice. Frank's Japanese, and he wears big square glasses. He always has an apron tied at his waist. He says it keeps his clothes clean. Frank's super nice to kids. He keeps the penny candy where we can reach it. The Lemonheads, candy bars, and packs of gum are on the shelves behind the counter. You need to ask Frank for those things.

Matty tells me I can choose five pieces of candy. I pick out Bazooka bubble gum, Atomic Fireballs, and Pixy Stix. He gets the same as me except he picks one green cigar instead of two bubble gums, and he has a jawbreaker instead of two Pixy Stix. I guess that's not the same as me, but the Fireballs are the same. We don't have to ask Frank for two bags. He puts each of our candies in our own bag. I love the sound the cash register makes. We say thank you to Frank. He says to drive safe.

We go back outside to our bikes. Matty whistles to Hansel, who's sniffing a telephone pole. I wrap the top part of my paper bag around my handlebar, after I put a big wad of bubble gum in my mouth.

It tastes so good. I blow big pink bubbles all the way back to our house.

CHAPTER 56

Electric Fence

It's really, really hot outside. I love summer, but not when it's so hot! Matty and I just ate peanut-butter-and-jelly sandwiches in the kitchen, and Mommy and Daddy are having a big fight in the living room.

"C'mon, Deidi, let's go outside."

"Okay."

Matty says he wants to go to the pasture.

We squeeze between the gateposts and the electric so we don't get shocks. I stare at the wires a little. I wonder if a person had to make all those little Xs? I bet they didn't have the electric on. I think those ties would be hard to make. It probably took a long time.

I hear Daddy yelling, "Matty and Deidi, get back here right now!" He sounds mad. We squeeze by the gate and run across the grass. Daddy wants to know who said we could go to the pasture. Matty and I say nobody, that we just went.

Daddy says, "Oh, smarty-pants. You 'just went' because you can 'just do' whatever you want?"

Matty shrugs, and Daddy looks mean.

His scary voice says, "Get your butts back in that pasture. If you're not there on the count of three, all hell's gonna break loose, get it?"

We both nod.

He says, "Go, one, two, three."

Matty and I are fast, but not that fast. We get to the pasture after three.

Daddy starts running to us. His heavy boots are hitting the ground like he wants to crush the grass, like he wants to crush us with his boots! My heart's going *thump, thump, thump, thump, thump.* It feels like it's breaking through my chest. He yells to sit our butts on the salt licks. He's got a wad of chew in his lower lip, but he's not spitting. That means he's swallowing. Matty said that makes Daddy talk fast.

Daddy's in front of us with his hands on his belt and his tummy sucked in. Mommy always tells him to suck in his beer belly. I'm scared. I'm afraid of what Daddy's going to do, and I am afraid my heart's going to blow up.

I look up at the sky and stop feeling anything. It's light blue with no clouds and I'm floating in it.

I hear Daddy's voice tell us to go over to the electric fence. To grab it.

I float over to the fence, still with the clouds, and grab the wire with both hands. Everything's silent except the *bzzzzz* in my head. I wonder if Daddy can hear the *bzzzzz*. I think I hear Matty *bzzzzzing*. My mouth tastes like I'm sucking on fifty pennies. I wonder if I'm drooling. I hear Daddy yell, "Let go."

I can't see very well, everything's fuzzy inside and out. It feels like all the stuff that lives on the inside of my body got pushed up into my head.

I hear Daddy's voice tell us to go sit on the salt until he comes back. Daddy says there's no talking allowed. He says, "I better not see one move or hear one sound out of either of you, get it?" We nod and walk back to the salt licks.

We sit on the salt licks for a long time. My blue sky's going night-night with the sun. I'm tired and feel sick from the electric.

Matty whispers, "Did you hear that?"

"What?" I whisper back.

He points in front of us. There's noise coming from some sage-brush. Matty whispers, "Snake."

I want to pull my knees to my chest, but I can't. A head pokes out of the bush. It's the same color as the dirt. There's a V cut in the end of its black tongue. It keeps shooting in and out, in and out.

I hear *ch, ch, ch*. A big snake body pushes out of the bush in curls. The head never moves.

Matty whispers, "Deidi," and I jump a little.

"What?"

Matty says, "That snake's coming to get us."

I didn't get what he said at first, but Matty's words go around again in my head. *That snake's coming to get us.*

I hear Hansel barking far away. The snake stops moving. It curls around and around itself. A tail pops up in the middle of its perfect circles. I see the *ch, ch, ch* beads on the tip of the tail. Hansel's bark is getting closer.

The snake lifts off the dirt and rattles more. Hansel's between us and the snake. His white teeth are showing. He never does that. His ears are back flat. His front paws and legs look like he's about to jump. His tail's straight and almost touches Matty's nose. He's bark-ing louder, faster, growling, stomping his front paws, and making dirt clouds. The snake disappears so fast we barely see the tail shoot under the sagebrush.

Mommy and Daddy are yelling and running up behind us. Matty and I don't care about Daddy's stupid punishment anymore. We grab Hansel and hug and pet him.

Mommy and Daddy are out of breath. Mommy's saying, "Wait, was that a rattler? Oh my God, that was a rattlesnake!"

Matty says, "Yeah, it was, Mommy. Deidi and I'd be dead if Hansel didn't scare the rattlesnake away."

Daddy says we need to get back inside. Mommy says the fun's over now. She says the next time we don't do what we're told, we won't be so lucky. She says they won't let Hansel out. Mommy wants to know if we want to sit on the salt licks longer next time.

Matty and I shake our heads.

Mommy says there are a lot more rattlesnakes back there.

We all go inside. Mommy and Daddy help Matty and me wash our hands and faces. Matty and Daddy flick water at each other and laugh. Mommy tells them to settle down. Daddy says let's make some popcorn and watch TV. I can't stop hugging Hansel.

We're all in the living room eating popcorn, drinking pop, and laughing when Daddy turns the station to *The Lawrence Welk Show*. Matty jumps up and pretends to sing like the pretty ladies in puffy dresses. I feel like I'm hanging from the ceiling watching us. I want to cry. I can't remember the last time we were all happy like this.

At bedtime, Mommy and Daddy both tuck us in. They tell us what great kids we are and how special our family is. They say we share a lot of special things and that makes us strong. They tell us not to make them send us to the salt lick again. I drift off to sleep making my promise.

CHAPTER 57

Animal Friends

"Your breath's stinky, but I love you, Hansel." He's chasing me in
the backyard and happy-barking. I roll onto the grass, and he keeps
trying to lick my face. His nose's pushing the side of my head and
tickling my ear to turn me over. The big black-on-brown tail's wagging. Hansel barks at me to run with him again.

I remember hearing the coyotes last night. I'm thinking how
different Hansel is than them. Grandma told me that coyotes by the
farm are part of the dog family. I've seen them race through the
pasture when it's almost dark. They look like the stuff that sparkles on Cinderella's dress when she gets ready for the ball. I think
coyotes are like dog fairies. They howl at night, and Grandma says
they sleep in the daytime. When bad things happen, I think about
the coyote howls. I go away with them, and we're friends running
fast in the fields.

I know I can't pet them, but I think they come by to show me
they're here and it's okay. I've seen them running across wheat fields.
They're fast and always have their head and ears straight up in the

air. Some coyotes look like they're running from something. I bet they're running from people. I bet they don't like people.

The grass feels good, and I don't want to move yet. But I know it's time to feed the kitties. I've been feeding them for weeks.

I remember when Hansel and I found them. Hansel's ears went up, and he looked away from me. I thought I heard something too. I asked, "What is it?" He started to walk around the side of the house and I followed. His head was up until we got to the big tree. I heard it too. It was the tiniest meow from a lot of cats. Hansel sniffed around the big tree. The kitties cried louder as we got closer. I was excited and scared.

Excited because I knew kitties were close by. I couldn't wait to see them. But scared because of what Matty would do to them if he found out. There was an old silver pan someone forgot at the bottom of the tree. Hansel looked over the top of it. I looked inside it and saw a pile of baby kitties. They looked hungry. If I fed them, they'd be quiet and maybe Matty wouldn't find them. This made me sad because I like to tell Matty if I find something special outside. But I knew I couldn't this time.

Hansel waited as I left the front door open and ran into the kitchen. I opened the fridge door and took the milk out. I found a pink plastic bowl in the cupboard. I filled it halfway with milk. I almost forgot to put the milk back. I reopened the fridge and pushed the milk on the top shelf.

"Here kitty, kitty, kitties, here kitty, kitty, kitties!" I called after I was back in the yard. Seven furry babies walked, fell, and tumbled out from under the tree.

I say to myself, *I need to get up off the grass now.* I think about how much I've fed the kittens since the first time.

The kitties can't wait any longer to be fed again. I feel like a mama cat and wish I could purr. The kittens are bigger than when Hansel and I found them. Whenever I'm sad, I think of the kitties and get happy. I think about how they rub their little whisker faces on me and how loud their purr engines are when I'm with them. Even if I'm not feeding the kitties, they love to be with me. I get so happy to see them every day.

Hansel lies down next to me. He likes to watch me feed the kittens. I'm sitting in the grass with my bowl of milk. I count all seven kitties climbing on me to get the milk. They don't wobble as much as they used to. They still get milk on their whiskers. There's Panda, he's black-and-white. Orangey is the orange kitty. Snowflake is the pretty white kitty. Sam and Mittens are gray-and-white kitties. Tarzan is all kinds of colors. Stripes has stripes on her face.

Panda's chewing on my hair, and Sam's untying my tennis shoe. Here comes mama cat, she's the same color as a Hershey candy bar with white paws. It's taken time for us to be friends. She pushes the side of her mouth on my elbow now. I say, "Hi, Brownie, have you been out hunting again today?"

She brings dead mice and birds in the yard. She dropped a dead mouse right next to me the other day. She stared at me like Mommy does if I forget to say thank you. I petted her head and told her she did a good job. Brownie arched her back under my hand and stuck her tail straight up.

She's purring louder than the kittens today. Hansel doesn't bark anymore when she comes around. He likes her, and she likes him. I think it's a little yucky when she licks his mouth.

The kitties are all rolling around me. Some are starting to get sleepy. Brownie stretches out in a sunbeam licking the kittens. She's a good mama kitty.

I lie down on my back in the sunny spot of grass next to Brownie and her babies. No one can see us behind the big tree. I whistle and lift my head. Hansel walks over and curls up right behind me for my pillow. The kittens are climbing up my shirt. They push each other around on my chest and curl up. I close my eyes and feel the purrs of my friends. I'm happiest with animals. I hear the robins working in the fruit trees. A meadowlark's singing. I don't feel alone.

I fall asleep thinking about the jackrabbit I saw this morning. I went outside after breakfast. The jackrabbit had a cute white-and-brown tail. It was fast and flew through the pasture. I said, "Thank you, Mr. Rabbit," because he made me forget my owies and made me happy.

I jump awake as Daddy comes out the front door. He says, "Hey, there's my sexy little Elly May." He thinks I'm pretty in my cutoffs like Elly May on *The Beverly Hillbillies.* I like that he's not looking at the kittens.

I say, "Hi, Daddy," as he heads to the garage.

The kittens are looking at me to make sure it's okay. I talk to them, pet them, and tell them to go back to sleep. The sun and kittens start making me sleepy again. I'm sleeping like a cat when the garage door bangs shut. I'm wide awake. I hear Daddy's footsteps on the gravel coming closer to me.

Something falls on the grass with a soft thud. Daddy says to go inside, right now. I ask why, and he says it again. He's not being nice. I get up and grab my bowl. I say bye-bye to my kitty friends. I see the gunny sack behind Daddy.

"What's that for?"

He says go inside. I run in the front door and drop the plastic bowl on the counter. I run back to close the front door and over to the window where I can see the yard. Daddy's where my kitties are.

I hear Matty in the hallway and tell him to come here. We're both looking out the window. Matty says, "Hey, where'd those cats come from?"

I shrug, and Matty says, "He's going to kill them, Deidi."

My heart stops and turns to ice. I ask how he knows, and Matty says his gun's lying in the grass. I see Daddy petting my kittens and Brownie. Matty says he's tricking them.

He lifts Panda, Tarzan, Sam, and Mittens by their scruffs and drops each kitten in his sack. The other kittens are rubbing their faces on his pant legs. They think he's nice like me. The kittens trust him because of me. He puts the last kitten in the gunny sack and pets Brownie. He lifts her up and drops her in the gunny sack. I feel like my legs won't hold me up. The gunny sack's moving all over. I open the front door, but before I can say a word, Daddy yells at me over the cries of the kittens to get back inside or he'll kick the crap out of me. I close the door.

I say I've got to stop him! I ask Matty what to do and he says tell Mommy. I know she won't help. I don't know why Matty just said that, he knows better. He says Daddy's walking back to the pasture. I run to the kitchen windows and watch my kittens go into the pasture. I feel my wet hands and start crying. I can't breathe. I can't go outside. I can't tell Mommy. I can't stop this, I can't save my friends. The dust puffs around the sack Daddy drops on the dirt. He's loading his big gun and standing over the moving brown sack. He's the scariest, meanest man in the world.

I hear Mommy hang up the phone. She asks what's wrong and Matty tells her. I make a loud crying noise when I hear him tell Mommy. She's putting her hands on my shoulders and says it's for the best. I want to shove her away, but I don't. I jump with each shot he fires. One, two, three, four bullets in a circle around the bag. They stop moving.

I'm sitting at the kitchen table when Daddy walks in. He washes his hands in the sink and sits next to me. Daddy says the cats had to be shot because they're strays. He's saying stuff about being sick, and I don't care. My head's on my arms and I can't stop crying. Daddy's telling me to listen and stop crying. He's making me want to cry more. I look at him and say he killed my friends. Mommy says they weren't friends. She says people are friends, not animals. Matty says

Hansel's his friend. Mommy says Hansel's different because he's our pet. These were wild, not pets.

I yell, "They were my friends!" I don't care what they say.

Mommy gives me a mean look.

I say again they were my friends.

Mommy tells me to go to my room and don't come out until I can talk nicely to everyone.

I'm in my room and glad. I don't want to see Mommy or Daddy for a long time. I bury my face in my pillow and cry. I'm so sad, so sad, so sad. My kitties are dead. My heart hurts too much. I'm falling asleep.

Daddy wakes me up. I know what he's going to do when he says, "Shhh." My pillow's still wet from crying. I see all my kitties' faces in my head. My guts are going to shoot out my bottom or my mouth. The second he says, "Shhh," again, my mind yells, *Kill me!* I see big piles of dirt dug out of the ground on the farm. That square hole in the ground is mine. I see my dead body lying at the side of the grave. My bare leg dangles in my new home. I feel like I can breathe. Everything's turning blurry and moving into something dark. I'm sitting here in the dark, there's no sound. Where am I?

Something brings me back to my bed. No, I don't want to be here, please stop, please. It's not Daddy. Is this light or something else? Isn't it nighttime? I can't see Daddy. Maybe this is dying. Something's here. All the kitties, the rabbits, the robins, meadowlarks, and coyotes. All the animals are here. Something else too. All okay. I'm okay. Sunshine and the meadowlark's song outside my window tell me it's morning.

CHAPTER 58

New Shoes

I'm glad it's almost time to go back to school.

I'm running into my room with my new box. I climb on my bed and open it. The tissue paper crunches, and I smell my new shoes. Mommy had the saleslady spray them. That way, if they get wet, my toes won't get soaked.

Today, Mommy and I had a "girls' day." My new shoes are light brown and kind of reddish. The laces have blue stripes. I wanted red Mary Janes, but Mommy said they're not practical. She said that means they won't last. I really like my new shoes.

I got to put my foot in the funny slider machine. The saleslady wore a bright-yellow dress and bright-yellow knee socks. Her dress didn't have any sleeves, and it was short. She had a bright-yellow headband on too. She told Mommy my shoe size. Mommy told her to bring one size bigger because I'm growing so fast. The saleslady put the shoes on my feet and told me to walk around. Mommy said to stay on the carpet. I had to see how they felt.

I heard the lady tell Mommy I was a very polite little girl. I heard Mommy tell her how smart I am. She said I never give them any trouble and I'm always happy. The saleslady said Mommy and Daddy must be great parents. I liked hearing Mommy talk about me. It made me feel good to hear the nice things she said. I got to pick out two pairs of white knee socks.

The saleslady gave me my new shoes and socks in a bag. When we walked away, Mommy said, "I think yellow might be her favorite color." We both laughed.

Mommy and I always look in the window at the jewelry store when we're downtown. Today we saw pretty gold earrings in their window. Mommy said they're called hoops.

We went to Tastee-Freez for lunch. We each had a cheeseburger and fries. Mommy had a Pepsi, and I had a vanilla milkshake. We sat outside and ate our lunch by the lake. We laughed when the wind tried to blow away our paper bag and napkins.

On the way home, we stopped at the drugstore. Mommy said she needed Aqua Net hair spray and cigarettes. I told her that Aqua Net doesn't smell so good. She said, "I know." She bought me a roll of butterscotch Life Savers. Those are my favorite.

I put my socks away and set my new shoes on top of their box in my closet. I run to find Mommy. She's in the living room folding clean clothes on the stereo. I say thanks again for my new shoes and for so much fun today. Mommy says, "You're welcome and thank you for a great day too." I ask if I can play with her jewelry box, and she says yes.

I run back in with her big white jewelry box. I sit on the floor, and Mommy turns the stereo on. I open the top lid and see the soft pink fabric inside. I like how it feels.

I know the song that starts playing on the stereo, so I sing along like Mommy does. Even if I sometimes forget what all the words mean, I can still sing them. It's about the sound of silence. I wonder, how can silence have a sound? I like the way the words rhyme in this song, like Dr. Seuss. *My old friend . . . again . . . in my brain . . . remains.*

I look at Mommy's crystal earrings. When I lift them up, I can see all kinds of colors.

I like this part of the song, when the voices get loud. They sing about words written on the walls and "ten-mint" halls. Mommy explained all the words to me before.

I pick up the ring that looks like her wedding ring. It's a cocktail ring, Mommy told me. You wear it to cocktail parties, and cocktails are alcohol drinks. I think a rooster's tail is a weird name for a drink.

Mommy has a watch and a necklace that match her wedding ring too. Her wedding ring has a pretty diamond in the middle. It sparkles blue, pink, and silver when I turn it in the sunlight. Mommy says it's antique, but not like old antique. It's antique style, she said. I guess that means it's kind of like antique.

We sing about dreaming and walking alone on cobblestones. Mommy told me that's an old kind of street that's made of big rocks.

Mommy says someday when I'm a big girl she'll give me some of her jewelry. She said I'll get the rest when she dies. I said, "You're never going to die, though."

She said she'll die someday.

I said but not for a very, very, very long, long time.

She laughed and said, "Okay."

We sing together, *The sound . . . of silence.*

CHAPTER 59

First Grade Drawing

I'm in the first grade now. I'm in school all day, not half a day like kindergarten.

My teacher is Mrs. Wallace. She was Matty's teacher last year. He said Mrs. Wallace is mean. He thinks she looks like the bad lady in *101 Dalmatians*. I guess she kind of does, but she wears pointy glasses. Mommy doesn't like Mrs. Wallace. She said Matty didn't do well because she's too strict. My friends Melissa and Jose are in Mrs. Fields' class. But Carrie, Brenda, and Mindy are in my class. We play hopscotch at recess. Carrie's mommy makes clothes for her and her sisters. David's a boy in my class. When he gets in trouble with Mrs. Wallace, she sends him to the principal's office for a paddling. Matty's been paddled too. He says it hurts worse than it sounds.

Our principal's name is Mr. Dunn. I like a boy in my class. His name's Bobby and he's nice. Randy's the tallest kid in my class. He was in Matty's class last year. Mommy said some kids get held back. I don't know why Randy was held back. Sometimes David calls Brenda and me "four-eyes" because we wear glasses. Mindy thinks

David calls us names because he likes us. Susie's one of the tallest girls in my class, but not as tall as Randy.

There're twenty-one kids in my class. Two ladies help Mrs. Wallace teach us. They're both nice. One lady wears purple shoes that show her toes and tie like tennis shoes. She told me they're made of suede. She said suede's like leather and comes from a cow. Melissa said she has twenty-four kids in her class and one helper lady. There's a black girl in her class with fluffy hair. I think she's pretty, but some kids are mean to her.

Matty has twenty-one kids in his class and one helper lady. His teacher's Mrs. Madigan. She wears short skirts and frosted eye shadow. Carrie calls her hairstyle a "bouffant." Brenda heard about a lady with a bouffant who hair-sprayed a black widow inside her hair. It had baby spiders, and she died from the bites. We have black widows in Moses Lake. They have a red hourglass on their tummy and eat their husband before they have babies. I've seen them in our garage. Brenda said black widows are more poisonous than rattlesnakes.

Mrs. Wallace gives us instructions, and we do schoolwork at our desks. I like being here. Everything's the same each day. When things change, you know why, or someone's nice if you ask. We eat lunch in the gym. I buy hot lunch if I have money. I bring my lunch if Mommy doesn't forget to make it.

I love saying the Pledge of Allegiance every morning. I put my hand on my heart and look right at the American flag. I say in my strong voice, "I pledge allegiance to the flag of the United States of America and to the republic for which it stands, one nation under God, indivisible, with liberty and justice for all." It's like a promise to be good to each other every day. I don't know what a republic is, but I know it's important. Daddy told me "justice" is like being fair to everyone.

Beverly read *Charlotte's Web* to me. Fern saves Wilbur from her daddy's ax because she says it's a terrible injustice to kill the little pig. She asked her daddy if he would've killed her if she were the runt. I don't think he would have. It would be an injustice.

If we have justice for all, that means we have fair for all. So people don't cheat playing Operation or cut someone out of a game if they don't like them. That's not fair. But that happens all the time. Mommy and Daddy aren't fair to Matty, and they aren't fair to me. The news says that lots of people aren't fair. Sometimes I wonder if grown-ups forgot the Pledge of Allegiance.

We have a project to finish today. Mrs. Wallace says "project" means something we work on. I get to draw and paint a picture of my family and our house. I have a large piece of nice white paper to work on. Mrs. Wallace says the directions are written on the chalkboard in case we forget. She said "directions" means how to do the project. I'm excited to do a good job on my project.

I've worked on my picture for a long time. Mrs. Wallace says I'm doing a very nice job. That makes me happy. I don't smile much, but I'm smiling.

Everyone's done. Mrs. Wallace's choosing three drawings to put up on the wall. They're the best in the class. Two nice drawings are picked and pinned on the board. The best drawing space is still empty. Mrs. Wallace's walking to my row. My tummy does some flips like I just went super high on a swing. She stops in front of my desk, looks at my picture for a long time, and then says that my drawing wins! Mrs. Wallace said it's the best one! This almost makes me start crying. I pinch my side real hard. I can't wait to tell Mommy and Daddy. Carrie, Brenda, and Mindy said I did a great job, and Bobby told me I'm a good artist.

I'm home from school and sitting in the kitchen with Mommy. She says Mrs. Wallace gave her the special picture she had on the wall. I'll miss seeing it at school. Mommy says Mrs. Wallace liked it.

I ask if she wants to put my picture on the fridge. Mommy says she doesn't think so. I watch her pull my picture from her bag. She takes it to the kitchen table. She spreads her hands across the picture to flatten it. She asks me to say what's wrong with the picture.

I shake my head. I don't know what she means. I don't think there's anything wrong.

Mommy tells me to look at the picture, not at her.

I stare at my picture. I think it's good. A long time goes by. Mommy's not talking. I keep looking at it.

Mommy says I don't get it, so she'll explain. She points to the thick line of blue across the top of the picture. She says, "The sky isn't a stripe, is it, Deidi?"

I'm thinking, *It can be,* but I shake my head.

Mommy points at my picture and says the sky doesn't stop here. She says the world isn't white after the sky stops, is it?

I shake my head.

She says this picture doesn't make sense. Mommy says my teacher thinks I'm slow. I ask what she means. Mommy says Mrs. Wallace told her I take time to finish my work. She says I'm not one of the best students.

I can barely hear Mommy because the owie inside my head is making noise like a car crashing on TV. Mommy's saying something about being worried because I don't have many friends.

Now Mommy's digging in the junk drawer. She pulls out a blue felt pen and hands it to me. She says I should go in my room and fix my picture.

I walk in my room, put my picture on the floor, and sit down in front of it. My picture won first place in my class. Why didn't my teacher say the sky was wrong? How am I slow if I do the work the same as other kids and win first place? How can I have more friends when I'm afraid to talk because I can never tell anything?

I'm scribbling the blue marker all over my picture. I keep scribbling until I can't see what I drew anymore. I hug my legs and look away from my picture. It's not a picture anymore. It's a baby's scribble mess.

It's a bad picture that a baby drew.

I'm crying like a big, fat, stupid baby and lift my head off my wet knees. I wipe my nose on my bedspread and tear the picture into little pieces. I throw the bits in the garbage can.

I hear Mommy saying, "Dinner's ready." I go in the kitchen and sit down at the table. Mommy doesn't say anything about the picture.

CHAPTER 60

Teeth and Cigarettes

More of my teeth are falling out. I lost my first teeth way back when I was little, but now they seem to be coming out faster. Mommy says that my baby teeth are coming out to make way for my big teeth. She says the big teeth are permanent. Mommy has nice teeth, but she doesn't smile much. I like when she smiles. Daddy's teeth are kind of yellow. He says that's because of all the cigarettes and chew. He had braces on his teeth when he was a teenager, so his teeth are really straight. I didn't know that people had braces that long ago. Daddy doesn't smile much either. When he smiles, he looks sort of like he wishes he hadn't. He looks like I feel when I get caught doing something I'm not supposed to do.

Daddy says that when I smile it looks like Ali, the boxer, knocked some of my teeth out. Matty and Daddy like boxing. I don't like boxing. It looks like it hurts. Daddy said that boxers lose a lot of teeth. I wonder how they eat food, and Mommy says fake teeth can be put in their mouths. That's good.

The state I live in is named after George Washington. He was America's first president, and Grandma from the farm told me that he had wooden teeth. She says his teeth fell out because they didn't have dentists back then. Or, if they had dentists, she said they didn't know what they were doing. Grandma told me that George Washington was born in the same state that Grandpa's family comes from. She said it's called Virginia. They should've named that state Washington. Grandma said she doesn't know if Washington ever even came here. I don't know where Virginia is. I wonder if George Washington knew my family?

Grandma has yellow teeth like Daddy. I don't know why, because she never smokes. I don't like cigarettes. I smell like cigarettes even when I'm at school and no one is smoking by me. Other kids smell like cigarettes too. We hate cigarettes, except the candy kind. Matty likes green cigars from Frank's store. You can't blow smoke out of them, but you can bite them and blow bubbles with the gum.

I'm thinking how I wish I had some candy right now, as I work on my Winnie the Pooh coloring book in the living room. I'm staying inside all the lines and using the same colors as the cartoons. It's not a project like Mrs. Wallace gives us, but I am trying to be careful with it.

Mommy and Daddy have the news on TV, and I don't know where Matty is.

A man with brown hair just came on. I hear him say cigarettes are bad for people. I remember when I was five years old and the president said cigarettes can't be on TV commercials anymore because they hurt people. Mommy and Daddy said they weren't surprised when the president did this. I asked if they were going to quit smoking. Daddy said, "We'll see, Deidi." Mommy lifted her shoulders up and down and then walked out of the room.

Whenever I tell them they should stop smoking, they get mad at me. Maybe they'll listen to the president.

I haven't said anything about smoking and cigarettes for a long time. I roll over on my bottom and sit up with crossed legs. "Are you guys going to quit smoking?"

Mommy sighs and Daddy curls his newspaper back. "What did you say?" he asks.

I say, "Smoking, are you ever going to quit?"

Daddy looks at me and says, "When the world becomes a different place, Deidi." He looks at Mommy, and she asks what that's supposed to mean. Daddy pulls his paper back and says she knows what it means. Mommy says something about everything being her fault now, and Daddy says, "Bingo, that's right." I try to ask another question, but she tells me to shut up.

I stand up from crossed legs without using my hands, pick up my coloring book and crayons, and go to my room. I close my bedroom door. I can hear loud voices, but I'm glad I can't hear the words.

CHAPTER 61

Water Fairies

There's magic light outside. The sun's night-night. The days are already getting shorter. I can see the pretty sky colors through my bedroom window. I want to run outside and see the sky up close, but my room is a mess, and I'm supposed to be picking it up.

Someone's walking down the hallway. Mommy stops at my door. She says to finish what I can in a few minutes and jump in the bath. She says I won't miss any *Mutual of Omaha's Wild Kingdom* if I get going.

I can tell tonight is going to be a good night. Mommy is in a good mood. I wonder what's on *The Wonderful World of Disney* after *Wild Kingdom?* It's always good. I love Tinkerbell before the show starts. She taps her magic wand on top of the castle and sparkles fly everywhere. I wish I lived in that magic castle with Tinkerbell.

Someone gave me a Tinkerbell toy for my last birthday. It had powder and perfume in a box. I love the pretty colors on the box. Light green and pink. I smell nice when I put the perfume on my wrist the same way that Mommy does.

I pull clean yellow PJs out of my drawer and head to the bathroom. I'm looking for my favorite pink box in the cupboard. Yes! We have Mr. Bubble. I turn on the big silver knobs. One is hot and one is cold. I test the water going into the tub, but it's a little cold. I make some turns and test again, that's nice. I remember to plug the drain. Now I can pour some bubble powder in. Not too much. Perfect. Now I wait for the water to fill up more.

I hear the furnace come on and remember how cold it is outside. I scoot over to the vent and put my toes on top. It's warm and cozy in here.

The tub's getting full. I lean over the side to stare at the curly, clear ribbons. They're magically floating over the bubbles. I wonder if there might be some tiny dancing fairies in the water.

I jump when Mommy's voice is right behind me. "What?" I ask because I didn't hear what she said. Mommy's cold hand is on the back of my neck when she pushes me into the hot water. Is my skin burning? I think this is what the field fire would've felt like if Hansel hadn't saved me that time.

Mommy's pulling me out of the water. I'm crying. My skin's burning. Mommy's talking really loud. Why does she want to know what I was thinking? She keeps saying the water was too hot to get in. She's wrapping a towel around me. She says I scared her and thank God I'm okay. I like that she's hugging me. I stop crying so hard. This feels nice. She asks what would have happened if she wasn't there to save me?

I'm thinking, *Nothing would've happened. I wouldn't have been in the too-hot water.* I was testing the water to make it right. She's confused me. Did I fall in the water leaning over the tub to find the fairies?

Mommy says to finish drying off, and she walks away. I didn't fall into the tub. I just looked at the magic ribbons floating above the bubbles. Mommy pushed me in the tub. This hurts my tummy.

It hurts my chest. My head feels like it has the steam from the bath-water in it thinking about what happened.

I never see Samantha do things to Tabitha and say she didn't do it. I twinkle my nose and Mommy is Samantha. I feel happy warm as I put the towel on my hair. I put my PJs on and run to the living room. Matty's in front of the TV. *Wild Kingdom* is just starting.

CHAPTER 62

The Purse

I'm sitting on my bed with Barbie and chewing red licorice. The front door slams and the whole house shakes. I hear Daddy stomping around and yelling for Mommy. I hop down and spit red waxy stuff in the garbage can. I hear her voice yelling with his. They're both getting louder. Matty's in the hallway when I walk out. He holds up a finger and says, "Shhh." I nod because I know what we are supposed to do. We step real slow down the side of the hall toward the light in the living room.

I see Mommy holding her purse on one side, then the other. I think Daddy wants her purse. They're saying, "fuck you" and "fucker." Daddy grabs the purse and pulls things out, saying, "Where is it?" I see him push Mommy down and get on top of her. Mommy is yelling at Daddy to stop and says he's hurting her.

Matty's in his yellow Batman shirt in front of me. I wish I was Robin. He runs into the living room and jumps on Daddy's back. Matty's yelling stop, stop and calls Daddy a fucker.

I think of all the times Daddy says this to Matty. Sometimes to me. Sometimes Mommy says it too. But mostly she says it to Daddy.

I think of when Matty told me that "fuck" means a boy pee thing goes in a girl pee place. He said this is "sex." When I think of this, it makes my pee place hurt. Go away, thoughts. Go away. He said this is how babies happen in mommy tummies. Mommy buys Kotex at the drugstore for her period. She says I'll get mine when I'm older. She's says it's part of how babies are made too.

Daddy grabs Matty with both big hands and throws him onto Mommy's chair, where he bounces up and down. Matty's on his back holding up his hands when Daddy jumps on top of him. The whole chair scoots into the wall behind it. Daddy says Matty's scared now, he better be scared now. Daddy says he shoulda killed him a long time ago. Then he says more bad words and something about a mother. He has his big knees on Matty, and I see one arm come up, go down, the other arm comes up, goes down. He pulls both of Matty's hands with his one big hand to the side and hits Matty's face with his other big hand.

Mommy's lying on the floor wiping her face with one hand. The other hand just lies there. It's a pretty hand and I want to stomp it. Her shirt's all bunched up and she's pulling it down.

Matty stops crying and his nose is bleeding bad. I think about how he gets nosebleeds a lot. Daddy said he used to get nosebleeds when he was a boy. Matty said he liked that he has nosebleeds like Daddy.

Mommy gets up with a sound like a mad cat, but louder, and pulls Daddy off. Matty's face is covered in nose blood and tears. He just lies in the green chair with his chest going up and down, up and down.

Mommy hits Daddy, he hits, she hits. He pushes her down and they're yelling bad words. Mommy says get out, get out. She says go, run to your mother. I think she means Grandma. Mommy calls Daddy a fucking asshole and says, "Go have another drink, I hate you. I always hated you."

Daddy says, "Gimme the damn money," and grabs Mommy's purse again. He pulls out the green papers and gets up. He goes to the door saying, "I'm gone, I'm gone," and lots of bad names. "See what happens." He says he'll tell everybody about Mommy and how she did bad things and lied when they got married.

Daddy slams the door so hard I can feel the wall that's holding me up move.

CHAPTER 63

No One Else

Cinderella's green dress feels soft and kind of rough in my hand. Soft and rough don't go together, but that's how it feels. My left thumb and pointer finger are going back and forth on the little yellow patch in the dress now. This is when she didn't have good clothes. She only had scraps to eat. But she's beautiful. My right hand is petting her blond hair. I think she looks like me more than ever. But I don't think I'm beautiful. Her eyes seem blue like mine, but grayer. She's in my lap. I roll back on my bedroom floor and hold her close to my heart.

I hear the front door open. No slam. Good. My door is barely cracked open and I see Daddy walking. I hear him and Mommy now in their bedroom. They both sound mean. I slowly walk to the side of the wall by their door. I see it closing, but it bounces off the latch and stays open a little. Matty's standing in his bedroom doorway next to theirs. I walk over and hold his hand. We can hear Mommy and Daddy just feet away from us.

Daddy says Mommy's a bitch. He says, "You know, like the female dog? It's called a bitch because it does one thing, fuck the male, have the kid." I think, *That's two things.* I wish he'd stop, but he keeps talking and we keep listening.

"You're all high and mighty, but you're as bad as they come." Daddy says his mom and dad tried to warn him about Mommy. They said she'd been having sex with everybody from Spokane to Seattle. Don't be fooled just because she's got a college degree. "You're more fucked up than any bitch whore in Vietnam," Daddy says.

Daddy says Mommy told him she fucked a nigger when they were dating. And other guys too. I know the name Daddy says is a really, really mean word for black people. My heart hurts when I hear the word. I know what it feels like to be called really mean names. Mommy told me never to say that word. I don't know why Daddy says it. He and Mommy got the picture of the black man on their honeymoon. I remember when the glass on it got broken in the living room. I never knew who broke it when they were fighting. Now I think it was Daddy.

Daddy says Mommy was pregnant with Matty before they got married. He didn't know if Matty would come out black or white. He still doesn't know whose kid he is.

Matty's hand squeezes mine so hard it hurts, but I don't care. I look at the side of his face looking at Mommy and Daddy's room. It looks hard, like it turned into a rock. I can't feel anything on my face or legs or arms, just my hand in his.

Mommy yells, "Stop it!" She's yelling about Daddy's women and his cheating on her. She says he's giving our food money to other women. She's laughing in a scary voice and says she's lost count of all his women.

Mommy says they're both not perfect. Daddy makes a noise like I make when I have a tummy ache. He doesn't sound mad now. Mommy says she's made a lot of mistakes. One of the biggest mistakes she ever made was trusting Daddy. She's crying. Mommy says she trusted Daddy not to tell anybody some things.

Daddy says, "Well, I trusted you too, you know." Now he's crying.

Mommy says she knows.

They're both quiet now.

Then Mommy says Daddy's parents never liked her. She says she doesn't know why, except no one would ever be good enough for his mommy's son. She says his mom said bad things about her to other people.

"Mom says things because of what you've done to me, that's why." He says he wasn't good enough for her parents either.

Daddy says, "Talk about my mom, your dad attacked you when you were a teen. Remember that?"

Mommy says, "At least my mom didn't strap me to the bed at night."

Daddy's talking really slow. He asks Mommy if she knows what it's like to get shocked if you pee the bed.

My face says *What does that mean?* to Matty, but he shrugs.

Mommy tells Daddy that she doesn't know, but it must've been horrible. She says, "I'm sorry, honey."

Daddy says he's sorry to Mommy too.

It's quiet again.

Matty pulls me back from the doorway into his bedroom and slowly closes the door. He leans against the wall behind the door. I put my arms around his neck and hug him. His eyes are droopy and almost closed.

"He's your daddy," I say.

Matty looks at me. "How do you know?"

I lean against the wall next to him. "All our family says so."

Matty says, "They could lie."

I step back in front of him. "Matty, look at Daddy's pictures when he was your age."

He says, "I guess so." Then tears run down his cheeks like a faucet just turned on. "You're the only one I have, Deidi."

"You're the only one I have too."

"No one else could ever know what we do."

"Unless we tell somebody, Matty."

"We can't, Deidi. They'd kill us!"

"No, when we're big like Mommy and Daddy and say what happened. But not mean."

"Yeah, maybe, but they still won't know what it's like now."

I nod.

CHAPTER 64

The Gun

Matty's playing Trouble with me on the living-room floor. The news is on the TV. I love the sound the bubble makes when it's my turn to pop it. He's always blue and I'm always red. I hear someone come in the front door. Matty whispers, "I think Daddy's home." I whisper back, "He's been gone so long." We don't move.

Whoever came inside went in the kitchen. It sounds like they knocked something over. I stand up to see what's happening. Matty turns the TV off and follows me.

Daddy's sitting at the kitchen table. We say hi to him, and he says hi back, lighting the cigarette in his mouth. He has his brown jacket on like he's leaving. Matty picks the tiki head up, puts it back on the brick bench, and runs around Daddy to the end of the table. I sit at the other end. Daddy's in the middle looking out the windows to the dark backyard.

I hear the basement door open and the loud dryer noise. It goes away when the door closes. Mommy walks upstairs with a laundry basket under one arm. Daddy keeps looking outside. She pushes her thick hair away from her eye to one side with her free hand. She says she's glad to see he finally made it home and walks into the living room. Matty and I stare at him, but he doesn't talk.

Matty asks Daddy if he's okay. "No, buddy. Not doing so good." I ask what's wrong, and Daddy says too many things are wrong. He's pushing a pile of cigarette ashes around his blue ashtray. Matty's watching Daddy and chewing the end of his sleeve. I hear Mommy in the living room snapping clean shirts and pillowcases before she folds them. The house is silent except for smoking and folding sounds. Matty keeps staring at Daddy and lays his head on his arm. I hear the furnace rumble downstairs. I like the heat on my toes.

Daddy coughs and puts one hand in his pocket. He sits for a while. It looks like there's something in his pocket. I wonder if he's not sad, but happy with a surprise for us. Daddy pulls his hand out. Wrapped in his long fingers is something small and black. He isn't smiling. He puts the thing on the table with his hand on top. Matty sits up and I get on my knees for a better look. Daddy slowly pulls his hand back. A small black gun wobbles a little on the table. The long part on top is shiny. The handle looks like there's ivy carved on it.

I saw Daddy's gun on his dresser one night when Mommy and Daddy were getting ready to go out. I was sitting on their bed. Mommy was naked. Daddy came in after his shower and dropped a green towel on the floor. He was naked too. Mommy told him to put his wet towel in the hamper. Daddy bent down to pick it up and Matty flashed a Polaroid camera from the doorway. I saw Daddy reach for his gun and stop.

I'm looking at the gun on the kitchen table now.

Matty looks at the gun and at Daddy, then he asks, "What's the gun for?" Daddy's shaking his head, wiping his eyes, and smoking at the same time. He whispers something doesn't matter. He says it hurts too much, it's too hard. Daddy puts his cigarette on the tray and picks the gun up. He turns the handle with both hands until it's pointing at his face. I watch the tip of the barrel disappear into Daddy's mouth. I hear it click against his teeth.

I scream, "No, Daddy!"

Matty screams, "Daddy, stop!"

We both jump up at the same time. Matty runs over before I reach Daddy's arm. He blocks me and whispers, "Don't touch him."

I hear Mommy walk in behind us. She stands next to the three of us and stares at Daddy's head. She walks to the kitchen sink and says, "Just get it over with."

Matty and I yell, "No!"

Matty's telling Daddy to please stop. I'm crying and begging him to put the gun down. Matty's crying and says he loves Daddy. I say I love him. Matty says we need Daddy.

Tears run down Daddy's cheeks as he takes the gun out of his mouth. He stops, points the gun up and away from everyone. He partly stands and pushes it to the other side of the table. He falls back into the chair, and his head drops on both hands like someone shoved him. I lift my hands and see my whole body's shaking. Mommy's standing next to the sink. Her arms are folded over her chest. She's the only one not crying when Matty and I wrap our arms around Daddy.

CHAPTER 65

Grandpa on the Farm

The sun's shining as we drive to the farm this morning. I'm staring at all the wheat fields zooming by my window. I count the only three things I see. Fields, telephone poles, and a road. Not one car or truck passes for a long time. These wheat fields are big like the ocean, and they are full of hills that look like waves. The fields never, ever end. Daddy drives fast on these roads. The wheat's green in the spring, real green if it rains a lot. It turns yellow in summer. One side of a road can be green and the other side's stubble and dirt. If a farmer burns his stubble, the dirt will look black. Daddy says they burn stubble to kill weeds and feed the dirt vitamins. It's fall now, after harvest, and it's either stubble, dirt, or black everywhere.

Matty and I are staying at the farm today. Mommy and Daddy need to do some things. I'm happy because Daddy said there's a new Ping-Pong table downstairs. I see Grandma walking out the back door when we pull in the driveway. I get out of the car, and Lucky stops barking because Matty's petting him. It's so quiet here, there's no sound. Daddy said a person could disappear out here and nobody'd know. The wheat fields around the house would just swallow them up. I think about Grandpa's nephew who fell in the wheat when he was twelve and everyone said he drowned.

I'm running behind Matty down the steps to the basement. I see the green table with white lines and a net in the middle. Matty says, "Let's play a game, Deidi!"

Matty wins three games. But not really. He hits the ball after it bounces twice all the time. I don't like it when Matty cheats.

I yell, "Stop cheating, Matty!"

He steps back, drops the ball, and throws his wood paddle at my head.

I'm bleeding and crying as I run upstairs. Grandpa takes me into the bathroom and closes the door. I want Grandma, but Grandpa says she just left for her afternoon walk and she'll be right back.

Grandpa says I better take my shirt off. He says there's blood on it. I hear water running in the tub. I pull my shirt up and see the doorknob jiggle. Matty's yelling that he's going outside to play. Grandpa says okay.

Grandpa says, "Take your clothes off and get in the tub. It'll be easier to get the blood out and rinse this shirt." I feel embarrassed but do what he says. I'm standing in water up to my ankles when he stops the faucet. The shower hits the back of my head, and he says turn around. I hear the shampoo bottle squeeze as my wet hair sticks to my face.

"I can do this, Grandpa."

But he says, "What? No, better let me. I'll make sure the blood's out."

He's rubbing shampoo in my hair and rubbing his hands all over me. I hear the glass door and feel something beside me. "Here, Deidi, soak this in the water. Don't want a stain."

I bend over and push the shirt in water as he pushes his finger in my bottom. The door's sliding back. He's making dog noises. I stare at my floating shirt. The glass slides again and Grandpa's pulling me in front of him. His pee thingy's in one hand. He's pulling the back of my head to him with his other hand. He's pushing my head down. He's rubbing his pee thingy all over my face. He's whispering in a slow voice, "C'mon, open up for Grandpa." He's pushing hard into my lips and teeth. He's in my mouth and I'm gagging. He's shoving my head from behind with his hand. My left hand's banging the glass doors. My right hand's pushing against his arm. I can't breathe! I'm gagging more. Drool, tears, and snot are running down my face. I can't breathe! Grandpa's pushing and pushing his pee thingy down my throat. It's like Mommy's finger when I'm choking on a butterscotch candy. Something hot and bad goes in my throat, it feels like fire. He stops. Grandpa tells me to dry off and come out to get dressed.

I'm wrapping the gold towel tight under my arms. I look up and my face is bright red in the mirror. There's blood by my nose and mouth. I turn the cold water on and splash my face clean. I watch bloody water fill the sink and go down the drain. I open the door to the bathroom, and Grandpa is in the hall. He tells me to follow him downstairs. I can't hear anyone else inside. I'm following him past the fruit room. He's opening the next door. I'm following him but can't see in here. I hear the door close. Grandpa says the thing he just picked up off the floor is for me. He says hold my arms in front and then he yanks my towel.

Something dark and scratchy covers my head. It smells like a gunny sack. It is a gunny sack! Why am I in this? What's Grandpa doing? My body's shaking. He says, "Oh, I like that." He says keep my arms inside. The scratchy sack gets tight on my tummy. It hurts. Grandpa pushes my head. The cold floor hits my bottom. I'm being pushed and rolled. Big hands are pulling my knees too far apart. I only see black. No air! No air! Get me out! Get me out!

My scream inside takes me bye-bye. I'm skipping across grass in a big garden. I don't have shoes on. Hummingbirds are floating.

Doves cooing. Meadowlarks singing. Pink roses climb over a big wall. A white hammock is tied to tall green trees. I climb up and lie on soft blue pillows. A little wind's rocking me. I'm smelling lilacs and lilies. I'm watching a doe walking around a tree. She lies down in the grass. Two white cats are curled up and purring next to me on the hammock. A dog like Hansel's licking my arm. I hear wind chimes far away.

I'm back and it's quiet. I push my arms out a little. I'm still in the gunny sack, but it's not tied on my tummy. I sit up, pull the sack off, and push my tangled hair out of my face. It's not wet anymore. There's a tiny light under the door. I'm patting the floor for my towel and feel something. It's kind of sticky, like the gooey rub Mommy puts on my chest at night when I have a cold. It doesn't smell the same. I find my towel, wrap it tight around me, but when I try to get up, I almost fall.

Everything hurts. I crawl toward the light on the floor. I stand and feel for the doorknob. I twist the knob, but it won't open. I'm trying again, pushing in and pulling slowly. The door opens and I see my clothes laid over a chair. It feels like happiness just got pumped in me like air in a balloon. I dress fast and race upstairs to the bathroom. My cheeks are red in the mirror and my hair's crazy. I'm brushing it out and taking lots of big breaths. The cold water feels good on my hot face. I steal a little of Grandma's pink lotion.

Grandpa is sitting in his big chair in the living room reading the paper and says somebody sure smells good. I say it's me because I stole Grandma's lotion.

I hear her voice say, "That's your lotion too, Deidi," from the kitchen. She's back from her walk. I race around the corner and jump in her lap.

CHAPTER 66

Marbles Bribe

Mommy got a red yo-yo for Matty and a yellow yo-yo for me. Matty knows how to do a bunch of tricks. He's teaching me how to "walk the dog." I'm not very good at it. Matty says, "That's okay, Deidi. You'll get the hang of it." He keeps telling me to relax my wrist. I don't think that's the problem.

Even though I can't walk the yo-yo dog, I love my yo-yo. I like to watch it spin up and down, up and down. It looks like a sunbeam when I get it going really fast. It's like I'm spinning yellow sunshine while Matty's doing a "cat's cradle." I wonder why so many yo-yo tricks have animal names.

Matty says he wants to show me something in his room. I drag sunshine down the hall with me. I can hear Mommy talking on the phone in the kitchen. Sometimes I can tell who she's talking to, but I'm not stopping to listen. Matty's bed is messy. I tell him he should make it. He closes the door. "Why'd you close the door?" Matty says because he doesn't want Mommy to see what he's got to show me.

Half of Matty disappears under his bed. I can see the word "Toughskins" on his jeans above his butt. I say "butt" sometimes with Matty and other kids. If I say it to Mommy or Daddy they might get mad, or not. So mostly I don't. I crouch down and ask what Matty's doing. He says, "Just a sec." He sounds like his face is smooshed in a pillow or something. One leg scoots out, then the other leg scoots out. Now he's standing, his face is all red, and he has a little brown bag in his hand.

"What's that?"

Matty says it's his special marbles bag.

I want to know where he got it, but he doesn't tell me. He just pours the marbles on the floor. These are nice marbles. He's got a cat's eye and a couple bumblebees. He's got two shooters that are blue.

"Wow, Matty. Where'd you get these bumblebees?" I ask.

He says he played a kid at school and won them in keepsies. I hope he didn't steal them; he does that sometimes when he really wants something.

Matty picks up a blue shooter and rolls it between his fingers. He's looking at me when he says, "Any guess how rare this one is?"

I shake my head.

He says it's the only one he's ever even seen. He says it's the luckiest shooter he's ever played with because he's never lost. That's how he says he got the cat's eye and bumblebees. I ask if I can hold it and he says yes but be super careful with it.

I hold the blue shooter up to the sunlight coming through his window. It's so beautiful. I say I wish I had a shooter like this. Matty says, "How much do you want one?"

I say a lot.

He tells me I don't have anything valuable to trade him for it.

I say I would trade my yellow yo-yo for this marble.

"Nope. Not valuable enough."

I tell him that's not fair, the yo-yo is so valuable.

Matty says, "Hold on, I'm thinking."

I'm rubbing the blue shooter on my T-shirt when he says if I show him my bottom and let him touch it, then I can have the blue shooter. I say okay but just once, and he nods. I pull my pants and undies down. Matty says to bend over the bed. I tell him to hurry up. He's poking around my bottom and then he pinches my pee place really hard.

I yell, "Owww!" and pull my pants up. I want to kick his face, but my undies are still stretched around my knees and stuck in the pants at my waist. I pull my undies and pants up and run out of his room down the hall to mine. I can tell Mommy's watching TV, and I don't want to see her.

I close my door quietly behind me, flop on my bed, and cry out all the tears inside.

CHAPTER 67

Archie Bunker

Daddy's smoking in the living room. He's waiting for the TV show he likes to start. "Hi, Daddy," I say and sit on the floor. I put Velvet in my lap so she can see. "Hi, Deidi," and the music starts. The only words I know to the song are *Those were the days*.

I wish the names and words were gone from the start of the show. I could see the neighborhood better. I know the family lives in New York. Their last name is Bunker. The show takes "a break." That's what Mommy and Daddy say when there's a commercial. They get a lot of breaks. I like some of the things I see when they break. They show shampoo, food, and toys. I tell Daddy that Eloise lives in New York too. He says he doesn't know her. I start describing the Plaza Hotel, and Daddy says, "Not now, Deidi. The show's back on."

I can hear lots of people laughing somewhere, but I can't see them. Velvet's doll hair is long and I'm practicing braiding. I hear people laugh the same way each time.

I think about another time I saw this show. Bad things happened in the Bunkers' neighborhood. The daddy's name is Archie.

He was scared and said he had to protect his family. He wanted a gun. Archie's friend loaned him a gun. Archie's married to Edith. Their daughter and her husband live in the same house.

I remember how Archie's family didn't want the gun. They all got mad about it. They didn't like guns. I like Archie's family. Archie tried to hide the gun. He kept it secret. He lied to his family and said he gave the gun back to his friend.

I think about how Archie makes fun of people. He's mean, but Daddy thinks it's funny. Archie hates black people. He calls them bad names. Mommy says Daddy's like Archie because he calls different-color people names. I don't think Daddy calls people bad names when he sees them. He does it when they aren't here. Archie does the same thing.

But Daddy doesn't call all different-color people bad names. Ali the boxer's black. He says he's the greatest. Daddy says so too. The TV says some people are mad at Ali because he won't go to the war. Daddy went to the war, but he isn't mad at him. And Daddy says he liked the different-color people he talked to who live where the war is.

Mommy says the war hurt Daddy. But then she calls him stupid all the time. Daddy says he can't be stupid and do secret things for the army. I don't think Daddy's stupid. Sometimes I think he's mixed up. I think Archie is too.

Big people are confusing. The show's taking a break now. I ask Daddy why he calls Mommy "Edith." He says it's because she's stupid like Edith.

I tell Daddy that Edith's not stupid, she's different.

Daddy whispers, "Don't tell Mommy that, 'cause then it won't bug her as much."

I whisper back, "That's not nice, Daddy."

He winks at me and lights another cigarette.

I like Edith because she's always helping people. That's not what Mommy does. But I think maybe Mommy does nice things for the students she teaches. Maybe she's nicer to them.

I think a lot about when Mommy's happy. Most of the time, she's not. Matty says she's happy about her students and her school. If Daddy's gone and Matty gets mad at Mommy, he says mean things about her students. He says she should go back to her school. Matty says Mommy likes them better than us. He says this a lot. Mommy was happy when she bought me new shoes. I'm glad I thought of that.

I jump when Daddy yells. The show's back, and Archie's daughter, Gloria, is talking to her husband. Daddy always yells at them. I can't hear what they're saying. But Daddy says Gloria's a women's libber, and he yells at her to shut up. I wish I could say she can't hear him, but I'd be in trouble, so I don't. I think Gloria seems nice like her mommy. My hair's like hers. I like her clips. Daddy's yelling at her husband now. Archie calls him Meathead. Mommy said it's not a nice name. I'm happy that Gloria and Meathead go out their front door.

I start thinking again about the show I saw before. Two black robbers broke into the Bunkers' when they were at a movie. A neighbor called and a robber answered. He pretended to be somebody, I don't know who. The neighbor said a store was robbed by two jigaboos. He said they're hiding in the neighborhood. Mommy said jigaboo's a bad name for black people. The robbers were black men.

The robbers walked down the stairs with a bag when the family got home. Archie's gun was in a robber's hand. Edith, Gloria, and Meathead got mad at Archie because he lied. The robbers used the gun to make the family let them hide at the Bunker house. They couldn't leave because no black people lived in the neighborhood and they'd get caught. They'd go to jail.

The robbers laughed at Archie and called him a bigot. Mommy says it means he can't stand people who don't think like him. The robbers laughed when they told the Bunkers about growing up with no food but lots of brothers, sisters, and rats. Edith didn't like this. The robbers liked Edith. It hurt her to think of kids with rats and no food.

I'm sad for the robbers. I think they laughed about things that are owies. Matty tries to make me laugh if I'm crying. He says he hates it when I cry. I wish that was true all the time.

Daddy says, "It's bedtime, Deidi."

CHAPTER 68

Jack's Bargain Barn

Mommy's at the kitchen table with lots of papers and stamps. I ask what she's doing, and she says, "Bills." I wonder if it's fun, and she says, "No." I sit next to the fireplace. I'm counting the rows of bricks from the floor to the bench. I count five. Eleven rows for the fireplace. I stand on the bench and count four rows to the white mantel. I jump down and walk backward to the kitchen. There are ten rows of bricks to the white wall. I skip by the front door and closet to the living room. I count twenty rows of bricks from the floor to the mantel. Same as the kitchen, but white. I count five dark wood bookshelves from there up to the ceiling.

I lie down in a sunbeam coming through the smaller window. It's on the same side of the house as my bedroom window. I bet I have a sunbeam in my room too. I run past the TV and the green bathroom to my room. There it is, another sunbeam. I run back to the living room.

Mommy says we don't have any food for dinner. We need to go to Jack's Bargain Barn. I heard her thank God she got paid. I love going to the Barn. They sell candy, pop, cookies, ice cream, and Pop-Tarts. It's a big store. Mommy lets me push the silver cart sometimes. They play happy music inside the Barn. Mommy said she doesn't know Jack. She buys meat from a man that cuts it in a big machine. He knows her name. She doesn't bake like my grandmas, so it's good they have a bakery. I can see their pies and cakes inside a glass machine that keeps them cold. Sometimes I get a free cookie sample. The Barn's always clean and smells like fruit. I like it when the wind blows in from the front doors. The red and white streamers twist. Somebody at the Barn makes a lot of signs that hang between streamers. If it's Christmas, the signs have Santas on them, and if it's Easter, the signs have eggs and bunnies. I bet today they'll have Santa signs.

I hear Mommy say, "Okay, kids, time to go." That makes me happy. I beat Matty in a race to the car for once. I'm bouncing on the front seat. He's not happy and says I cheated, but I didn't. Mommy tells Matty to stop whining. I watch her put on sunglasses and turn the key. One of her mommy's plastic flowers from Davenport Flowers hangs on her key chain. The flat flower glows in the dark. We drive down our gravel road, and the water tower across the street gets bigger. I hear *tick-tock, tick-tock* and we turn right onto Highway 17. I see Wheeler Road up ahead. Different-color trucks pass each other. If we turned right again, there'd be one bad thing and two good things on Wheeler Road. Good is we'd see lots of cows and cross the little bridge over the river. Bad is we'd go by the stinky potato plant and smell farts. I'm glad we're turning left.

Mommy says we're going to the post office first. I'm looking out the window and there's our library. I wish I could get a new book, but I'll wait. I want to be inside the Barn! I see the stores and food places downtown. I tell Mommy there's a dress with orange flowers in a store's window that'd be pretty on her. She says she'll have to look later. We're going too fast for me to count rows of bricks on part of a building.

The post office has lots of papers taped to the glass door. I see Mommy mailing her envelopes through the window. A big American flag's waving outside. It's the same as the flag at the library. The green flag next to it is Washington's flag. It's kind of boring with a yellow circle in the middle. Mommy slides her purse on the seat and closes the car door. We're on our way to the Barn now. A really noisy motorcycle pulls up behind Mommy, and Matty goes crazy. I hear him talking to himself about speed and sound. I wonder if there will be any oranges at the Barn. I love to eat and smell oranges.

Mommy's saying, "Deidi, Deidi, goddammit! I'm talking to you."

I turn from the window to look at her as the round part of her fist hits my head and ear. The other side of my head hits the window, and everything is nighttime with sparklers in the dark. Light comes back, but everything is blurry. Did my head break? My hands grab the side of my head, and my glasses slide off my nose. *Why did she just hit me? Why?* I'm yelling inside. I didn't do anything. She's not talking. I rub my wet eyes. Still blurry, but not as much. Through my snot-covered fingers and tangled hair, I see her hands squeezing the wheel. She parks the car and tells me to wait here. She says to think about what I did. The doors slam, and I watch Matty skip into Jack's Bargain Barn next to Mommy. He looks back and waves at me with a sad face. I can feel bumps on both sides of my head. It makes me jump in my seat it hurts so much when I touch them.

I roll the knob on my door to let the window down and fresh air in. I listen to the banners tied to the store's rooftop flapping in the wind. Another car pulls up next to me, and two teenage boys run inside after they slam their doors. I wish I was one of them, but a girl.

CHAPTER 69

Protecting Daddy

Mommy's yelling at Matty and me that dinner's ready. He says, "Race ya to the kitchen." Matty gets a head start and wins. My head still hurts from where Mommy hit me. He's getting bigger, faster, and stronger all the time. I just seem to be getting taller and skinnier. Daddy's smoking at the kitchen table. Light gray ashes circle the green tray he's using. I tell Mommy it smells good in here. She tells us to set the table. Matty whispers to me, "That's your job, Deidi. Winner sits."

Daddy tells Matty to sit next to him. He stops for a second. When Daddy says to pull a chair over, a little smile starts to show. Matty's eyes open wider as he pushes the greenish, bluish chair closer to Daddy's. He climbs up and puts his elbows on the dark-brown table-top to hold his chin. Daddy messes Matty's hair. Matty reminds me of a wiggling puppy. Daddy drags a shiny magazine from the middle of the table in front of them.

I hear Matty saying "Wow" and "That's so cool" over and over while I set the table. I see the magazine's pictures of guns and hunt-ers when I set Matty's place next to his elbow. Daddy's telling Matty all about some special rifle at his daddy's house. Matty gets to use it when they go hunting at Duck Lake. I wipe off Daddy's ashes and fix one of the ties for the white drapes on the kitchen windows. I pull stiff white fabric back to the side of the big middle window and slip the hole in the tie over the gold hook on the wall. I finish setting the table.

Matty asks Daddy if they can target shoot for practice before they go to Duck Lake. Daddy says, "Sure, we can do that." Mommy brings dinner to the table. Daddy and Matty are talking about bullets and moose and deer hunting. I hope they stop talking about guns and shooting. I look at the fried chicken, green beans, and mashed potatoes on my plate. I'm so hungry! Matty and Daddy start eating Mommy's yummy dinner. Matty wants to know if Grandpa's going hunting with them, and Daddy says yes.

Mommy says of course he is. "Your daddy must always be with you too." She has a mean voice, I don't know why. I see Matty watch Daddy look at her with a sad face. Matty pushes his plate away. He puts the magazine in front of Daddy's face and asks about a picture.

Mommy drops dishes in the sink with a loud bang. I see Daddy wipe his forehead and blow his nose with his handkerchief. He shoves the handkerchief back in his pocket as Matty starts talking faster. When Mommy walks back to the dinner table, her face looks like a face rock that can't ever move, except to blink. Mommy takes the last dishes away and drops them in the sink. It sounds like breaking glass this time. Daddy shakes his head.

Mommy's in front of me and shoving Daddy and his chair to the floor. She's yelling and saying he's a "sonofabitch." He does whatever Grandpa wants and never gets the money we need. She pushes his head on the floor with her foot. She says, "Are you going to run to your mommy now?" She throws her foot behind her and kicks him in the back so hard his whole body moves to the wall. She's kicking his sides and long legs. Something flies past me. I see Matty tackle

Mommy like those big men on TV football. He holds her legs as she falls hard on the floor. Everybody's on the floor but me. Mommy's yelling at Matty to get off. Daddy sits up holding his back and yells for Matty. He looks over at Daddy. Matty gets off Mommy with a shove from his heel and runs to Daddy. Daddy stands up slowly with Matty glued to his front. Mommy's lying on the kitchen floor looking at the ceiling. Daddy looks at me and waves for me to come over.

I hop off the chair, push Mommy's chair out of the way, and wrap my arms around Matty's and Daddy's backs.

Matty and I jump when Mommy starts yelling at Daddy. She wants to know if he just saw what Matty did to her. She wants to know if he knows what a monster Matty is because of him. Matty yells, "I'm not a monster." Daddy stands up with Matty in his arms and me holding his leg. Mommy says to Matty that's not what she meant. I don't know what she's saying.

Daddy takes us into the living room, and we sit on the floor together for a long time. No one talks. I keep hearing the swish of a match and the click of an ashtray moving on the table in the kitchen.

CHAPTER 70

Looking Inside

I'm glad it's a new year, and I'm glad to be back at school. A lot of kids wish they were still on break, but I don't. I'm happy at school.

School's over today and I'm skipping down the sidewalk to find Matty. I hope he's okay after this morning. He knocked over a glass of milk in the kitchen. Daddy hit Matty's arm with the back of his hand. He said he's told Matty a thousand times to watch what he's doing. Matty said it was an accident. He kept saying he didn't mean to. Daddy started hitting Matty's other arm with the back of his hand. He said, "Oh, didn't mean to, baby boy?" and hit him. "Didn't mean to spill, baby boy? Huh?" He hit him again. "Just too big a baby to not spill? Huh?" and more hits. "Oh, is the baby gonna cry now? Does that hurt?"

Mommy started doing the dishes. She walked to the sink saying, "You asked for it, Matty."

Daddy hit him over and over until Matty slid into the corner. Daddy punched his arm with a big fist. He shook his hand like it was wet, turned and walked out, slamming the front door.

Mommy was putting on her coat and grabbing her purse when she told Matty thanks for ruining the day. "I'm late now," she said. "How many times have I told you not to talk back to him?"

I stopped on the sidewalk in front of the school. I don't see Matty anywhere. I walk down the street past our school, and that's when I see him tackling another kid in the grass. Matty's sitting on top of a boy with both hands on his neck. The boy's arms are flying around like he's swimming. Matty punches his tummy. The boy twists and Matty punches his back. He jumps off and starts kicking the kid's head. I yell Matty's name and he stops. The kid rolls over and runs away. I don't see any grown-ups.

Matty grabs my hand and pulls me along as he starts running. He says he doesn't want to get in trouble. We run down the hill all the way to Frank's. I'm breathing fast. My chest feels like it's burning. Matty asks, "Got any money?"

I shake my head and hold my knees.

"No candy then," he says.

I don't care about candy right now.

Matty says, "Don't tell what happened, okay?"

I say, "I won't, but stop fighting!" I tell him he's scaring me.

Matty promises he'll stop fighting. He makes me promise again not to tell.

I nod. "Is that boy okay, Matty?"

He says, "Yeah."

I ask how he knows.

He says, "I just know."

I say *I don't know* to myself.

After we get home, I walk into the living room, and Matty's on the floor looking at a book about race cars. It's more pictures than words. He can't really read. Mommy says nobody knows why. Sometimes he writes letters backward and doesn't know it. Matty can't read out loud very well either. He reads super slow. He sounds out hard words but gets them wrong a lot. It's easy for me to read. I can write but can't spell lots of words. I read better now that first grade's almost done. There's a boy in my class at school that can't read like Matty. His cheeks get bright red when Mrs. Wallace asks him to read out loud. Why does she make him read in front of everybody when he is so bad at it? If Mrs. Wallace asks who wants to read, I put my hand in the air every time. I like to read, but mostly I don't want her to pick on somebody else who isn't very good at it. It makes me think of Matty.

Mommy's on the phone in the kitchen. I hear her saying Matty's doing much better. But I know he's getting in more fights all the time. Mommy tells whoever is on the phone that Daddy's spending more time with Matty, that he's taking him hunting. But I know Daddy's not here very much, and when he is, he's almost always mean.

I sit in the flower chair listening to Mommy and staring at the back of Matty's head. I think about how he got in a bunch of fights this week. I saw him pick up a branch and smash it on a kid's head. The boy just fell in the dirt and didn't move. I thought he was dead, but he got up and ran home bleeding and crying. No grown-ups were there. Another time he shoved a kid and broke the boy's glasses. Matty ran after him laughing and yelling that the boy peed his pants.

Mommy tells the phone person the other boys start the fights and pick on Matty. Sometimes I hear her say, "As a teacher," and then why nothing's Matty's fault.

When I hear her hang up the phone, I run into the kitchen and ask, "Mommy, does Matty's teacher make him read out loud in front of his class?" She wants to know why I'm asking. I tell her about the kid in my class who is really bad at reading too. She says different kids learn differently. She says Matty's learning to read slower than his class, but he'll catch up soon. I wonder how she knows.

Mommy didn't answer my question, so I ask again if Matty's teacher makes him read out loud at school. "It happens sometimes." I feel my face getting warm. I tell her that's not fair. I say some kids are mean to the slow reader in my class.

Mommy says it doesn't bother Matty to read out loud in class. If I was in a comic book, a white cloud would float over my head with a yellow light bulb inside. I bet she makes slow-reader kids read out loud in her class. I say, "Okay." But my mouth bursts out, "Teachers and grown-ups don't tell kids that slow readers aren't stupid. And it's stupid to be mean to them!" Mommy's eyes are getting big. I can't stop. "They don't say kids learn different." Mommy's eyes are real big. Her head leans to one side. "You're not better than Matty because you read faster, Deidi," she says in her mad voice. My brain feels like it's breaking. "I didn't say that, Mommy."

She grabs my arm and pulls me into the living room next to Matty. Mommy looks at me and says I need to be reminded of some things. She says Matty's a better athlete than me. She says he wins more sports games. I nod, and Matty's smiling. She says he's better at shooting guns and hunting. I nod and so does Matty. I don't say because I don't hunt. Mommy says Matty has a lot more friends than I do. I nod, but my heart explodes. Matty stops smiling and looks at me. She says people like Matty more because he's funny and smart. He likes to be with people. Mommy says I'm too shy, and that makes people think I don't like them.

I should say the kids Matty beats up don't like him. I should tell her how Matty lies when Daddy gives him black eyes and how he says he fought a bad person and won to make kids like him. I should say I'm shy because I'm scared of saying something by accident, and if I do, Mommy and Daddy will leave me in the basement forever or shoot me in hide 'n' seek.

Mommy's voice is just noise now. I'm thinking how much I want to yell at her. I want to yell how much I hate that Matty hurts people who didn't do anything because he's so mad all the time. I want to yell that he's a bully because he has too much hurt. I want to yell in her face that she makes Matty and me have too much hurt. We're always mad, we're always sad. I want her ears to feel like they're going to pop because I'm so loud when I yell, "You're mean. Daddy's mean. You both want to be mean! You never stop it! You don't stop it because you don't want to stop it!" All these words spin in my head like a tornado. Mommy looks scared and wants to know why I'm rocking. I look at her and think two words: *I can't.* Tears roll down my cheeks instead, and I blurt out, "You're not always right about stuff, Mommy."

She points her finger to the window and tells me to go outside and cool off. I walk through the kitchen to the back door. I sit in the grass for a while and cry. The cold outside makes me cry even harder. I watch my tears fall on my knees and roll down to the grass. The Velveteen Rabbit's tears bring a fairy from the flower. Cinderella's tears in the garden bring her fairy godmother. I watch each tear drop below me. I don't think anything like that will come from all these tears.

"Deidi." I look up at Matty standing above me. "Mommy was nice to me but not to you."

I nod.

"Why does she say those things?" he asks.

I shake my head.

I stand up and say, "Does Mrs. Madigan ever make you read out loud at school?"

Matty's looking at me but not talking. His head moves to five after on the clock. I'm learning to tell time. No words. His face looks sad. No, he looks mad. "Why, Deidi?" He doesn't ask very nice.

Some butterflies are in my tummy. Maybe I shouldn't have asked. I start talking too fast and tell him about the kid in my class and how other kids make fun of him. Matty spits in the grass and stares at me. I'm getting scared. He's not talking. A lot of butterflies fill up my tummy.

Matty tackles me to the grass. He wrestles me to my back and pushes his butt into my tummy real hard. He pins my arms above my head. I'm wiggling a lot but can't get loose. What happened to my glasses? His hand is on my throat. He squeezes my neck so hard the light starts to go away. His other hand digs into my wrists. Hansel's barking at both of us. I'm trying to scratch him. He lets go of my neck, and I yell, "Get off me!"

I flip over. I'm almost facedown in the grass. He's punching my back. I push my back up and down to get him off. He keeps punching. My hand is free. I throw one arm behind me. I feel and hear it smack into Matty's face. His weight gets lighter and I buck him off.

I watch Matty holding his face. I sit down cross-legged and rub my tummy with one hand and my back with the other. "Matty! Stop hurting me!"

He looks down at the grass. "Why do I read so slow?" He's shaking his head.

"I don't know, but you're as smart as anybody."

He asks, "How do you know?"

I say, "Because I'm with you all the time." I'm smiling a little. So is he.

"Thanks, Deidi. Sorry." He gets up and walks away.

I stand on the step to the back door, lean into the kitchen window, and push my face between my hands. The sun is on the other side of the house, but it's still bright out. The glass feels cool on my face. The kitchen's empty. Through the walkway to the living room I see the top of Matty's head on Mommy's lap. She's petting his head, and I hear her start singing to him.

Hansel's pushing his wet nose on my elbow. Animals know when people hurt. I don't know how they know, but they do. I slide my back down the side of the house to the concrete. I sit down and stretch my legs in front of me. Hansel's paws cover my knees and he lays his head on me. He stares at me. I stare back at him. Hansel's helping me, but no one else is.

It's so quiet outside I can still hear Mommy's singing. I close my eyes and sing with her in my most quiet voice. We sing about a senor and senorita who want to be married, but they can't unless the bells ring. They aren't supposed to ring, but then they do. They *chi-i-i-ime.*

I wipe my wet face and snotty nose with my purple sleeve. This makes a streak down my arm. It sounds like Mommy's walking into the kitchen. I hear Matty talking in a happy voice.

I'm smelling something good for dinner when I hear Daddy's car in the driveway. Hansel and I walk around the garage. I say hi to Daddy as he gets out of the car. Daddy gives me a one-arm hug as he puts a cigarette in his mouth. "Hey, you almost scared me. Why're you walking out here in the dark?"

I tell him I'm in trouble with Mommy.

He says, "Let's go inside."

Matty runs up to Daddy. His cheeks are red. He says they made a spaghetti dinner for us. Matty says he set the table. He's talking about draining noodles and washing radishes for the salad. I should be happy, but I'm not.

CHAPTER 71

Garage Stairs

It's still winter but getting closer to spring, and it doesn't feel as cold all the time. I've seen little green buds on some of the plants and tree branches outside.

Mommy's gone, and Daddy's friend is here. He looks like Daddy, but shorter. I guess his hair's darker too. They've been drinking a lot of brown bottles. Matty and I hear gunshots and run into the kitchen. We can see through the kitchen window that Daddy and his friend are shooting their empty bottles off a fence post.

We hear Daddy's friend say he needs to take a piss. Daddy follows him in the house. He opens the fridge. He sees us, wobbles and says, "Hey, what're you two doing?"

Matty says we're watching them shoot.

Daddy's getting more bottles when his friend comes back. He says he's got a great idea. Matty and I can't hear what they say to each other. They're looking at us. Daddy says to follow them. He opens the front door and pushes Hansel inside. We go out the door and walk on the cement to the garage. Dark-gray rain clouds sit on top of the fields as the wind whips hair across my glasses. Daddy opens the garage door and hands his bottle to his friend. Inside he flips the light switch and reaches for the hanging blue bead. He yanks wooden stairs out of the ceiling. Daddy jumps on the bottom step and leans over the middle until we hear a snap. He says, "Let's go!" I watch the back of Matty's tennis shoes take one step at a time. He stops for a second and looks back at me. His face looks like I feel. The stairs again. We don't say anything. Daddy and his friend are ahead of us laughing. I want to jump over the rail to the pink flowers on my bicycle seat below.

Daddy holds the door at the top of the stairs. There's stuff stacked by the walls and spiderwebs hanging from the ceiling. Daddy tells his friend the widows don't like it up here because it's too warm. I know he's talking about black widow spiders. Daddy closes the door, and I open the front door to Grandma's house in Davenport.

There's a closet door on one side and Grandma's desk on the other side. She says it's in a nook. I like that word. Sun from a small window shows the shiny wood top that rolls up. It matches her chair. I can't see where the top goes. Inside is the place Grandma writes. There are stamps in one little drawer, blue pens and black pens in another. Her pencils, all sharp, are in their own drawer. She has paper with flowers on the bottom part. She uses it to write letters. I don't know who she writes to, but she said there are lots of people.

My throat's burning as I look through Grandma's cards. She buys these before birthdays and special days, she said. My hand's shaking, and I drop a card. I'm choking on my throw-up. Matty sounds like he's gagging. I see Daddy's friend hitting him. Daddy growls and says he can't believe the little fucker bit him. Matty's not making a sound now. Daddy shakes him until he coughs. My bottom hurts a lot. I have sweat all over me when Daddy and his friend leave.

I go back to Grandma's house.

CHAPTER 72

Gunny Sack

After buying a Tootsie Roll and tiny-size Chiclets at Frank's, Matty and I ride our bikes to the park. The sun is a bright-yellow ball. We were supposed to go home, but we don't want to. A new station wagon is parked by the water tower. It's blue on top with wood like Beverly's basement on both sides. Matty unwraps and bites the short Tootsie Roll in half to share with me. We watch a mommy and daddy carry coolers and baskets to a huge blanket they laid in the grass. Lots of kids pile out of the car and follow them to the blanket. Cold chicken, potato salad, and watermelon slices fill the paper plates. I chew my Tootsie Roll and pour tiny Chiclets into my hand. I hear laughter, the snapping of pop tops, and soft voices for a fussy baby. Matty wants the green and purple pieces. I get all the pinks and yellows. I split the oranges to be fair.

We watch the daddy walk back to the car with one of the barefoot boys. They have the same shiny black hair and pretty skin, like the color of caramel apples at Halloween. I chew my gum as the daddy opens the tailgate and hands something to the boy. He runs back to his mommy. The kids start jumping up and down when their daddy returns with a pile of sacks. Each of the kids gets a gunny sack, and they run to get in a line together. I watch them hop inside the sacks feetfirst. The smallest girl has to fold the sack in half before tucking it under her armpits.

My gunny sack is on headfirst. Daddy stopped yelling and kicking me, but if he hears me breathe now, he'll kick again. I'm lying under the ceiling string he just pulled. No more light's coming in the burlap on my face. Daddy says to think about all the things I've done and shuts the door. My bare feet are cold on the cement. Daddy's thin rope around the burlap feels like it's cutting my ankles in half. I'm lucky now because he used to tie the end closed with my feet inside. I can still fit all of me in the gunny sack, but I act like I can't when he's tying me up. My heart starts scary pounds when I remember being all the way inside the gunny sack. I push the fabric away from my face a little, but my heart pounds harder. It's pounding in my ears. A wave of scaries squeezes my tummy, my throat, my head. I'm going to die without more air.

Go back to the picnic!

I'm not sure, but I think the oldest boy let the oldest girl win the first gunny-sack race. I think he fake-fell at the end. Matty thinks so too. We sit in the grass together and watch the races from far away. The girl is so excited. Her black ponytail waves back and forth when she jumps up and down. The smallest girl skips to her sister with a red, white, and blue ribbon. It looks like the kind I've seen at the fair for the best sheep or bunnies. This one is homemade. After more races and ribbons, the family sits down for dessert. They sing "Happy Birthday" in a language I don't know. A girl in a red sundress and two braids sits on her heels in front of a big chocolate cake. She blows five candles out with help from her brothers and sisters. Everyone claps and cheers.

The doorknob clicks. Quiet cheers in my ears! Daddy pulls the light bulb on. I've been down here for a long, long time. I'm wet all over. I feel warm fingers untying my ankles. Daddy's voice sounds nicer now. The burlap scratches my nose as he's pulling the gunny sack off. I grab Daddy's chest with a big hug as soon as my arms are free.

"You're the very best Daddy in the whole world! I'm sorry, sorry, sorry for all my bad things I've done!"

Daddy says, "Okay, princess. I'm glad you've learned your lesson." He pats my back a little.

I can breathe! I don't care about a lesson. There's no lesson. There's never a lesson. I don't know what bad thing I've done. I don't care.

"Just please don't make me do this to you again, okay? You need to understand this is much harder on your daddy than on you. Okay?"

I nod. It's not true and I don't care. I'm alive. I'm ollie ollie oxen free.

"Good, Deidi. Remember that."

I race ahead of Daddy up the stairs into the kitchen. Mommy's at the kitchen sink. "Mommy!" She turns and I run into her with the biggest hug. I look up at her as she wipes her hands on a kitchen towel above my head. "I'm sorry, sorry, sorry, Mommy!"

She pulls wet strands of hair from my cheeks and says maybe someone's learned a lesson. She turns back to the sink. I hear a top pop off a brown bottle, and Daddy says he thinks so.

He's squatting next to me as I'm hugging Mommy from behind. Daddy pulls my ear to his face. He whispers what he always whispers now. If I tell about the bad things, I'll never get out of the next gunny sack.

I nod and turn to face Daddy. I give his head a big hug.

Mommy says, "Good girl, Deidi."

CHAPTER 73

Strip

I'm so sleepy. I put PJs on and climb in bed. I want Baby with me. I jump up and get my doll. We're snuggling under the covers when the door flies open. The hall light makes a long square from the corner of my bed to my face. Daddy walks in and turns on the bright ceiling light. He slams the door behind him.

I'm sitting up with Blankie by my mouth. He yells, "Get out of bed." I jump out, and he says, "Strip." I'm taking off my yellow PJ top as he unbuckles his belt. I see his shaky hands unzip his pants and push them down. He kicks the pants behind him and puts a hand in his underwear. He points without shaking and says, "Take those off." I'm bending over and pushing my undies to my feet when he says, "Don't move." He's moving toward me. He's pulling his underwear down and grabs my chin. He lifts my head up. His hand squeezes the sides of my jaw. He pushes his pee thingy in my mouth, and I leave.

I remember the Blow Pop I had yesterday. It took a long time to get to the gum in the middle of the sucker. I don't like Blow Pops as much as I like Tootsie Pops. Chocolate Tootsie Pops are still my favorite. I have chapped lips. The sucker left a sore on my tongue.

My whole mouth hurts and I taste blood when I see Daddy's black socks walk behind me. I think blood's pounding in my head. I don't know what he's doing. A hand's pushing me, and I step forward. It looks like his knees are bent behind me. Is he sitting on my bed?

Something wet and warm slides on my pee place and bottom. What's happening? No, no, no. Is Daddy licking me? My head yells *Stop!* My pee place feels tingly, like I need to pee, but not. What's happening? Daddy's moving around behind me. His hand's covering my face. My bottom feels like a knife's tearing it.

I'm at the ocean. Water sprays my cheeks. Baby, Hansel, and I run in warm sand to the blue waves. I feel scared and look behind us. Small white wings fly near me, and I stop. It's like a hummingbird, but not a hummingbird. It's a bird, but something else. The something-else bird says, "Remember, Deidi." I ask how the something-else bird can talk. Tiny red lips kiss my cheek. The tip of her wing touches my finger, and I remember. I'm not scared. I'm not cold anymore.

Warm softness wraps my hand. It looks like Baby's hand. I follow the plastic hand to the arm to the body and head as the parts melt into real baby skin. She doesn't have any teeth in her smiling mouth. Baby's smiling at me. I can't see it, but the shape of a hand takes her other hand. How can I see something that's not there? The same hand holds my hand. We're in a circle. I jump when water covers my toes, feet, and ankles. Water covers my legs, bottom, tummy, chest, shoulders, arms, hands, neck, and head. I'm feeling warm and clean. I think all my hurt's washed off. I look for Baby. She's gurgling and floating in a white blanket. My hand moves with the jerks of her arm. I look for what's holding our hands.

The tiniest breeze tickles my face. She whispers, "I'm sorry," in my ear. It's so loud everything shakes. None of it was supposed to happen. More shaking. She knows me, every hurt, every icky. She says Baby's me. Everything's better, and I sleep.

I'm still sleeping when two black dots push my eyelids open. Daddy's gone and my room's different. Where're my drapes? There's a new shade on my window. A light, a strong light's pushing under wavy edges of the shade into my room. I'm scared. I think I want to hide. What is this? My room's full of something big. I can't see it. Inside my head, I hear a sound I know. I breathe, close my eyes, and sleep again.

I wake up to sunshine coming through the drapes I've always had, into the room I've always had. Something's moving on the wall. I turn to see the tiniest wing leave sparkles floating in a sunbeam.

LEAVING FIVE

The sun moved, and the leaves stopped dancing. The light covers two moving boxes now. I get up and push the boxes out of the way so I can sit inside the warm sunshine on my floor.

These moving boxes are getting full. The room waiting for me in Bellevue is empty. All my memories make me feel empty, but there's something heavy in my tummy. I feel empty and heavy at the same time, like I swallowed a big rock. I love pretty rocks, but I don't like to see rocks in the guts of dead animals. All the times Daddy made Matty and me look at dead animals from hunting swim around my head.

I remember when Daddy came home after duck hunting with his daddy. He told Matty and me to go in the garage, to help. I watched him cut a duck in half with the knife from his belt. He pulled the duck's guts out on the table. That's when I saw rocks inside. Daddy made Matty pull guts out of a duck. It covered his hand in red slime. I started to gag, and Daddy yelled at me to stop. He said if I didn't stop, I'd be digging guts out of four more ducks. He put his arm around Matty's shoulder and said, "You did a great job." Matty begged Daddy to let him gut the next duck.

He cut it open with Daddy's knife and didn't look sad or scared at all.

I remember when Daddy shot a deer and hung it by the hind legs in the garage. He made Matty and me watch him stick a knife inside the shoulder, cut around his hand, and pull the bullet out. He put the bullet in my hand. It looked like a mushroom. He said, "One bullet took this big deer to the dirt." He patted its side and said, "This here's just another dead animal. Reminds me of all the bones buried at the farm." He walked behind the deer, lit his cigarette, and said, "But nobody knows about nowhere." Daddy said to think about the bullet. He said it cut all the skin, organs, and bone. He gave me a big hug and picked up his gun. I felt better when he said, "Don't be scared, Deidi."

Then he cocked the gun and said one last thing. If Matty or I ever talk about what happens in our house, there'll be more than dead deer hanging in the garage. "Do you understand me?"

Matty said yes right away, but I was too scared and just nodded.

Daddy shoved me hard and yelled he couldn't hear me.

I said, "Yes."

I remember the deer's big brown eyes were open, just staring up at me from the brown slats its head was lying on. I thought the deer face would be scared, but it wasn't. It didn't look scared at all. It looked beautiful. I don't know why, but I was glad the deer didn't look scared to be dead.

Daddy said he knows how to kill things. I heard him tell Matty never, ever go up to the animal you just shot from anywhere but its rear end. He said if the eyes are closed, it's still alive. Daddy said only city hunters cut big game when it's down to see if it's alive. He waved a long knife in the air. He said if someone shoves it in a downed animal, watch out. "If it ain't dead yet, anything can happen." I'm not sure what happens. I didn't ask.

This makes me think about how hunters like Daddy trick animals. The horn they blow to call ducks brings the birds close, and the hunters shoot them. Mommy's daddy, my uncles, and Daddy go hunting for elk and sometimes for moose. Those are big animals. Somebody makes the sound of a baby moose in trouble to trick the mommy. She comes running to help, and the hunters kill her.

Mommy says there's no hunting allowed in Bellevue. I hope that's true. I asked her if there're coyotes in Bellevue, and she said no, but Daddy said there might be. I'm going to miss the coyotes. I've listened to them howl since I was a little girl. Last time we drove home from the farm, the coyotes were howling. I think they were saying goodbye.

I push a moving box with my purple sock foot and stare at the ceiling, thinking about how Grandma in Davenport says big daddy elk, or bulls, like to roll around in their own pee. She says if elk meat ever touches the skin of a bull, it's not allowed in her house. Daddy rolls around in some animal's pee before he hunts. I don't remember which one, but it's another trick.

I've been tricked before. I remember when I was tricked at school. It's like I'm there again and I'm happy in first grade. We're running outside for recess. Some of the girls ask me to help look for four-leaf clovers on the playground. I pick a yellow flower and I'm twirling it, when I see two boys waving. Are they waving at me? They're in Matty's grade. I tell the girls I'll be back. I hope they see where I'm going. They'll wish they were me.

I skip across the grass to the boys. They ask if I'm Matty's little sister, and I nod. One boy's wearing a blue velour shirt with a big circle on the zipper. He says, "Matty's cool." The other boy's wearing long sleeves with brown and beige stripes. He says, "Matty's got a cute sister." Really? I can't help smiling a little. He just said I was cute. This is the best day ever! They tell me to follow and we go around the corner of the school. They like me. They picked me to play with. We're standing in front of cardboard boxes by the school garbage. They say it's a secret. We all crawl inside the biggest box. The boy in blue says, "Nobody can find our hideout." This is a hideout, and I'm in on their secret!

I'm feeling a little squished in here. I don't like small places. My heart's starting to beat a little faster. Why's blue shirt scooting behind me? He says we're playing a game. I need to let him hold my arms. Okay, it's just the game. Brown-stripe boy's in front of me and says, "Okay, go." He pushes his hands up my skirt so fast. His nails scratch my legs. He's pulling my undies and shorts. What's he doing? The boy behind me squeezes my arms and says, "Get her!" I twist until I bend my arm and elbow his chest. The boy facing me leans over and pushes his hand between my legs. He's grabbing my pee place real hard inside. I kick the boy's face. He hollers and grabs his cheek. The other boy's hands loosen when I twist and elbow him again. I pull my clothes up as I fly outside. I'm running back to my classroom when I hear the recess whistle blow.

Mommy said she told the principal it's not like me to kick somebody for no reason. I like remembering this. It seemed like Mommy stuck up for me. I don't like remembering what else happened when I got home.

But I like remembering one other thing about this. Matty said he was going to beat up those boys. I don't know if he did. But I liked it when he said that. I don't like it when he beats up other kids for no reason. I'm scared of how much he hurts them. I'm scared of him getting hurt. I'm scared he'll hurt me.

I'm lying in the sunbeam, trying not to think of this anymore. I'm a kitty getting warm.

But now I'm thinking again. Mommy and Daddy play tricks on me too. I'm happy when they're happy. I'm not happy when they're not happy, but they trick me a lot.

Daddy gets real mad at me and says it's because I'm flirting at school. But he tells me I'm the best little girl. I hear him tell grown-ups I'm the best little girl. I don't flirt with boys. I'm too shy. Daddy says I try to be sexy with boys. I don't. But then he's happy when he says I look sexy like Elly May on *The Beverly Hillbillies*.

Kids at school say the big purple house on the way to Moses Lake is a whorehouse. Ladies live there and have sex with men they don't know for money. Mommy and Daddy says sluts are ladies who have sex with men they don't know, not for money, but because they're bad.

Daddy says Mommy's beautiful before they go out at night. He says he's the luckiest man in town because he always has the prettiest lady in the room. But when they come home, sometimes Daddy yells that Mommy's a slut and a whore. He says she sits on men so they can touch her bottom and have sex. Mommy yells the same things about the ladies she calls his "girlfriends." Then they hit each other.

One time Daddy said I make other kids mean to me because I'm a slut. He said parents talk about girls like me. I ran to my room crying, but Mommy came in and said, "Just ignore Daddy." She said it wasn't my fault and told me how Daddy's girlfriends tell him bad things. She said they're not true.

Mommy told me I was beautiful and said everyone tells her so. She said I'm smart and can be whatever I want when I grow up. I was so happy. I thought about a lot of things I could be. I worked hard to think what would make Mommy the most proud of me. I promised to work harder in school. I was happy for the longest time. Bad things happened and didn't hurt so much. I thought of what Mommy said to me, and the bad went away.

But it was just a trick. She's mostly mad at me.

Mommy said she's sorry for being mean to me before. She said Daddy's so mean to her it makes her mean to me. I felt sorry for Mommy. But Mommy and Daddy are mean to each other. Why does that make her mean to me? Sometimes I wonder why I feel so sorry for Mommy and Daddy when they're so mean to me. I can't help it.

I stomp my foot because this makes me mad!

I squeeze my fingers into fists.

My head's shaking back and forth. It's dark in here. Where am I?

I don't want. I don't want. I don't want Daddy to come in my room. I stomp both feet. I don't want. I don't want Mommy to come in my room and take me to the bathroom. Stomp. More stomps. I don't want. I don't want to be here. The lights are on. I'm back.

I'm stretching between moving boxes. The sun moved away from me on my carpet, so I scoot to it.

PART V: AGE SEVEN

CHAPTER 74

Grandma and Grandpa

Everything has happened so fast since I turned seven. It's like looking through my glasses in a steamy bathroom. I finished first grade two months after my birthday, and it's all been a blur since Mommy and Daddy told us we're moving to Bellevue this summer.

I've been packing so much. My dolls, toys, books, and clothes are just about ready for the trip over the mountains. I close my eyes and remember the day after we started packing.

Mommy, Matty, and I are taking a break from packing and driving up to Grandma and Grandpa's house in Davenport. It's super hot and smells like it's going to rain. We walk to the back door, and Mommy says the grown-ups need to talk. After Matty and I hug Grandma and Grandpa, we ride bikes to the tennis courts. Grandma and Grandpa have bikes for us. I love riding bikes, but sometimes I'm like a cat. I don't like getting wet. I feel sprinkles from the dark clouds and tell Matty I'm going inside.

I walk up the back steps and hear talking through the screen door. I quietly open and close the door behind me so no one hears. I sit on the top step of the stairs to the basement. No one can see me, but I can hear some of what the grown-ups are saying in the living room.

Grandma says Matty behaves better when he's with them. Grandpa says, "You can't deny this." I hear Mommy say she agrees, but something else I can't hear. Mommy says Daddy has problems from Vietnam. She says he's a different person when he's not drinking. She says he's a good man and they know what he's like. No one says anything.

Mommy says she's tried to get help from Daddy's parents, but they told her to stop saying their son's a drunk.

My mind wanders and I think about when I heard Mommy say on the phone that her daddy can't drink. I don't know why. I heard Grandpa tell Daddy and my uncle that he can sneak a sip when Grandma's not looking. He said if she catches him, all hell will break loose. I think about how I've never seen Grandma or Grandpa drink.

I hear Grandma saying, "But he is a drunk." Mommy's voice sounds a little mad, and she says, "I know, Mother. That's not the point." Grandpa tells Mommy to simmer down. She says, "I can't simmer down, Daddy. You're telling me to give my son to you to raise because I'm not doing a good enough job!"

Grandma's voice is loud when she says, "Good grief. That's enough!" Grandpa tells Mommy they're just trying to help her. Mommy's crying and says how hard and scary everything is because of the money, the drinking, his parents. Grandma says quietly, "And the other women." Mommy's voice is loud when she says, "What are you talking about?" Grandma says softly that everyone knows. She says Daddy doesn't try to hide it, and people talk. Mommy's crying harder when Grandma says she needs to face something. Grandpa says she's got to think about her children first.

Mommy sort of yells that's all she ever thinks about, the kids and how we're going to survive. Grandpa says Matty's problems are scaring everyone and it's not getting better. Grandpa says he may not be on the school board anymore, but he still talks to people. Mommy says he has no business talking behind her back. Grandpa says, "It's most definitely my business."

I'm thinking about Matty. They know how much he needs help! I'm scared and happy all at once. I'd miss Matty so much, but maybe Grandma and Grandpa could help. Grandpa says something about Matty not being with them for good. He says everyone could try it for a while when we move to Bellevue and see how things go. Mommy says that's not going to happen. She says Daddy would never agree. She says Matty's his son too. Grandpa says Daddy needs to start acting like a father.

Mommy says, "What about Deidi?" But no one says anything. Why are they all quiet? What about me? Does anybody want me? Mommy says how well I'm doing in school, how much everyone likes me. Really? She says how well-behaved I am. She wants to know how she can have such an amazing daughter if she's such a horrible parent. Amazing daughter? She thinks I'm an amazing daughter? Grandpa says they aren't saying she's a horrible parent. Grandma says people are worried because of Matty. And because of things they see Daddy doing.

Grandma says if the children are Mommy's priority, she needs to consider a divorce. I know that means not married anymore. My chest freezes. Then it breathes bigger than ever. Back and forth. Grandma says times have changed, and people get divorced nowadays. Mommy's sighing and says, "You don't know what you're talking about." Grandma says she knows exactly what she's talking about. She says a lot of names. She says they're all people they know who got divorced.

I remember when Mommy said on the phone if she ever divorced Daddy he would tell her parents bad things about her. Mommy said he would tell them she slept around. Mommy said Daddy told her his parents would do something to make sure she never saw her kids again. But why are Grandma and Grandpa talking to Mommy about divorce to help us if we wouldn't be with her? They said everybody knows about Daddy doing bad things.

Grandma says, "Mothers get the children. In your case, there's no question."

I hear Mommy tell Grandma to stop. She says she's not divorcing Daddy. Everybody's quiet.

All the words I've heard feel like they're crashing against the walls of my head inside. Anything that happens is all bad, all sad. I need fairy helpers to come.

Then Grandma says she needs to get dinner started. I tiptoe down the stairs and go out the shop doors. I run up the steps to the back door and walk into the kitchen where Grandma is. She says we're having ham, potato salad, green beans, and carrots for dinner. Grandma says, "Guess what I made for dessert, Deidi?" I smile and say, "Pound cake?" Grandma nods, and I say, "Yeah! My favorite!"

I want to see the magic face. I walk through the living room and the hall to the guest bedroom. The angel's face and wings are still on the wall, but she's not here.

I can't feel anything.

My eyes open to the spot on my wall where I see her. I wish I could wrap her up and put her in one of my boxes.

CHAPTER 75

Last Memories

My bedroom is almost empty. The boxes left are almost full.

I miss Hansel so much my chest is bursting. It bursts even more when I think of Grandma in Davenport. She says we'll see her a lot, but we'll be a long way from her.

I'll be a long way from Beverly's house too. I think about walking to her house after school. We always looked for the big green tree in her front yard. Her house was real close to Lake Hill and Frank's Market. I'll miss those places too. I spent so much time at Beverly's. She always made me happy. I know she likes me too. I stop thinking about Beverly because it hurts too much.

I'm rolling back and forth on my carpet from bottom to back.

I think maybe I want to move more than stay. Lots of people will be there. Mommy and Daddy act better around other people. They don't do bad things to us around other people. Neighbors' houses will be right next to us, not far away in endless fields. I'll be able to see Sophie a lot. Maybe I'll have more friends from the new neighborhood and school where more kids are. Maybe everything will be better.

Matty keeps telling me he doesn't want to move. I asked him why. He said we won't have grandmas and grandpas, our school will be different, and we won't have friends. He said it's going to be scary. He told me he thinks Mommy might keep us in Moses Lake. I don't think that's true. Matty said he has a plan if she doesn't. He makes plans to get monsters and bad guys.

I think about how Grandma and Grandpa want Matty to live with them. I wonder if they would like me to live with them. I don't think so. I only heard them talk about Matty. I don't want to leave Matty here because I'd miss him. I'd be scared without him. And I'd be scared about what would happen to him. Even though he scares me too.

I don't think Matty will stay in Davenport without us. But if he wants to, maybe he'd get better and not have so many hard things happen. I would have the hard things, but maybe Matty wouldn't. I think Grandma and Grandpa would be nice to Matty. But Grandpa might lose his temper like he did with Mommy. He pushed her down when she was a teenager and started punching her face. I heard Mommy and Daddy say this. It made me mad at Grandpa. I've only seen him be nice to people. I heard Mommy say he got his temper from his daddy. She told Daddy that Grandpa's daddy used to beat the crap out of his kids. Matty beat the crap out of me a lot. Not very long ago, Mommy caught him and got real mad. She pulled him off me and threw him around the room. Mommy punched Matty real hard.

I remember one time when I fell asleep in the car on the way to the farm. Daddy was driving with Mommy in the front seat. Matty and I were in the back.

I woke up when Daddy hit the brakes. I was scared and didn't know what happened. I heard Daddy and Mommy yelling at Matty to get out of the car. Mommy was turned around in the front seat. She'd unbuckled Matty and was pushing his shoulder to the door.

Matty looked like he didn't know what to do. They yelled even louder until he got out of the car. His door was shut and Daddy drove away fast. Matty was screaming and running. We were far away when Daddy stopped the car. Matty kept running and running. When he climbed back in the car, his face was brown from dust. He was breathing real loud. I grabbed his hand and squeezed.

I remember when Daddy was driving a motorbike around and put Matty on the back to go for a ride. Daddy said to hold on tight. Matty was smiling when he wrapped his arms around Daddy's waist. Then I heard Matty crying in the front yard. I ran outside and saw him sitting in the grass. His legs were cut and bleeding. I asked what happened, but he couldn't talk very good. His voice was all scratchy. Matty said Daddy drove through a wheat field. He said Daddy wouldn't stop when the wheat started cutting his legs. Matty said, "I was screaming, but he kept going." He said they stopped someplace and Daddy disappeared. He left Matty on the motorbike for a long time. His legs were bleeding, but he couldn't move. He told me he thought he'd die because the motorbike was still running.

I remember the times I've seen Daddy sleeping in Matty's bed in the morning. It makes me feel like bad ghosts are in the house. Matty says Daddy wakes him up and makes him take garbage outside in the middle of the night. It wakes me up when I hear Daddy yelling at him. Sometimes I see beer bottles all over when I get up in the morning before anyone else.

I remember all the beer bottles when Daddy took us to a babysitter's house one time. He got in a fight with her before he left that night. They sounded the same as Mommy and Daddy do when they fight. Mommy said later that's because she's his girlfriend. The babysitter said she knew Daddy let Matty drink. She gave Matty a beer. She gave me a beer, and I barfed after the first sip. Matty likes beer and drank the whole bottle. He drinks beer with Daddy more and more. They used to do it when Mommy was gone. Then they did when she wasn't. Sometimes she said, "You really shouldn't," to Daddy. Then she didn't say anything. Matty seems wobbly and really, really happy when he has beer. I don't like it. That's how Daddy is at first when he has beer.

I remember when Matty and I were watching Grandpa, Daddy, Hirsch, and other people harvest the wheat. Grandpa and Daddy said a storm was on the way and they had to move fast.

The combines cut the wheat, stop next to the big truck, and fill it up. Daddy said they had to "fill on the go" to save time. Matty and I were sitting next to Daddy inside the dusty cabin of the combine. I don't know who drove the truck. We were going up and down hills. Grandpa's combines were made to stay flat on hills. The truck stayed right next to us. Daddy watched the truck, the sides, the back and front, all at the same time. The combine engine noise changed when he moved gears and pushed buttons. I could barely hear the truck engine over the loud combine. I knew from rides I'd taken in the trucks that the driver was pushing and changing big gears too.

Daddy yelled, "Steady! Here it comes." I saw a jet of gold berries shoot into the back of the truck. Daddy yelled, "Pick it up, pick it up, c'mon!" The truck had to be under the combine's auger when the wheat poured. It's like an arm. The dust started blowing up, and it was hard to see. They were moving fast.

When they finished and Daddy cut the engine, my ears were ringing. Daddy wiped the sweat and dirt off his face. He looked at Matty and said, "I hope you got all that 'cause you're next." Matty's eyes got big. I said, "What does that mean?" Daddy said Matty's going to work on the farm and drive the truck next harvest. Matty stared at Daddy. It would be so scary to drive one of those big trucks, I thought. Even scarier to think of Matty driving one. I remember trying to figure out if he's big enough to reach the pedals.

Daddy was wiping down the cabin windows. He said Matty gets to stay at the farm for harvest. Matty's eyes got even bigger. I asked, "How long?" and Daddy said, "Few weeks or so."

Matty told me he didn't want to go to the farm for harvest. He knew it was coming up soon. He kept saying it made him sick to think about going. I told him it'd be good to get paid money. Matty said he didn't care. I know he takes money from Mommy sometimes when he's not supposed to. He keeps it in a Folgers coffee can behind toys under his bed. I helped him clean up once and found it. I promised not to tell. I've seen him get in Grandma's purse on the farm too.

Matty said Mommy and Daddy want him to go away for harvest to get rid of him. I asked why. Matty said Mommy and Daddy are giving up on him. I asked what that meant. He said they don't care about him anymore. He said he's too much work and has too many problems. Matty said he's heard them. They don't want him. He said it doesn't matter what he does, it's never good enough. He thinks they hate him.

I said, "Mommy and Daddy don't hate you." But Matty thought I was just trying to make him feel better. No, I wasn't, I said. Inside I was afraid I was lying. But I hoped not.

I roll to my side on the carpet, lay my head on my elbow, and stare at the moving box in front of me. I keep staring and staring. My eyes hurt from not blinking. I close them.

CHAPTER 76

Janie

I jump when Matty opens the door. He says to get up and grab my shoes. He's down the hall when I hear him say something about Mommy and errands. I go outside, and Matty's already in the front seat next to Mommy. I climb in back and shut the car door. Mommy says to roll the windows up so dust doesn't get inside. She lights a cigarette. I ask her if I can go to the library while she does errands. Mommy says, "Sure," out of the side of her mouth. She brushes Matty's leg with the back of her hand and says he should go with me. Matty says, "Nah, I'll help you, Mommy." She says that's nice of him.

Mommy pulls into the library parking lot by the front doors. She says have fun and they'll pick me up in an hour. I wave and run inside. It's cooler in here than it is outside. There're a lot of people in the library today. A tall man with pens in his pocket says the presentation's about to start. He says it's for grown-ups, and kids can stay in the children's section. That sounds good to me. I wish this wasn't my last time here.

I hope no one else's in the bathroom. I'm walking by the front doors when I hear a lady's voice. She says, "The first time we looked at who's abusing children in Washington State was four years ago in 1968." She says they'd never kept records until then.

I slow my steps. What's "abusing children"?

She says, "These records show that parents hurt children more than anyone else."

I stop behind a rack of paperbacks and pretend to read. Abusing means hurting?

"The state reports that over half of all child abuse in Washington was committed by a parent."

Air's stuck in my throat like a lemon drop. My face's hotter than the worst sunburn. Why's the lady talking about me? Are they looking at me? I'm too scared to look. I squeeze the yellow paperback in my hands to stop shaking. I step back with my head in the book and my eyes looking up. No one's looking at me. She said "over half." She said "children." She's not just talking about me.

The lady says something about programs to help parents. "But protecting children needs to come first."

Then the lady says, "Almost one in five of the cases were sexual abuse."

The burning sun outside the library window hurts my eyes. The ice-cold blizzard inside makes me start coughing. I feel like I'm falling off a cliff. I'm grabbing sky over the scary rocks at my back. What did she just say? Words turn into bald-eagle screeches mixed with a long red-tailed-hawk cry. Two soft heads hit the middle of my back. I lose my tummy when the eagle's wings lift me like an angel. The hawk's not keeping up with my lower half until a snowy owl takes my feet. I'm laid at the top of the cliff as she blinks yellow eyes back to the book in my hands.

The lady says we have a new law. It helps protect abused children. She says, "It means all doctors, nurses, teachers" and words I don't know "must report child abuse if they think it might be happening." She says if they don't tell, they are "legally responsible." I think about Mommy being a teacher. Is she in trouble for not telling on herself and Daddy?

I cross my legs so I can keep listening and not pee my pants. She asks if there're any questions. Another voice says, "I've seen a man hit his kid and shove him to the ground. Is that abuse?" The lady says, "Yes." I can't wait anymore and run to the bathroom. I pee and race to wash my hands. I walk out and people are everywhere. The program's over.

I walk slowly to the kids' section. I hear the lady's voice that was talking. She's a black woman. Her name tag says "Janie." She has gold hoops in her ears and a cloud of soft hair around her face. I like her white blouse with the big collar. The long sides of her tan vest match the length of her black skirt. Her boots are almost the same color as her brown legs. I stop at the shelves behind her and try to listen.

A tall lady with glasses covering most of her face asks a question about the new law. Janie says, "See, here's the thing. Anyone working with kids must report if they think a child's being abused. Hurting children is the worst thing. Remember what I said, kids die from abuse in Washington every year."

The blizzard whips up inside me again.

Another person says something I can't hear. Janie says, "Anybody can have a baby. Raising a child is a different thing. There's an old saying, 'Blood is thicker than water.' But love is thicker than blood. Children aren't property."

Someone asks, "You mean taken from their family?"

"Yes, if they're hurt too much. They need to be with a family that really loves them, really takes care of them. We have a long, long way to go with all this. There's barely anything set up right now to keep kids safe."

I'm glad Mommy's late picking me up. Almost everyone's gone. Janie's putting papers in a box. I've been watching her from a little table. She grabs a purse and starts walking to the front door with her box and a folder under her arm. She's telling the library workers thanks. I jump up fast and run to the door. I hold it open, and she says, "Well, thank you so much, sweetheart." I run to get the second glass door for her too. She thanks me again. I can't help following her.

I say, "Can I help?" She stops walking and looks at me. I look at her. We're just standing in front of the library. I don't feel shy for once.

She starts to smile, and I see her perfect white teeth. She says, "What's your name?"

I say Deidi.

She says her name's Janie and it's very nice to meet me. Janie points and says her car's right there. She says if I can hold the folder while she opens her trunk it would be a big help. I follow her to a red VW bug. "The trunk's in front, Deidi." There's an extra wheel in her trunk, but nothing else.

Janie bends over and puts her box inside. I hand her the folder. She sticks it between the box and the wheel. She tells me to stand back before pushing the lid down. I watch while she digs through her big macramé purse. She says, "I hear you, but I can't see you. There you are." She pulls out a big silver ring of keys.

Janie says, "Where are your parents, child?" I tell her Mommy's running errands with my brother, and I don't know where Daddy is. I blurt out, "Do you live in Moses Lake?"

She probably thinks I'm a weirdo, but she's nice and says, "No, no, sweet girl. My job brought me here for just a couple days."

She stares at me. "You know something? You remind me of my daughter. She likes to know about people too. That's a good thing."

I ask what her daughter's name is. She walks to her car door and says, "It's Ahanti. It means eternal and indestructible."

I ask what eternal and the other thing she said mean.

Janie smiles and says, "It means she can never be broken."

I'm embarrassed when I get tears in my eyes for no stupid reason. I kick a pebble with my shoe and say, "I like that."

Janie puts her hand out to shake mine. I want to hug her but shake hands instead. I've never touched a black person before. Our brown and beige hands look like the colors belong together. Janie's still holding mine when she squats in front of me. She says, "Look at me, child," in a voice no one else can hear. I look at her. She has the darkest chocolate eyes I've ever seen. She says, "You are eternal and indestructible, Deidi. Don't ever let anyone mess with you, child. You hear me?"

I nod, and Janie says, "Tell me."

I say, "I hear you," and then can't help myself. "You're so beautiful!"

Janie smiles and says, "That's because of what's inside me, Deidi." She points to my heart. "I don't know how, but when you keep trying to do good, even when it's so hard and scary you can't see straight, beauty always somehow comes outta that. You understand?"

I say yes in my strong voice.

She stands back up and thanks me for helping her. She says it was so nice to meet me. Now she's got to pick up her little girl. We wave and say goodbye. I stand in the same place and keep looking at her car drive away. I keep looking after I can't see it.

I hear a car pull up behind me, and Matty hollers, "Hey, Deidi, let's goooo!"

I climb in the back seat of Mommy's car. I say, "Goodbye, Moses Lake library," to myself, but I'm not sad. I keep saying *Ahanti* over and over in my head.

CHAPTER 77

Coyote

Mommy picked up a bucket of Kentucky Fried Chicken on the way home from the library. She gave Matty her change. He said he's saving money for something important. He won't say what.

After dinner Mommy says we need to go outside and look at the sky. The sun's going down, and it's bright orange and yellow with some white clouds stretched in between pink colors. Matty says, "It's nice," and goes back inside. I put my hand in Mommy's while we stand together for a second. She takes her hand and says she needs to finish cleaning up.

I'm in my bedroom thinking I ate too much chicken. I fall on my bed. My tummy feels big. I like how Mommy came and got us to see the sky. I hold my tummy and think about Ahanti. When I have a real baby someday, she'll be Ahanti. I'm so tired and not tired at the same time. All I can think of are Janie and Ahanti. I feel like I'm flying away with them. We fly like birds. Then we float. We're napping on white clouds. I wake up on my bed. I'm thinking, *I can't tell Matty, Mommy, or Daddy about Janie and Ahanti.*

I jump up to get my jewelry box. I lift the white lid, and the tiny ballerina twirls to music. I pull out a pink square and see the two dollars I've been saving are gone. The music keeps playing as I tiptoe to the hallway. I hear Matty's voice in the living room.

I walk quietly to his open door. I wiggle under his bed and see his toys piled in the corner. I dig around and find the coffee can. My elbows pull me to the square of light coming from the hallway. I take rocks out of the can and pull up the silver circle. Matty made it to hide his secrets. That's what he said when I watched him cut the tinfoil. There's some money, Bazooka bubble gum, gold bullets, and white paper rolled up in a thick rubber band. I unroll the crinkled paper.

This is Matty's writing.

It says *fisT day o scol in belVu.*

What about the first day of school in Bellevue?

Underneath is *gun, nives, gas, machs.*

Why does he need a gun, knives, gas, and matches?

I flip the paper over and read *BeRn scol.*

Burn school?

My heart and my head boom at the same time.

I roll the paper and rewrap the rubber band. *Boom, boom, boom.* I put everything back in the Folgers can. I shove it to the corner and pile toys around it. Everything's pounding. I get out from under the bed and run to my room, closing the door behind me. These booms are going to blow me up inside. I'm on my bed.

What do I do? What do I do?

I'm falling through my bed, through the floor, through the ground, through all the dirt in the world, into space. Never-ending space. I'm leaving everything.

I jump from the sound of a crash in the hallway. Daddy's home. He's yelling something about his gun. I crawl to the end of my bed, stretch to grab the knob, and open my door a little. I see Matty slumped against the wall by the blue bathroom. He's wiping his nose. Mommy's screaming, "Why did you take Daddy's gun?" Matty says to shoot people. Daddy reaches down and picks him up by his shoulders. Matty's gone until the crash sound happens again. Matty's sliding to the floor. Daddy screams, "You're a fucking devil!"

I see Mommy by Matty's door with both hands on her mouth. Matty's in the air again until his head bounces off the wall. He falls to his side with a thud. He's not moving, crying, or making a sound. There's no sound anywhere. Nothing's moving anywhere. They're both standing and staring at something crumpled on the floor in the hallway. It's like one of Matty's spitballs after it falls off the ceiling.

Cold sweat has pulled my glasses down. I breathe without breathing. No finger, toe, or muscle's moving. My eyes are staring without blinking. Mommy's on her knees next to the wadded-up thing. She's looking at Daddy standing in front of it. Huge slow words spill out of her mouth like foam. "I think he's dead."

Daddy just stands up straighter and stretches his long arm like a baton. His watch is undone and dangling at his wrist. Mommy's eyes follow his moving arm past Matty and the empty hall. One finger releases from his fist like a bullet shot between my door and the wall.

The coyote scream explodes outside. I fly across my bedroom, turn the latch, and lift the glass in my window. My hands and knees hit the wet grass.

Lightning flashes and I see everything like the sun exploded. A growl turns my head to black-lined amber eyes.

He's in charge.

It's like someone dipped a big brush in speckled gold and painted one stroke from his black nose to the tip of his long tail. All the fur beneath glows white like the moon. Sharp ears point me to the trees.

The wind that's almost knocked me down so many times when it came in waves and circles on the fields pushes me up.

I'm running as fast as I can. Past the big trees that scratch my arms and legs until we're in the open field.

I follow the dust from the coyote's paws hitting the wheat and dirt. His big tail is moonlit. It's pointing at me as I'm following him.

I need to think fast.

I need help.

My head screams, *You can't die, Matty. I can't die. Run.*

Headlights are moving toward me faster on Highway 17 than I'm moving toward them.

Run! I can't stop.

I can't keep running. I'm falling. My hands are hitting the ground. Coyote's in front of me. I feel his fur and see his face.

I know this face. It's her.

Coyote's the magic face. She's the coyote. They're the same.

I jump back up.

The wet nose wipes my leg and pushes me across the highway to the park on the other side. I hear voices. Someone says, "It's okay, sweetie, it's okay. Just slow down." I feel people lifting me. I say I think they killed him. I point to the only house across the highway.

CHAPTER 78

Maybe

I open my eyes, but everything's blurry. My heart's racing. Who was holding me? Where'd they go? Where are the people?

I pull the tangle of wet hair off my face and see a moving box in front of me.

My lungs won't let enough air inside. What's happening? I grab handfuls of blue carpet. I hear nothing. I feel hands squeezing my shoulders and see two black Converse tennis shoes with loose bows that belong to only one person.

"Deidi, what the heck? What're you doing?"

The sound of his voice shoots through me and lifts me to my feet. I grab Matty and pull him into my room. I'm crying and talking fast. What happened? What happened! Are you okay?

Matty says, "You're weird. Why're you wet? Let go of me."

I let go and say I need to know where Daddy is.

Matty says he's not here. He says I know he's not here. Matty walks backward to the hall. He says we'll see Daddy later, in case I forgot that too.

I'm alone again.

It was a dream. A dream. A dream. A dream? A dream!

I never met Janie. I wasn't at the library today. She was never there.

There's no Ahanti.

I'm so sad I can't move.

But how did I know all the things Janie said? Where did I learn that?

Stop. I remember. The news. It was on the news. I heard those things about how we have a new law and protecting kids. It will come back to me where I heard *Ahanti* before too.

More pictures float through my head. I wish Janie and Ahanti were real. Everything aches so much it feels like my bones are cracking.

They were so real in my dream. But so was Matty, and he's okay. That was a dream. But he's real, and Mommy and Daddy are real, and the scariest things that have happened are real, and the coyotes are real, and I've seen the magic face before.

Wait. I can't remember what I did today. Everything in my head is swirling. Why can't I remember?

Wake up, Deidi. Wake up! Maybe I fell asleep after we went to the library and came home.

Wait! What if I fell asleep after I came back from Matty's room? What if he really wrote those things?

I'm throwing up spit.

I can't go look now. He's in there. I can't ask him if we went to the library. I have to figure out what to do first.

I squeeze my eyelids shut. I still can't move.

I open my eyes. My jewelry box is sitting on top of the dresser.

It's open, but the ballerina isn't moving. She's looking at herself in the circle mirror inside the lid. She can only dance to the music for a couple minutes. I haven't heard any music since I woke up.

I walk to my dresser like a robber afraid to get caught. My fingertips touch the top. I lean over the pretty white box.

I see the pink square inside. It's sideways at the bottom. I don't think the two dollars I saved are under it. I don't want to look. What if the money's gone?

Stop it, I tell myself. Even if it is gone, so what? Matty could've stole it before. I don't remember the last time I looked. But the top's open.

I never leave it open. Because the music won't play.

But I left it open in the dream and it's open now.

So how can it be a dream?

I lift the pink square and see the empty space.

Hot spit comes up my throat again.

How can I know?

And if I look in Matty's room, how can I know if he wrote the bad things? He could've thrown it away.

But what if I found it?

More hot spit.

It's all real, even if it isn't! I'm seeing everything that's happened since I can remember. Even what I know was a dream has almost happened! I'm seeing everything that's hurt me. I look down at my body. I see every piece that was hurt.

What can I do?

Think, think. I'm thinking, *Maybe Janie and Ahanti are real.*

Does *Ahanti* really mean she can never be broken?

Maybe I'll find them someday. Maybe they're where I'm going. Please let them be where I'm going.

What if I was Ahanti? Maybe the sads and mads and scaries and owies wouldn't be on me. Maybe I wouldn't feel so sorry so much for Mommy, Daddy, and Matty. Maybe I'd have a family that didn't have things so wrong with them. Maybe nothing would be wrong with me. Maybe seeing the butterfly outside my window wouldn't be the only time I was happy today.

Sometimes I think there are giants playing with us, like I play with my dolls. We can't see them because they're invisible. They put us in places they want us to be.

Sometimes I wonder if they put me in the wrong story. I don't fit with my family. I see how much I'm not like them. I think maybe there's been a mistake. I don't feel like I belong here. It's like I'm always outside watching them through a window.

I think about the magic face. I want to see her again. I need her. Maybe she'll come later. Maybe I'll see her where I'm going.

Maybe.

AFTERWORD

By Kerry J. Todd, MSW, LICSW

Over the course of my thirty-five-year career as a clinical social worker in the field of child abuse, I have had the pleasure of meeting and working with Lisa Blume. She requested that I review the novel she was writing and has now completed, *Little Girl Leaving*. It is based on the true story of a child's earliest experiences of sexual abuse, as well as physical and psychological abuse and neglect.

As a professional who has worked in the field since 1983, I do not believe I have ever seen a piece of literature on these issues written solely from the point of view of a very young child, in the first person, present tense. To be honest, I questioned if this could be done successfully. However, once I started to read this compelling story, I was captivated. The author has so poignantly captured how a child, from three years old to seven years old, experiences sexual abuse, as well as physical and psychological abuse and neglect.

As a licensed clinical social worker, I have been on the front lines of investigation as a child protective service worker. I have been a forensic child-interviewer. I have provided counseling for child victims of sexual abuse. I have trained law enforcement officers, forensic child-interviewers, and child protective service workers on proper child-interviewing techniques, as well as provided trainings to professionals throughout the United States on the topic of child abuse. Among others, I have provided the above at Harborview Center for Sexual Assault and Traumatic Stress (1988–2010) and Harborview Medical Center (2011–present); as chapter board member (1999–2011) and board president (1999–2000) of the American Professional Society on the Abuse of Children (APSAC); as affiliate clinical instructor at the University of Washington's School of Social Work (1995–2010); and as a consultant providing training and consultation on the topic of child abuse and trauma, investigative interviewing of child victims and witnesses, and supervision of social work licensure candidates (2010–present).

Children have the right to be safe and protected from sexual abuse and all forms of abuse. The statistics are staggering. One out of four girls and one out of six boys are sexually abused by the time they reach eighteen years of age. The numbers are even higher when including physical abuse, psychological abuse, and neglect. These statistics come from the Centers for Disease Control and Prevention (CDC)-Kaiser Permanente Adverse Childhood Experiences (ACE) Study. The United Nations cited the CDC in 2016, reporting that as many as one billion children around the world have experienced physical, sexual, or psychological violence.

Most adults cannot wrap their heads around the fact that so many children are abused. We want to bury our heads in the sand and pretend these horrific things don't happen to children. But with this book, the author moves the reader to take Deidi's hand and travel with her through her heartbreaking journey.

In this era when sexual abuse is increasingly prevalent as a social issue, *Little Girl Leaving* could not be timelier regarding the most important aspect of the issue, the protection of our children. This has always been timely and always will be.

Deidi's story represents the context wherein children are the most statistically at risk of being sexually abused: in the home.

Sexual abuse is an exceptionally destructive violation of a young child at their most vulnerable stage of life.

While based on a true story, *Little Girl Leaving* is a work of fiction. It is the only way I know that can so eloquently convey the thoughts and feelings of a very young child who is experiencing abuse. As a clinician, I've heard hundreds of accounts of abuse from young children. The author expertly uses concepts and language to depict Deidi's experiences that are congruent with what I've heard from so many young children. The style in which this book is written allows the reader to feel intimately acquainted with Deidi, and to begin to understand what a young child-abuse victim experiences. The author's purpose in writing *Little Girl Leaving* is not to focus on any particular individual in the story. Rather, by writing a novel, the author's goal is to present a universal depiction of childhood abuse and to fully capture the child's view.

Deidi's story is not easy to read, but statistics prove it is not unique. What is unique is the author's ability to immerse the reader in a child's world and thereby describe the thinking and behaviors that unfold during the most critical period of a child's development. Deidi goes from pure innocence to questioning and realizing that what she is experiencing is not right. It is a story that needs to be told. The author is a survivor of child sexual abuse. Only a survivor could write this novel.

Writers bring their own experience to fiction in varying degrees and ways. However, the author intends to maintain a boundary between her personal experience and her work as an author. I fully support this. The boundaries a survivor may require about revealing or discussing the specifics of their personal experiences are the decision of the survivor. This needs to be respected so as to not contribute to re-victimization or further trauma. It is also essential to the author that the novel is the focus of the reader. The true story it is based on is in many ways a composite of the true story of countless survivors. Tragically, this larger true story can be confirmed by seemingly endless personal accounts, reports, and studies. It is this larger true story, through our connection to Deidi and her story as a character in a novel, that can connect us to the countless children who need us to see their reality.

This book is, paradoxically, incredibly sad and hauntingly beautiful as it captures the fullness of both childhood and abuse. It also captures, in a way I've never seen, the experience of a child's increasing dissociation in order to survive the abuse. Further, it captures elemental aspects both of childhood in general and of survival from abuse through connection to nature, animals, books, music, a few people in various degrees—including her brother who is tragically both co-victim of her parents and other adults and who also victimizes her—and a sense of a larger good in the universe which offers at least the hope of protection and love.

Little Girl Leaving is so very aptly titled. The context of the story is a seven-year-old girl in the process of leaving her rural home for the big city. Leaving with memories, good and bad, in some ways as any child would, from the only home she's ever known, as well as from a way of life and an environment very different from where she is going. It is also set in a historic time, beginning fifty years ago, in which much was being left behind in society at large, in both wrenching and positive ways—a process ongoing still today. It is most importantly the story of a little girl being forced to leave her innocence behind from the start, at the same time never letting go of it, with increasing consciousness from three years old to seven years old. It's the story of a little girl forced to dissociate in order to survive, leaving her body and traveling in her mind to different places as she tries to detach herself from the physical and emotional pain inflicted on her. It's the story of a little girl who, as time goes by, starts to internally leave the family system that is abusing her, seeing with confusion and empathy and pain what is happening to her, and yet still longing for love and goodness for herself and everyone. And in the end, it's a story in which the author leaves the reader with questions as to what happened to *Little Girl Leaving*.

Deidi's story evokes powerful emotions. We want to reach out and embrace her. We want her to feel safe and protected. I want every adult to read this book. It is rich with material that demands responsible adults fully grasp the reality of the sexually abused child. Current prevention programs rely heavily on children reporting or exhibiting behaviors as the precursor to intervention. The threat to psychological and physical survival generally prevents children from reporting, and victims are trained to present well. The experiences of Deidi illustrate this heartbreakingly. It is common for child sex abuse victims not to fully recognize, realize it was not their fault, and report until well into adulthood, often decades later if at all. This a measure of how much all of us in our society need to open our eyes and hearts and create protection for children, safety for child victims, and support for adult survivors. Statute of limitations reform for criminal and civil action against perpetrators is being pursued by child and survivor advocates. It has increasingly received public support and been enacted in various ways in a number of states. However, it is still very much a work in progress that will depend in the end on the actions of citizens.

Child sexual abuse has always been there. For many years, it was a taboo subject, something that was not talked about. It was one of those horrific situations thought to only happen to children from lower income families. In families rampant with physical abuse, domestic violence, and/or substance abuse. It never happened in well-established families. Not in families with a mother and a father. Not in families that had good standing in the community. Not in families where children were well dressed.

But as a society, we learned this wasn't true. Child sexual abuse knows no bounds. It happens in families of lower economic standing. It happens in families with wealth and status. Just as physical abuse, domestic violence, and substance abuse do. We know the offenders are most often someone the child knows and trusts. We know that sexual abuse offenders are usually male, but that females also offend. Both females and males physically abuse children.

We know that a plurality of offenders are family members, often the parents themselves, which is particularly difficult for us to look at as a society. A child, especially a young child, naturally sees the parent as the psychological and physical source of nurturing and survival. The rights of children and their best interest are, or should be, pre-eminent, ranging from local to international law and practice. Common sense and decency put children first, but there is still a conscious and unconscious treatment of children as belongings by some people and institutions that must change.

Children belong in only one place, by law and morality—wherever they are properly cared for. It is the responsibility of all of us to make certain this occurs. The science on early childhood has continually shown the drastic difference that occurs when a child is nurtured in every way versus being neglected or abused.

Deidi's story isn't just for professionals who are providing treatment for young victims or adult survivors of sexual abuse. It is for everyone who has a child, child victim, or adult survivor in their life. For everyone who knows a child, child victim, or adult survivor.

Childhood abuse—whether one incident or ongoing, whether committed by clergy, teachers, coaches, family members, or others—impacts the adults these children will become one day. Left untreated, many victims/survivors may experience problems such as alcoholism, depression, illicit drug use, violence, incarceration, and even suicide. Such results impact society at large. Some victims/survivors become adults who repeat the horror of what they endured. Some become adults who face and overcome the horror of what they endured. The possibility of a healthy adulthood is there for all, but we cannot underestimate the challenges that should never have to be faced by anyone.

If you are an adult victim/survivor, and you need help and support, I recommend contacting your health care providers or other trusted sources for therapeutic support and information about other individual or group support.

In 1974, the United States Congress passed the Child Abuse Prevention and Treatment Act (CAPTA), which provided funds for child protective services. Mandated reporting was required for the first time for states to receive these funds. Professionals working with children were required to report any suspected abuse. Child abuse was finally being talked about openly.

But how far have we really come since that time? CAPTA leaves reporting requirements up to the states, which range from mandating that some professionals report abuse to requiring anyone suspecting abuse to report it. Even in states where all adults are mandated reporters, our children are still being abused. And they are most often being abused by someone they know and trust. We all must think about the children in our own lives, whether our own child, the children in our extended families, a child in our classroom or our church, or our child's best friend. We must do more to protect our children and keep them safe. And we need to listen. Again, presently, the onus remains on the child to disclose in most prevention programs.

It is the adults in a child's life who have the responsibility to keep a child safe. Child sexual abuse, especially at the hands of the adults entrusted with the child's safety, severely impacts the child's view of the world. It skews a child's view so that the child no longer feels safe. If the adults entrusted with the health and safety of a young child are abusing the child, how will this child ever feel safe in the world?

Deidi helps us better understand the experiences of a young child, and what we need to do to stop the cycle of abuse. We all know a child who has been abused, whether we are aware of that or not.

We are all mandated reporters.

We all have a responsibility to protect our children. It is our first responsibility as adults. We need to educate ourselves and hold our institutions accountable. The institutions will not work otherwise.

I know. I've been working with them for thirty-five years.

I want to thank the author for writing this tragic yet inspiring story. I know personally how extremely difficult this was for her to write. But like her, I am hoping people will read Deidi's story and think about all the children in their lives. And that they will dedicate themselves to ending the scourge of abuse inflicted on children and defend every child's right to a life of love and protection and nurturing.

ACKNOWLEDGMENTS

Special thanks to Girl Friday Productions for their editing, production, and, most importantly, unreserved moral support for me, and conviction about the importance and quality of the novel.

Another pivotal factor in deciding to work with Girl Friday Productions is the fact that it is a women-owned and women-led firm, which, as its website states, "is clear that women need to build, create, and lead."

Emilie Sandoz-Voyer, senior special projects editor, skillfully guided the overall production of the book and was a particular gift. Her professionalism, intelligence, accountability, sensitive nature, and kind heart helped make an often overwhelming process of writing more manageable. From the start, meetings with Leslie "LAM" Miller, co-founder, and Kristin Mehus-Roe, executive director of publishing partnerships, created an atmosphere of insightful dialogue and caring commitment. Co-founder Ingrid Emerick offered thought-provoking developmental editing. Laura Whittemore and Nick Allison provided adroit proofreading. Finally, Rachel Marek crafted brilliant artistry and design.

I need to express my immeasurable gratitude to Kerry Todd, not only for her generous and magnificent afterword, but for her essential support as I went through the ineffable process of writing this book. Kerry is that rare accomplished human being who seeks no fame or recognition. Her historical contribution to addressing childhood sexual abuse is as much about what she helped create as it is about what she refused to be part of. Kerry has my utmost respect and admiration.

As much as I love words and relish the ordering of such, one particular acknowledgment is greater than any I could ever choose or combine. My husband.

There are far too many people, and experiences, critical to me in the journey that led to this book and the writing of it to mention here. The acknowledgements would go on for pages and still be incomplete. These names, and stories, will remain my private treasures, etched deep inside my heart.

My inspiration for *Little Girl Leaving* has been, quite simply, all children. Not just in families of origin, families of choice, and related families, but all children, everywhere. Ultimately, they are what gives me hope. Many friends, colleagues, professionals, and family members in the above all-encompassing sense, both living and dead, have loved me and supported me over the years. A distinct salute needs to be given to the many survivors who've helped me. You all know who you are.

Last, but certainly not least, my thanks to all the readers, now and in the future, of *Little Girl Leaving*. I hope Deidi's story will help adults to experience life as a very young child who needs them does.

ABOUT THE AUTHOR

LISA BLUME has been a principal and executive producer of public service media and research projects for more than thirty years, focused on hunger, child and maternal health, education, environmental protection, and numerous socially beneficial efforts. Her projects have been supported by the White House, members of Congress, and local governments and agencies. Her public service campaigns have been honored by Women in Film Nell Shipman Awards, Addy Awards, Telly Awards, the New York Festivals, London International Advertising Awards, Global Awards, and others. In recent years, her primary focus has been on issues of global sustainability and ensuring basic needs, rights, and protection for all children.

This is the author's first novel. She lives with her husband in Seattle.